A SHADOW OF EAGLES

Books by Jane Barry

THE LONG MARCH
THE CAROLINIANS
A TIME IN THE SUN
A SHADOW OF EAGLES

A SHADOW

OF EAGLES

Jane Barry

DOUBLEDAY & COMPANY, INC.

GARDEN CITY, NEW YORK

1964

All of the characters in this book are fictitious, and any resemblance to actual persons, living or dead, is purely coincidental.

For Tramore and Carl Hoelscher

A SHADOW OF EAGLES

The renegade longhorn called Rojo by Mexicans and Texians alike was seen by four travelers in a single day, within a thirty-mile area north of the border.

Out of the gray morning of a February day he came into full view of two men riding south, turning his great horned head to them and standing his ground. Late in the afternoon, when the harsh light lay long on the land he was seen by a woman coming alone across the flat and by a man who lay concealed in a sandy wash watching the woman.

No one of the four crossed the other's traces on the dry blowing earth, under a sky intensely blue, deep, wide, filled with flying clouds. Beneath it, dust coiled and spiraled. Wind blasted the brakes where the longhorn cows lay hidden with their calves. The border country glittered under days hard and reflective as golden glass, nights thick with snapping stars. The sun was a long time burning off the cold.

In the last dawn the two men saw the huge block of the steer

1

against the chaparral and halted, waited, tensed to run. A heavy-shouldered boy with a dark narrow face; the other a year or two older, sandy, bluntnosed, with a wry relaxed mouth.

A fresh saffron light came with the coming of the sun.

The eight-foot span of horn gray, black, white as bleached bone, the rough red coat, the high wild head, the heft, height, and power of the big steer held them. The horses were edgy, judging distance to the curving lances of horn. Four, five hundred feet. They were cow horses which would take the bits and chase. Their feet worked. The dark boy was up in his stirrups.

"Rojo," he said.

"Easy," the other said. "Easy, he's lookin' at us."

"Over a year now since anybody's laid eyes on that red hide. Wait'll Pa hears." The dark boy settled in the saddle again, pushing his hat up. A lock of thick hair sprang on his forehead. "What's he up to? I never see a critter just stand like that, out in the open."

"Don't mind he's seen, looks like. We could maybe bring him down from here, Frankie."

The boy laughed a short single sound, showing white, slightly crooked teeth. "Pa'd break my back and you'd be drawin' your time, Shiloh." The grin was gone. "I git like Pa, I hanker to see the end of the trail for that old snake. Crossed the border now, ain't he? Runnin' our range one of these days, too. Pa's goin' to herd him right into a boxcar this time."

"Oh yes," Shiloh said, looking off at the sky, narrowing his mild blue eyes against the light.

"I got a mind to head back and tell him."

"I got a mind to kick that fool horse out from under you. I got work to do and I ain't about to lock horns with that red steer."

They rode on, turned warily in their saddles. When they had passed beyond him, the longhorn swung his head for the first time and began to move away, walking when he started, but ending in a thunderous gaunt-hipped hollow-backed run, nose in the wind and a squall of dust exploding around him as he went for the brakes.

2

Twenty miles to the south, Captain Aaron Lightbourne Bonaventure, Company D, First Texas Rangers, was lying on his back in the wash waiting for nightfall.

Not that his papers were not routine. He had drawn and signed them himself, two weeks ago. In the days which followed, he had got over the notion that giving yourself orders somehow made them more valid and now held the thought that it made them less valid. The problem was that it was getting harder all the time to explain why a commanding officer didn't command somebody else.

He had been in Mexican jails before. This time he carried a legitimate commission, and maybe it would work if he was picked up.

And maybe it wouldn't. Three out of four said the chili-eaters who corralled you couldn't read anyway. So there you were, in with the cockroaches again.

The westering sun was striking him in the face. He covered his eyes with his forearm, yawning. He ought to sleep, because it was going to be a long sleepless night, but what he wanted to do was think about Buster. What Buster had done. Where Buster might be now. Mexico City, if he had any sense, but Buster never did have much sense. When he thought about Buster discipline and dispassion were strong in him, sprung from the half of him which was Quaker-English. But his eyes were the warm amused eyes of the Creole, black and forgiving. The misfortune was that one did not, could not forgive, and stay within the limits of duty.

He saw the woman before he saw Rojo. Lowering his arm, opening his eyes, he turned his head from the sun and his ear, against the ground, caught the sound of the horse. He rolled and looked over the lip of the wash.

He went and slipped a feedbag over the horse's nose and drew him farther into the shelter of the thicket at the end of the gully. Prone again, he saw that the rider had come to a halt three hundred feet away.

She was bareheaded in the sun. The wind had torn her hair loose. It blew across her shoulder and back a slick black scarf. The rough leather coat, dark divided skirt, dusty boots were graceless and rude. But the horse was not plain, a big black with a Berber

3

head, sixteen hands easy. A pale flat-crowned hat with a wide brim hung latched to the woman's belt. Strapped to a folded serape behind the cantle was a yellow-faced guitar.

Rarely in Mexico he had seen women ride astride. While he watched she drew one foot out of a box stirrup, its *tapadero*, the protective hood, larded with silver, and raised a knee to the saddle as if to ease her position. She did not turn her head, but one hand dipped suddenly into the breast area of her coat and came out again bearing an object too small for him to identify. He watched the motion of her hands, the forward bending of her head and saw that she had rolled and lighted a cigarette. It shocked him agreeably; there was a faintly aphrodisiacal element in the act. After a moment it occurred to him that she was watching something directly in front of her. He looked to the right and saw, on the flatland facing her, the red steer.

His instinctive thought was to leap up and go crashing over the edge of the wash, to deflect, if he could, the onslaught of the longhorn. He could feel his muscles gather and pull together, willing him, before his head took over. As it stood, she didn't seem much afraid of the steer and he didn't look to be much bothered by her. So he watched both: the bare-headed woman smoking serenely, knee drawn up on the big horse; longhorn standing, head lowered, so still he might have been pasted against the sky and backlighted by a sun which fringed him with reddish fire.

Bonaventure pulled the Winchester up and set his hand around it. Then he thought about what it might take to stop the longhorn. More than a rifle. Maybe a brass cannon. Bonaventure knew him, every man in the border country knew him. The biggest longhorn he'd ever seen and something more. They said of this Rojo that he had killed two men in Mexico and another in Texas. They said of him that except for the crew which brought him in and castrated him and branded him with the brand of a ranch which no longer existed, the red steer had not been brought in again.

He looked back at the woman. If she was aware of her danger it did not show. She sat easily in the same unconcerned attitude.

And he remembered her, watching her raise the cigarette to her

4

lips. He recalled the meeting, four or five years ago, on a street in San Antonio, a hard brown little hand in his and eyes that looked up calm and withdrawn. She was a child then. She didn't look to be much bigger now, and he thought she would not remember. Or recognize him if she did, with the dark stubble of beard and the worn trappings of a saddle tramp, a drifter.

He knew men would give a year's wages to be where he was, looking at her and she not knowing it.

He saw her pitch the butt of the cigarette into the sand and drop her foot to the stirrup. When he turned his head Rojo was gone. He loosed his grip on the rifle and knew for the first time how hard his hand had been closed around it. Rising dust marked the way the red steer had run. The land dipped sharper than he thought and then flatted away to thickets and low slopes and gilded horizon. Rojo had gone into the sun. Now the woman would go.

For a long moment her face was turned full to him as she twisted in the saddle, checking the rawhide thongs which bound the guitar behind her.

He was restless after she passed, and the only thought he had room for now was what she was doing alone in the middle of nowhere. And knowing he had no choice but to intercept her, offer escort, whether she wanted it or not. He drew out his watch and looked at it. He would give her half an hour.

Twenty minutes later he saw with relief and regret that she was not alone. A string of five Mexicans passed, driving horses. One of the riders was a woman, not young by the squat solid set of her, head wrapped in a *rebozo*. Three were young men in wide-brimmed straw hats, stiff blue Levi jackets buttoned to their throats. The horses were wild but driving, which meant they had been picked up at some isolated *mesteñero* camp, maybe over the big river. There was a single pack mule. The fourth man he knew: Tiburcio Uremáy, *peon* boss of Tres Reyes.

Afterward the thought came to him that he had seen two legends. Most men never got to lay eyes on a legend in a lifetime, and he had seen two in one afternoon: the daughter of don Ramón Dominguez and the outlaw steer called Rojo.

5

He did not sleep. When night fell he mounted and rode down the long bleak silent land and before dawn came touched the narrow waters of the Rio Grande and crossed the border into Mexico.

ONE

The day they began to make the paper feast lanterns at Tres
Reyes was the day Rojo killed Ben Richards' night horse and
swung on the downed rider, Jonah McLean. So that the boy
called Shiloh had to ride down to the *casa* and tell Ben Richards,
not only about his horse but about Jonah being hurt. He stood
turning his hat around in his hands, not looking at Ben Richards
and trying to say it so it somehow didn't sound as bad as it was.

"I'll go back with you," he told Shiloh.

None of the *casa* people were around when they rode out, except for a girl kneading and rinsing an altar cloth in the courtyard pool and singing in a thin voice. Water made a trickly
sound coming off the lip of a fountain and rippling down to
where the girl was bent dark-haired in the sun. The finches were
restless in their cages, hopping and leaning into the light. Siesta
wasn't an hour old.

They rode through the gates. Around them was the flatland
with the long spurs of the *brasada*, the brush country, angling into
it thick and lethal along the Nueces River. It was the first in a

7

long time Richards did not look back, leaving this house, this community which called itself Three Kings. Within the walls it was green and white and there was the sound of water. Shade moved smoky and purple up and across white adobe. There was a shock of red bud and blossom, neat lined-out kitchen plots, clean orange-colored roof tile, heavy brass-studded doors. Jacaranda, and lime trees in tubs rose against slim Moorish arches leading into places of song and silence and out again to the symmetrical fans of wheat and bean fields, with the oxen coming yoked across them.

For a time, a little time, he belonged here.

"What's he doin' for doctoring?" he said to Shiloh.

"Got Sid Lunt, ain't he?" Shiloh's voice contained that pride which men sometimes bear in other men whose accomplishments are to them mysterious and inexplicable. "Sid can doctor anything. Hosses. Mules. Men. Dogs. Even a banged-up old wolf, one time. They say you got to have a license, though. He could make a fortune if he could hang out a shingle."

"Wouldn't matter, you needed him," Ben Richards said.

He had a thin quick bronze mobile face that just missed being severe. Under the dented-crown hat his hair was long and straight, colorless. The eyes were deepset and framed in squint lines, an indeterminate light shade which might have been blue or gray or green. Sun had burned and bleached him. He said shortly, "Is Jonah bad enough hurt to die?"

"I mighty well hope not," Shiloh said.

"I didn't ask you that, goddam it, Shiloh."

"Don't get yourself up on me, will you, Ben? I ain't see him since they got him in. Sid wouldn't let nobody see him first off. Not even her. Not even his own wife and kid, if you can figure that."

"How'd he look?" Richards said.

"I ain't see him, I tell you."

"You tell me you saw it happen."

"That. Sure. Yes." The boy's frank uncomplicated face was turned to him, without expression. "First off he didn't look good, I admit. I figured he was a goner for sure. Then he groaned some, so as soon as I see he was still with us I took care of Glass before I done anything else."

8

"Glass was . . . you couldn't do anything?"

"Ben, I hate to tell you, honest. That old Rojo put a horn in Glass's belly and ripped him to hell."

"Leave it there," Richards said bitterly. He looked straight ahead. "The best night horse I ever had or hope to have. A man comes by a horse like that maybe once in a lifetime."

"You was a damn fool makin' the loan of him," Shiloh said.

"I know that now. Jonah was crazy for that horse. I couldn't say no to him, all he wants to do is ride him." Something burst in him, anger boiling over so hard he could feel his heart grow uneven with it. "What in *Christ* was Jonah doin', brought Rojo down on him?"

"You want to know the whole story, Frankie comes in and says there is two mavericks runnin' up and down in ropin' distance and Jonah has got to grab up your Glass, and him and me and Frankie goes out for them little fellers. Frankie is whoopin' it up like always and Jonah is tryin' to keep him quiet so the little fellers don't head for the brush, but all good natured and all, and you know tryin' to keep Frankie down is like tryin' to corral the Three in One in a hog wallow, and sure enough, we come up on the dogies and start chousin' 'em and by then Jonah is havin' himself a fine time and kind of eggin' Frankie on to it. We gits up on that table north of the Crushin' Stone and I look up all at once and there on top of that rise is old Rojo himself, lookin' like he owned the country and me along with it, just like he looked that day me and Frankie seen him."

"When was that?" Richards said.

"Six, seven days ago. Early in the morning. He's been gone a long time, Ben, over the border, we figure."

"Then Jonah was lookin' for him."

"Jonah's always lookin' for him, you know that. By the time I spot him, Frankie has gone latherin' off after the little fellers and don't hear me holler. Jonah hears me, though, and he pulls Glass in and looks up and just sits there and you can see him breathin'. I never see a man breathe so slow. Then he says . . . but not talkin' to me, I don't think he recollects I'm there . . . he says, 'I been waitin' a long time for this. I ain't never got you within distance of my rope. I wanted you a long time and this

9

time I aim to have you.' And he starts walkin' Glass right up that ridge, easy as you please, takin' his time and snakin' out rope all the way."

Richards closed his eyes. "Where were you and Frankie?"

"I tell you. Frankie is off rippin' himself up in the brush, you can't even see where he's gone to. I just sit there, bein' surprised and all like I am."

"Packin' guns?"

"I reckon so," Shiloh said. "Yes, I reckon I was. I had a pistol and I had a rifle in my boot. And I would of got 'em both turned on me if I had put one or the other on that red steer." Again he looked at Richards. "Jonah wants that steer. Eight, nine years now that steer's been lordin' it, right on Jonah's range. Jonah wants him."

Richards could feel sweat under the rim of his hat. "How far did Jonah run him?"

"If you mean how far did he run Jonah," Shiloh said, "not far. Not far 'tall. He just stands a minute or two watchin' Jonah come for him and then he charges. Better'n any charge I ever see. Straight's an arrow, no tricks, no pawin' or snufflin', nothin' like that. Straight. All his weight in the shoulders and his tail swingin' and the hair standin' up on his backbone. Better'n them bulls I see in Mexico supposed to be fighters. Ben, his horns is bigger'n the Holy Ghost."

Richards didn't say anything.

"Jonah ain't a fool," Shiloh said then.

"No?" Richards said. His voice was almost pleasant.

"No. That horse of yours was took for some fancy ridin'. Jonah angled him in and drew Rojo right on past, but he missed with the rope."

Richards could feel his face grow stiff. "And if he didn't? What did he think he was goin' to do, rope that longhorn in and have my horse hold him? My horse? Good God, Rojo must go sixteen hundred pounds without tryin'."

"I'm just tellin' you," Shiloh said. "He missed, that's all. He didn't even git turned around again when Rojo stopped on a coin and give him change. He hit Glass broadside and toppled him and swung in on him. Jonah pulled loose and lay quiet, but it was kind of uncanny the way that steer had it all figured and went for the old man."

Richards' mouth pulled back. Shiloh could see his teeth, clamped like he had a case of lockjaw. The sweeping horror of the moment was with him: the raging steer, a near-ton of unreasoning fury, the grinding crash of the collision, the frantic horse with the horn tearing out his life, the man maybe knowing, sensing, that the horn would find him too.

"I don't know what you're thinkin'," Shiloh said, "but I want you to know I pulled my rifle."

"What made you so hasty?"

"What I live by," Shiloh said, "is what Jonah McLean tells me. I draw my pay off'n him. When he looks up at me over the saddle of your horse and tells me to hold fire, I hold it, but I ride for him and by then that steer's turned and is goin' for all he's worth, and he's sure worth some, I would say. Jonah makes a funny noise and drops out of sight behind Glass. I reckon he's dead . . . Glass, that is, not Jonah, so I let him have it through the ear." Shiloh gestured wildly. "You understand I don't shoot Jonah, I shoot Glass. Then Jonah makes some more noises, only what it is is his belly is growlin'. I swear it, Ben. It sounds like the big guts is eatin' up the little guts. Then I see his leg is bleedin'. The shot brings Frankie in. I stay with Jonah while Frankie goes back for the wagon, and all that time Jonah is layin' with his eyes closed and his guts rumblin' like that, the damnedest thing I ever hear, and I am sweatin' terrible and shakin' like I had the flits at the same time. I keep sayin', 'Jonah, kin you talk, kin you hear me?' but he don't answer. Sid comes out with the wagon. He don't say nothin' either and he ain't said a word since."

Richards didn't say anything for a time, then he said, "Well, I'm beholden anyway, Shiloh."

"What for?"

"Glass. Me."

"He was done for, Ben."

Richards said, "Jonah hired you and you stick by him. No brush popper's worth his salt if he doesn't stick by the boss. But this is me and you, Shiloh, and you might as well bust down and say it:

Jonah McLean did the biggest damnfool thing I ever heard of and I've heard of some damnfool things in my time."

"It don't make it any the lesser if I say it," Shiloh said.

They rode into the ranch, scattering chickens. The house sat solidly, neat, weathered, uncompromising, with liveoaks around it. Off to the left, along the corral fence, a windmill took the wind; it was well greased and made small sound. The colors of house and spread were gray and graygreen and dun under the bright winter sky. Shiloh cut off toward the corral, picking his way over the wagon wheels which lay in the front yard. Avis McLean planted flowers between the spokes every year, bringing water from the hand-dug well to keep them alive.

He went in without knocking, hearing her voice when he closed the door behind him.

"Shiloh?"

"It's me, Avis," he said.

She came to the kitchen doorway, drying her hands on her apron, looking at him, and he saw her mouth tighten in a gesture which traced fine hard lines at either corner. He took off his hat and stood holding it.

"Shiloh told you," she said in a voice which seemed shy of the breath to carry it. She put up a hand and touched the tight coronet of braids on her head and clenched her apron again. "I ought to of known. Come in and have some coffee, Ben."

He came and sat at the kitchen table with its covering of blue and white cloth and waited while she filled a cup for him. She did not sit down, but stood opposite him, her hands on the back of a chair. "He's goin' to be all right, Ben."

He burned his mouth on the coffee. "How bad is it?"

"Leg," she said. She picked up a corner of the apron and dug at her eye with it, but she was not crying. "That damn red steer . . ."

"Avis."

"Oh what's the use? He's a fool, a perfect fool, that's all. How many years people been laughing about him and that red steer? You think I don't know it, just because so much of the laughing got done before I married him? The minute he gets a chance he's got to risk his life over it. His *life*, Ben. What is he, an old tom-cat, he thinks he's got more than one? The steadiest man on two

12

feet and he goes clean out of his mind if you so much as mention that red steer. I made the mistake of believin' any wild notions he's got in him, he's passed 'em all on to Frankie. But no. He's not only got to do what he did, he's got to have Shiloh with him, and Frankie, to watch him do it. And Shiloh too dumb or too loyal to shoot when he should of shot, and Frankie . . . Frankie . . ."

Richards flashed a look at the door leading to the back room, where he figured Jonah must be. It was closed, but Avis' voice was clear and high. "Sit down, Avis," he said, and when she only stood, clenching the back of the chair, said it again, quietly, firmly. "Sit down."

She pulled out the chair and sank into it, leaning on her elbows. "Don't preach at me. I got hardly a brain left to think with, between Jonah and Frankie." She laughed. He did not miss the bitterness. "Sometimes I think I'll go clean crazy. I'll tell you something, Ben. Whatever troubles the McLeans got, there's no king steer ever lived goin' to make 'em worse. If I ever lay eyes on that old Rojo I'm goin' to shoot him dead as a hung coyote."

He didn't smile. He didn't even want to smile. He could only look at her across the table, wishing that the time might come when he could look at her simply as a girl he knew, a casual acquaintance with whom contact was sporadic, random, conditional upon the demands or lack of them, of both their lives; a time when he might look at her as Jonah McLean's wife and believe, know, that this was so and that nothing was going to change it. It was not only her age, which was near twenty years short of his, it was the correlation of age with that of the gray and crusty widower who was already father and now, again, husband. She was always Avis McLean and she was always somebody's half-broke filly daughter, in looks anyway, and the two wouldn't reconcile for him. It was one thing to be lighthearted, hospitable, easy, with lonely men she maybe didn't even know thought of her, except in passing, but he was part and parcel of a lonely, silent way of life and knew that lonely, silent men did dream of her and despised himself that he too should have been brought to that brink of ignoble dreaming. He felt that she knew this about him, however little she knew of the world of men. Or however

13

much. Always when she met his eyes, clearly, candidly, he felt she knew his strength, his weakness, his want. And often, as in this moment, he could sense something spilling over in her, like steam lifting the lid of a kettle. In the clean quiet warm kitchen, her own domain, she made massive contrast: nervestrung, taut as stretched rawhide, poised to break and run. He had seen this in range women before. But they had chosen their own way. No. Did any woman choose?

He said, "I don't look for you to go huntin' Rojo, Avis."

"I thought of it."

"No."

"You don't reckon I can?"

"No."

He hurt inside when he looked at her, but what he hurt for, now, was to help her some way. "Avis, you don't come out any more. Señora, she asks about you. And Cayetana."

Her eyes were as grayblue and clear as cold still water, cutting him off. "Ah, what's the use?" she said again. "I'm too busy to be lonesome. There's nothing wrong with this life, Ben, and if there was talking wouldn't change it." Her flat acceptance hurt him too, the more so because he felt her capable of, perhaps even dependent upon, the latent rebellion he knew was in her. Her eyes went beyond him. "There's times I don't find it easy to talk to a girl's got the whole world in the palm of her hand."

"She's an easy listener."

"So's my old spotted dog," she said. She smiled, but her face had gone still, a little pale.

"You look awful tired, Avis," he said softly.

"Yes," she said. "I can remember sayin' that to my ma, Ben . . . sayin' it and sayin' it. By the time she was thirty she was wore to a nub. And all us kids." Again he saw the faint lines at the corners of her mouth. "But that's one matter I ain't got to worry over, I reckon. You want some more coffee?"

He shook his head. What she had said shocked him, as if she had deliberately flaunted her position in this house. Yet he knew she had said it simply, naturally, because he was a friend, he was close, and friendship, closeness, were things of high value.

14

"I'm a great one, ain't I," she said, "goin' on like that when we ought to be talkin' about Jonah."

He said, "Avis, I know Sid's here, but what about a doctor in San Antone."

"Jonah wouldn't stand for it. You know that. Sid says . . . The wound ain't too deep. He's a strong man, Ben. Sid says the only thing he might have to worry about's maybe greenflesh or something like that, and Sid's watchin' it."

He looked down into the dregs of his coffee. What she had said was that Jonah was being stubborn, which came as no surprise. There was no doubt in Richards' mind that Jonah McLean would rather quietly die than act in any way to injure Sid Lunt's pride.

While he still had his head down her arm came out across the table toward him in a giving, a sympathy. "Ben, we're awful sorry about your horse. It's what comes of wantin' what ain't meant to be yours. Jonah wanted that horse, just like he wants Rojo. He thought too much of it. Things bein' planned the way they are in this world, it was the horse had to suffer."

He watched her. Her voice was controlled, but the stark cruelty of what she said was mitigated only by the truth of it. He put out his hand and covered hers, where it lay on the table, and felt her fingers curl up hard around his own. She did not seem as astonished at the contact as he did, and it was he who had initiated it. And even then he did not know what he was going to say to her, looking at her cool eyes and flushed fairness, aware of the tenuous warmth and nearness of flesh, blood, bone, warmer and nearer than any thin stuff of dream could devise, fabricate, made absolute by the curling fingers locked upon him.

Her hand went away from him with the opening of the door and he looked up and saw Sid Lunt come out of the back room. Lunt's broad red face was bland, almost vacant. He came halfway across the room.

"Howdy, Ben. Thought that was your voice."

"I reckon you mostly heard me," Avis said matter-of-factly. "Is Jonah awake?"

Lunt nodded. He too, Richards saw, looked fatigued. More

15

than that, both Lunt and Avis looked as if they had been forced to deal, on a major issue, with a recalcitrant child.

"He wants to see you, Ben. Don't let him wear hisself out."

Richards rose reluctantly. He didn't want to hear any more apologies about Glass. He swung his head to avoid Avis' eyes and went into the room off the kitchen, walking lightly, as if he went into a church, or a death room.

"Close the door," Jonah McLean said.

He lay in the big ugly four-post bed with the sheet so close wrapped around his chest it was like a bandage.

Richards closed the door and came to stand, looking down at him. "If I had a list of fifty men and you were on it, I would of said, here is the one man on this list will never do a damnfool thing."

McLean's chest rose and fell heavily, under the sheet. His face was twisted and grotesque with the steady pull of his pain. "I don't expect it seemed so damnfool to me at the time," he said. He half-turned in the bed, heaving his big bulk around awkwardly. "I owe him one, now, Ben, and by God, he's goin' to have it before I'm through."

"Next time he'll kill you," Richards said.

"He'll never git another chance," McLean said. The eyes were steady in the lined, sick countenance. "Any other man, he'd post a reward for that steer, dead. Not this man. I ain't about to be bossed by a outlaw longhorn." His eyes shifted and came back to Richards. Then he said, "Talk's cheap, ain't it, Ben?"

"I wasn't thinkin' that," Richards said.

"Sure you was. I was thinkin' it myself."

"You ain't goin' to be able to fork a horse till hell freezes over. I don't expect you feel kind of thankful for just bein' alive, do you?"

After a moment McLean's big meaty hand moved down and rested on his thigh. "Next to Sid Lunt there's one other man in the world I'd say this to, Ben, and that's you. I don't know what come over me. It was . . . hell, you can laugh if you want to, but it was like something told me to do it, I couldn't lose. I seen Rojo and Almighty God Himself was ridin' with me, sayin' it was all right, I had him, I could do it." His laugh was wracking. "Goes to show you even God can git sidetracked, don't it? Jesus. The kind of thing that wild-haired son of mine wouldn't put up to." The hand came up and gestured at Richards. "Pull up that chair in the corner there, Ben."

"No," Richards said. "Not this time, Jonah. I don't want you bustin' a lung. Sid . . ."

McLean's face stopped him. "I know what Sid says. Or what he don't say, I reckon. I'm talkin' to you now, Ben, so sit down."

"Can't it hang fire?"

"I want to show you something," McLean said. He pushed the sheet away with both hands, lifted out his leg, and pulled up the hem of the flannel nightshirt. His hands worked carefully, unrolling the wide bandage, and after an interminable time Richards stood looking down at the great wound. The horn had torn a ragged eight-inch trajectory upward into the thigh. Lunt had sewn it together with black thread. The stitches were as neat and precise as those a woman might set in a bridal quilt. It was draining heavily. Richards didn't say anything, and after a minute McLean began to rewind the bandage. When he was finished he said, "Now I want you to see this, Ben," and his hands moved the nightshirt up disclosing a flat square of sheeting across the lower abdomen. As he worked at it, sweat began to pour down his face, and when he had pulled it away he sank back on the pillow gray and exhausted.

The hole in the abdomen was straight in, just the diameter of the horn, and it was this wound which made Richards hot and sick. Clenching his teeth against the nausea in his throat, he saw McLean half-sit up again, saw the hands move to replace the bandage, heard McLean's voice.

"The leg might lame me, Ben. This hole'll kill me."

He looked up levelly, but his voice was thick. "That's why I said talk's cheap. Sid knows about this, and you and me know about this. But Avis ain't to know, or Frankie either."

Richards sat down slowly on the edge of the bed. They looked at each other.

"Jonah, you're forgettin' something. Avis is your wife. Frankie's your son."

McLean was shaking his rough leonine head. "I got to spare

17

Avis. She's been good to me, Ben. I can't ask of her now that she be good to me out of . . . out of pity."

"And Frankie?"

"Frankie's my cross. Maybe it'll teach him a hair or two of responsibility. He always did kind of go for the unexpected."

Richards was shaken in the knowledge that it was impossible to gauge another man's attitudes in the face of adversity. He felt, but could not know with certainty, that his own reaction under this same given circumstance would be the opposite of Jonah McLean's. He would want a wife's pity, a son's promise of atonement.

"Ben, you know what I'm goin' to say."

"I reckon I know some of it," Richards said.

"How soon you startin' Dominguez' gather?"

"We been gatherin' all winter, you know that. I'm settin' up cow camp in a few days. I aim to head out the end of March if the weather'll let me."

"How many head? How far?"

"Three thousand, into Montana."

"You got a contract," McLean said. It was not a question.

"We got a contract on Tres Reyes, prime, steers only. Reservation beef for Todd Allenby."

McLean nodded against the pillow. "That's a big herd. A long way to trail 'em. I got Frankie and Shiloh and whatever poppers I can pick up to boss me in fifteen hundred, mixed, for Dodge City." His voice was coming slower. "This is the first summer in more years than I want to count I won't be goin' up the trail, Ben."

Richards leaned forward. "Jonah, you're tougher than hell and twice as stubborn. You won't get a doctor because you're afraid of hurtin' Sid's feelings."

"Cut it, Ben," McLean said suddenly, harshly. "Sid's as good as any medicine man on the range and there ain't nobody good enough for this. I wanted you to see, I wanted you to understand. When I go, I will go fightin' every inch of the way, but I ain't foolin' myself and I don't want no kind words from anybody. All I want now's to keep Avis from knowin' and some help from you."

"You want me to trail your herd with the Tres Reyes, as far as Dodge railhead," Richards said.

"That's what I want."

Richards stood up. "You're askin' me to ramrod forty-five hundred head. It's too big. Ten, twelve of us can handle the Tres Reyes. Throw in your fifteen hundred and another six men. That's a lot of grass and water. That's a lot to make go and make go right."

"I don't fight that," McLean said. "I'm goin' to tell you the facts, though. I got a son can't seem to git through one week of the year without bein' in some kind of trouble. I can't rely on him to give me the right time. I got Shiloh, been up the trail all of once, and in a pinch I'll use him. I might of got Lon Davis, but he's foldin' and pullin' out, goin' back to Louisiana. I got this one year to make me a decent enough profit so Avis won't starve till she can git her a man to run things." His voice was unemotional. "I don't worry about Avis . . . she'll be took care of, I reckon, but I don't never want her to go hungry, not for one day of her life. I need this year, Ben. I got to have it, because it's the year that's goin' to take me out of the red, pay off my debts, leave me something over."

Richards was looking at the raised design on the high, varnished headboard of the bed, not really seeing it. The eternal cry of the cattleman: one more year, the year that was going to do it, the year that was going to pay off. He had heard it a hundred times.

McLean said, "Somebody's got to trail my herd, Ben. I'd as soon it's the best trail boss in the business. Because I'm one of them knows it ain't every range man can boss a herd. Know it's born in a man. Like it was born in you."

Richards said uneasily, "I'm grateful, Jonah, but it doesn't change anything."

"I can't offer you a cut, Ben. I would if I could."

"That's square. But you better take Shiloh."

There was silence. Richards felt now that an odor hung in the close, stuffy room, and he knew it was the odor of the draining wound. His nostrils flared against it. McLean said, "I'm talkin' too much. Don't matter now, though. I got to tell you what I feel, Ben. You're my friend, and for near a year now I felt mighty friendly to you. You got to know in your own heart no matter how polite a man is to your face what he's most probly thinkin' is: this here Ben Richards is a hell of a good man . . . ought to be bossin' his own spread, and instead of that he's not only bossin' the biggest spread in southwest Texas but the spread of a rich old greaser to boot. Not loose-ridin' it there, either, but bunkin' right in with the family and got to change his shirt for dinner." McLean cleared his throat. "I got nothin' against Ramón Dominguez, he's white as I am when you come right down to it, and a lot truer to Texas than some gringos I could name. It'd take a small man to envy his spread and a fool to laugh at a name he can trace to the best blood in Spain, so they tell me. He can buy and sell me twenty times a year. But you ain't his blood, Ben. You're my blood, and I'm askin' you a favor."

What did you do with a favor, when it was asked from a death-bed? He said, "I can't do it, Jonah."

"You don't think Dominguez will stand still for it."

"Maybe."

"Maybe. But you won't. I can't talk to you, Ben. I can't make you see. Take a good look at what's ahead for you. You think you got the bear by the tail at Tres Reyes. What do you think's goin' to happen if Ramón Dominguez' wife dies? Face it, your time might be runnin' out just like mine. Hell, man, this is 1875. Dominguez ain't a citizen. He married a Yankee and put Tres Reyes in her name. Ain't that the truth of it?"

Richards said wearily, "There's things you don't savvy, Jonah."

"No, there ain't," McLean said. "Not about this. I got a hunch Dominguez'd be squarer with me now than you're bein', Ben, and he ain't so close to me as you been."

"Jonah, for Christsake, you're askin' me to handle too big a herd, to maybe put Tres Reyes in jeopardy because of your few . . ."

He stopped. McLean's face was white. "My few. Yes. Mighty few, mighty small alongside the Tres Reyes spread, but the few that might wipe my books clean for the first time. If you'd said yes, Ben, you might of give me back my life, you know that? I ain't too proud to beg, but I've begged all I'm goin' to now."

"Jonah, I work for Dominguez. Look where I stand. Stand where I stand."

"I see it," McLean interrupted. His voice was beginning to rattle. "I see you, a goddam drifter who never had a fork to eat with until you begun gittin' yourself a name for bossin' trail herds. I see there was only one man had what it took to pay off a Ranger for . . ." Then he said, "I'm your friend. But light your shucks. Now, Ben."

And Richards only stood there, looking at him.

"I left somethin' out?" McLean said, and saw that Richards' eyes were questioning, confused, and thought, I said too much. He don't know. I said too much. God curse me, I deserve to die. And even while he stared at Richards, saw the blood leave his face and a hardness like rock come into the eyes.

Richards said, "Throw 'em in with the Tres Reyes."

McLean's head turned to the wall. A huge yellow stain had appeared on the sheet, so wet that it moved while Richards watched.

"Dominguez?" McLean said hoarsely.

"I'll handle him."

"Thanks," McLean whispered. His eyes were closed. "Go down and take the pick of my horses."

"I don't want to do that, Jonah."

"You got to, Ben, if you want me to sleep tonight. I spent too much time today thinkin' what I done to Glass. I'd be pleased if you'd take that old mud-colored Portero of mine. He ain't much to look at and he couldn't touch Glass with a fence post, but he's got a good night eye." McLean's hands had begun to pick, pluck, at the sheet. His eyes were still closed. My father did that when he lay dying, Richards thought, and so did that old man died in Reed's soddy after the winter was over and spring was coming . . . lay for days and picked at the sheet with unfeeling, unknowing, dying fingers.

Lunt came in. "Got to see to him," he said, not looking at Richards, inviting him out with the single sentence.

"He's goin' to take some seein' to," Richards said.

Now Lunt looked at him. "I reckon you know, then."

"I reckon I do," Richards said.

"Tell Miss Avis I would like some water and some tore-up sheets," Lunt said.

Richards left the door ajar when he went out. Avis stood at the stove with her back to him. When he relayed Lunt's request she removed the lid from a big pan of water, drew away from the flooding steam, picked up her apron to take the hot handles. She set the pan down inside the door of McLean's room and went to a cupboard and took out clean sheeting and lay it on the kitchen table. She did not raise her eyes.

"Are you goin' to take the herd, Ben?"

"Yes," he said.

Her hands stilled. She looked up at him. A lock of fair hair slipped from its braid and lay across her cheek.

"But you don't hanker to, do you?"

"No, I don't want it, Avis."

Her hands began to tear at the cloth. "Yes," she said. "Too big a job. Because if anything goes wrong you got to look out for Tres Reyes first. Not Jonah McLean. When Jonah McLean has a grown son ought to be handlin' his pa's interests. It's hard, ain't it, Ben? I expect you can see it looks to get harder."

"I don't reckon on trouble with Frankie about it."

Her eyes slid away, as if she could not meet the directness of his look. "I'm grateful you'd do this for Jonah."

Lunt came out and took the pile of sheeting and went away again, closing the door.

Richards said in a hard, slow voice, "I reckon you'd ought to know how it stands, plain. I'd do a lot for Jonah. I ain't doin' this all for Jonah."

She met his eyes now. "I like to think you are."

"I don't reckon I got a thing to say about your thoughts, either, but I would like for you to think straight as you can, Avis."

She received, nervously, seeing the grim set of his mouth, the gift he had made her. And she knew intuitively that he was aware of something she was not aware of and was not to be made aware of. His feeling for her was so solid and tangible that it was like a weighted block, a dense mass which she could put out her hand to and take upon her taut palm. Because she knew he was trying to protect her, to keep her shut off from this knowledge he possessed, she kept herself under control. "Then I thank you, Ben. I'll always be beholden to you."

He did not want her gratitude, her obligation, but it was better than nothing. "Any change in Jonah, be sure you let me know. I want to see Frankie in a couple of days and I want to see him on Tres Reyes, not here. And tell him to bring Portero when he comes."

"I'll tell him," she said, standing, watching him while he watched her, as if they waited for some spark to ignite the tinder-dry air between them.

"Well, I'll be goin'," he said at last, and walked out of the house with the sense of too much left unfinished, too much said which could not be unsaid. Yet even when he pulled free the reins, the horse standing three-legged at the rail, and had mounted and begun to turn away, even then she was not through with him but had to come to the doorway and then into the yard, where the wind could pick at her hair and mold the graceless apron to the tenderness it commonly concealed, and call to him.

She came across the yard and looked up at him where he sat above her, holding the horse with its head turned into the wind.

"Ben!" Crying it. "Something's wrong."

"Not to my knowing."

"Ben, don't *lie* to me."

"I wouldn't lie to you."

"Is it Frankie? Is he in trouble?"

"I ain't heard so."

"Shiloh ain't goin' to pull stakes on us?"

He felt as if he was yelling, against the wind. "Honest to God, Avis, there's nothing wrong."

Her face was the face of a child. On it was fused sly innocence and conscious perception. And he knew that Jonah would be the last consideration in her mind, simply because Jonah lay within sight and touch, inert and helpless, embattled only hours ago, defeated, and now safely out of harm's way. The childlook passed as if the wind had blown it away, and she fell back a step, away from him.

"I'm sorry, Ben. I didn't mean to do that. I reckon I got more unsettled about Jonah . . . about this morning . . ."

23

"I know," he said, ashamed for her shame. "Hang on, now, Avis, like a good girl, will you?"

She nodded in that quick, vehement way she had. "You come back, Ben."

"I will," he said.

"Tell Caye to come on over one day."

"I will."

And backing away from him, walking backward, between the futile flowerless wagon wheels, with the wind swirling her skirts around her ankles and her hand up to shield her eyes from the sun. He saw in her something forlorn and yet unforgiving, as if she were angered at him and still held to him against her will.

Out of sight of the house he pulled the horse into a walk and gave it its head. Jonah McLean said he was going to die. A man could talk all he wanted to about town doctors and what they could maybe do, but it didn't mean anything, it was a sop not to the dying but to the powerless watchers at the bedside. Jonah would die, and what he left would belong to Avis and Frankie. What he left would be Avis and Frankie: a woman barely grown out of girlhood who had left an emigrant train of Arkansas rednecks, father, uncles, brothers, to marry a man near old enough to be that same father; a son, from a long-dead first wife, who seemed ear-notched and branded for troublemaking from the day he was born.

And Jonah, out of as composed, hypocritical, and righteous a meeting of death as Richards had ever observed, still had the raw strength to strike out in defiance not of his own impending lot, which would be comprehensible, but against the honor and pride of another man, that he might still use the man. What in hell had he been saying? Paying off a Ranger. He was out of his head. Nobody paid off a Texas Ranger. Nobody.

He needed time to think about it, time to throw up a barricade against the suspicion which had begun to settle on him, time to cut sign of something he didn't even want to know about, in case it was true.

Inside the walls of Tres Reyes the wind was shut out. Inside the walls the world ended and another world began, a world which he was paid to exist in, to be part of. No eyes saw him return but those of two young coyotes who stood leaning against each other companionably on the edges of the brush spur, pelts thick and ragged with the winter, and ruffled wrong way to in the wind.

TWO

The day's main meal was eaten early. When he went up the stairs, past white wall, dark exposed beam, gleam of hanging silver and copper, he would have sworn the house was empty and yet knew that the table would be ready and Lupe singing in the kitchen. The door to the Señora's room was closed. He went into his own room, catercorner from the closed door, and pulled off his shirt. The girl Soledad came in with hot water. He stood there naked to the waist while she put the basin and *olla* on the heavy chest with its tier of little cupboards and inquired if he desired any other service and went away when he said he did not, *guaraches* creaking on the thick wooden floor.

He was putting on a clean shirt when he heard the Señora's door open and close and the dry whisper of the rubber-tired wheels which propelled her chair down the hallway. Feliciano would be pushing it. At the head of the stairs he would stoop and lift the Señora in his arms and carry her to the chair at the foot of the stairs. Then he would return for the wheelchair and take her in to dinner. Some nights she did not come down. She had not

26

appeared in three days. He thought, she must feel better today. Either that, or she smells something in the wind.

He finished tying the black string tie as the triangle sounded. Out of undeviating habit he strapped on the single Schofield Smith and Wesson .44, stretched his neck out of his collar, and stepped into the hall. The triangle sounded again. Going down the tiled stairs, he chewed over what they were most liable to ask about McLean. There wasn't time to practice any answers.

He had stopped being uncomfortable about wearing a gun at table because it had been so casually ignored. "Señora," he said, bowing to her. "Don Ramón."

They were barely seated and the soup placed when Cayetana came in still in riding clothes, apologizing but not offering excuse. "*Lo siento, Padre. Madre.* Ben." From beyond the door into the kitchen, Lupe's voice ascended the scale, faltered, broke off in an exasperated burst of rapid-fire Spanish. The Señora's eyes probed the closed door with annoyance. Don Ramón was indifferent. A small smile touched the girl's mouth and went away again.

Soledad took the soup plates away and replaced them with platters of chicken under a *mole* rich with chocolate, refried beans, tortillas. The beer glasses were filled. The meal progressed quietly and they spoke little. Richards didn't feel hungry. Behind the Señora, Feliciano waited, dark and silent, in the event his mistress required some service. Not until the shivering orange *flan* appeared and was consumed did Ramón Dominguez lean back in his chair and regard with affection and satisfaction the faces of wife, daughter, and even, at last, the man he had hired to manage the herds of his country, his kingdom, Tres Reyes.

They spoke English, but with Dominguez it was a gentle, formal, archaic, idiomatic English. His Spanish, and Cayetana's, was the Spanish of Castile; he knew only one of the Mexican dialects, and this was the Indian of his mother. He pronounced his name Domeenhayth and neither objected nor became accustomed to the pronunciation Do*mingezz* used by other men. "So, Ben. How is it with McLean? I returned too late or I should have gone to him."

There it was, and now all he had to do was answer it. He looked around the table and saw they were all watching him, waiting; saw too, that they had figured it was really some minor accident magnified out of all proportion, growing with every fresh report. Dominguez had had it from Tiburcio, who had had it from one of the field hands who had had it from Soledad's sister who had happened to be out by the fountain when Shiloh rode in.

Richards said, "It could of been worse." No lie there. Jonah could have been killed on the spot.

Dominguez was reaching for a cigar. "But is the truth that the big steer put his horn into McLean?"

"Yes," Richards said. He saw don Ramón's hand pause, arrested midway between the edge of the table and the carved wooden box.

"¿Muy grave?"

"Rojo hit him in the leg, after he got Glass."

"Oh, Ben," Cayetana said. "Not *Glass*."

He did not answer, avoiding her face, not wanting to see how she looked with horror and sympathy shadowing her eyes. And still knowing how deeply she would know, that don Ramón would know, that there are times for a man who has nothing as for a man who can buy anything, when his most valued possession is a horse. Vaquero, wrangler, cowman, every man had a horse he would have come close to selling his soul for. For the first time, under the strain of anger, remorse, concern, he felt grief come up a hard hot mass in his throat, and he had to speak the lie around it. "Lunt thinks Jonah'll pull through, but it's goin' to be a long time of just sittin' in a chair for him."

"Nonsense," the Señora said crisply, from the end of the table. "Sid Lunt will have him on crutches within the week, if he has to make a pair with his own hands."

Richards had never been this close to mention of illness or crippling in the Señora's presence. It was a subject he kept shy of, in an awareness that the time rolls around when you see a man with a cane and you begin to speak spontaneously and with nervous volubility of the lame and the halt. As if there is nothing else to talk about. Now the time had caught up with him, and she had made it easy. He half-smiled, looking down the table at her, seeing the ironic acceptance in her downdrawn, deliberate mouth.

Her crippled right hand lay, as it always did, uselessly in her lap. She was quite fair; the hair drawn back severely and knotted at the neck was a coarse reddish gold, beginning to dull with gray. The face contained vestiges of if not great beauty, great awareness, great magnetism. But the body was small and old, as if it had withered and dried with the withering of her arm and leg. The left hand, holding a silver coffee spoon, showed skin so white it was like frost, and as fragile, traced with little blue veins. But the chin was resolute and the eyes were the pale eyes of the Anglo-Saxon, and they were veiled and secretive.

Her name had been Alice Graves Dawes and he had known her story before he set foot within the walls of Tres Reyes. Forty years ago, before he had been born, the story had appeared in numerous American newspapers, lacking certain essential facts, but accompanied by extensive editorial judgments and facsimiles of pen and ink sketches which, with the exception of one profile drawn from life, were mere artists' conceptions. Years later, American newspapers neither noted nor cared that she had paid a debt with the ruining of her body. This was a theory she shared only with the people of Tres Reyes, who knew everything about her as innately as Mexicans in small villages know every detail of one another's lives. She had lost of herself, of what she had been, all but the flat Midwestern voice. She was doña Alicia, Mamacita, the Señora, and she did not merely pretend, but believed, that what had come before had never been, that she had been born and raised at Tres Reyes.

From some unrecognized yearning, some unconscious backward reaching into the culture in which she had been bred, she found it pleasant to have an American in the house. She had heard of Ben Richards long before she set eyes upon him. When Dominguez hired him, she inquired only if the man Richards was as capable as rumor had him; Dominguez laughed and said that capable was not the word he would have chosen. She had her spies in the household, the closest and most trusted of whom was Feliciano.

Sí. Señor Richards had a name for knowing the country, knowing the trails, knowing men and cattle. Tiburcio, Esteban, *si*, they too knew cattle, but as everyone knew, *Mexicanos* handled horses better than cattle. It had always been this way. Then too, there was a thing . . . yes, and she knew, the Señora knew, what this thing was. It was a feeling, almost an enmity, which gringos had about Mexican trail herds. Now, if there was a gringo bossing the herd, a man like this Señor Richards . . .

She remembered being mildly disappointed when she saw him, expecting something out of the ordinary, perhaps even phenomenal. The novelty of the acquisition drained away on the presentation of this man with the old-young taciturn face and the slight build and the pale dull hair which needed cutting and the quiet self-contained eyes. Within a week she had sharply noted and credited to him efficiency, firmness, interest, unobtrusiveness, loyalty. She liked him for his very lack of intricacy. He was in direct contrast to this house of sleep, song, gossip, sentimentality, peculiar passions. And having seen this, she accepted him by ignoring him, as she ignored everything else in her great preoccupation with prayer. It was only lately she had seen the slow patient humor. He, and only he, had been as amused as she at the deliberate remark about Lunt and the crutches, and she applauded him for smiling at it.

She was a knowing woman, but not as knowing as she felt she was. When it was demanded of her, she could think like a man, precisely, logically, and because of this she knew what other ranchers thought: Richards was a machine and someday the parts were going to wear out. A machine like this could be kept in good condition at a place like Tres Reyes. Well enough. She, and Ramón, would supply the oil, and who knew how long a machine, even if worn, could continue to run? He was still young and Tres Reyes was rich. Either in spite of its wealth or because of it, Tres Reyes had to continue to operate smoothly and never in the red, and when it came to trailing the big herd north in the long blinding summer, that was what Richards was there for.

The machine was now a member of her family, a part of Tres Reyes and under her protectorate, and she would never again regard him with any other eyes and would pray for him as a mother prayed for a son when he left.

She finished her coffee. Opposite her, Dominguez was lighting his cigar. At her right, Cayetana sat with one elbow on the table, cheek and mouth cupped in her hand as if she were sorry she had spoken of the dead horse. What ails the girl, she thought, with rising irritation, what ails her every moment of the day . . . ? Her mouth drew up again and tightened. She looked at Richards. He was still half-smiling into his empty cup.

"Feliciano," the Señora said.

He moved forward, all solicitude.

"I wish to go to the *capilla*." She was blunt. "I must pray for Jonah." Her good hand braced against the edge of the table. "Well, Caye," she said.

"I was thinking of Avis," the girl said. She looked at Richards over the cup of her palm. "How did she take it?"

"She's kind of upset. Sid won't let her do anything. She said to tell you come on over one day. I reckon she'd like some company."

"You used to go to McLeans' more often, Caye," the Señora said. Her voice was thoughtful. As if she reminded her daughter of a duty, Richards thought. He broke in.

"Avis always says she's too busy to get lonesome, but that's just talk. She said be sure and tell you, Caye."

For a moment the girl's dark eyes rested full on his, and he thought, keep talking, keep talking, you damned fool, tell her all there is to be told. Yet he read nothing in her expression, nothing at all, not even interest. She had the saddest eyes he had ever seen, outside of a yearling cow, and he couldn't even make himself laugh at the comparison.

"I'll go in the morning," Cayetana said. "Pardon me, please, *Padre*. Ben." They stood up. "I'm going down with Tiburcio. Ebano's throwing lame and I want to look him over."

"Ah, too bad," Dominguez said. He was already preoccupied. "Ben, I must take from you an hour or two this night."

Richards nodded. It was a rule of the house at least three nights a week, the two of them and sometimes Uremáy, closeted in Dominguez' office with wine and cigars, checking reports, going over the books, attending to the thousand and one details which went into the operating of the ranch. Dominguez put his napkin down in a crumpled heap. Cayetana had already gone. Feliciano drew back the Señora's chair with practiced gentleness.

In the hallway outside the dining room, Dominguez paused to relight his half-smoked cigar. To the left, Richards watched Feliciano wheel the Señora through the slender iron gates of the chapel and down the single center aisle, until she sat directly beneath the altar. Above it, from a deep sheltering niche, the Virgin of Guadalupe looked down, her smooth brown tragic Mexican face touched on the cheeks with pink paint, her dark head tilted slightly to one side, her body girlish and slim in the folds of the sky-blue robes. It must be hard for the Señora, she can't kneel, Richards thought; maybe she prays to be able to kneel, sometime. Anyway, she prayed. Dominguez too, on Sunday morning. The priest in the house, the Franciscan Father Berrades, was in Mexico, so there was no regular Mass. But the whole population of Tres Reyes, man, woman, and child, trooped in on Sunday morning, and between times too. There wasn't ever a time you went by the chapel somebody wasn't down on their knees, or lighting candles in front of that altar. In the beginning, he felt awkward about it, but Dominguez had laid it out in black and white for him right away.

"I do not know what your beliefs are," he said, "or if you have beliefs. That is not my concern. But I wish you to feel free to enter or not enter this place."

"Right now I don't feel free," Richards said, after a time.

Dominguez grinned his big white grin. "I confess that as I grow older the benches become harder and my knees sharper. Perhaps both."

It had never been mentioned again. He had not been inside the chapel, although sometimes he had stood outside and looked at Guadalupe. But one time he thought she moved, and when it happened he almost jumped out of his boots. It was like a bolt of lightning went through him, and his heart beat so hard it felt as if it had pulled out of place. He never stood and looked at her again for any length of time; he just let his eyes glance off her. It struck him, standing there, seeing the Señora wheeled to what had become her occupation, waiting for Dominguez, that the only person at Tres Reyes he had never seen inside that chapel was

Cayetana. Because you never came through and caught her, that's all, he told himself, but knew with curiosity that this was not so, that Cayetana didn't go through those gates. Pray, he commanded the Señora, from inside himself. Pray like hell, on account of Jonah needs it.

It was chilly and cluttered in Dominguez' office, and there was a fine sandy dust on everything. It was a fair-size room but it had been chopped up with a partition, so that about a third of it was storage area, with a couple of old chairs. The women of the house were not allowed to enter, although sometimes Cayetana came in to struggle with totals in the ledgers and check the Cattleman's Association book, which was registered in the Señora's name. Seeing it now, lying on the desk, Richards was reminded of Jonah McLean's words. Dominguez is not a citizen. Not a Texian. Not a gringo. A greaser, who's ranching here with all his holdings in the name of his American wife. Say the Señora did die. Cayetana was a citizen. Cayetana was half English- or Irish- or German-American, or whatever the Señora's family had been, even if you looked at her and couldn't see it and said *pura Mexicana*. Tres Reyes was to be Cayetana's and nobody had to say so or put it in writing. She would be sole survivor. Unless McLean had the idea they were going to descend on Tres Reyes and throw don Ramón Dominguez clear out of Texas and over the Rio Grande if the Señora died. You never knew. There might be men felt that way, small men, envious men. God Himself might have liked to own Tres Reyes. Maybe Cayetana would have a fight on her hands, given the proper circumstances. Then he thought, maybe Caye doesn't give a damn. If she didn't, she'd ought to let her father know about it now, while there was still time. Jonah had been using every threat, no matter how remote, and Richards hated the fact that he had forced Jonah into it.

As had become customary, he poured the wine and selected a cigar. Dominguez was making entries in the ledger. Richards lit up, leaned back in his chair and began to think how he was to broach a subject had to be broached. He watched his *patrón* intent on the books.

Much of what he had been in youth remained in Ramón Dominguez. He was middle height, big headed, with a shock of iron

33

gray hair, thick iron gray mustache, skin the color of parchment under the copper overlay of years of sun. He had been, and was, a handsome man, with dark kindly eyes, slow moving, slightly bowlegged. His father had been Sevillano; his mother, his father's second wife, Mexican out of an almost pure Indian tribe. A half brother lived still in Seville, where Ramón had been sent for schooling. The schooling, the *Andaluz* way of life, had stayed with him, but he was filled with the dark, earthy, sometimes gentle, sometimes barbaric graces and dignities which were inextricably portion of the Mexican *gente* and of their land. He laughed easily, not only with his mouth but with his eyes, a man with *alma*, soul. He was a good man and he loved his people. But he was also a man of *sentido*. He had continued to build and improve Tres Reyes, out of the little mud village his father had taken over before there was a United States, before this big rough country had been called Texas. The prime of his life had been spent expatriated in Mexico; he had given up quickly on legal action to restore and hold his property. When he returned to Tres Reyes for good, years of revolution had torn Mexico and he had fought and lost a war which gave Texas to the United States. He was a Mexican, and he wanted to live on his land as his father had lived; to be honest, content, comfortable, respected, to sell his herds, raise his horses, care for his people. That Tres Reyes was situated on American soil was of no particular importance to him. He crossed the border as he pleased and maintained a reputation for unequivocal fairness. He had fought against Texas and now he was Texian.

And like other good, just men, he would commit untold follies, practice any deception to protect, if not perhaps his life, the way of it, and the continuing certainty of the way of it.

He closed the ledger and reached for his glass. "Now, Ben." He picked up a scrap of paper and studied it. "Ah, Tiburcio . . . he will not desist until he has spent the last dollar of Tres Reyes. Two new men he has taken on . . . good vaqueros, he says." Dominguez laughed, shaking his head. "I cannot hire all of Mexico and yet Tiburcio will have it so. There is here also a letter from Allenby. In his words, then, you know how he operates and he knows how you operate and he expects that you and he will run together like clockwork." He looked up. "You have driven for Allenby before. What is it he must do that asks for this clockwork?"

"He likes to meet us along the trail," Richards said. "You pull into some town and the boys are all ready to go see the elephant and down some brave makers only their pockets are empty, and there's Allenby buying drinks and handing out credit. I reckon I'd rather deliver a herd to him than any man in the business."

"Mexicans?" Dominguez said, smiling.

"Todd's square as they come, don Ramón. As long as a man ain't set for trouble, popper or vaquero, Todd will stake him."

"And if he is, as you say, set for trouble?"

"Then I reckon Todd Allenby can make more trouble for him than he ever looked for."

Dominguez swung back in his chair and lighted a second cigar. "These things it pleases me to know about this man. Ben, you see the annoyances with which I am faced here. My position is . . . *que raro*, perhaps. Fifty, sixty years ago, here, among the *Californios*, this was a way of life. The way of life is fading, it goes from us. I am not one of those who must band with his neighbors and drive all the stock together. I am alone here, with more good beef than ten small ranchers can gather for one drive. Always, I must do it alone."

"Don Ramón," Richards said, "it's kind of common knowledge you've staked more than one rancher when he needed it."

"Staked? Ah, the loan. So what does this mean? What man would I be to hold back so little from a man who needs so little? No, this is not what I am saying, Ben. What I wish you to remember, always, is that I am alone, that I am a Mexican, and that I am living well in your country."

After a minute Richards said, "And that I work for you." He stubbed out his cigar. "Don Ramón, there's something I got to talk to you about. About Jonah. I made a promise to him I wouldn't tell what he showed . . . told . . . me, but then he went and put me where I got to break it. It means a lot to me he doesn't know I told you."

Dominguez had pushed back his chair. "McLean? What is it, Ben?"

"It's hard sayin' it, but it looks like Jonah's goin' to cash in. After what Rojo did to him."

"Cash in? Die, you mean. *Sangre de Cristo*, but you said . . ."

"I had to. Jonah did get gored in the leg and that was what looked the worst, on the outside. But the horn went in his belly. I saw it. It doesn't seem to me he could make it, with what the horn did to him."

"*Dios*," Dominguez said. "But Lunt. What does Lunt say?"

"Not much, like always. Jonah won't have a doctor, he won't hurt Sid's feelings, even if he dies for it."

"And the son. And the little wife." Dominguez sounded as if he was talking to himself.

"He won't tell 'em. I had to go along with that."

"It is hard to accept this. How much time do you think there is for him then?"

Richards was sitting forward in his chair, hunched over, hands on his knees. "I don't know. I think, for a fact, that whatever can be done for him Sid can do. Maybe tomorrow, maybe next week. *¿Quien sabe?* Not even Sid, I reckon."

"What can I do in this?" Dominguez said. McLean was his neighbor, his friend, they lifted their glasses together, they consulted and discussed their problems, he went to McLeans' to see a new horse, the McLeans came to Tres Reyes for the saints day feasts and the bull baiting. He knew McLean as a big vigorous bear of a man, overhasty sometimes, prone to temper sometimes, the kind of man you could count on living to a testy old age. Yes. The red steer. Rojo.

"I will pay well for his hide, this killer," he said, swinging back and reaching across his desk for paper.

"My God, no," Richards almost shouted it. "He wouldn't stand for that, don Ramón. You know him well enough to know he wouldn't stand for that. If he dies, then's time enough, but for now he's got to think about Rojo just like he's always thought about him."

Dominguez looked at him. "And how is it he thinks of him?"

Then Richards said slowly, "I ain't sure. Sometimes I reckon he thinks of him bein' dragged in and shipped off to make beef, sort of punishment for bein' how he is. And the punishment always handed out by Jonah." He shrugged. "Then sometimes I reckon Jonah thinks of him just bein' wild and free and never havin' to bend to anything or anybody and maybe thinkin' that's the only thing that's worth it, worth livin' for, to be free."

Dominguez was watching Richards' face. "And is this the manner in which you think of Rojo, Ben?"

Richards looked up. "I reckon it is," he said.

Dominguez said nothing, only sat there, watching Richards. Then Richards said, "You asked what you can do. Do you want me to tell you? Because I got to tell you. He's got fifteen hundred head. He wants to throw 'em in with the Tres Reyes, as far as railhead."

Dominguez did not look surprised. Richards could see he was figuring in his mind, tallying, totaling. "It is a big herd, Ben."

"Yes," Richards said.

"It is in your heart that you would do this thing for him, no?"

"I tried to make him see that my responsibility was to you and to Tres Reyes, and if there came a time when I had to make a choice the choice would be with Tres Reyes. All the way. Every mile."

"You do not tell me, now, that he does not understand this?"

"He sees it, I reckon. He just didn't seem to feel it was any reason for turnin' him down. Like there wasn't any risk."

"And the risk . . . you feel this risk, Ben?"

"Don Ramón, if I was drivin' six head of longhorns from here to Montana, I'd be watching the risk."

Dominguez leaned back and put his booted feet on a corner of the desk. Richards could not have given him a better answer. "And if I should offer my refusal, what will he then do?"

"Turn the herd over to Frankie and Shiloh."

"This Shiloh is a good man."

"Green. Give him three, four summers, he'll be top hand."

"You do not tell me your thoughts on Frankie."

"Don't reckon it would get us any further," Richards said.

"For myself, I do not find the dislike for Frankie," Dominguez said after a time of regarding his feet, crossed at the ankles, on the desk. "I would put him out with Tiburcio for six months. After that he would look out at the world with other eyes."

37

"And see that it doesn't owe him a thing?" Richards said. "Don't misunderstand me, don Ramón. I like Frankie. But I wouldn't put a trail herd under him, and I ain't keen on havin' him in my crew. I don't expect he's bad, I just don't trust him, on account of if there's a fight or a bottle anywhere where he can smell 'em, he'll drop everything and go after his nose."

Dominguez considered the ceiling. "It comes to me that this is the drive which will take McLean out of debt, no?"

Richards nodded, staring at the floor between his feet. For a bare second he felt a flash of anger. It was easy for Dominguez to speak of this, and, while he was in no way patronizing, Richards caught the cynicism in his voice. Tres Reyes longhorns could range from here to Durango this summer, and don Ramón Dominguez would be little poorer for it. He said, "I reckon McLean took on like he did because the last thing he wants is pity. I don't know why it is a man can't stand to be pitied, even if he thinks he's dyin'. Sure, he's countin' heavy on this drive."

"Then it is settled. It may be that the medicine he needs most is to know that you will take his herd."

"I don't know. I'm kind of confused about the whole thing, tell you the truth, don Ramón. He was bad today, off and on . . . kind of delirious, I expect you'd call it."

"*Que lastima.* Whether or not that is what he wishes," Dominguez said.

"He said a lot of things he wouldn't of said if he'd been feelin' better, or in his right mind. I didn't understand some of it."

"It is the fever," Dominguez said. He picked up his glass and drained it. His face had gone sad, thoughtful.

"He didn't seem feverish, is the funny part of it. He was makin' sense enough till he got to the part about payin' off a Texas Ranger."

Dominguez turned his head slowly and looked at Richards. "It does not, indeed, seem that his mind is sound."

Richards leaned back in his chair, shifting his gun belt. He thought, I ain't any good at this, no good at all. He sees through me like I was a sheet of glass held to the sky, but what I aim to see is what he's goin' to do about it. It took him a little time to realize that Dominguez was not going to do anything about it. He was calmly pouring himself another glass of wine, offering the pitcher to Richards with uplifted brows. Richards shook his head, refusing. He said patiently, "As good as I can remember, it was something to do with me bein' a drifter and only one man bein' rich enough to pay off a Texas Ranger. Or anyway that was part of it, before he maybe realized he shouldn't be sayin' what he was sayin' and quit."

Dominguez sipped at his wine, regarding Richards over the rim of the glass. I might not be good at this, Richards thought, but he is. He is. He knows exactly what he's doin' and the right thing to say if it ain't swinging his way, and how not to say anything at all. He can ride out and get himself as dirty and sweaty and blood-stained as any popper, runnin' down steers and heatin' an iron and puttin' in twenty-four hours a day with the best of 'em, but when the chips are down, he knows how to play, with the cards right up against his chest and not a change of expression on his face, and that is what money and name and education and the good things in life teach you: ease. How to be easy.

"On the other hand, though," he said, "I don't reckon a man would make an accusation like that right off the top of his head. Against a Ranger, I mean."

"Rangers," Dominguez said. "Rangers have to their credit a great accomplishment, no? They have made men in all walks of life, in every corner of Texas . . . yes, and Mexico, too . . . know that they are not to be taken as a game. They have built for themselves a great name, great as the names of the saints. They are true as the summer day, they fear God, they are brave as the panther, they will die without question to perform their duty." He pursed his lips. "Do you know how it is the Rangers have done this, Ben? No? Allow me to tell you. They have managed it because, I suspect, it is largely true."

Richards smiled.

"Ah, you think I make the joke," Dominguez said. "No, I tell you what I believe. But let us look again. Do you not suppose that among these many there may be one or two who may be called away from this devotion, this duty. Who may find, let us say, money, a woman, *agujeta* . . . what you would call boredom . . .

reason to leave the ranks and go upon their way without notice, perhaps without thought of betrayal?"

"Yes, I reckon so," Richards said. "If the temptation was strong enough. Why not? I might. You might."

Dominguez got to his feet. He scratched his head, looking almost amused. "Is it possible? Can you look, long enough and far enough, and see Captain Bonaventure betraying Texas for a handful of gold. Or Shipley, that fine young man we see now and again. Pure as this pitcher, Ben." He picked up the silver pitcher and looked at it reflectively. "And Lyons . . . what is the name by which they called him . . . Buster." He pronounced it wryly. "Buster too is pure, I think. You know them all. Where would you find better men?"

"I wouldn't," Richards said.

"Do you believe any one of them could be 'paid off,' as Jonah would have it?"

Richards didn't answer right away. When he did his voice was quiet, almost cold. "I wouldn't want to speak for Bonaventure. Or anybody else."

Dominguez said it outright, suddenly. "But who would this rich seducer of Texas Rangers be?"

And Richards, standing now, looking at him, said, "I reckoned maybe you could answer that for me, don Ramón."

Dominguez' eyes showed the beginning of laughter; they were for a moment shrewd and merry. "Ben. *Amigo*." For the first time he seemed aware that he was holding the pitcher. He set it down on the desk, but he did not turn his eyes from Richards while he did it. "I did not phrase well what I wished to ask. Let me begin again. Let us pretend that I did not ask this man's identity. Let us, instead, inquire of ourselves, you and I, why it would be necessary to buy a Ranger."

He faced Dominguez across the desk. His face, voice, were weary. "Maybe the fault was mine, don Ramón, in not sayin' it right out in the beginning. I never worked for a man like you before. I got kind of used to bunkin' with my crews. I never had a boss called me in for supper and passed around the *vino*. The cigars. I like it this way. I can live without it, but I like it this way. I like you and your family and everything about Tres Reyes. All my life I been like this: if something gets in my way, gets in the way of what I'm bein' paid to protect, or even what I ain't paid for, just what I happen to feel inside me I got to protect, I reckon I don't take too much time thinkin' about the ways in which I'm goin' to do it. I do it whatever way comes to mind first and easiest. Words, maybe. My hands, maybe." He stood with his head lowered. Dominguez could hear him breathing.

Dominguez said, "¿Y un pistolero, talvez?"

Richards said levelly, "You said it. I didn't."

"Please. Speak, Ben."

"For a long time, over a year, I looked for Rangers. I went out of my way to keep away from Rangers. After a while I got to see Rangers didn't pay any more attention to me than they would of paid to a spavined horse. Then a Ranger came to Tres Reyes. I passed him out there." Richards swung his arm toward the courtyard, as if he could touch tile, fountain, water, through the wall. "Right out there. Lyons. Buster Lyons, Tiburcio said his name was. I never saw him before. I ain't laid eyes on him since. A Ranger came here and people on Tres Reyes saw him. You saw him. He talked to you. Six weeks later Jonah McLean lays busted up with steer horn and tells me you paid off a Ranger." He bent forward, bracing his arms on the desk. "I got to know why, don Ramón. You got to tell me why."

Dominguez sat down again. He drew his chair to the desk as if he was about to resume work, placing his arms flat out across the clutter of papers. "First you will tell me, Ben, whether I have ever offered you the lie."

"Far as I know, never," Richards said.

"Were there times when you felt I might have made the lie, without effort for myself."

"No, don Ramón."

"But, at this time, it would be very simple for me to lie, would it not?"

"Sir," Ben Richards said stiffly, "I expect I don't know just how simple it is for you to lie."

Surprise flashed across Dominguez' face. "My own returns to me, eh?" His eyes did not conceal his amusement now. "If I say to you that I do not lie to you, will you accept my word?"

"Yes," Richards said.

"I do not know the reason for what you tell me of yourself. It does not matter. I ask you no questions. The Ranger called Lyons came here because he was crossing the border and wished to contact some people to whom I could give him introduction. What passed between us was a paper with three names and addresses upon it. He then paid his regards to me, to Cayetana, and to Tiburcio, delivered the regards of Captain Bonaventure, and left Tres Reyes."

When he had finished speaking he saw that Richards' face was strained and pale; it had that look of severity which Dominguez had noticed before, when Richards was under pressure. He almost leaped out of his chair when Richards held out his hand, across the desk; when he took it he winced at the grasp.

"So. It is an end to this, Ben?"

"I reckon they knew where I was," Richards said. "Jonah took a windstorm by the tail and milked what he could out of it, on account of he wanted something and wasn't goin' to be stopped gettin' it. I'm beholden to you, don Ramón. More'n you could guess."

Behind the desk, Dominguez was surreptitiously nursing his hand. Richards picked up his hat and said good night. When he closed the office door behind him and stepped into the hall, he saw that the chapel was still lighted, and that the Señora still sat under the altar. She was motionless in her wheelchair, slightly twisted to one side with the ravages of her affliction, so that all he could see of her was a slight edge of her warped body, a rim of shoulder line above the woven rawhide chair back, a fall of black lace over her head, held in place with a high tortoise-shell comb. He went to the gate and pressed his forehead against the cool iron-smelling palings and looked at Guadalupe for a long time. His face was wet with sweat. Guadalupe's sorrowing eyes held him. She did not move. He went out the massive carved door, into the night, and unbuckled his gun belt and felt it slip from him as twice its weight and stood holding it at arm's length, the gun swinging against his leg, and drew clean sharp air into his lungs.

THREE

When darkness had fallen he came out of the brush and made for water. The tip of his right horn was thick with dried blood. Bits of horse entrail still clung to it.

He stood looking over the flat grassland to the river. Around him cows were grazing in the night, calves left in the brush under the protection of other cows. One by one they rotated the grazing, the watering, each cow returning unerringly to her own. A few steers grazed with them, but the bulls had not come in from winter range yet to do battle with one another for their territorial rights.

He went to water slowly, breathing deeply, with a snorting sound. Cows moved out of his way. He drank for a time, standing knee deep; then he raised his head and looked about him, upstream, down, across to the near shore, and came up out of the water. When he found firm footing he began to paw. The sharp polished hoof dug deeply into the earth, throwing the black bottom dirt high in the air. He felt it on back, haunches, head, tossing his head to meet it. When he was covered with dirt, he sank the stained horn deep into the earth, until he felt dampness. He worked the horn, scouring it. When he had cleaned it, he sank the other horn and worked it. At the last, he worked both horn tips into the lightly sloping bank, but he could not bring the earth to his forehead, for the spread of his horns was too wide.

This done, he moved from water to graze, walking more slowly now, with his ropey tail flicking. When he reached the edge of the grass he stood again, seeing his kind against the sky, using the dark as man used daylight, preparing to go restored to hiding when dawn came. Water was near, but had it not been, he would have walked twenty miles to it and returned to graze this same area and not gone for water again for three days.

He was red, but he was an uncommon deep dark red. Other things about him men marked as uncommon: the horns whose tips curved up and out, the first foot of their spread, close to his head, marked with ever-widening concentric rings which gave an appearance of wrinkles and marked him a mossy horn; his size, which at ten years put him two to three hundred pounds above the weight of a grown steer in prime. He was rough-coated, shaggy, seamed with the scar of an old, barely legible brand, swaybacked, heavyboned. But he had the legs of a racing horse. Along his backbone ran a lobo streak, a thin line of lighter colored hair, and the fringe of thick hair around his ears and muzzle were lighter still. His eyes were clear, wild, black, remote, picking up points of light.

In him was the blood of Andaluz. His forefathers had come from the green rolling *pasturas* of don Gregorio de Villalobos, themselves the stock which produced the Spanish fighting bull. They came in the sixteenth century, with men who followed the dream of gold in the new world, and before that century was a quarter done, they were running free in the fastnesses of Mexico: *mesteños*, mustang cattle; *cimarrones*, the wild ones. They fought anything which moved: men, bears, wolves, horses, snakes. In time, their savagery was diluted by the blood of more docile stock brought in from the southern states, but here and there some escaped the dilution, living, sireing, dying in the mountain and desert wildernesses where man did not seek them. The wild strain remained, strong in the *cimarrones*.

44

When he was eight weeks old, Mexicans who worked an American ranch separated him from the pale red mother cow. He was taken shivering and bawling every step of the way for the familiar warmth he could no longer see or smell. The mother cow followed. She had long slender deadly horns and would kill if she could. They roped her and cut a knee tendon in her foreleg. Now she could walk but not run, and still she followed. He had never before smelled men, the sweat of men, blood, fire, burning hair. The smell was all around him, bringing his tongue out in terror. He was thrown to the ground. Hands held him. There was a rushing sound and the stink of his own scorched hide. Fire ran along him with the branding iron. He never lost his voice. He did not know what pain was, now pain came to him in the white hot iron which dedicated him to ownership, the blade which slit his ears, the bloody knife which gelded him. In a vortex of dust and shouting, bawling of cows and calves, splattering of blood, he was on his feet and running, crying his fear and agony through the bedlam of the cow camp, the mutilated calves, the grieving cows, until he found, with his nose, his own semi-crippled mother, and went to her swollen bag and felt her rough tongue on him in that same fierce affection with which she had once torn the belly out of a panther for his life.

He had never been claimed. That same mother took him into mountain canyons, into hiding places which were faced unbroken with rock walls, into brakes so high and densely woven that men could not penetrate. With her, he crossed rivers and recrossed them. With her, he saw men, horses, wolves, coyotes, his own kind. In the spring he saw the bulls fight, not for the cows, for the bulls did not cut out a string of cows as stallions cut mares; a cow was for any bull who wished to take her. The bulls clashed horns to decide their range rights. At two, he was ready to be driven to market, and rope never touched him. At three, the ranch whose brand he bore joined the scores which folded in the wake of the War between the States.

He did not know when the old cow died. He had been long since free of her, a loner who did not seek the company of his own kind, and men called him *ladino*, outlaw. In the coming warmth of a new year, despite his steerdom, he would follow the cows for a time, yearningly, impotently. Then, when men and cattle moved in great masses upon the land, he would go to sanctuary, remembering and hating man, who had wrought pain upon his body, sensing instinctively the finality of bondage to man.

He was no longer afraid of men. He could run, like wind in the mountain places. His endurance, the endurance of the long-horn, was greater than that of any other animal, and the more his endurance was tested, the stronger it grew. In a well-armed race, his armament was superior. The country itself was partisan. There were cow trails in the brush that a man encased from head to foot in leather could barely reach. Nor did he fear thirst, for he could exist if he had to on the wet pulpy mass of prickly pear until darkness removed whatever threatened him and allowed him to water in his own time.

Educated in the eluding of all known menace and quick to put vast distances between himself and the unknown, he was now lord of the brasada and had begun to show himself as such.

He had proved it again today, with the slow horse, the slower man.

In the courtyard under the Spanish glass-and-iron lamps which were smoky with burning oil, Richards saw two small points of light moving toward him, out of the darkness. While he stood there, holding his gun belt, the lights slowed and suspended inside the arch of the gate. They looked like the eyes of an animal, but he knew they were cigarettes glowing. One glow disappeared briefly, and he heard the thud of the main gates closing, the bar grating as it was lowered, the clang of the iron inner gates; then the glow rejoined the other. House *mozos*, he thought, walking toward them, and then saw that it was Cayetana and Tiburcio Uremáy.

"*Baynhaméen*," Uremáy said. "*Hola.*"

"*Hola, Tiburcio. ¿Como es Ebano?*"

"*¿Ebano?*" Uremáy said. "*Huh. Ebano vivien.*" He spread his hands. "And he lives, the ebony horse, because this one, this flower of a thousand places, feeds him *peloncillo.*" They both looked at Cayetana in the dim light. She was holding, along with

46

the cigarette, Richards noticed, a spill of twisted paper, used to carry the brown cones of Mexican sugar. "Listen to what I say, now, *amigo*," Uremáy said. "The ebony horse, for whom this flower puts forth her most beautiful petals, what does he do? He steps into a hole, perhaps? He is feeling . . . how shall I say it . . . *muy infantil* . . . and he does not put all that black weight properly upon the earth? So it is. Now he limps and the flower will not ride him. As if that weight of the flower would matter. No. I, Tiburcio Uremáy, I go myself and I bathe the offended foot and I see that there is no swelling in the hoof. I make a nice warm maguey poultice and put it upon the leg. I comb and rub and soothe and place a blanket . . . the best blanket . . . upon this Ebano, so that he does not shake with the cold and catch a devil, and I go and remove the blanket so that he does not steam in the night and catch a devil. But what is it that makes the black horse as good as the day he slipped from his mother?" He threw up his head to the sky, as if studying the stars. "I will tell you. *Peloncillo*."

"Tiburcio," Cayetana said, unmoved. "I only gave him one cone."

"Truly," Uremáy said. "*Es verdad*. It is all that is needed, one cone." He pushed the big straw hat he wore to the back of his head. His soft eyes shone in a broad, square face stamped Indian. Levi canvas covered his squat agile body from ankle to neck. His boots were worn, old, with very high, slanting heels. Under the thrown-back hat his hair stood up a stiff gray brush, and the mustache on his full red upper lip was also gray, and pencil thin. He was of an age with Dominguez, near sixty. In a sense, Richards knew, Uremáy was Tres Reyes: he had managed its people from field hand to vaquero for over twenty years. He had handled Dominguez' trail herds. Now he was too old. It was his pleasure to affirm . . . and he had related it so often that he now believed it . . . that Tres Reyes had been a grant from Carlos the Second, a full league, four thousand four hundred and thirty-eight acres, made to the Dominguez' in times as long dead as those of the Seven Cities and the martyred Church. The acreage had as long since numbered well over one hundred thousand, and as to the Sevillano who fathered don Ramón and built Tres Reyes from a cluster of mud huts, he professed no knowledge, secure in pride of tradition.

Cayetana dropped her cigarette and ground it under her boot. Her free hand rested on Uremáy's arm. "*Gracias*, Tiburcio," she said.

Again he shrugged. His words were for Richards. "The flower is all gratitude. And for what reason? Because I go with her in the dark to see that the horse chews his sugar well." His voice was very soft. "So all is trouble this night, eh, Ben?" His eyes were soft too, but they glinted in the pale light. The words seemed to Richards more than an allusion to the lame horse. Sometimes he thought, there are Mexicans with a sixth sense. Maybe a seventh, and an eighth. Then Uremáy straightened. "Since I see you before the sunrise, what is it you will tell me when the sunrise comes?"

Richards ran a hand over his jaw. "Well, I'm supposed to tell you to quit hirin', for one thing. Other than that, I expect you can just get up tomorrow and do your usual four days' work before nightfall. I reckon to do a little scoutin' the next day or so, see if there's anything around with horns worth bringin' in."

Uremáy laughed soundlessly. His teeth were huge, square and white. "Nah. There is nothing out there worth it. *Nada*. I tell you this before sunrise, however. All day a *manada* of women . . . God still their tongues . . . is gathered to make the paper lanterns. You know my *gente*. Well then you know they will not think one thought of money . . . the steer is money, no? . . . until the lanterns are hung and the meat is roasting. After that it may be they will think of work again."

"I expect you are talkin' about your fiesta," Richards said.

"But of course. When the spring comes and we prepare for the trail it is reason enough for many pleasures," Uremáy said. "You see that it is not all work here, but that we reach out for even the smallest excuse to enjoy life. It is the soul of Tres Reyes."

Richards wasn't sure whether he meant the annual feast or Cayetana. The *peon* boss was still looking down at the girl, and her hand still rested lightly on his arm. Richards remembered that he had heard men speak of the affection between the daughter of *casa* Tres Reyes and her father. But it seemed to him, had seemed to him since he came here, that despite the bond between father

48

and daughter, there was something hairfine, subtle, empathetic, between the girl and Tiburcio Uremáy which went beyond blood. No one he knew had ever remarked on it, as they did on the paternal alliance. It was an open thing, easy, informal, yet it was a thing he could see was a form of love. What its depths were, or why, he did not know, but he wondered, in this moment, if Ramón Dominguez was aware of it.

"I will tell you more," Uremáy said. "There will be good tequila for those who are sick in their very guts of all this wine of civilization. Also pulque which would grow hair on a stone. There is a certain stone in the Tres Castillos where Coahuila pulque was poured, many years ago. Each spring it covers itself with hair as fine as that of the Holy Child."

"Sure," Richards said. "And another stone that comes over and combs out the lice."

"*Bueno*," Uremáy said. "The gringo makes the music of the *Mexicano* after all. So. I go find my Natividad and we drink a little glass together."

"Tiburcio," Cayetana said anxiously, "in the morning . . ."

"In the morning, small gray dove, you will stay in your pretty blankets and wait for your *chocolate*. The first voice to speak your name will be mine, and I will hold Ebano up by his ears, outside your window, so you shall see that he still lives. *Buenos noches*, Ben. *Buenos noches, Morena Flor*."

"Good night," Richards said. Until the darkness took Uremáy he watched the blunt, bowlegged figure disappear toward the cluster of houses which fanned out behind the big house.

Cayetana stood by the fountain holding the cream-colored hat by its throat latch. She had pulled a heavy woven blanket over her shoulders, and by the smell of it he guessed it had come from the stables. She stood looking down into the pool, which might have ice on it by morning, the way it felt now, he thought. There were some twigs floating in it. "Ben," she said, "I want to tell you something. I haven't told anyone but Tiburcio."

He felt a mild surprise. He knew Cayetana as well as any man could who sat opposite her at table, sometimes rode with her to look over the interests of Tres Reyes, engaged her interest on a level somewhat less than brotherly. There were hours, days, when they did not see one another and he more or less forgot she existed. Even now, wrapped in a horse blanket, he wondered how it was he could overlook what a superb woman she was. Beauty such as hers was rare, and in this harsh country shortlived. The border sun was merciless, it would sap the oil out of her in a few short demanding years, unless she took infinite pains to see that this did not happen. She took none. She was younger than Avis, barely twenty, and he forgot this also, for she seemed older to him. Not in face or body so much as in the settled demeanor, the self-contained and self-sufficient bearing which came from having largely grown up with adults in an unconventional caste. She was tough, hard, thin, as well put together as a cat, and above it all was that exquisite face, Uremáy's Morena Flor, the brown flower. It was a grave, somber face, and the eyes looked to have opened on the world knowing too much, and sad. Despite the toughness, the maturity, she had a tendency at times to be a shade out of touch, just over the hairline border of saying, doing, not quite the right thing, and recovering when it was too late. She was not quick to give her confidences, except, he now believed, to Uremáy, and her spontaneous offering to disclose some apparently guarded secret might have amused him, made him gently encouraging if he didn't know how important and absolute the secret would be to her. Reality, for her, was always twice as real.

She had a low voice with an edge in it, almost a roughness. The Castilian influence was faint but discernible. "I saw Rojo," she said. "I was close to him. As close as we are to the gates. I think it was the same day Frankie and Shiloh saw him. We were on our way back from the *mesteñero* camp."

"You were with Tiburcio."

"I rode ahead. When I first saw him I was . . . alarmed." She gave him a wry smile. "He didn't object to my being there. He acted as if he'd set himself out for me to look at. What does a longhorn do when you come upon him? He goes like the wind. Not that longhorn."

"You ran for it," Richards said.

"I couldn't, Ben. I couldn't move. I sat there on Ebano and watched him. If my father knew it . . ."

"Girl, if he did, he'd raise the roof and be right in doin' it.

50

Where I come from that would of meant a trip to the corncrib with a switch. Teach you sense."

"It was as if Ebano had grown there. I didn't move and Rojo didn't move. Just long enough to smoke a cigarette and he was gone. I had the oddest feeling . . ." She stopped. He wondered if whatever she had been going to say had been said to Tiburcio.

"That's another thing," he said. "Smoking. You go to the corncrib for that too."

Her voice was vague suddenly, drifting off. "All the old *Mexicanas* do it. It makes you grow old quickly."

He let it pass, but he felt unsettled inside to hear a young girl say a thing like that. He couldn't imagine Avis smoking, or saying out loud she wanted to grow old. What in hell would a woman want to grow old for, except perversity. Because when they were old they all wanted to be young again. If you did any thinking about it at all you would pretty soon begin to find out that women were just one big heap of contradictions; only you never seemed to find out in time.

"Well, which did you want to do, post a reward, or shoot him?" he said. She didn't miss the bitterness. The words came out sounding scalded.

She said, "When we made camp that night I drank a little wine and I said to myself, this is for you, Rojo. May you always be free."

He stood looking down at her. He knew the sentimentality of the Mexican, expressed at times in a tone so choked with feeling you thought he might burst into tears before he finished. The dedication of passion might range all the way from the Queen of Heaven to a dehorning saw. He liked that in the *gente*, yet Cayetana's simple statement of fact was disarming. When she was at her most uncomplicated was when he felt most awkward with her. "Now listen, Caye." His face was severe, paternal. "It ain't my place to say it, but if you lay eyes on Rojo again, you go for cover, hear? You say anything you want to when you're wettin' down the dust, but do it from cover. It ain't natural for a long-horn to stand like that unless he figures he's got the whole world his way. And about Rojo . . . or anyway kind of about him. I'm goin' to be trailin' Jonah's herd along with the Tres Reyes."

51

She was silent a moment, considering. When she spoke he knew she still thought of the red steer. "Ben, did you think how strange it is . . . how long Jonah has talked about Rojo, and when the meeting comes, it comes like this? I thought we should send word we would not have the *barbacoa* now, but too many people look forward to it. Our own, most of all. The McLeans, the Davises . . ."

"Jonah says Davis is foldin' and goin' East."

"Is it that bad with him?"

"Last year was rough. It was a blizzard year in '73. And '72 was a drought year."

She smiled wanly, fleetingly. "But '72 wasn't a bad year for Ned Selvo, because you trailed his herd out from the Panhandle. He recouped two years' losses on that drive, didn't he, Ben?"

"Maybe," he said uncomfortably.

"Selvo borrowed from my father a few years ago. You should know something, Ben. I could run Tres Reyes if I had to."

"I expect you could," he said.

"But don't boast, is that what you're thinking?"

"No, what I was thinkin' is that probly you could sit in that office where your *padre* sits and do a bang-up job of it, but you'd still need a man around."

"As long as I have Tiburcio . . ." She shook her head. "I won't always have Tiburcio, will I? He grows old. Ebano grows old. Only I do not grow old."

"I'll make a little bet with you," he said lightly. "I bet you will. If you figure out a way to stop it, I'll pay up, too."

She did not smile. And he knew something for the first time. A man. There must be men from here to Philadelphia Peeaye wouldn't turn up their noses at marrying with Cayetana Dominguez and falling into a paying proposition like Tres Reyes. Her chances weren't worth a damn, though, and unless don Ramón went to a lot of trouble to make some fancy arrangements, she was going to marry, if she married at all, out of her world, out of her class. Also, she didn't seem to him like the type of woman would just meekly side up with the man her old father picked out for her. She had a problem he'd never even thought about, and what puzzled him was that she didn't seem to worry about it any.

52

At least not out where it showed. Maybe it explained those big sad eyes. And maybe it didn't. He could remember his prim elder sister, born virgin and dead virgin, saying through tight lips that there were worse fates in this world than being an old maid. The sour judgment had been made to a neighbor in the act of plunging into a huge washboiler with one hand and fighting the kids off with the other, and he recalled his sister didn't so much as twitch when the woman said, you damn right they is, girl, and you lookin' at one of the worst of 'em. "Caye," he said, "why do you go out with the mustang crew?"

It seemed to him that the somberness died out in her eyes. He knew, saw, her latent warmth the first time he met her, in this same courtyard, when she had asked that he call her by name and not by the careful *Señorita* he had counted on. "Why? Oh Ben, I love it. We cross the river and the *mesteñeros* come in with those funny, crazy horses and Tiburcio and I go about and tell them which we want. We are very clever, Tiburcio and I . . . or at least Tiburcio is. I learn from him." She sat down on the low tiled wall which bounded the pool. "We look a long time and then we say, see what they try to pass off on us. That one will never make a work horse. This one, look, he has a gall on his leg, he will never do. And Tiburcio says, see the one with the white nose, bypass him, for he is the best of the lot, and we will take him grudgingly at a low price. But in the end, you see, we do pay the price, and we are satisfied, and the *mesteñeros* are satisfied. We have horses and they have money. Then we sit at the fire and Natividad has cooked for us, beans and more beans and coffee. Then we sing. All the old songs of Mexico, and of Spain. They love the Spanish music. I play them *paso dobles* and *Sevillanos*. The coyotes sing with us, always, and sometimes we hear lobos. Do you know what I wished, Ben? I wished the coyotes and the lobos would come to our fire and sit with us and not be afraid and sing. I thought this was foolish, but Tiburcio says no, he has wished this all his life. I never knew he wished this. In the morning we take our string and start back to Tres Reyes. Now we go again soon. The brothers Gómez have promised us a good string."

"You make it sound mighty pleasant," he said, searching her

face, seeing she had omitted any reference to cold or heat, fifteen miles a day in the saddle, lack of privacy for any or all functions demanding privacy, plain hard muscle work chivvying mustangs, a hundred other things he could think of. Safety for her person did not enter his head; he knew, as did she, that she was as safe in Mexican or American camps as she would have been within the walls of a church, that if she had ridden in depraved and stark naked the only hands to touch her would be the hands which sought to cover her and dry her tears. Brasada men, vaqueros, gave that to their women without thought. It was an unwritten code. But she sure as hell wasn't safe if she was going to go around looking at and being looked at by a killer steer.

She stood up before he could reach a hand to help her and began to walk to the door. "And it is something to occupy me and I am sorry if it makes me seem so dull and stupid."

She was only a child after all, and it didn't seem enough to say that she wasn't any such thing, but that was what he said. He recollected once or twice giving a compliment to Avis when she was feeling self-pitying as women did now and then, and trying to downgrade herself, and that she had flushed up and countered with, pshaw, or something like it, but when he contradicted her now, this child with her odd adult bearing, she only said quietly, "Thank you, Ben."

They had reached the doors. The light gleamed like oil on the high planes of her cheekbones. "Has my mother gone up?"

"She was still in the chapel."

"My father?"

"In the office, when I came out," he said.

She made a slight sighing sound. He knew she would go directly to her father when she went through the doors. The father could draw her. Ramón Dominguez was indulgent with his only child, but the mother exercised the greater indulgence. Because the girl had allied with the father, he wondered what the Señora thought about her daughter living so free and easy, apparently without guidance or interference. Don Ramón seemed to approve, and somebody ought to warn them both you could overdo indulgence. He had seen Cayetana cold as ice, but he had never seen her either willful or imperious; she got her way, went her way, whichever you chose to make it, without resorting to a gambit which might have come easy to her. And it was too bad to have to grow up so much alone.

"Caye, why did you come back home?" he said.

She turned, looking at him. "Why do you ask me that?"

"Pure curiosity. I'm sorry I asked."

"No. You did ask. I want to know."

"It just seemed to me you might of been happier with young folks, your own age."

"What makes you think that I am not happy?"

He was sucked into it now and he couldn't stop himself. "You keep it hid," he said.

Her hand was on the door latch. "I spent a most . . . most agreeable visit with my uncle's family. I was taught the guitar, embroidery, and how to conduct myself in an open carriage. None of them seemed to me to be terribly useful when it came to running Tres Reyes." Then she said, "And I was homesick, for all this."

She had answered him. But she seemed to be falling apart before his eyes. Her hand was unsteady on the latch, her stance against the door was the stance of a trapped animal. He put out his hand and took hold of the horse blanket, gathering it up in his fist. "Caye, I didn't mean to sound like I got such a long nose."

"Oh that's all right, don't say you're sorry, I can't bear it when people are sorry . . ." Her hands came up before her, clasped, and the blanket slipped off her shoulders. If he hadn't had hold of it, it would have fallen to the ground. He swung it around her again, his hand resting on her shoulder. "In the morning I'm goin' to go down and let a mule kick me," he said, trying to ease her off, seeing that she was close to tears.

She was equal to it, but her voice was shaky. "Now I will ask you something."

"You owe me one," he said.

"Why are you carrying your gun belt?"

It had hung so long in his hand that he had forgotten it. He looked down at it. "Why," he said, "it was pullin' my hips down into my knees. I could see it wasn't goin' to be too long before I couldn't mount up any more."

55

Her head was tilted to one side; she looked up at him as a child might look. He swung the door open for her. She crossed the hall to Dominguez' office, folding the blanket as she went. "Good night, Ben," she said gravely.

"Good night," he said. When he reached the foot of the stairs he saw that the Señora had left the chapel, but that a candle still flickered near the altar. Guadalupe's face looked dark and drawn with suffering in the faint playing light.

He did not go near her, but he spoke to her for the first time, inside himself.

"Gaudaloopy, if you can savvy this Tex-Mex of mine, I would take it kindly if you could put something in the way of my bein' a bigger fool than is necessary at any one time. If I got to light one of those candles for it or anything, I would be pleased to oblige."

Without knowing he did it, he waited for some sign from the figure in its shadowed niche. While he watched, the candle flared briefly, guttered, hissed, went out.

FOUR

Richards was preparing to mount in the courtyard three days later when Frankie McLean came through the main gates riding a chunky cow horse and leading the mud-colored horse called Portero.

The day had come up warm. There was the feel of a weather break, as if winter's back was cracking under the weight of sun and warm air, a sweet taste in the morning, part stirring dust, part rain traveling in big graying clouds, part green scent as if the yellow grass stirred its roots to grow again.

"I'll take him right now," Richards said. He unbuckled the latigos of the rim-fire saddle and hauled it off, settled the blanket on Portero and flung the saddle up.

"Where you headin'?" Frankie said, leaning on the horn.

Richards didn't look around at him. Portero was being fractious and he had his hands full. "Just goin' to look things over some, Frankie. You want to ride with me?"

"You callin' it," McLean said carelessly. He grinned, watching

57

Portero sidestep when Richards went to put his foot in the stirrup. "Notional. He's used to Pa," he said.

Richards was in the saddle. "He'll get over the notion. How's your pa this morning, Frankie?"

"About the same. Hell, he wants to git into a chair and Sid won't let him."

"How's the leg comin'?"

"How would I know? I ain't managed to squeeze past Sid since yesterday. I tell you something, Ben, though, I think the old man looks like hell."

Richards didn't say anything. Off to the left of the main house there was a coming and going of cotton-clad field hands, movement of vaqueros and horses. Richards pulled around the *casa*, past three house servants standing under a woven brush *ramada*. Frankie followed, his eyes on the slim shy girls. They rode past the small whitewashed houses. Both men and women spoke to them in soft, low voices, so much, so often, that Richards only touched the brim of his hat. *Hola, Señor Richards. Buenos dias, Señor Richards. ¿Señor McLean, como se encuentra usted? ¿Que tal, Benjamin?* They skirted the crop fields, the irrigation ditches, passing yoked oxen and a wagon with high wooden wheels. The mustangs were racing in a dusty circle in their corrals, waiting for the tough vaquero breakers. Beyond was grassland, studded with clusters of horses. Richards cut well below them and headed out into the open, toward the brasada. When Frankie angled in alongside him, he dropped Portero to a walk.

"You lookin' for something?" Frankie said.

"I kind of keep my eye out," Richards said.

"You got any idea when you're startin' north?"

"Early, if this weather sticks." Richards looked up at the sky. The blue was hazy and thin and the clouds moving up from the south had rain in them sure.

"Avis says you wanted to see me," Frankie said. "I figured you wasn't in no hurry or you would of said so."

"No hurry," Richards said. He put out his hand and rested it lightly on the horse. "Easy there, now, easy, let's walk some, you got to get the feel of me just like I got to get the feel of you. You talked to your pa about your drive, Frankie?"

"Naw," Frankie said. "I reckon there ain't much to talk over. Pa ain't goin' nowhere this year. He ain't goin' to be outta bed by next Christmas, with Sid around. Shiloh'n me, we reckon to pick up some men in Antone and hit the trail early as we can move."

Richards had a sinking sensation, followed by anger. Damn Jonah. He hadn't talked to Frankie, and Frankie had come over here with it all planned out how he was going to handle the Mc-Lean herd and maybe downright gratified his old man wasn't able to bend his leg to a saddle. He pulled Portero to a halt, letting his eyes sweep the flat brown country, the thickets of thorn. After a time he reached into the pocket of his brush coat and pulled out cigarette makings. "You want a smoke, Frankie?"

"Don't mind," Frankie said.

Richards poured tobacco and passed over sack and papers. He rolled and lit up and told Frankie.

"I figure your pa's bad off and all, Frankie, but it seems to me he might of talked things over with you. He's had three days to do it in." He drew on the cigarette thoughtfully. It went down a third of its loose length. Even Avis hadn't found fit to talk to the boy. He forgave Avis, right after he thought it; it wasn't her place to tell him. But he didn't exactly feel it was his place, either, and now here he was, stuck with it.

"Talk it over?" Frankie was saying. "You ain't worried about my drive, are you, Ben?"

"No," Richards said dryly. "I worry some about your pa's, though. I got to tell you that your pa asked me three days ago if he could throw in with Tres Reyes this year."

He saw the blood come up in the boy's face, flushing it all at once, as if a vein had burst. The teeth glinted behind the drawn-back lips. "Throw in with you? Then that means you're bossin' our herd to Dodge?"

"That's what it means," Richards said.

Frankie flung down his cigarette. "You sure as shootin' right on one score . . . somebody ought to of told me before I come over here actin' like I was the best trail boss ever got borned." The blood had left his face but his voice was bitter.

59

"I didn't look to be the one to tell you, Frankie." He eyed the boy levelly. "You got any objections?"

"I got one," Frankie said.

"Let's have it."

"I got to object some on the grounds that when my pa can't handle something it ain't your job to handle it, it's mine."

Richards nodded agreeably. "Only you maybe ought to stop and think a little about that, Frankie. Kind of try and add up on your fingers how many times your pa depended on you to do something for him and you didn't get it done."

Frankie stared at him. After a long time he said hopelessly, "I ain't got that many fingers, then, if that's the way you want it."

"Anything more? I'd be obliged if you'd say it because I ain't aimin' to hear about it a month from now."

Frankie said, "You're makin' me *segundo?*"

"No, I ain't makin' you *segundo*, Frankie. If I can manage it, I'm takin' Uremáy."

The boy flushed again. "My herd," he said. "McLean stock, and I ain't even goin' to be allowed to second 'em, is that right?"

"That's right. And in case you think I'm braggin' on this job, let me put you straight. I'm trailin' three thousand steers and you're goin' to be throwin' in a mixed fifteen hundred. That means she stuff droppin' calves and bulls on the prod all the way to Dodge. You want to boss that? Or second it?"

"You think I couldn't?" Frankie said.

"I know you couldn't. I ain't sure I can. No trail boss in his right mind would take on a herd that size."

Frankie said bitterly, "So what are you makin' me, then, night-hawk?"

"I ain't thought about it. Somebody's got to ride night herd on the remuda. You keep stumblin' on things like that, Frankie, and you might fall in the right hole yet."

The boy's mouth was savage. "I want to git one thing straight with you, Ben. I ain't scared of you. I never been scared of you."

"I never gave you any reason to be scared of me. I hope to God I never have to. I was kind of aimin' for you and me to get along and make it as good a drive as we can. I've driven a lot of herd in my time, a lot of 'em mixed brands, and I never had any trouble with the men owned those brands. I don't reckon to start with the McLean brand now. Your pa and me, we been friendly. Your pa's bad off and he asks a favor of me, of don Ramón, and far as I can see it's settled. So you get it all out of your gizzard, Frankie. Get it out now."

McLean blurted it, the words like gunfire. "Sure you and Pa been friendly, I wonder how friendly Pa might feel to you he knowed you was holdin' my mother's hand right in our kitchen three days ago, right out where me or Shiloh or anybody could of seen you through the window . . ." He stopped. Richards' eyes were so flat, cold, colorless that they cut off his words like a bullet.

But over his own calm voice Richards could feel his heart pumping sickeningly. "I ain't got to explain anything to you. I hate the idea I got to explain anything to anybody would have to snoop through the windows of his own house. If you couldn't see right from the start Avis needed something to hang on to, if you'd been talkin' it out with her, if you'd tried to give her a little help, I don't reckon she would of grabbed on to me. I ain't her family and you are, by law anyway. One thing else you ought to sort of keep in mind: she ain't your mother." He wheeled Portero, not waiting to see if Frankie was with him any more. After a while he heard the creak of the boy's saddle behind him.

"Ben."

He let Frankie catch up with him.

"Ben, I'm sorry for sure. I don't know what gits into me sometimes. My mouth goes off like a repeatin' rifle, don't it? After all the hell's raised I git around to thinkin' about what I should of said instead of what I did say."

Richards waited. He still felt sick inside but over it he was fighting rage.

"What I should of said is that we're damned lucky to be able to throw in with you and I'm obliged."

Richards turned on him. "Did it cost you anything to say that, Frankie?"

"Cost me . . . ? No, goddam you, Ben. No."

"You say what you feel. I don't aim to be softsoaped."

"All right, will you *listen* to me?" There was desperation in the voice now. "I'm tryin' to say we're grateful, me . . . Pa. Avis

61

too, I reckon. I won't give you no trouble, Ben. I mean that."

"You sure as hell won't," Richards said quietly, softly. He put his gloved hand out quickly as a snake striking and closed it on Frankie's arm. "I'm goin' to need you, Frankie, and I don't reckon I can look at you like your pa does. When I tell you a thing's got to be done I'm goin' to expect you're doin' it."

His face was abashed. "Aw hell, Ben, I won't let you down. You ain't sore?"

Richards shook his head and withdrew his hand.

"You want to shake on it?"

"You reckon we went so far we got to?" Richards said.

Frankie laughed. "You always one up on me, ain't you, Ben? You always try to stay one up on everybody."

"Sure," Richards said. "Why in hell should I let another man up on me."

"My feelin', on the nose," Frankie said fervently. "Only when I do it . . ."

"You are ridin' a wild dream, boy," Richards said. "You never do it."

Frankie looked at him. "You don't trust me, do you, Ben? Well, I would like for you to know something. I'll ride nighthawk if that's what you say. But if I do, I am goin' to be the best nighthawk you ever seen on the trail."

"If you make it, I'll be the first to tell you," Richards said.

They were riding between the Nueces and an ever-widening strip of brush which ran for several miles. Liveoaks and hackberry lined the river. They rode along a strip of sere grass, before the dense island of mesquite, catsclaw, prickly pear, topped over with black chaparral, thrust itself at them. Richards reined Portero and sat looking into the brush.

"You see something, Ben?" Frankie said.

"Listen."

Frankie listened. "Pig, I bet. You ain't goin' in there, Ben? . . . I ain't dressed for brush."

Richards hesitated, looking down at his own thighs and wishing he had leather on them. His eyes took in every line of the barricade: branch, thorn, leaf, intertwined and laced to shut out the rest of the world. He could hear Frankie breathing, and yet it seemed to him that a great hush lay over everything: no wind, no snap of twig, in the silence of the land. The desire to enter the brush came up in him a craving, a power. He had half-kicked the horse forward when a great crashing and cracking stopped him. Down the line a small bunch of longhorns broke out of the shelter of thorn and spine and went at a hard run down the grass strip.

"Hey," Frankie said. "*Hooopeee.*"

"Cut it," Richards said sharply. Gauging for the future where the bunch had been lying, he started down the strip at a slow gallop. He had nearly reached the trail end where the bunch had come out when there was a second explosion of breaking brush and a lone longhorn crashed into the open and braced to a halt within feet of him. For one wild moment he was looking full into the wet black eyes.

He spun Portero, feeling with gratitude the split-second response of the horse, shouting as he turned. "Move, Frankie! For God's sake, move!"

But the boy was ahead of him, tearing down the strip toward the river, bent over in the saddle. Portero was streaking now, catching up in an eye-rolling, open-mouthed burst. At the river edge, under the liveoaks, they hauled short, looking back, seeing exactly what they had seen moments before: Rojo standing high-headed on the same spot from which he had confronted Richards, facing down the slope, pawing earth.

"That could of been close," Richards said.

"That was close. Jesus, he's snaky." Frankie pushed his hat back and wiped sweat from his forehead with the palm of his hand. "He sure scared the hell out of me."

Snaky was right. Mean as they came. Richards felt cold, but his hands were sweating. This was how the big longhorn must have looked to Jonah, only coming at a dead run, not braked to a stop, with his head down and ready for the swing. I saw him before he saw me, Richards thought. Another few feet and he would of hit Portero broadside, just like he must of hit Glass, and even if he hadn't had his head down the weight of him would of knocked us both into a heap of broken bones. He knew how Jonah must have felt, lying behind the torn anguished horse and maybe praying and maybe closing his eyes so he wouldn't have to see that massive hulk bearing down on him with the violence of a twister. He half-turned to Frankie, almost said the words Jonah had made him swear not to say, and when he looked at the boy he saw that his face was reflective, and gone sullen.

From the shelter of the liveoaks they saw Rojo wheel and run, not following where the longhorns had gone.

"If he's runnin' with any stuff, he's runnin' with Tres Reyes," Frankie said.

"Were they all our brand?"

"I seen one of our M Bar L's. The cows was yours."

"They looked like tame stuff."

"That's good," Frankie said. "Rojo's runnin' with tame stuff, that's good."

"I ain't about to ask you why you think so, Frankie," Richards said with a long sidewise glance at the boy. His face was still sullen. He did not answer.

A few spatters of rain, big drops, fell on them. They rode up from the river, retracing their steps until they could see Tres Reyes laid out like a small village, the white of its buildings whiter and sharper under the darkening sky than it ever was in sunlight. It stood out, chalky and soft, secure, ageless and full of great grace. Up on the pasture slopes, horses were being gathered.

Following ancient custom, Ramón Dominguez kept his horses separated by color, each *manada* of mares, colts, and the stallion to which they belonged, cut out and kept apart as grays, roans, bays, blacks, paints. The practice marked the vaqueros of Tres Reyes as singular horsemen. Many of them had been raised in this tradition which was still widespread among the *hacendados* of Mexico. They were bunching the horses and driving them out, cutting and leading, selecting and harrying. Richards edged around a fresh-plowed field and across the foot of the *casa* cemetery, high-fenced with prickly pear, its plots protected with rock cairns and guarded by white crosses wreathed in faded paper flowers. Off to the right near a grove of liveoak he saw Dominguez, riding a big-muscled gray and leaning from a heavy stock saddle. He was chiv-vying two mares so pale they were nearly white.

"The old man can sure fork a saddle, can't he?" Frankie said.

"I admire to watch him." A moment later Richards heard him say very softly, "Hey, Miss Caye," as if it came from behind his teeth, and looked and saw Cayetana sitting a small roan mare on the far side of the grove. She was turned to them, but she made no sign that she saw them.

Frankie said, "I would kind of like to go and say howdy to Caye."

"Go ahead," Richards said.

"Aw come on. Just because you git to sit down to supper with her every night. Anyway, we ought to tell her, I seen Rojo twice now."

Richards rode up with him. He did not want to see the dark sad eyes. He felt that the look of them might lodge and remain, trapped, in the back of his mind.

The barred door closed behind him. He stood wearily against it, surveying the room with its three-legged stool, corn-husk mattress, latrine trench. He breathed very slowly, very deeply, taking the stink of dust, crumbling adobe, urine, darkness, into his lungs. After a while he took off his hat and ran a hand through his hair and down the side of his stubbled jaw. His gun belt, the .44, the Winchester, watch, knife, and papers were gone.

He went over and sat down on the mattress. A rat ran out and disappeared down the latrine trench.

There was not one lonely soul out there he knew, or knew of. Not one. Not one face which rang a bell, not one ear which had heard the names he named. He knew Juan Procuna. No, they knew no Juan Procuna. Also he knew Lozano, Sergeant Pedro Lozano of the Rurales. No, they knew no Lozano. Christ, why were they all named Juan or Pedro? Would they try to locate Sergeant Lozano. Si, they would try to locate Sergeant Lozano. Sometime. Someday.

He didn't want to let himself think how long he could rot here.

After a while he leaned back against the wall, which felt, unbelievably, damp to his shirt, and stretched out his long legs and crossed his feet and whistled. He could hear them coming and going in the outer room, laughing, thumping bottles and slapping down the monte cards. He whistled about a ten-dollar horse and a forty-dollar saddle and how he was going to trail Texas cattle. Then he got up and went and examined the bars of the single window, which was about two feet long and a foot wide and close to the ceiling. The bars were firm, even though the surrounding adobe had begun to come away in chunks. Where the latrine trench ran outside there was a rectangular hole about the size of a greenback. He began to pry out some of the loose adobe.

"Hut, hut, hut," the voice said disapprovingly and he turned and saw a fat, smiling Mexican standing at the door and shaking his head. At his side was a wheezy old dog. "I do not blame you, Señor," the man said. "But we do not allow this. No." He seemed to be an officer, or anyway an official of some sort.

Bonaventure came to take the bars of the door between his hands. The Mexican moved back a step. His smile was almost contagious.

"You speak English?" Bonaventure said.

"¿Inglés? Ah, no, Señor." He looked regretful. Then his face brightened. "Dice, 'allo'," he volunteered.

Bonaventure sighed. There were times "hello" was an all-right sort of word, and there were also times it wasn't worth much. He got it out in good Spanish. "How long before I can speak to somebody in authority here?"

"Me," the Mexican said. "I am in authority. I am Captain José Pedralbes Morisco. And you are . . . ?"

"Captain Aaron L. Bonaventure, Company D., First Texas Rang—"

The little Mexican was holding up his hand. His smile was broader, wider. "Please to pardon me, Señor. This you have told us before. What is it I can do for you?"

"You can let me out," Bonaventure said.

"Ah," said the little Mexican. "You keep the good spirit, no? Now, what is your name?"

Bonaventure took a good grip on the bars. "Captain Morisco, you have my orders . . ."

"The orders, yes." The smile was gone; he looked unutterably sad. "But I ask you, man. When I am going on a service, do I sign my own papers? Do I say, Captain José Pedralbes Morisco is hereby entitled to cross the Rio Bravo, and sign it myself?"

66

Bonaventure lowered his head and chewed on the end of his thumb for a moment without taking his hand off the bar. When he looked up he saw Morisco staring intently at him. "I regret it," Morisco was saying. "You cannot be Captain Bonaventure. One man here, he has seen Captain Bonaventure. At Matamoros, it was. During the misfortune at Running Creek in which some cows were stolen. My man saw him. No, Señor, you cannot be Captain Bonaventure."

Bonaventure gritted his teeth. "I wasn't at Running Creek." He stopped. This wasn't going to get him anywhere. Morisco's face was almost pressed against the bars now. "No, Señor, Captain Bonaventure is taller than you, much taller." His glance swept up Bonaventure's six feet odd and trailed off somewhere near the ceiling. "His hair is yellow and his eyes blue. Also he has a fine white horse."

Bonaventure was nodding, teeth sunk in his lower lip. This was the end of the line: if some Mexican had seen him, he had seen him, and there would be no talking him out of it.

"Now, Señor, tell me what it is you do in Mexico?" Morisco said briskly, sympathetically.

"I'm looking for a Texas Ranger," Bonaventure said.

"Ah! Of course. You are looking for Captain Bonaventure."

Have it your way, Bonaventure thought.

"He is in Mexico, Señor? But we have had no word of this. Your government has not asked us . . ."

"Captain Morisco, the authority of my government is in the orders I carry. You have them."

"But, Señor, I do not understand. Why must you be hiding in the night? No, this is not possible. I ask that you tell me the truth, Señor. The truth."

They looked at each other. Bonaventure felt more pessimistic now than at any time since they had picked him up, near midnight, from a retama thicket. It wasn't Morisco's fault, it was simply the way they operated. They were bored, lonely on their outpost duty, eager for relief, waiting for the day a Rurale troop would ride in across the long desolate miles to check their post, maybe a month from now, maybe three. And then, with any luck

67

at all, he would be transferred to a city jail and could reach the proper authority.

"The truth, Señor?" Morisco said imploringly.

Bonaventure came near feeling sorry for him. If there was any chance of making that jail transfer, he would work for it. "Very well, Captain. I see I can't fool you. I'm a fugitive from justice. They're looking for me in Texas."

Morisco stepped back, drawing a quick breath. "A fugitive? You have robbed the *banco*? You have killed a man?"

Silently Bonaventure stuck his hand out through the bars and held up four fingers.

"*Four* men! *¡Ay de mí!*" Morisco's mouth worked; he did not know whether to be jubilant at his catch or to weep. Bonaventure turned away from the door, the last hope burning in him like fire.

"So I suppose you have got to turn me over to the Rangers." He swung back suddenly. "The money . . . I'll split the money with you, Morisco."

The little Mexican was red with outrage. "The money! The money which you have taken from the bank, the money you have killed for? Ah, Señor, *now* you make me angry. To think that you believe that I, José Pedralbes Morisco, can be bought with money! I will show you how I can be bought! I will show you by giving you over to the Rangers with joy in my heart."

"When?" Bonaventure said mournfully.

"The time will come, Señor, the time will come." Morisco turned and took two steps away. The dog sat and looked at Bonaventure. Morisco turned back. "It is my sorrow that I myself cannot take so black a gringo to the river. When my promotion arrives, then I will not have to wait for any man. Were it left to me, I would take you from this place today. This morning. This hour. You understand? Now I shall send word to my Rurale captain, and he will come with the steel bracelets for your wrists, Señor."

Bonaventure was leaning against the door again. "When you send for him, don't let him tell Sergeant Pedro Lozano about me, will you?"

"No favors," Morisco shouted. "No favors, gringo."

Bonaventure was leaning his full weight on the door now. He felt as if a horse had just got up off him. He knew that Morisco, out of pure meddlesome inquisitiveness, would see that Lozano heard the whole story.

He was aware that Morisco had taken two steps back and was again standing in front of the door. He appeared to be undecided, and was examining his dirty fingernails.

"I can't say anything more, Captain," Bonaventure said. "I wouldn't want it used against me."

"In truth, you have said enough," Morisco said. His voice was soft, cautious. "I only wish to know . . . I must know . . . where is the money, Señor?"

Bonaventure walked across the floor of the cell and sank on the mattress again and leaned against the wall and looked out at Morisco and then at the ceiling and was silent.

"Did you see those devils go?" Dominguez said, pulling the stallion up so short it tossed its Arab head and showed its teeth. He was smiling and flushed with the chase; beyond him the two pale mares were gathered into a very small *manada* led by a pure white stallion. A vaquero hazed them out on the slope.

"*Muy bien*, don Ramón," Frankie said. "That was some gather. We just come up from seein' Rojo down on the brush spur."

"Rojo? Here? On Tres Reyes?" Dominguez was sweating heavily, breathing hard.

"He might be runnin' with your stuff," Richards said.

"We damn near plowed right into him . . . 'scuse me, Caye," Frankie said. He laughed. "Two more feet and Ben here would've been stretched out alongside Pa."

Dominguez flashed a look at Richards. "How is your father today, Frankie?"

"He's doin', I reckon. Wasn't for how he feels, though, I expect I would of been ready to put a shot in that old steer a while back. That'd kill Pa sure." Richards winced. Again his eyes met Dominguez'; the older man's face looked strained. For the second time rain struck them in big flat drops. Uremáy came up from the direction of the house, greeted them, spoke a brief aside to Cayetana.

69

"I have turned Ebano out, Señorita. I want him to use the leg."

She nodded. "Whatever you think best, Tiburcio." Uremáy rode on. "*Padre*, we are going to be wet in a moment. Come to the house. You too, Frankie. Ben, I meant to ask you, what horse is this?"

"Meet Portero," Richards said.

"Portero? *Hola*, little gatekeeper." She leaned and touched Portero's nose. "Come," she said, "the rain is cold."

Yet they made no haste returning to the house. The rain was still a shallow uneven fall, spotting the earth. A peculiar unpleasant odor which would soon be lost in the sweet scent of wet greasewood came up from the dry land.

"I'm thinkin'," Frankie said. He was walking his horse, hands clasped on the horn. He looked at Cayetana, beside him. "Ain't you goin' to ask what I'm thinkin', Caye?"

"What are you thinking, Frankie?"

"I'm thinkin' that I will take Rojo along with the McLean herd, unless you Dominguez got any objections."

She turned her head quickly, looking at him. "Take Rojo?"

"Sure. Bring him in with our gather and take him all the way to Dodge. Wouldn't that there be something to see?"

"Don't know about see," Richards said. "But I know about do."

"Maybe yes, maybe no," Frankie said. "We know he's here. Me'n Shiloh, we'll lay the ropes on him and neck yoke him with a ox and let him sull for a spell. Then, wham. Beefsteak. Hey, Caye, you look like you reckon I can't do it."

"I hope you cannot," Cayetana said.

"You hope I *can't*. Well by Friday, if that ain't some way to look at it. This old steer is rampagin' around killin' folks and stickin' his horn in my own pa and you hope I can't take him, when I got something to pay him back for."

Richards saw Cayetana set her mouth, a little contemptuous, a little pained. He said, "I reckon what Caye means, Frankie, is that she kind of admires Rojo for bein' what he is, but if anybody has to bring him in she hopes it's you. Am I right, Caye?"

Her eyes gave him her thanks, and something else. He couldn't

70

read it but it made him feel somehow mournful inside. "Ben said it for me, Frankie," she said.

"Well, all right," Frankie said, "but it don't make sense to me. You admire a sidewinder for bein' what he is?"

"I'll have to think about that, Frankie," she said.

"Hey, Ben, it's your drive, you care if we take Rojo, providin' we can git him in?" Frankie said.

Richards looked up and past Cayetana and said, "He's not wearin' my brand, nor Tres Reyes' either."

"Well, thanks," Frankie said. "You so eager about it, it really fires me up. Thanks. I reckon to do it then, since you give me the go-ahead."

"I leave you here," Dominguez said. He turned to Frankie and his eyes were as somber as his daughter's. "You wish to catch the red steer, I will not say no to this. I think maybe he belongs to you now." He reached out and covered Cayetana's hand with his own. "Caye, tell your mother I may ride with Tiburcio if the rain holds off. You stay to eat, no, Frankie? *Adiós*, then. Ben, I meet you later."

The rain began lightly but steadily. The stink came up off the earth in a wave, compounded of the sudden wet against the dry soil. Richards shut his breath against it. They picked up the horses and raced for the house and around into the front courtyard where a boy waited to take the mounts. Soledad was removing the cages of finches, hurrying them inside. A low wind rustled the vines on the inner walls.

Richards was out of the saddle and on his feet when the horse pounded through the arched white gate. He turned and had only a swift searing picture: the little paint mare with its head thrown up and back, Avis hooded and cloaked against the rain, sidesaddle and clinging to the horn. At the far end of the pool the horse seemed to fetch short, stopping so suddenly that Avis lurched and slid from him, off balance and hanging to the stirrup. He caught one glimpse of Frankie's astonished stance, half-dismounted; of Cayetana's startled face as she began to swing out of the saddle; and then he was moving forward and Avis was running through the rain with the cloak flying open and the hood fallen back, run-

71

ning until her full weight struck him and his arms closed around her and her face wet with rain or tears was on his shoulder and her voice said his name twice, three times, and he knew Jonah McLean was dead.

FIVE

Uremáy's face was running sweat. The dust rose so thickly that he worked largely by feel and instinct, eyes narrowed against the grainy yellow cloud which surrounded him. He had grown used to the noise, as though it had always been there, would always be there, unchanging and unceasing. The sounds of the cows ranged from anguished deep-throated mooings and murmurings to high-pitched wailing; sometimes a cow would scream when it smelled blood. There was the quavering bawling of calves. The hoofs of horses flashed by. The hoofs of cows and calves thundered and stumbled. A wave of heat from the coals of the branding fires flared over him.

The spring branding had begun. Across from Uremáy, Esteban waited with the iron. A rider came in with a roped calf. Behind him, other riders held off the frantic mother cow. The calf went down in the practiced hands of José and Teófilo, raising a new cloud of dust as it was half-slid, half-slung, into position. The iron with its three crowns in pyramid was pressed on its side, near the flank. There was a little time of scorched stinking hair before

73

Esteban lifted the iron. Uremáy waited patiently with the knife, fresh lifted from a pot of water boiling on the coals. The Tres Reyes herds wore no ear bob; the three crowns of the three kings were enough. José and Teófilo slid the calf across the three feet of earth which separated Esteban and Uremáy. In one slashing motion Uremáy slit the scrotum, popped out the testicles as if he popped fruit from its skin, and cut the cord. Without looking he tossed them over his shoulder and onto the edge of the hot coals, where they spit and seared. Now and then a rider coming in leaned low from his saddle without a break in the pace of his horse, scooping up the delicacy and tossing it into the air until it was cool enough to eat.

Two miles out, crews were driving in gathered steers. The work would go on for some days, rain or fair, although it seemed now the weather pointed to an early spring, an early start. The little herd of tame steers captained by a thoughtful-faced old leader named Hondo moved out again and again to bring in the obstinate angry longhorns, playing out their Judas roles, telling the market steers, follow us, it is all right, nothing to fear here, follow us. The men of Tres Reyes ranged far, covered in leather even to their horses, in and out of the brush, scratched and torn despite their heavy jackets and *chaparejos*. Only the very young riders were not yet marked from brush riding. The old hands wore scars like stitching, like saber cuts. Some had misshapen bodies, as if they permanently dodged the knives of the brasada. Some were marked with odd lumps and swellings, as if festerings which never healed dwelled under their skins. Some carried in their systems from time to time painful poisons injected as though from the fangs of a snake. They rode scarred horses seasoned at running steers out of the brush and calves into the branding camps. Rarely, a man was adept at using a rope in the brakes; mostly it was hard and heavy chasing through thickets tough enough to cut leather. Now and again a troublesome dangerous steer would be forcibly yoked to an ox to be led in. Once driven into the winged corrals where his fellow steers milled and settled, he learned acceptance, though he sometimes refused to eat or drink for hours.

The work was in its third day, almost without pause. The fiesta was over, and the only men at liberty from the gather crews

74

were those whose saint's day it was. This was the doing of the Señora, who believed that no man should work on the day which belonged to the saint whose name be bore.

There was a great annual joke on Tres Reyes concerning a man who owned a dog named Xavier. This man, they said, cautioned his dog that on the day of San Xavier he must not run a rabbit or scratch a flea. This was also a joke on the Señora, for the people of Tres Reyes knew that the Señora knew it.

Richards was annoyed the first day. There were three men sitting in the sun whose hands and horses he had counted on. Uremáy only shrugged, smiling a little. Today he didn't see anybody sitting in the sun.

Portero had proved his night eye and was being held in reserve. Richards sat a big buttermilk gelding with a white mane and tail, rolling a cigarette, watching the calves get up from knife and iron and go barreling off to freedom with their outraged mothers. It would be another three or four years before they were brought in for market, and by then they would be big rangy unpredictable longhorns. He nursed the back of his hand with his mouth, where it had torn open on catsclaw. Sweat had soaked clear through his brush coat. At least he could feel it. Today he could feel everything: the warmth of the sun, the scalding coffee, the pain of the tearing thorn; he could smell fire and sweat and horses, could taste *frijoles* and chili. Three days ago he could feel, smell, taste nothing, and he knew now what pulque could do to you if you let it.

Dominguez came up, mounted in a carved work saddle. An hour before he had nearly had words with Richards. Or maybe it was the other way around. There was no need, he reminded Richards rather sharply, for his foreman to be brush riding. After a moment Richards told him he aimed to see his riders kept in mind that anything they could do the boss could do. Dominguez, who had been brush riding himself, flushed with a color which was more than exertion. Now he seemed to have forgotten it. "So, Ben, it goes well," he said. His mustache was gray with dust. "Clockwork, as our friend Allenby says."

Richards nodded. Chances were if you were prepared for the unexpected and dealing with a smart rancher, it was bound to go

75

well. There was not a man here who didn't know his job to the last detail and if he had to, would invent new details. Every corral had been built around a hand-dug waterhole, every horse, cow, steer, and bull had been allowed free range to the best water, grass, and unmolested sanctuary, and the stock was in fine shape because Ramón Dominguez, unlike the majority of Mexicans, practiced gelding. Only a few miles distant, over the border, Mexican stock was allowed to deteriorate through the casual methods of its owners. Dominguez drove good herds and he knew how to build them up. He would not sell below market because he did not need to, and in bad range years he brought in as many cows and calves as he could and fed and watered them at the *casa* corrals. Poor and sick stock were shot off as a matter of course, as were temperamental animals who were sure to cause trouble on the trail. Any steer with so much as a peculiar cast to its eye was disposed of, for he could remember the day when Texas cattle carried an infectious fever and were not allowed to pass through certain states. The dreaded Spanish fever had turned out to be caused by a tick which could not survive the winter, but Dominguez could recall the furious reaction of southern and Midwestern ranchers in those violent years, and he was anxious to see that anything going up the trail under the Tres Reyes brand was in good health. The end of the Mexican War had seen the greatest growth of his holdings, and the trade restrictions due to the fever tick had come close to hurting him. During the Civil War he had gone quietly about the business of building up his herds and shipping them into Mexico and Cuba. Federal troops held the Mississippi River, and there was no way of supplying the Confederacy, which he would have done. By the end of the war, he was faced with the fact that there were perhaps six million longhorn cattle in Texas, and that a prime steer was worth only pennies.

The booming economy of his adopted country saved him. The Kansas Pacific Railroad came into Kansas. The cattle towns of Abilene and Wichita sprang up. The Chisholm and Goodnight-Loving and the smaller trails which branched off and paralleled them took thousand upon thousand of longhorns on the final journey to northern and eastern markets. It would not be long, he knew, before railroad track replaced the old trails, and the only driving he would do would be to the nearest railhead. In a sense he welcomed that day and in another he viewed its imminence with sadness, for he saw in this progress the end of another loved facet of his way of life.

To spare Avis and Frankie McLean he was bringing the M Bar L stock in with his own, where and when he found it. It meant extra work, keeping the cows, calves, and steers separated from one another, but he threw the steers in with the Tres Reyes' and there would be no need to cut them out until they reached railhead at Dodge. It had been his own offering to widow and orphan, and while he knew with sly certainty that Richards had been going to ask for it, he delighted in having beat his foreman to the punch. He also knew what Richards had done on his own: left several good M Bar L bulls ranging it, so that the McLeans could restock without counting on the services of Tres Reyes even if their branded stuff ran together. Pride. He knew about pride, who had many prides.

A running cow nearly blundered into them. Richards swung his hat at her, grunting, and she swerved off, searching for her calf. Wherever it was, it would find her the moment it was on its feet again. Richards looked at Uremáy, crouched with the Indian patience of centuries, streaked with dust and sweat. The men around him laughed now and then, so that Richards knew he joked about the work. Uremáy had been crouched in that position for hours, yet he too had his prides; if his face was blank, his eyes narrowed so that there was nothing to be seen in them, Richards knew the weariness of the man and the stoic refusal to bow to it.

"I'm goin' to relieve Uremáy," he said to Dominguez.

Don Ramón looked startled; then he smiled as if he savored the idea. "Speak to him of this, and he will fight you," he said. "Or perhaps he will fight you if he does not ignore you. Or ignore you if he does not disobey you."

Richards called to him. "Tiburcio."

They all looked up: Uremáy, Esteban, José, Teófilo. When he saw that Richards did not move, Uremáy rose to his feet and came around the fire and walked to them, his bowed legs bent from squatting.

77

"Relieve every man running an iron and take a break yourself," Richards said.

Uremáy's dark eyes went with disbelief to his *patrón*, noted the agreement in Dominguez' steady gaze, flashed back to Richards with amusement. "So be it," he said.

And don Ramón was out of his saddle and handing the reins to Uremáy. "So, old friend, you have been bested, and worse, you have let yourself be bested. There is age upon you, Tiburcio."

"So be that, also," Uremáy said. "But where is there a man better, to rob these poor children of little bulls of the greatest joy in life?"

"He is here," Dominguez said, and took the knife out of Uremáy's hand and went to take his place at the fire.

Uremáy mounted Dominguez' horse slowly, shaking his head. "God help them all, the little bulls. He was never the man at this that I am."

Richards was grinning for the first time in days. "I reckon you got bested twice," he said.

Uremáy turned the horse's head. "You are slow to learn, Benjamín. Slow as Jesús Pequinas bringing his ox to market. One must wait. The market waits, and the ox comes. I waited." He looked around him, eyes ruined for the day by the dust of the camp. "When one is set at what one must do, he does not see. All this dust, all this excited flesh. Nor smell." He glanced at Richards out of the corner of his eye. "It is as if one had drunk too much pulque, eh, *amigo*? Come, let us go to the river."

Richards followed him out of camp and down to the Nueces, under the budding willows. Uremáy went and dipped his big straw hat into the river and sloshed water over his head several times. When he returned Richards was slumped against a tree with his own hat tipped over his eyes.

"Would you be so kind as to offer me a *cigarillo*?" Uremáy said.

"Sure. Have a cigarette?" Richards voice was muffled by his hat. He held out makings to Uremáy.

"You are still not well and whole," Uremáy stated, running his tongue along the edge of the paper.

"Listen, old *pistolero*," Richards said, "you shot me, now you ain't got to rub salt in it, do you?"

"So now you believe it, about the stone which grows hair, do you not?"

"Hell yes," Richards said. "That stuff would grow hair on the ace of spades."

Uremáy chuckled and then was silent. After a while Richards pushed his hat back and saw that the *peon* boss had gone to sleep on the ground, the cigarette still burning in his fingers. Richards reached over and removed it and ground it out and sat back against the tree again. He studied Uremáy's face. It was funny how you never thought about age, or if you thought of it at all, it was always something that happened to everybody else, it was never going to fasten its fingers on you. That was until you got to see age in a working state, working on somebody you liked and were kind of close to. You saw him getting old and you felt a chill for the first time about it. There was an underlying acceptance, but there was the chill. Somewhere in the back of your mind you began to count up the years that were left, not just to live out, but to work in, to be whole and well, as Uremáy put it, to maintain the very living soul of your manhood. Maybe Uremáy was too old to go up the trail this time. Richards wanted him and probably Uremáy wanted to go, but maybe, in the space of one season, he was suddenly too old. Or maybe it was next season he would be too old, in which case you felt you had to give him this one last time. He sat up straighter, feeling the chill again and tasting something which reminded him of the aftertaste of the pulque.

He had been incredibly drunk. But he had managed not to disgrace himself, not with Cayetana, or Avis either, and maybe not even with Uremáy. The *barbacoa* was over, and no pall thrown on it, either, thanks to Avis, who had more grit than a barnyard full of roosters. That she had come at all, with Jonah only two days in the ground, had been Cayetana's doing, and since it was what any cowhand would call she-stuff, he stayed as far away from it as he could. He couldn't stay away from the burial nor from what preceded it, and that rainy day of the ride

79

back to the McLean ranch with Frankie and Avis had been in its way the longest and the shortest ride of his life.

While Frankie was at Tres Reyes, Avis gone to the well for water, Lunt with a cow having a calf, and Shiloh riding brush ten miles away, Jonah got out of bed. He walked as far as the kitchen door, fell so heavily that he left the skin and flesh of his face on the frame, and died on the floor between the two rooms. Avis found him, the great black-haired trunks of his legs exposed, the belly of his nightshirt running red and yellow where the horn wound still drained, and knew instantly that he was dead. Without calling Lunt she had saddled her mare and ridden through the rain to Tres Reyes in a state of deep shock. Yet once there, she would not stay, and after her first outburst she was calm and almost coldly silent. All the way back she rode without speaking, shaken now and again with a tremor that seemed to sway her whole body. Twice Richards saw her hand go out and seek Frankie's where he rode at her side.

It was over when they got there. Lunt had Jonah back in bed and covered with a clean sheet. The big man sat in the kitchen, slumped in a rocking chair with his face in his hands. He did not look up or speak, until Avis crossed to him and stood in her dripping cloak with her face hard as rock.

"Did you know he was goin' to die, Sid?"

Lunt took his hands down slowly.

"Sid. Did you know he was goin' to die?"

"I knowed," Lunt said. He looked up, his big simple face contorted, his eyes blank. Briefly he gestured at Richards. "He knowed too."

She turned and her eyes found Richards. For a moment he could barely face her, barely realize that she was Avis McLean, with her eyes so furious and her mouth gone grim and straight. Her soft light hair had come down and hung lank and rain streaked about her shoulders. Her hands were balled into fists.

"You knew, Ben? You knew when you walked out of my kitchen after tellin' me you were goin' to take the herd. That was what you wouldn't tell me that day?"

"Yes," Richards said. "I knew."

She turned again. "Frankie?"

"No," he said hoarsely, shaken, pale. "I swear it, Avis."

"It was to spare you," Richards said. "You and Frankie. It was how he wanted it, Avis."

Her eyes swept them all, without sorrow, at war with them. "Thank you," she said scornfully. "Thank you for sparin' me." She went into the room where Jonah's body lay and closed the door behind her.

Jonah had wanted to be buried on the ridge north of the ranch where there was a big boulder balanced on the rim. He had always called it the Crushing Stone because, as he had been fond of pointing out, if it ever fell off there, and on you, it would sure crush you. There was a handful at the burial: Lon Davis and three other area ranchers and their families; Dominguez, Cayetana and Uremáy, Richards, Shiloh, and two wandering hands who happened to be passing through and were spending the night at Tres Reyes. One of them read the burial service in a soft, uncertain voice. It was a raw day and they stood on the ridge near the Stone, high under the gray sky, and buried Jonah in a coffin made at Tres Reyes, under a cross carved by Uremáy. A wind moved on the ridge and there was a rustle of women's skirts. Richards stood apart, not sure he wasn't still being warred with. It seemed to him that Avis was unnaturally tall in the black cloak which swept the ground, near as tall as Frankie. They stood close, hands clasped as they had been clasped on the ride home two days before. Richards felt a deep grief, the same grief he knew Dominguez felt. They had been primed for this and still the anticipation in no way softened the shock. A big hard honest man who had made a living for himself and his family in a big hard country was gone for good, and for days afterward you would catch yourself speaking and thinking of him as if he still rode into the McLean ranch for his dinner, and have to stop and remind yourself that he was up there by the Crushing Stone.

Richards looked down over the rim of the ledge and saw the golden country beneath him, the green-black islands of scrub, the faint overlay of fuzzy new green, the forbidding battlements of the brasada. It was right up here Rojo had been standing, and Jonah had glanced up and seen him. A last, fatal glance on a last, fatal day, for Glass and for Jonah.

There was an uncontrolled snuffing and bawling, as if a calf worried for its mother. It was Lunt, and where men and women at the burial site had been merely mournful they were now discomfited, shifting their feet and turning uneasy eyes from the man who showed his feelings outside. It was a bad moment. Richards saw Avis' mouth harden, in that way it had, and Frankie's face go lopsided with distress, disgust, the stress of his own bereavement. The traveling cowhand paused in mid-sentence, took a gulp of air and continued at twice the pace. He could not go fast enough. Before he was finished, Lunt had turned and gone plunging down off the ledge, toward the ranch.

Richards looked at the ground at his feet until it was over. The women gathered around Avis with murmurings and cluckings, like old black chickens: women who had kept their emotions to themselves, unshared, through years of privation and drought and discouragement, women who were sallow husks with nothing inside, women whose burned-out eyes silently told the widowed girl, in time you will look like us, you will be like us. She allowed herself to be taken away. The men filed after, not speaking. There would be time to speak when the coffee and pie were served, and then there would be no mention of Jonah, but talk of longhorns, of the drive to come, of the weather, and at the leavetaking the set standard simple words which would mark the hour of their ordeal: I'm awful sorry, Miz McLean. Sure am sorry, Miss Avis . . .

Turning away, Richards saw Cayetana standing close to the ugly mound of the grave. Her black lace scarf had slipped from her head and the edges of her skirts were trailing in the dirt. Unaware of him, she crossed herself in a gesture which seemed to him too quick, too impatient, and then leaned forward and touched the cross Uremáy had made, a long lingering touch which was almost a caress.

He, and the Tres Reyes people, were the last to leave. He had sat outside with the men, but twice, entering the house, he was aware of the strain in the air, something more than the occasion. He knew that it was because of Cayetana; he knew too that she would have made her effort, admired a young one, offered a solicitous inquiry, commented, smiled, and failed. She sat with these women and could not have looked, not have been, more alone, under their probing eyes. Once, when she rose to take a tray and left the scarf lying across the back of her chair, he saw the sad-faced Harter woman reach over and touch the soft rich stuff, not with envy, not with curiosity, not with disapproval, but with no expression whatever. When he insisted on taking the tray from her, he felt that her hands were cold and wet. Half an hour later, helping the swarm of Davis children into the wagon, he heard the Davis woman say in her prim small-mouthed way, "She rides astride," and knew that the disdain and condemnation of the women had been at last spoken aloud, in three short words.

When he came back in the front door he heard a woman laughing, a gay, releasing laughter, and was not surprised to see that it was Avis. There was color in her cheeks now; she had pushed up the sleeves of the rusty black dress and tied a big apron around herself and was going about cleaning up with that feverish intensity and energy people fall prey to when they are entertaining after the funeral of a loved one. He stood in the doorway, watching. Shiloh was seated at the kitchen table, taking large doleful bites out of a wedge of pie.

"I hope I didn't crack this cup," Cayetana said.

"Oh, that old thing," Avis said almost merrily, snatching it out of her hand and plunging it into the gray enamel dishpan. "Hurry up, will you, Shiloh. I can't wash that plate while you're still eatin' off it."

Cayetana was drying dishes, awkwardly. "Avis, I want to tell you . . ."

"Mercy, Caye, you're gittin' water all over that pretty waist. Here, take an apron."

Richards watched Cayetana fumble with the apron strings. Her face was utterly hopeless. "Avis, it's about the fiesta."

"I hadn't even thought on it," Avis said. Her hands were fiery red when she took them out of the dishwater. "There was so much goin' on here . . ." She stopped, as if the full meaning of what she had said hit her square and hard.

Cayetana put the sacking towel and the plate she had been drying down on the table and went to Avis and took her by the shoulders and turned her around. "Avis, I want you to know this. I wanted them not to have the fiesta. Because of Jonah. But

83

we couldn't do that. Our people would understand but they wouldn't be happy. It's important to them."

Avis looked startled, Richards thought; maybe even a little displeased at the other girl's touch. "Sure, I know, Caye. You don't have to explain. You shouldn't make so much of it."

Cayetana was shaking her head. "What I am trying to tell you is that you must come. You and Frankie. It's important to you."

"Important to *me*?" Avis said. "Caye, you've gone plumb crazy. What in the world ever do you expect those women were kind enough to come here for this burying today would think of me if I went gallivantin' off to sing and dance two days after?"

"You don't have to do that. Avis, you don't have to do anything you don't want to do. But you must come. You must let them see that you aren't beaten."

"Oh-oh," Shiloh said. "I'm done now, Miss Avis."

"Be quiet, Shiloh," Avis said. She was looking Cayetana in the eye, a little disconcerted, but shrewd too. "You tryin' to tell me about those women, Caye? I know all about those women. I know how they think and feel about everything."

Her voice was quiet; she did not know what cynicism was. "I too, Avis. But you have your own . . . your own soul to account to."

"But what will they think?" She wailed it, but there was laughter in it too.

Cayetana said, "Do you care what they think? Why do you care? One of the finest moments of your life is going to be when you discover you don't care what anybody thinks."

"I say go. Go," Shiloh said.

"Shiloh, will you please for just one minute keep quiet," Avis said. "Nobody can get a word in edgeways here. I'll have to think on it, Caye."

"If you think about it you won't do it. You come down early in the morning. You have to do this, Avis."

Richards stepped into the room. "She's right, Avis. For yourself, you got to."

There was silence. A clock struck the hour with a hard metallic sound. Then Avis said, "I will. I'll come." She was looking at Richards over Cayetana's shoulder, disheveled, determined. He

84

felt his heart go out to her, a giving now, a need to comfort and help rather than a wanting.

She gave him her hand, after the Dominguez had entered their barouche and before he had mounted.

"I hate leavin' you alone, Avis," he said.

"Oh, Frankie's here," she said. "I ain't exactly alone."

He released her hand. It had none of the warmth and tenderness it had had the day she had given it to him in the kitchen; today it was a moist, nervous hand. He turned to Frankie before he mounted up. The boy had taken his father's death hard: he was silent, perceptibly self-controlled, but he was not stunned. Inside he smoldered like a fire which has been badly doused, and Richards knew it. He wanted to say a thousand things which were of immediate importance: be good to this girl. Take care of her, she's your stepmother and she comes before anything else, she and this ranch your pa worked so hard for, so stay out of trouble, don't make extra work and heartache for her. He said nothing. There would be time for that. All the time in the world.

He looked back toward the ranch, following the barouche and the two traveling cowhands. Frankie had put his arm about Avis' shoulders. They were moving slowly back to the house.

Two days later they rode into Tres Reyes early in the morning. Richards did not see them. He was with Uremáy and the cook crew, watching where the steers had been roasting all night in pits lined with red-hot rock. Every woman on the place was slapping out tortillas and cooking big pots of *nacionales*, the staple bean of the Mexican. The paper lanterns were being strung in the courtyard, and the weather favored it all. He didn't even know the McLeans had come in until he looked up and saw Frankie, on foot, rounding the last house on the way to the pit site.

"Sid took a freight last night," the boy said by way of greeting.

"I don't claim to be surprised," Richards said. "How'd Avis take it?"

He lifted his shoulders. "Hard to say right now what Avis's thinkin' about anything. Sid took a lot off her shoulders and Pa's too, but I don't know if she figured him worth his keep. Minute he got ahold of anything was sick or had got hurt he wanted to keep it. You wasn't here when he give us all that trouble with a busted-up old lobo he had. Meanest damn critter I ever see, couldn't tame him down for nothing. Finally took a hunk out of Spot one morning and Avis ran out with Pa's rifle and shot him dead." He shook his head. "Anyway, Sid was crazier'n a bear with a belly ache."

"No," Richards said. "Not crazy. Like a little kid never grew up. He couldn't help it."

"Well, him and Avis wasn't too much took with one another anyhow. I reckon we'll git along without him."

"Where's Shiloh?" Richards said.

"Doin' chores. He'll be along." He called to Uremáy. "Hey, Tiburcio, how long before those old cows are ready, I could eat one all by myself."

Uremáy looked up. "They prepare one only for you, Franco, a very bony one. Very old, very tough."

"You ain't too thirsty, are you?" Richards said, trying to keep his tone light.

"Say, what in hell is this anyway, Ben? You tellin' me to go easy on the *vino* or something? I aim to race this afternoon so I ain't goin' to be drinkin'. Not yet, anyway. If you ain't too busy, you supposed to come over to the house for coffee."

"I'm busy," Richards said.

And that was the end of it. He didn't want to see Avis, didn't want to sit and do nothing, and he missed the absence of work. Quit lyin', he told himself finally. What he feared was the sharp, knowing, seeing eye of the Señora.

All day he ate and drank and made work for himself. On the flat by the river the men of Tres Reyes leaned from their saddles to scoop up roosters buried to the neck and played at distracting a small bull, twisting its tail until it plunged into the river and won its freedom. One of the new men Uremáy had hired won three out of five races on a big gray gelding, and when Richards went to pay his respects to the Señora, watching from the barouche, she asked him who the man was.

"His name is Manuel Vega. Tiburcio hired him."

"And what horse?" the Señora said, head thrown back sharply under her lace.

86

"His own," Richards said, grinning now. "Or so he says."

A knowing little smile was on her mouth. "Look at that horse when you pass him, Richards. He's got a burned-over brand on his right flank. The hair has grown down, half over it."

"Yes ma'am," Richards said admiringly. He passed the gray on the right and saw that the Señora knew what she was talking about, crossed behind the horse, and just missed being kicked for his pains.

By nightfall he was drunk. Somehow, somewhere, he and Uremáy had become inseparable, and he could not remember when Uremáy had first passed the bird-shaped stone jar to him. Uremáy remarked nothing on the contents and drank of them himself and all the time Richards felt his body growing numb and dead, like frostbite had set in, and he hoped that nobody would move him up to a fire because he knew he would howl with pain, like a trapped wolf. It seemed to him that all his faculties were clearer and sharper than they had ever been in his life, and he could not understand why his voice came out sluggish, halting, toneless. He could think the words with precision, but he could not push them out and he felt himself shaping his mouth around every syllable.

One thing he remembered. He and Uremáy had got up on the front wall and seated themselves, with the stone jar between them, so that they could look down on the inner courtyard. He saw clearly the warmth and color, the lamps and candles, the reflection of light in the pool, the glow from a big copper *brasero* on the little platform where the women sat. There was the music of guitars and a mouth organ, and the *gente* were singing and clapping and laughing, full of meat and wine and weary of dancing. The Señora sat in her wheelchair, with Feliciano and fat Lupe behind her. At her feet was Cayetana with the yellow guitar cradled across her. Avis was at the Señora's side, a rosy shawl about her shoulders. Richards could not recall what he had said to her or what she had said to him, briefly, in the few moments they had spoken. It did not matter. He was satisfied to sit on the wall and watch her.

"Have a care," Uremáy said.

"I ain't goin' to fall, if that's what you mean," Richards said.

Then he knew he had not said it, but only thought it. There was a burst of laughter and applause from below and he saw Shiloh jump to his feet near Avis and hold up his hands, looking shy and pleased.

"Everybody be quiet," he said. "Everybody quiet down. *Silencio*, now. Guess who drawed the black straw. Miss Caye."

There was a moment of silence, then more laughter and clapping. Richards managed to turn his head without snapping his neck, which felt thin and brittle as glass to him, and saw that Uremáy was looking at him and that his face, even in this half-light, was taut and strained. "The black straw," he said. "Now the little dove must take that flower from her hair and go and give it to the man she loves." There was an angry catch in Uremáy's voice. "Every year those fools cursed with *vino* must shame some woman with this thing." He leaned closer to Richards but his balance did not seem precarious. "One year I remember it was a poor soul born the year Christ died. Who was she to love, I ask you? Who was to love her, this ancient? She went to her house and gathered a little handful of paper flowers and took them into the *capilla* and laid them at the feet of *El Señor* where He hung on the cross, and still they were not shamed. And one year . . . *ay de mi* . . . my own Natividad, when we had been man and wife for fifteen years. Fifteen years, I tell you." He straightened and stared morosely down into the courtyard. "At least she brought her flower to me," he said, after a time. "It was in my mind that she thought to take it to Vicente Brega . . . ah, well, that was long ago. But the little *morena flor*, I would not wish this for her."

Richards looked down. Cayetana was already on her feet and coming across the courtyard, between her people, unsmiling, a swift flash of black swirling skirt and white lace. Only a moment he saw her hesitate; then she bent her head and with both hands took the red blossom from her piled hair and presented it, with a gesture which was more genuflection than curtsy, to don Ramón.

A great cheer went up. She reached for her father's hand and then raised her eyes, quickly, deliberately, in a solemn searching of faces, until she looked full on Uremáy, on the wall. Then she led her father back to the platform, smiling now, and reached across her mother and took Shiloh by both ears and pulled his head down laughing and kissed him on the cheek.

"Shoot," Shiloh said. "I thank you, but I was aimin' for the flower."

The laughter died and it was quiet and Richards saw Cayetana had taken up the guitar. The songs were the familiar songs of Mexico, and beside him Uremáy sang under his breath and drank and passed the jar and Richards grew more and more numb, condemned to move only to raise the pulque to his mouth. He was never sure of the moment the singing ceased and Cayetana's was the only voice he heard in the still starred-over night. This was music he had never heard before and it touched him in a way he could not define, deeply, so that he thought of old sorrows and knew there were sorrows to come, not separate, not single, but as a merging of unidentified sadnesses in the very core of him. The girl's dark husky voice was suited to this music, but it seemed to him now more animal than human; her fingers moved from the strings to strike the wood of the instrument and returned to the strings. The rapidity of deliverance, the peculiar extension of the same line, sung again and again, the spoken exclamation which broke the words, the range of the scale, were alien to him and he was baffled that he could understand no word of her Spanish, so distorted was it to his ear. There was a primal wildness in this, an overtone of almost unbearable pain, and he did not like it.

When it was over the day was over. With great purpose of mind, seeing the *gente* begin to leave the courtyard, Richards got the words out. "What did she sing?"

"An old song," Uremáy said in a low voice. "From the old country. It is the way the gipsy people sing. Unhappy songs from the land of her grandfather. She asks that a man not boast that she has loved him." He picked up the jar. "She will not sing the things of joy again, I think."

Richards didn't think so either but he didn't know why he thought so. He was frowning. He wanted to say something more, but he could not remember what it was.

"Ben, *amigo*, what is that you now wish?" Uremáy said.

"Sleep," he said.

He wanted to tell Uremáy he couldn't make it to the house.

The thought of the stairs filled him with fury and despair, and the knowledge that he would have to face the women, face Avis, cut like a knife. The last thing he recollected was stretching out flat on the wall and trying to shape more words. He woke up in the morning, feeling beaten and blinded, in the bed which normally would have held Uremáy and Natividad.

Watching Uremáy asleep now, against the tree, Richards knew that he had slept on the floor that night, he and the little woman he had once feared might give her flower to another man. Uremáy's face worked as he slept; it was ferocious, violent, teeth bared. He sat up with a jolt and opened his eyes.

"Did you kill him?" Richards said.

Uremáy's misshapen, work-hardened hand came up and moved across his brow. He took it down and looked at it as though he were astonished to see it. "Blood of Christ. I dreamed. How I dreamed. The *Mexicano* sleeps in the daytime, and I am as fond of this as the next man, but it is not well for man to sleep in the daytime."

"Unnatural," Richards agreed.

"Would you offer me another *cigarillo?*"

"You want a smoke?"

"I would be honored."

Uremáy lighted the cigarette and Richards saw that his hands were unsteady. "Tell me, my gringo," Uremáy said. "You were in the big war, eh?"

"Not long," Richards said. "I stopped a rifle ball early. It never did heal right while I was on my feet, so they pushed me out."

"Good fortune attends your every move, I see," Uremáy said. "I tell you. I fought a war there, while I slept. A man sleeps in the daytime and he may fight a devil or two which has come for his soul, but to fight a war is very difficult. I ask. How can a man fight a war alone?"

"Get the general right off," Richards said.

Uremáy looked up at him. His eyes were alert and, it seemed to Richards, a little suspicious. "This I did. I have killed the general while I slept. How do you know this?"

"I didn't know it," Richards said. "It's just plain sense to shoot the officers first and hope the troops'll lose their spirit and run the other way."

"Gringo sense," Uremáy said. His voice was a growl. "Since you have all this fine sense, I will give you a small warning. Use it."

"Somebody on the prod for me?" Richards said. Uremáy saw that his expression did not change, but he caught the changed timbre of voice.

"Of this I know nothing." The smoke curled slowly from Uremáy's nostrils. "I am saying that a man lies in his grave and his soul struggles in hell and other men must have a care that they do not walk too swiftly over that grave."

Richards stood up and pushed his hat back. "You got a long nose, Tiburcio. What is it your people say: a long nose makes for lean sides."

"Your heart has turned against me," Uremáy said. "For this I am sorry. But I am your friend."

"Sure, I'm madder than hell at you," Richards said. "I'm so damned mad I ain't goin' to ask you if you want to play *segundo* on this drive."

"Ah," Uremáy said. "I had the fear in me that you would not ask. All the words I have said, I will take them back into my mouth. Into my heart. Tomorrow, at the first coming of day, take the best horse on Tres Reyes and ride to the McLeans'. Waste no word . . ." His voice trailed off. Richards stood there, looking at him. He rose slowly. "So," he said. "We must return. I am certain that thanks be to the *patrón* more than one splendid animal is now good for nothing but to be butchered."

Richards still said nothing; he wondered if he might come to hate if not Uremáy, that sixth sense in the man which he thought he admired. They mounted up and started back to the camp. As they neared it, Uremáy said casually, "As to your desire that I go with you on this drive, it is my belief that the *patrón* will agree. But I must give it much thought. Much."

"Sure, you think about it," Richards said, amused in spite of himself. "If you can manage . . ."

"Perhaps I may," Uremáy said. "*Talvez.*" He dismounted, not looking up at Richards. "One word I did not say, so I will not have to take it back to myself. When I was in the great city of Seville, my Natividad and I, with the little *morena flor*, I knew a man, a *caballero con grandeza*. Today, while I slept, he was the *generalissimo*, and I killed him. While we were fighting in my dream, you fought also, but it was not a *generalissimo* you fought, and you did not kill him." He tossed the reins of Dominguez' horse to the ground and walked away. When he had gone several steps, he turned and looked up at Richards. "*Cuidado, amigo*," he said. "Have much care when you are with the young McLean."

SIX

The gather was over. Richards had never worked harder nor held a job in which he was required to do less. For him, this was only the beginning; what lay ahead would make the spring work schedule seem a game. Already weary, he focused on what he knew would be, even if it went without incident, the hardest trail drive of his life. There were already problems: the size of the herd, a drive crew which would be wholly Mexican except for the men of the M Bar L, mixed stock which, small as the mixture might be, would add to the work load. He thought of the trail boss's stock summation, which applied twice over to the trail boss himself: you hands got all winter to sleep.

With the hard work behind, there was an air of release on Tres Reyes, singing among the house servants, field hands, and vaqueros taking in and bringing out the *manadas* and selecting their strings to form the remuda for the drive. Richards did not share the air of well-being but he did not let it show. He had three days' grace in which to prepare himself, in which to say what he had to say to

Avis, and he felt that it had to be more than a good-by, that it had to be an understanding.

The time was not right for it but it had to be settled now. He would be gone eight months. Maybe, if it wasn't settled, there would be no point in his coming back. No point but Tres Reyes itself, and he supposed he could spend the rest of his life here if he wanted to. He was being paid double the price of a trail boss, two hundred dollars a month and found, and found, for him, was not a bunk shack and a pot-bellied stove, but as good as the house had to offer. A man would have to think twice about throwing over a situation like that. Yet something drove him relentlessly, a burning inner energy which sapped him while it pushed him on, and against which he was powerless. He dreaded the time it might burn out in him.

He was grateful the drive lay ahead. If Avis left him hanging it would be the means to make a clean break. Money didn't matter, it had never mattered, what did he need it for? He had spent all his life in the saddle and there were always jobs to be had and a plate of beans to be picked up when things got tough. Inside, he knew it was wrong to believe he didn't need anyone, anything. The Ben Richards inside him wanted to mount a horse only when he wanted to mount it, and when he had mounted, to look out at some thing, some possession, no matter how small, which belonged not to another man but wholly to him.

When he shaved that morning he cut himself badly and cursed the razor. Little Soledad, coming for the water basin, laughed behind her cupped hand and he only shook his head at her. He was always clear eyed and good tempered in the morning, and she knew she could laugh at him. After he had dressed he had the feeling that he had forgotten something and he stood casting for it in his mind.

When it came to him it came in the voice of Tiburcio Uremáy. He opened the top drawer of the chest and took out his gun belt and the .44, looked them over automatically, loaded five cartridges, and dropped the hammer on an empty chamber.

Damn fool, he said to himself. Lettin' Uremáy get under your hide.

When he went out he glanced toward the Señora's room. The

door was open and he hesitated. But while he made up his mind to go and say good morning to her, Feliciano looked out at him and closed it. He shrugged. That took care of it. He stepped around a pile of wet cleaning rags and a small woman on her hands and knees, put one hand over his still-smarting jaw, and almost collided with Cayetana coming at a near run toward the staircase. She stopped and stared at him.

"Ay, Ben, you've cut yourself."

"Near bled to death," he said.

"Are you going to McLeans'?"

"I want to talk to Frankie's hands," he said.

"I would like to go with you."

"Come ahead," he said, trying not to let his face show resistance, trying not to let her know that her company at McLeans' was the last thing in the world he wanted.

"I cannot. I'm trying to pick up Ebano. We're getting ready to leave for the border and I don't want to go without him." Her voice was rueful. "He's ranged. Tiburcio is so kind to my best horse that he leaves me without him."

"Leavin'?" Richards said. "You won't be here when we head out? Tiburcio . . ."

"Tiburcio takes my horse and you take Tiburcio. I am going with Esteban. But not until you leave." Her eyes were grave. "It is bad luck, you know, unless I am here when you leave. It was because I was not here last year to see the drive off that Pedro Mendoza drowned at the Brazos crossing."

He remembered that drowning, and he was uncomfortable at the memory, and at her assertion. "Is that a fact?" he said.

"You can think what you like, Ben."

"I believe you, I do for certain, Caye." He scratched his head, knowing he'd come up square against another of the many superstitions in this house. Maybe you could even say this house was run on superstition, and if you hung around long enough, listened hard enough, it would begin to get to you, until it was seeping into your skin like alkali and you not only never did get entirely shut of it but pretty soon you began to run on it too. He had got used to running on what his head told him.

"I'm going to miss you, Ben," she said. The set of her head

95

was that of a sedate child, considerate and considering. She knew no other way than to be open and frank. "All summer I'll wonder where you are and how the drive goes. If they would let me, I would go along."

He gave a short laugh that was half grunt. "Nothin' against you, little Caye, but I expect I would cut my throat first."

She looked at his face, not quite smiling. "Your hand is not steady enough, Ben."

He laughed, then. "I hope you pick up Ebano."

She went on down the stairs, turned, and disappeared in the rear of the house. Lupe caught him at the front door and wanted to put some tallow on his face, but he pushed her off and was glad to get out without meeting anybody else.

It was a good day and he nursed the wish it had been the day set for moving out. When he rode into McLeans' he saw there were men in the corral, so he passed the house and went on. Frankie, Shiloh, and the two hands picked up for the drive were sitting on the top rail and looking over the horses, figuring what they wanted to cut out.

"On your feet, girls," Shiloh said. "Here comes the ramrod."

"Stay set," Richards said. He swung from the saddle up on the rail with them. During the gather he had crossed paths briefly with the two McLean hands, Emory Hedges and Tom Corrigan, but he'd had no chance to size them up. They both said, "Howdy, Richards."

"Hedges. Corrigan." He looked them over without seeming to and pegged them in their late twenties, with worn clothing and work-hardened hands. Hedges was dark and pockmarked, middle height. Corrigan was red-haired and deep chested, half a head taller than the average. "Where you boys worked?" Richards said. He knew better than to ask them where they were from. That was the one question you never asked any man.

"Worked all the way to Wyoming," Corrigan said. "This here makes ten years I been trailin'." He jerked his thumb at Hedges. "Em'ry here, he's been foolin' around cows since he was born. We aimed to do some travelin' this year but we run out of money in San Antone, so we figured to take a drive."

"How'd you come to light here?" Richards said.

"Picked up the name from the list at the Association office. Seen McLean only wanted a couple men, so we figured it was a small drive. About ten old muley cows."

"I ain't keen on throwin' cold water on your hopes," Richards said. "Did McLean tell you the facts?"

"Man, yes," Hedges said. "Ain't that a whopper of a herd, though."

"You ever worked with Mexicans before?"

Corrigan had a flashing Irish grin. "Hell yes. Worked with 'em, lived with 'em, and slept with 'em."

"All I wanted to know. You goin' to have enough horses, Frankie?"

"Sure," Frankie said. Richards heard the thin, acid note. "We got enough right here, after I crack my goddam back findin' out which of 'em'll be rode and which won't. And if I ain't, you'll make me the loan of some, won't you?"

"I won't," Richards said levelly. "Dominguez will."

Frankie jumped down off the fence. "You see that little dish-face with the white blaze? He's throwed Shiloh four times. I aim to ride him."

"I aim to stay and watch," Shiloh said. "I wouldn't miss this here for a bucketful of new socks."

Richards got down, on the outside of the fence. "Break a leg, Frankie, and you're out of business."

"I'll stay home with the ladies," McLean said, not looking around, watching the horses.

"The hell you will. You're goin' to your Christ-begotten railhead if I got to take you there in the chuck wagon."

McLean looked around at him, grinning. "Sure, boss man. Ain't you goin' to stick here and watch me do it?"

"No," Richards said quietly, sadly. He looked up at Hedges and Corrigan. "Day after tomorrow, before sunrise. We're takin' ten horses a man and you better do the same."

"Man," Hedges said, "if I got to try out ten horses between now'n then you might have to take me in the chuck wagon."

Richards mounted the buttermilk and went back to the house. Avis had been scratching around in the dirt between the wagon wheels and had strung some pieces of red cloth to keep the birds

97

away from the seed. He knocked but didn't wait for an answer and pushed open the door and went in. For a moment he felt so close grained he almost turned and walked out again, and then it was too late and he was in the kitchen and Avis looked up at him from a chair by the window.

"I saw you go down to the corral. Now I'm shamed you came by and caught me busy at nothing." He saw her mouth come open.

"You're absolutely right, I cut myself," he said, smiling, forestalling her. "You goin' to offer me some coffee?"

She set out a cup for him. "I reckon you're ready to go. Anxious for it, too."

"I'm ready," he said. "I hope Frankie is."

"Frankie?" She turned sharply, holding the worn coffeepot, with a corner of her apron around the handle. "Don't you know what's ailin' Frankie?"

"Avis, I don't know a thing about Frankie. All I know is he goes off half-cocked when you least expect it and comes up mild as milk when he'd ought to be tearin' off the roof."

She came and sat by him. "It's because he ain't been able to get so much as a sniff at Rojo. He was countin' on it. He was goin' to hogtie that red steer and take him to Dodge."

He had forgotten Rojo. He had not given more than passing thought to the killer longhorn, and not a man on Tres Reyes had sighted so much as a corner of red hide. As far as he was concerned, that was one problem licked and out of the way, and he wasn't going to have Frankie sulling like a frustrated bull because he hadn't done what he wanted to do. He picked up his cup. "I'd be lyin' if I said I ain't glad nothing came of it. Rojo's probly back over the border by now . . ."

She interrupted him. "Killin' whatever gets in his way and maybe rememberin' your horse and my husband. Well, I'm glad too, Ben. But if I see one inch of his horn on my range while the boys are gone, I'm goin' to do what I reckoned to do when . . . before . . ."

He saw she hadn't looked for his consent. "If you don't, you're goin' to have another McLean spendin' the best part of his time tryin' to pull down that steer. You got to promise me, though,

Avis. Don't try it alone. You understand that. He ain't Sid's wolf. You ain't goin' to stop him with one rifle shot."

"Yes," she said. "I reckon I know that. Tres Reyes's near enough so I got help, no matter what."

"I'm sorry Sid left like he did. It ain't goin' to be easy bein' alone here, Avis."

"Well, he's gone, and that's an end to it. I don't expect I could of stood him around long anyway. I got plenty to keep me busy."

He watched her. She wore no sign of bereavement now, or of indecision. There was no doubt in his mind that she aimed to stay right where she was and run the ranch as Jonah had run it. Maybe, judging by the way she could harden her mouth, she even felt she could put the traces on Frankie and keep them there, and he longed to ask her if what Jonah had told him was true, if this drive would take them out of debt and leave something over. "Avis," he said, "I got hopes for Frankie. Maybe this drive'll mean more than just a drive to him. Maybe it'll teach him something, steady him down. Make him see he's got a fair proposition here if he handles it right. He can make a living at it, this ranch. Maybe he won't be flush, but he shouldn't have to go broke either, unless the bottom falls out of cows. I'll help him all I can."

She folded her arms on the table. "Ben, you'd ought to know something. Frankie is just eight months younger'n me. If he ain't a man now I ain't a woman. Jonah couldn't handle him. I don't expect you can. But there's something you got to give him. Except our herd's thrown in with the Tres Reyes now, there's no reason he couldn't pick up a few more men and pull out by himself. For the first time in his life he's mindin' what Jonah told him."

She was deadly serious and he was moved. She cared about Frankie; Frankie and what became of him were important to her. He was not merely an irresponsible kid she had acquired through the accident of marriage, but her responsibility twice over, now that Jonah was gone. He had thought about it before: in a sense, even now, Frankie was his responsibility too. He looked at her, stirred not only by the look of her, but by the resolute stand she was taking. His voice was only a hair unsteady. "Avis, you're a

99

young woman and maybe it ain't right to speak of it so soon, but you got to marry again, you can't stay like this."

Color came up under the fair skin. Yet she looked, Richards thought, more caught-out than caught off guard. "You know what I'm goin' to say, don't you?"

The color stayed in her face. "Maybe I do and maybe I don't. If you said it right out, then I'd know for certain, wouldn't I?"

She was not arch, but blunt. And he saw that none of this was going to happen as he had wanted it to happen, that he was, rather, reduced to sitting before an empty coffee cup, looking her in the eye, and saying it point blank, when he now knew that he should have come into this kitchen, taken her into his arms, and allowed her to say nothing, absolutely nothing, but said it all himself. He had not been cast in that mold.

"I don't expect I'm able to say the kind of things you'd like for me to say, Avis. I never been good at that sort of thing. I'll be back the end of November, beginning of December. I got some money saved up. About three thousand dollars or so. If you could wait that long. I'm askin' you to marry me."

She sat looking at him, eyes wide but only slightly astonished. "Ben," she said. "Ben Richards."

"Are you all that surprised? I didn't reckon you would be." He got up from the chair and took her by the shoulders, wanting to find some spontaneous and genuine response in her. "You knew I loved you, Avis, you knew it a long time ago. I might of kept it hid from Jonah, but I never could from you. You knew it the minute I let you know I was takin' the M Bar L's for you, not for Jonah."

"I . . . yes," she whispered finally. "Ben, I'm sorry."

"Sorry?" he said. "Sorry? If that's what you are usin' in place of no, it won't do, I won't take it for answer."

"Ben . . ."

"Listen," he said, "there were times I was with you . . . I don't know how many times . . . when you . . ."

"What," she said, "what did I do?"

"I don't know . . . I can't make words of it. It wasn't anything you did, or said, it was something I felt. Something you let me feel. Maybe something I thought you felt."

"Ben, I can't help what you felt."

"Yes, you could of," he said ruthlessly. "All you had to do was make one sign I wasn't to feel that way and it would of been the end of it."

"And you would have stopped how you felt?"

"No," he said, "but I wouldn't have stayed around where I had to keep feelin' it."

Her voice rose a little. "Ben, give me *time!*"

"I got no time," he said steadily. "I kept everything I felt for you inside myself for too long. I got to know if there's any sense my comin' back."

She put her hands on his arms. "Do you know what you're sayin'? Did you think about anything more'n me? Did you think about this ranch? About Frankie?"

"I thought of him," Richards said.

"This is his ranch too."

"If he's got any feelin' about it we can start someplace else."

She took a deep breath and he saw her eyes fill. "Ben, I don't know. I don't know." She could feel him drawing away, feel a tensing of muscle in his upper arms, and she raised her hands and drew him down to her and kissed him, gently, a peace offering, a link in the chain to hold him. "Ben, please . . . just till you come back. Please. Give me that time. I'm so tired and confused now. I want these weeks alone, I need 'em. What do a few more months mean?"

"And when I come back?" he said.

"Then I'll say what . . . what I have to say. Don't you see? Even if we kept it between us, it wouldn't be . . . be decent now."

He looked at her for a long time and then he bent and kissed her again. "You're right, Avis. I didn't mean to push you when you don't want to be pushed. I reckon there's a lot I didn't think about, like you say. How maybe you might like to look for somebody wasn't puttin' the years behind him quite so fast as I am. I want you to know I'd be good to you, Avis."

"You don't have to tell me that. Ben, now I don't want you to go. I want you to stay, and if you don't go I won't never get to think on it, or remember you, or . . . or . . ."

"Or what?" he said, smiling, feeling a first blind faith.

"Miss you, I reckon. I can't miss you if you ain't gone."

He could feel his elation, a warm living thing with a heart of its own, spreading like fresh blood in his veins. But only for a moment. Unlooked for, unwanted, Cayetana's somber open countenance passed his mind, and the similar words, and he knew without question how honest the words were when she spoke them.

"Ben," she said, "don't tell Frankie how we . . . about this."

He shook his head. "I didn't aim to say anything to him till I saw how you felt."

He saw her draw a long breath, as if in relief. "It ain't enough, is it, Ben?" she said. "You'd like for me to say something more."

"I'd like for you to be able to say something more, but I don't expect you can, now."

She rose, reached up, and touched his face, touched the ugly slash the razor had left. "Poor face," she said. "Such a stern face, sometimes. Ben, you're a good man."

"No," he said. "I wouldn't keep anything back from you, Avis. I just aim to do the best I can. Could you write to me sometime, this summer?"

"Whereabouts should I send it, Ben?"

"Dodge City, but I'd get it for sure care of Todd Allenby in Fort Benton, Montana."

"I'll write," she said.

"I expect I'll come back, then," he said.

"Did you reckon you mightn't, Ben?"

"I questioned it, some. There ain't any question now." He didn't touch her again. The hope was still warm in him, but he felt too a longing, a pain, as if he were already weeks away from her. "I expect don Ramón'll keep his eye on you, but you take care, won't you, Avis?"

"I'll take care."

"And you'll think about it. About us."

"Yes," she said. "Yes, I'll be thinkin' on it."

So it had not been settled, and when he came into Tres Reyes the afternoon was half gone. Esteban Ibarra met him in the courtyard and stopped him before he could dismount.

"Ah, Señor Richards, I look for you. The Señorita Cayetana, she says you have gone to the McLeans'."

"Something wrong?" Richards said.

Ibarra was young, lithe, hawklike, with a big handsome head and thick blue-black hair. He said that he had been born on a horse while his mother was on her way from a day's work in the bean fields to the more suitable surroundings of her house, and that was why he was the best horseman on Tres Reyes. Richards strongly suspected that his mother had got down off the horse to have him, but he didn't argue with the rest of it. One day, Uremáy's nose was going to be out of joint because of Esteban, who no matter under what circumstances he had first seen the light of day, was born knowing as much about horses as Uremáy had taken a lifetime to learn. "I do not know if it is wrong, exactly," he said. "A little while ago the *patrón* and Uremáy ride out and they find a good steer is lying on the edge of the brush, badly torn up. Torn to pieces, in fact. They look at him now."

"Where are they?" Richards said.

"You know where the brush begins, by the river. There are one, two, three trails, very clearly marked. Just beyond the third trail is where they find this steer."

"What tore him up, did you say?"

"I did not say, Señor." Esteban looked about him, making certain there were no other ears to hear. "Not a panther, not a javelina. No. What is it that has horns and uses them to kill?"

"Other steers," Richards said wearily. Something in his mind said, Rojo.

"Aha," Esteban said. "Other steers, you say. What else has horns, Señor?"

"I wouldn't want to disappoint you," Richards said. "You tell me."

"*El Diablo*," Esteban said triumphantly.

"I'll watch out," Richards said, and rode back out again and toward the river.

He counted off the trails and found the steer. Dominguez and Uremáy had gone on, probably looking to see if they could find some clue; he picked up their tracks in the soft earth. He sat the buttermilk looking down at the dead steer. It was a big one, about three years old, which had either been overlooked or let alone because it wasn't mature yet. He gauged it had been dead maybe a day and a half or two days. Buzzards and crows had been at it and probably pigs too, but he could see that what had killed it was its belly had been torn open. There was a big round hole in the side of its head, like it had been horned after it was down. His eyes went beyond the trailing guts, the noisesome flies clustered on eyes and muzzle, and saw something white beyond it, lying in the dirt under a sweeping huisache covered with yellow blossoms. He dismounted and walked around the dead steer and bent down and picked it up. It was an envelope, heavy cream-colored paper, stained with dirt and bent at the corner. He turned it over and saw that there was one word written on it: *Cayetana*.

He stood tapping it against the palm of his hand and looking down the line of brush. There was no sign of Dominguez and Uremáy. Sometime or other, Cayetana had been out here and dropped this, or it had maybe blown in from somewhere. Or she had thrown it away. He half-started to toss it down again, but he didn't. He had never yet seen a woman throw away anything on paper without first either crumpling it up or tearing it in about two hundred pieces.

He stuck it into the side pocket of his coat.

He was barely mounted when he saw Dominguez come out of the brush some distance away, followed by Uremáy. "What do you think, Ben?" Dominguez said when he rode up.

"This critter? I think he got in the way of another steer didn't want to be got in the way of."

"Like Rojo?" Uremáy said.

"Like Rojo."

"Well, it is unfortunate," Dominguez said. "I think now that our friend Frankie has not made good his boast, I shall send out a party to hunt down this *ladino*."

"I reckon you ought to," Richards said. He felt a kind of deliverance at the idea, but there was an underlying reluctance in him too. "If you do get him, don Ramón, I wish you'd let Avis McLean know. She's goin' to be on the lookout for him."

He looked at Uremáy and saw a small smile on the *peon* boss's mouth. He looked away again. "You goin' back to the house, don Ramón?"

"No, they are still working some of the new horses. We go to the corrals. If you go back, tell them to send some men to bury what is left of this poor brute. We will smell him all the way to the *casa* by nightfall."

Richards rode for the house. Once when his arm rested against his pocket he felt the stiffness of the envelope. Probably he had done something foolish. He might better have given it to Dominguez and said, "Here, I reckon Caye dropped this," but it didn't occur to him. Living in this household, he thought it might come easy to him to believe he was fated to do fool things. Guadalupe hadn't been any help at all, blowing out the candles like she did.

He rode around to the back of the house and dismounted in front of the *ramada*. Somebody's kid, dressed in white cotton, eyes black and bright, took the buttermilk horse. He could remember the day if somebody reached for the reins of his horse he would have reached for the .44. Now he didn't even have to rub down a horse or saddle it, unless he felt like it. He went through a storage room and into the kitchen. Lupe wasn't there but she had some thick slabs of beef laid out for supper and an iron pan of tallow to fry them in. He was hungry. He picked up a cold tortilla left over from the middle of the day and began to eat it.

A door slammed somewhere on the lower floor. He tried to figure out where it was, but he came here so seldom that it was hard to get his bearings. There were two doors leading out of the kitchen, one into the dining room and the other into the hall. Beyond the dining room, which was dead ahead to his left and separated by another hall, was the chapel. On the right was Dominguez' office, the continuation of the intersecting hall, and then the main room with the timber-framed fireplace and easy rawhide chairs and massive Spanish furniture and big colored rugs. It had been the office door he heard. He went out of the kitchen and into the hall, in time to see Cayetana crossing to the stairwell. He groped in his pocket and found the envelope and called to her, his mouth still full, and met her at the foot of the stairs.

"Oh, you're back, Ben. Is everything well at McLeans'?"

"All set to go," he said, and swallowed the last of the tortilla. "You get Ebano?"

"He hadn't gone far, he just wouldn't let Tiburcio find him."

"Well, you're set then, too," he said. He handed her the envelope. "Here, I found this. Figured you must of dropped it."

She took it and turned it over in her hands. A frown came on her smooth, clear brow. "Where did you find this, Ben?"

"Down on the brush spur," he said. "We were lookin' at a dead steer."

Again she turned it over. The frown did not go away. He was struck, then, with the feeling that she had never touched this envelope, never seen it, before. "It's yours, ain't it?" he said. "It's got your name on it."

"Yes," she said in an odd, uncertain voice. "Yes, it's mine. Thank you, Ben." She turned away from him, removing the contents of the envelope, and started up the stairs again.

He was about to go up himself, but she looked as if she didn't want company, so he decided to go into the office and look over the tally sheets and see if maybe she had got ready the letter of credit he would carry. He was halfway across the hall when he heard a sound from the stairs. If he had been asked what the sound was, he couldn't have said: it was a little like a whimper of despair crossed with subdued rage, and then crossed again with a sharp and unendurable anguish. It brought up the short hairs on his neck. He spun around and saw that Cayetana was on her knees, halfway up the stairs, still holding the envelope and whatever it had contained in one hand and clinging to one heavy carved rail with the other. If she hadn't been hanging on like that he would have thought she had fainted. He jumped for the stairs, skidding like he was on ice when he hit the first rise, and running the rest of the way and reaching down and lifting her around the waist and feeling the lean smooth flesh under his hands, under the white cotton shirt. She was astonishingly strong. He had to tear her away from the railing. She didn't fight him, she just had a mind of her own.

"Caye, for God's sake . . ." he said, and then she went limp and fell against him as if all the strength had drained out of her at the sound of his voice. He pulled her up and she let him, leaning against him. For the first time he saw her face and knew the strength had drained away because the blood had drained away. At least there wasn't any left where he could see it.

"I'm all right," she said, but it was a gasp. "I'm all right now."

But she couldn't seem to stand. He supported her full weight the rest of the way up, not that she weighed much, but he knew it would have been less awkward to carry her. At the top, it was on the end of his tongue to mention that Feliciano was probably close at hand, but he didn't say it. Her room was at the opposite end of the hall from the Señora's, and he didn't think twice about leading her there, opening the door with his one free hand, and taking her in.

"Caye, if you're sick or something . . . look, you got to lie down."

But she did not. He let her down on the edge of the bed and she sat there, bent over and clutching at her middle, still holding the envelope. She looked like she had a belly ache but he didn't think he ought to ask her.

"You want me to get Soledad?" he said, inspired.

"No." She cried it at him. "Close the door. Close it!"

He went and closed it.

She was still sitting in the same position, head down. "Ben . . . wait a minute . . . give me a minute. I have to talk to you . . . ask you." She didn't say any more.

He was patient, knowing she would pull herself together if he waited. His eyes went around the room, seeing that with the exception of the rich hangings at the window which faced out into the courtyard, it was peculiarly sparse; roomy, but just on the other side of what he figured Father Berrades' cell might be like. The furniture . . . bed, clothes press, chest, chair . . . was the same heavy carved Spanish stuff which had been used throughout the house. But there wasn't even the usual crucifix or garishly tinted portrait of one saint or another. Then he saw something. There was a niche built into the corner of the two walls which met at the left of the bed, and there was a figure in it. It was a girl's figure, three feet tall, but he knew it wasn't Guadalupe. No Guadalupe ever looked or dressed like this. This Virgin wore gold, so stiff and heavy with embroidery that it stood out around her like the housing of a bell and trailed off behind in a rounded train. And it wasn't just a crown she had on, but a great golden headdress that pointed out like the rays of the sun coming up. Her face was the most beautiful face he had ever seen, more beautiful than any face a man could make up for himself in his own imaginings. It was a face of agony, the perfectly carved scarlet mouth open a little, the eyes great with suffering, but it was a face glossed over like satin, and in no way distorted. On one cheek, destined to fall forever, were three perfect tears, and he knew from where he stood that they were not glass. They were something more than glass, diamonds, maybe. There were no paper flowers at her feet either, only low little candle holders set in thick Mexican silver. He couldn't take his eyes off her; he'd never seen anything like her in his life, and he had seen his share of Mexican saints in Mexican churches. He stood there staring at her, until he realized Cayetana had raised her head.

For one flashing instant he thought he saw so strong a resemblance between the Girl in gold and the girl in worn riding clothes, that they might have been interchangeable.

He went and hunkered down in front of Cayetana. "You all right now, Caye?"

There was something terrible about her composure. She nodded once. "I have to know. This letter. You found it down on the spur. How long ago?"

"Not more'n an hour," he said. "It was layin' under a bush, and I expected you had dropped it, so I picked it up figurin' to give it to you. If I'd known it was goin' to get you so upset . . ."

"But this is only the inner envelope. There was nothing else? You're sure?"

"Nothin' else," he said.

She wasn't looking at him, but over his head, at the bare wall.

"Caye, are you in trouble?" he said then. "Is it anything I can help with?" And he saw, as he had seen the night she lost her poise in the courtyard, that she was fighting tears.

"I don't know," she said shakily. "I don't know if anyone can help." She leaned forward and put her hand on his shoulder. She was biting her lip. Her face was the face of an animal in pain.

She whispered it, on a breath of sudden fury. "My father. All this time. *My father.*" She stood up so quickly she nearly took him off balance. "Did you mean it when you said you would help me?"

He rose. "I wouldn't of said it if I didn't mean it, Caye."

She said harshly, "Even if it is something that only you and I must know?"

"What you mean," he said, "is something that your father wouldn't take kindly to, that it?"

"Yes," she said flatly. "That is what I want."

He didn't stop to consider. No matter what had caused it, it was good to see something in her eyes besides that sadness, to know that she was capable of anger, receptive to pain. Whatever she wanted of him, it was worth it, and he felt this with an amazement which was like the prick of a knife, but without comprehension. "All you got to do's say it," he said.

"When you are finished in the office tonight go to the kitchen door and wait by the *ramada*. I am going to give you an answer to this letter. I want it to go to San Antonio."

"How?" he said. "Who am I goin' to send?"

"You must ask Tiburcio for the best rider and the most trusted."

"Then I reckon Tiburcio has got to know too."

"Yes. Always. Tiburcio knows everything always. Now, this . . ." She held the letter, back in its envelope, out to him, but when he reached for it her fingers clung to it as if she would never let it go. "Take it back and drop it where you found it," she said.

"What?" he said. "But it's yours, Caye. What do you want to put it out in the brush for? Most likely they've buried that dead steer by now and any one of those hands diggin' around down there would of found it."

"Then drop it anywhere," she said. "Somewhere between the main gate and the river. So that he finds it again."

"If that's how you want it," he said. He wasn't going to ask any questions. He didn't feel entitled to ask any. He knew for a fact, now, that while the letter was hers, she had never seen it. Because of that one fact he intended to do whatever she said she wanted done. He was reaching for the door handle when she said, "I forgot to thank you, Ben."

He turned around. "I figure there's nothin' to thank me for, Caye."

She said it quietly enough. "Ben, I think for my life."

He went out of the room. He had figured that too.

Somebody was calling his name, a long way off. He turned over groaning and saw that the sun was far up. It was funny how you could get used to sleeping late when you had a chance, and just as funny how you could lay out in the open all night and rest just as good as you did in a bed and be able to operate, alert as a wolf, on a few hours sleep.

He didn't open his eyes. Something blurred across his mind he wasn't sure he felt like thinking about, but his mind was waking up and he didn't have any choice.

He remembered, an hour after he'd dropped the letter, Dominguez coming in, absent and sharp tempered, when he should have been elated and keyed up, like he got when he was watching them work the horses. By suppertime he was himself again, so it was plain he had found the letter, right where Richards had dropped it, a few feet off the spur. Supper was the worst meal he ever got through, and he recalled how those big beefsteaks had looked in the kitchen before they got cooked and smothered in tallow gravy and wondered that he had ever been hungry for one. The Señora was feeling so bad she had taken to bed, and Cayetana got up halfway through the meal and said she had a headache. That left him to talk with Dominguez, and he had to set his mind to it to answer questions and sound like he was untroubled and sharp as an eagle when he was torn with his hopes and fears about Avis and his new concern for Cayetana and a growing curiosity about Dominguez.

After Lupe had left the kitchen and put out the lamps, Cayetana came down and gave him the letter and he in turn crossed behind the house and went down the little street of adobe houses until he reached Uremáy's. Uremáy came with a lamp in his hand. Inside, somebody was crying, Natividad, he guessed. Richards didn't say anything, seeing how Uremáy looked almost as ferocious as he had looked the day he killed the general in his dream, and he handed over the envelope without looking at it. As he was turning, Uremáy reached out and gripped him by the shoulder so hard he came close to flaring up. But Uremáy wasn't mad. It was something else he saw in Uremáy's face, menace, and a grim protectiveness, and he knew what Uremáy was protecting.

"Not to a soul, Ben," he said. "Not to a soul. And for myself, I thank you."

He went back to the house and went upstairs to bed and thought first of Avis and then of Cayetana and then of that strange saint with the tears on her cheeks, all wrapped around in gold, before the grinding strain of the day caught up with him.

The voice went on calling, below. Then there was a knock at the door and he heard Soledad's voice.

"What is it?" he said.

"Señor McLean," she said, against the door. "He wishes to see you quickly, Señor."

He got up and pulled on his shirt and pants, struggled into his boots, grabbed jacket and hat, and went for the stairs.

Outside, Frankie and about two dozen of the Tres Reyes men were standing around talking and hooting and calling his name. He was just out the door when McLean came for him, looking feverish and ragged, as if he'd spent ten days in the brush.

"I done it, Ben," he yelled. "I done it. I got Rojo."

Richards stopped jamming his shirt into his pants and stood looking at him.

"I got him," McLean said, "and I'm havin' hell's own time with him. The way he's goin' it now, I'm goin' to need twenty men."

"Where?" Richards said, somehow not believing it, half-hoping it wasn't so because he didn't feel up to it right now and didn't know if he ever would.

"About two miles out of here snubbed to a tree. I got two ropes on him and he's goin' to snap 'em or pull that tree out roots and all. I got to have a ox. For Chris' sake, git a horse, will you?"

"Horse," Richards said to a kid standing looking up at him. "*Caballo*." The kid ran off, the loose legs of his cottons flopping around his ankles. Esteban Ibarra came out of the admiring bunch around Frankie and said, "I wish to go, Señor. I wish to see."

"All right, I'm goin' on," Richards said. "Bring up an ox fast as you can, Esteban."

By now they were coming out of the house and in from the fields. A vaquero in a big hat and fancy spurs that were more show than work had intercepted the kid and was coming down with the buttermilk horse, saddled. Men and horses were milling around by the gate and dirtying up the courtyard. Richards mounted and they swept out, into a day unseasonably soft and warm. Frankie was all wound up, half-yelling so Richards wouldn't miss any of it.

"You should of seen what I done, Ben, so neat I couldn't hardly believe it myself. I chased him right into Shiloh."

"You what?" Richards said.

"We was on our way here to look things over, me and Shiloh. We wasn't talkin' any and it was kind of quiet and all, and Rojo busted out of the brush just like he done that day by the river. I got rope on my saddle so I grabbed it and swung for him and he turned and run right into Shiloh and hit Shiloh's horse in the chest, between his horns."

Richards stiffened. If what McLean was saying was the truth, and he didn't have any reason to think it wasn't, it had taken nerve to ride at the big longhorn with a rope.

"Shiloh horse and all went down in a heap," McLean said, "but Rojo didn't keep goin', he turned on me. I had my rope all the way out then and I got him on one horn, first throw. He didn't come on me like I thought he would, he pulled off. This little old horse was with him all the way too. We didn't git far before Shiloh catches up and throws the nicest loop you ever see, right around both horns. By then he's tryin' to fight his way off and Shiloh'n me are haulin' like hell, and we got him right up to a good old tree and snubbed him."

"Shiloh ain't hurt?"

McLean laughed. "Says all his bones is jarred loose, and he's got a few spots comin' up black, is all. Well, what you got to say, Ben?"

"Congratulations," Richards said, after a moment.

"I wish you'd seen it."

"I'll see it," Richards said. "Quit worryin', I'll see it."

Frankie took them through a short trail in the brush, the chattering vaqueros following. When they came out the other side, Richards saw Shiloh sitting guard and Rojo roped to a stout tree and fighting it, braced and arched in fury and trying to swing the lethal head. He made no sound until he caught sight of the men. Then a low violent grunting began in him. The tree creaked and shook and branches cracked off it.

"Put a couple more ropes on him," Richards said. Two vaqueros rode out and doubled the strength of the snub.

They waited until Esteban came up with the ox. It was an old blue named Constante, tame as a house cat. The Spanish-blooded oxen were the best at this work and the blue had been at it for years.

"I will yoke him, Señor," Esteban said.

"He ain't a horse, Esteban," Richards said.

"That is true, Señor," Esteban said. "But the ox does not know Señor McLean. He knows me."

They rode in on the raging red steer and circled him. Manuel Vega rushed to grab his tail, dodging a flash of swift lifted hoofs. The tail was so long it came close to dragging the ground. Constante came up with Esteban, tranquil as if he had been turned out to pasture, steady and without fear as Esteban maneuvered him. He moved in under Rojo's horns at the first opportune moment and was out of danger. Then the ropes went around his neck, and around the neck of the red steer, binding them together. When it was done, McLean slashed the ropes which held Rojo to the tree.

For a dazed moment the great steer stood, trembling in the flanks. Then Vega, who still had hold of his tail, twisted it, hard enough to break it, and he tried to swing his head, swinging Constante's head also, and seeking with his horns. Richards yelled at Vega: the one unnecessary brutality enraged him, and marked Vega in his mind as a man brutal with animals, not uncommon among Mexicans but not tolerated on Tres Reyes. The blue ox nudged at Rojo, and then they were moving.

They ran, without regard for gullies, holes, rocks, but it was the blue ox who led. It might be the most roundabout way there was, but eventually he was going to end up at his own pen, and still yoked to him would be the *ladino* steer. They went weaving, staggering, slashing, bowling over big mesquite, as if they deliberately sought the most difficult path, the greatest obstacle.

"Follow 'em up," Richards said.

But there wasn't any hurry. They could follow at whatever pace they wanted, knowing that Constante was going to work his way home whether Rojo wanted it or not. He sent the vaqueros back to Tres Reyes and rode on after the clumsy pair who wanted nothing more than to be free of one another.

Within sight of the walls it happened. It might have been accident, but Richards had a feeling Rojo knew to the last instance what he was doing. He had been running free too long not to be smart, not to be cunning in ways a man could not begin to understand. There was an old hackberry standing out of a low clump of brush. Ox and steer were headed straight for it. It looked as if they were going to hit it head on, and Richards could see the blue ox straining away, pulling to the left of the trunk. It seemed to him that that was the way Rojo wanted it. At the last minute the red steer veered to the right and the tree loomed between him and Constante.

By the time they got there it was close to being over. The rope was too short, Rojo's tremendous weight too much. The blue ox's legs were buckling; he hung on the ropes straining, voiding, tongue out, eyes half-shut, snorting to breathe. Given another minute Rojo would have choked him to death as methodically and efficiently as brush poppers roped and choked a trapped lobo.

There was one rope among them: Esteban's. He tossed his knife to Richards and put the *reata* over the red steer's horns as lightly as a wreath of mist settling, and Richards leaned from his saddle and cut the blue ox free. Constante lurched upright, drawing great breaths; water sheeted from his distended eyes. Richards grabbed the severed rope and hauled, moving him out of the way at the same moment Esteban swung around the tree with the length of the *reata*. This time Rojo had got himself head against the trunk, both horns on either side of it, and if the rope held he was in no position to make trouble. Richards left the blue ox standing and went for the house.

Half an hour later he saw Constante and Rojo yoked for the second time. Rojo was still fighting, in some final unyielding burst of energy, but the fight was over. Constante had won. Practice and instinct led him across the edge of the fields, toward his own pen and the reward he knew awaited him: brown sugar, an apple, a sweet lime.

Uremáy came in from the horse pasture to watch, and for a long hour there was no work on Tres Reyes as the *gente* stopped to see the red steer brought in.

"So, Franco," Uremáy said. "What will you do with him now?"

"Take him to Dodge and shut the car on him myself," Frankie said. He was pouring sweat, his eyes were blind with it.

"No," Uremáy said. "Now."

"Now? Git him in that pen, I reckon."

Richards shook his head. "Don't cut that ox off him," he said. He rode on, looking over the spread of the corrals. In the second one out there was a bunch of a hundred or so steers which had been brought in early in the gather and had tamed down quickly, as much as they would ever tame down. "Head 'em in here," he said.

Esteban and Shiloh cut Constante off and turned him on the first swing. Frankie got the gate open, flapping his hat and hollering at the steers until they backed off, and then there was a rush by him and Rojo was choused in, among his own kind, which he had avoided as guardedly as he had avoided men.

Frankie closed the gate and turned around and leaned against the timbers in exaggerated weariness, arms flung wide and grinning. "You made a promise, Ben," he said.

"I did?" Richards said.

"Near. You said if I got him, I could take him."

"Yes," Richards said, "I reckon I much as did."

Uremáy looked at him. "Benjamín, my friend," he said softly. "You are *un hombre valiente*. A very brave man." He gestured at the corral. "And he is the kind who will die first."

They sat for a long time, watching Rojo circle frantically among the steers, making no sound, thrusting with that intense, power-ful, unwavering defiance, still yoked to the patient blue ox and doomed to that yoking until he was moved out on the long trail north.

SEVEN

On the sixth night of April, Esteban Ibarra was eating *nacionales* in the desert of Nuevo León. He had never felt better in his life, but he had a facility for remaining tranquil even when he was elated. True, it seemed strange not to have Tiburcio Uremáy's subtle hand in sight, drumming out small signals with knowing fingers when bargaining time came around, not to observe his keen eye appraising horses, to learn if Uremáy's eye saw what his eye saw. He had always known he could manage without Uremáy and yet he felt the loss of Uremáy's presence.

All else was the same. Natividad had come to cook, as always; she had a cousin in Nuevo Laredo of whom she was fond, and while they did not always pass that way, she would not miss the opportunity to visit. The two Juans, Sanchez and Porrumba, and Felipe Herrera. The Señorita Cayetana, who belonged not to all the *gente* of Tres Reyes now, but to them, the few, for a little time. And the horses. He thought mostly of the horses, and he knew the brothers Gómez had kept their word: it was a good string. Little wild ones and big wild ones, soon to be tamed, bred

117

or made work horses or cutting horses or riding horses. He had selected thirty out of forty-five, leaving only a couple of sorefoots, several whose eyes or legs or barrel he did not like the look of, one with bad teeth, and the paints. Paints were for Indians and children, so inbred they could not be relied upon for stamina, strength, or speed, except in short bursts. The prize was the little albino mare with eyes as blue as sky . . . what the gringo poppers called glass eyes. He knew a certain pale stallion on Tres Reyes who would be filled with joy at sight of her in his *manada*.

Or perhaps all was not the same. The little Señorita, for example. Why was it that at times she seemed in such a hurry, so anxious, so eager to expend all her energy, and at other times so lost and sad, as if her soul had gone away from them. Tiburcio might have known, but he, Esteban, had not yet replaced Tiburcio in all things.

There was still light and color in the sky, rose and pearl and smoky sapphire which would be lost in a flush of raw scarlet at sundown. The string had been watered and grazed and now must be kept together content and reconciled. The land was wide open, so that the band was in a corral woven of rope and rawhide *reatas*. He, the two Juans, and Felipe could string this corral in minutes, right around the horses, as night herders of trail remudas sometimes did on the long drives. Further, Felipe and the two Juans would take their turn at guard in the watches of the night, and to show that he was as important as Uremáy, not to speak of being just and honorable, he also would take his turn. Only Natividad and the little Señorita could not be expected to work at this. Anyway, Natividad worked each night at the cooking, and the little Señorita got herself hot and dusty and, it seemed to him, tired to the bone, chivvying the horses.

"Tiburcio will be jealous of you when he sees the white mare," she told him, and he soared. Everyone knew the Señorita and Uremáy were like two trees growing from a single root. He dreamed innocently and without malice of the day the old tree would topple and a younger support be required to take its place.

Not until the darkness was nearly down, with a last clear red line of light in the sky and the air filled with the richness of flowers and starlight, did the girl say with surprise, "Look, Esteban. Off there. There are lights."

But he did not trouble himself to look. "It is an old station, left from the revolt. There are soldiers there now. Only an outpost."

"If we see their lights they see our fire," she said.

"But I have the bill of sale, my Señorita," he said, smiling. "The horses are ours."

Two men from the post, wearing big soft hats and crossed bandoliers of cartridges rode in and on Esteban's invitation ate freely from the pot of beans. They sat and eyed Cayetana, one morose, one curious. When they had eaten they asked to inspect the bill of sale for the horses, and she saw the words, the identification, form on Esteban's mouth and forestalled him. "Give them the bill, Esteban."

He handed it over. She knew they could not read. After much muttering and fingering they passed the bill back to Esteban. Don Ramón Dominguez' name had been lettered large upon it, but the letters meant nothing to them.

"For two months now we do not see one Rurale," the smaller of the two was saying to Esteban. "Two months." He had long drooping mustaches which curled around the corners of his lips. "For two months we have only Captain Morisco and he is like a man mindless, one hour all smiling and the next hour sharpening his knife to cut a throat." He leaned and spat into the fire. He had never taken his morose eyes off her and she returned his look steadily. "If they do not soon come and give him his promotion and take him elsewhere, we are all dead men."

The taller man was very thin. The twin ridges of his collarbones humped under the open neck of his shirt. He smoked thoughtfully, squatting, narrowing his eyes against the smoke. "It is the gringo prisoner who makes him mindless," he said. "He picks at the bars of the window, so that we must watch him. If he does not pick at the bars, he whistles. Always the same song. One would think that his mouth is dry as a withered branch."

Cayetana felt a faint pity for the tormented captain; she envisioned him rushing to prevent his prisoner from picking out the bars and rushing away with his hands over his ears. She heard Esteban say courteously, "Your captain is perhaps more favored than he knows. How long since he has had a prisoner? Does this not contribute to his chances of promotion?"

The small man grunted assent. "So much that we are not to take him to the border, but must wait for the Rurales, so that they can see what Morisco has caught. And they never come. The devil has dropped them all in a hole and sealed it with rock. A very important prisoner, and Captain Morisco will let no one know he holds him."

"What has he done?" Cayetana said.

The morose eyes bored into her. "Taken money from a bank in Texas and killed four men. A black gringo."

"Worse," said the tall one. "He has lied to Captain Morisco."

She tried not to smile. The man tormented by a restless whistling prisoner had also to contend with matters of truth and virtue. Why did the lie matter, if the man had stolen and killed?

"Worse even than the lie," said the small one, "is the nature of the lie. To say that he is a Ranger."

"Worse than to say he is a Ranger," said the tall one, "is to say that he is Captain Bonaventure."

Cayetana turned to Esteban and saw that he was looking at her, his face alert, questioning.

"Yes," said the small one, "that is worst of all. When I myself have seen this Ranger captain, with these two eyes, and would know him with these two eyes closed."

Cayetana said. "Esteban."

He rose. "Do you wish me to . . . ?"

"Go to the post." She stood up and looked down at the squatting soldiers. "How is it you know this prisoner of your captain's is not Captain Bonaventure?"

"It is as I say, Señora . . . I myself have seen him, a tall pale man with hair like the sun at noon. Alone of this post, I have seen him." He gestured at Esteban. "Beg your Señora to seat herself and have no fear."

"She is not my Señora," Esteban said, shocked.

Cayetana said quietly, "I am of the house of Tres Reyes. It is my father's name upon the bill and these are his horses."

They got to their feet slowly, staring at her. She saw the working of the tall man's Adam's apple, up-down, up-down, in his throat. He said, "A thousand pardons, Señorita. We did not know."

"No harm is done," she said. "But perhaps there has been harm done, before we came to this place. You must escort Señor Ibarra to your captain."

They backed away stricken, thanking her for the beans, for the coffee, begging their thousand pardons. Cayetana put her hand on Esteban's arm. "Do you know this man Morisco?"

"No, Señorita. What am I to do if it is Captain Bonaventure?"

"You are to see that he is released," she said.

"And if it is not Captain Bonaventure?"

"Then we must assume that he is a bank robber who has killed four men and tells lies. God be with him."

When they had gone, she settled again, rolled and lit a cigarette, and poured herself coffee. Herrera came in to eat and was replaced on horse guard by Juan Sanchez. Natividad, her *rebozo* thrown back, was gathering and scraping plates angrily. Her brown face was round and shiny, and the eyes were small and shrewd in it.

"You see how it happens?" she said. "The very time Tiburcio is not here. The first time. A thing like this must happen. If Tiburcio were here, he would know at once what must be done."

"We are doing what must be done, Natividad."

"Where Tiburcio is not, there is trouble."

Herrera looked up from his plate. "What is it, Natividad?"

She shook her head at him, refusing to answer. He looked at Juan Porrumba. Porrumba shrugged and lay back, smoking, face turned up to the soft sky.

Where Tiburcio is not, there is trouble. And there are times when there is nothing but trouble where Tiburcio is, Cayetana thought. That is how he has learned to face it, because he has seen so much of it. She had forgotten Tiburcio in her prayers, for there had been so much to pray for these last days. *Now I shall pray only for Tiburcio, and I shall ask that from this day to the last day there will be no trouble for him.* It did not seem to her an unreasonable request. Why could there not be an end to trouble on some appointed day, at some exact moment, before death ended all troubles.

When she thought of Tiburcio she thought of the herd, for Tiburcio was with it now. And Richards. A sudden feeling of well-being, of security rose in her close to the point of exhilaration. Let there be no trouble there. Let the whole northbound herd feel as secure, as well cared for, as she felt in this moment. And let them come back some far off autumn day, Tiburcio and Richards and the sweating, laughing vaqueros and the handsome McLean boy and Shiloh who made her smile. Because life was good, and for no other reason, and now, now that the letter had come into her hands, let there be a sum of singing golden summers yet to come . . .

Was life good? She sat up, frowning. Aaron Bonaventure. He was dark, not fair, and he had sharp fine grained features, like a bird of prey, and kind eyes, but would she know him? Would Esteban know him? If they saw to the freeing of a stranger she would have been duped and possibly got Morisco in trouble to boot. The thought made a breach in the good feeling. She reached for the guitar and began to test it, playing nothing, but coaxing small plaintive sounds from it. The fire pulsed in its bed. Natividad sat huddled, looking at her, waiting. She put the guitar aside and lit another cigarette.

An hour passed before they heard horses. She saw Esteban first, and the two soldiers who had come to the camp. Behind them were a rotund little man in tight dark clothes which looked like the tag ends of several uniforms, and a tall man with a hat low on his head. She kept her eyes on him. When he dismounted and turned, he took off the hat and she saw a face with a dark beard and a blocky ill-trimmed mustache. He came directly around the fire to her and she looked up at him and knew that she had not, after all, made a mistake.

"I believe I owe my freedom to you," Bonaventure said in English.

"It is your good luck that these soldiers thought it their duty to question our string," she said. "And also that they talk freely."

"You know me?" he said.

"I know you."

122

"I thought perhaps . . . it was over four years ago. And I was out of a job then . . . most Rangers were. I regret this." His hand came up to the beard, dropped, touched the worn clothes. She could barely see his mouth under the thick mustache.

"Please," she said. "I understand. If you ask do you look as I remember you, the answer is no. But I would know you."

Bonaventure took a deep breath. "I thank God for that, Miss Dominguez. Would you kindly verify it for this crazy captain?"

She had only half-turned when Morisco rushed forward, nearly falling over Natividad's feet, and in an impetuous gesture reached to clasp her hand in both his own. She drew back in astonishment, repelled by his attempted touch, the breathless outpouring of words.

"Señorita Dominguez, for me to have the pleasure . . . ah, I cannot tell you, my heart is breaking within me for this terrible thing which has happened to me. To Captain Bonaventure. To you. You see that I am perfectly blameless, perfectly innocent. If the man had only *told* me in the beginning who he was, none of this would have happened. But no, he must have his little joke, he has stolen the money from the bank and killed four men. I cannot understand why he should wish to stay in my jail . . . of course, I run a clean, fine jail, it will stand inspection any hour of the day or night . . . if it had not been for you . . . ah, a thousand thanks, a thousand pardons . . ."

Sweat poured down his face. He turned and grasped Bonaventure's hand, raising it as if he would kiss it. "And for this poor friend, this comrade in arms . . . a great man, no? . . . but one whose jokes I do not understand . . . it has been an ordeal for him, he has grown quite thin . . . not that the food is not of the most nourishing at my post, Señorita. But the heartbreak. Ah, do we not all have bursting hearts, this night? Captain, though I do not deserve it, if you would give me your pardon it would make me the most fortunate, the most grateful, the mos—"

"Say," Bonaventure said, "how about giving me back my papers?"

Morisco's hands fell away. "Papers? Ah, of course, your papers." He reached into the inside of his jacket, brought out an envelope, and thrust it at Bonaventure. He was shaking his head. "But I ask you. Do I sign my own orders? Do I say, Captain José Pedralbes Morisco is hereby authorized to cross the Rio Bravo and then sign it myself? Never. You should be very careful, very careful when you do this thing, Captain."

"My watch," Bonaventure said.

"Of course, the watch."

"My rifle," Bonaventure said.

Morisco turned and shouted at the small soldier. A horse whinnied in response. The soldier placed Bonaventure's possessions on a blanket and handed Esteban the Winchester. Morisco smiled hugely. "All in order, as you can see, Captain. Now you are prepared to travel back to the river, and in good company too, such a beautiful traveling compan—ah, I cannot tell you, Señorita, how it pleases me to meet the daughter of my very old, most respected friend, don Ramón Domin—ah . . ." Cayetana's frozen face brought him to a trailing halt. He turned suddenly, flatly, to Bonaventure. "I regret it, Captain. You understand that I did only my duty. If it is known that I kept you prisoner for so many weeks there is no doubt that I will never so much as touch a finger to my promotion."

"I expect you deserve one," Bonaventure said, "just for being so set in your ways. You do me a favor and we'll call it square. You tell Sergeant Lozano you saw me and I said howdy. Will you do that?"

"There is no Sergeant Lozano," Morisco said bitterly. "He is a myth. All day I watch for him, for someone, day after day, and no one comes." He brightened. "But I will tell him if I see him."

He followed Bonaventure anxiously back to where the soldiers stood. Bonaventure checked the contents of the blanket and stepped close to the small soldier and looked him in the eye. "You the one who saw me at Running Creek?"

"I was not at Running Creek, Señor," the small one said on an intake of breath.

"Neither was I," Bonaventure said almost indifferently. But his hands reached out and took hold of the crossed bandoliers and jerked the small one forward. "My name is Aaron Lightbourne Bonaventure, and I am a captain in the Texan Rangers and if you ever set eyes on me again, anywhere, I want you to know me. Look at me."

The small one looked up and then dropped his eyes to Bonaventure's belt buckle. "I will know you, Captain," he said.

"You'd better," Bonaventure said, "because I'll remember you."

Cayetana had come to stand at his side. Morisco was now talking full speed to Esteban, explaining and apologizing, inquiring where the horses had come from, making first a derogatory and then a complimentary remark about the Gómez brothers, the *mesteñeros*. Cayetana walked around him and stood looking at the horses they had ridden in, Bonaventure's sad thin sorrel, the soldiers' worn mounts, Morisco's gray, distinguished by a fancy striped blanket showing beneath the saddle, and *tapaderos* mounted in silver, similar to those Ebano wore. She saw the horse shudder, a huge ripple moving from withers to flank and walked to his off side and saw the great open sore on the upper edge of his belly.

Morisco came to mount, joyous, sweating, glib, voluble, and it was not until he was in the saddle that Cayetana spoke.

"Your horse has a bad wound, Captain. There are worms in it." Her voice was icy. "Why do you not treat him or put him out of his misery."

Morisco looked down at her, smiling. "Ah, I have been meaning to care for it, Señorita. Many thanks for reminding me. Many thanks, my friends, my dear friends one and all. And have no fear. With my post at hand, you are safe as in a cathedral."

They were gone. Turning, Bonaventure came close to running into Natividad. She was holding out to him, silently, a plate of beans and tortillas.

"*Bestia*," she said.

"Thanks, little lady, I can sure use this," he said. "But what are you calling me a beast for?"

"Not you," she said impatiently. "That other. *El Capitán*."

"*El Capitán Bestia*," Bonaventure said. "I expect that's a good way to think of him. God knows, though, I don't plan to think about him any more than I can help." He dropped down and began to wolf the beans. When he had finished he turned to Esteban.

"I was as glad to see you as I can ever remember being. Do I know you, man?"

"Esteban Ibarra," Esteban said. "I was with the *patrón* when you met in San Antonio. I too remembered you, in spite of the fact that you hide in the brasada."

"Hide in the brasada?" Bonaventure said.

"You grow it upon you, the brush," Esteban said.

"I must look like all hell. Excuse me, Miss Dominguez. Is there any more coffee?"

Esteban poured him another cup. Without thought, Bonaventure rolled himself a cigarette, leaned forward and held out makings to Cayetana. "Can I offer you a smoke?"

He knew his mistake too late. Cayetana was looking at him strangely; he thought he detected a hair of amusement in her eyes. She said composedly, "Thank you, I have my own."

He covered himself quickly. "You know, I don't even know what day it is. I didn't want to ask."

"No," she said. "They might have held it over you. It is early in April, the sixth, I think."

"Your drive must be on the way now," he said. "Is Ben Richards still working for you?"

"Yes," Cayetana said. "You know Ben?"

He noted the softening of her face, the pleased, anticipatory look of it. "We've met once or twice. I expect everybody in the Nueces country's heard of him. Where's he taking your cows?"

"Into Montana," she said. "Fort Benton. A million and a half pounds for the Indian reservation there. And the M Bar L herd into Dodge City."

"How's that?" he said. "Must be quite a lot of cows getting acquainted with one another."

"Did you know Jonah McLean?"

"Your neighbor. I know of him."

"He died five or six weeks ago. He was gored by a steer. The *ladino* they call Rojo."

Bonaventure looked up from sinking the butt of his cigarette. The picture was so clear in his mind he didn't have to close his eyes. Rojo. And this same cool child-woman sitting in his path without a nerve in her body and him lying in that wash and wondering if he could stop the red steer if he had to. He said, "I know Rojo, I've seen him. McLean was after him for years, wasn't he? Have they hunted him down yet?"

"He is on his way to Dodge City with the McLean herd. They brought him in two days before the drive."

"That seems . . . you might say unnecessary," Bonaventure said.

"Not to Frank McLean. He has his revenge now."

"Something besides that, maybe?" Bonaventure said. "Doing what his father never managed to do?"

She had caught her lower lip between her teeth. "Pride, then? Yes. That too."

"I'm sorry, about McLean. About all of it."

"About Rojo?" she said.

His eyes narrowed, watching her. Her face was without expression and without softness. "No, not about Rojo," he said. "If it was only he was a wild one, I might, but he's a killer, and killers have to pay the price."

"Ranger training speaks," she said. Now she did begin to roll a cigarette. "But killing is his way of life."

"That doesn't make it right. He's an animal."

"Man is an animal. Is his way of life, right, as you put it?"

"Man is some jump away from a killer steer," he said, baffled.

"Man is crueler, Captain Bonaventure. What Rojo does by instinct, for self-preservation, man does by careful thought and planning. Rojo kills quickly, and it is over. Man kills slowly, by degrees. And inflicts all the torture and pain he can devise while he does it."

"You have a point," he said, after a moment. "But that's for self-preservation too."

"Of course. What else is there? What does it matter if it is right or wrong? What I am saying is that the methods differ but the end is always the same." Her smile was small and sudden. "Forgive me, Captain. It can't be pleasant for you to walk out of that pit over there and into an argument with anyone as willful as I. I meant only to say that it is a big herd which went out of Tres Reyes this year . . . Richards thinks too big."

"Honest reluctance on Richards' part?" Bonaventure said. "They say he's a singular man."

"Why singular?"

"You people are in the business and I expect you know what I mean. What he knows about cows. Something a man like Richards is . . ."

"Born with," Cayetana said.

"As I am born knowing horses," Esteban said. "Born on a horse, is how this knowledge comes to me."

"Horses," Bonaventure said. "The same with a trail herd. Some men trail with herds all their lives and never make top hand. And a few, a very few, go up the trail twice and have it all right in the palm of their hand."

"In the heart," Cayetana said.

"Maybe you're right, in the heart. How's your father these days, Miss Dominguez?"

"Well, as always."

He thought her voice was toneless, without feeling, maybe even without interest. "And the Señora?"

"She too is as always . . . some days well, other days unable to leave her room."

"Will you present my compliments when you get home?"

"Thank you, I will." She leaned forward, clasping her hands on her knees. "You are welcome to ride with us, Captain. If you return to your headquarters, perhaps you will be our guest at Tres Reyes."

After a moment Bonaventure said, "I appreciate the invitation. But as it stands, time's short with me now. I'd like to get out of here in another hour or so, with your permission."

"You mean to ride ahead, tonight?" She looked up quickly, telling Esteban with her eyes, and Esteban rose and walked out of hearing. "Captain, I do not mean to pry into your business. But surely it can wait until daylight."

"I think not," he said then, not so much wondering how much he should tell her as the way he should tell her. And there was a lot he could tell her, and maybe she would really fight him when it was over and done, disbelieving and angry. He said in a low voice, "Miss Dominguez, I owe you a debt I'm never going to be

128

able to pay. It still seems like it couldn't have happened as it did . . . your being here and those fool soldiers talking, and me walking out of there free again. I still feel shaky on my legs. Shaky inside too. But I'm where I am for a reason, as you must have guessed, and a month or so in Morisco's jail doesn't change it."

She said, "You are not going back, then. You are going on into Mexico."

"That's the how of it," he said and got himself set for the questions. But they did not come. She sat looking at him for a long time and then she said, "I do not think you are in any condition to travel. Certainly you can't ride that horse without him collapsing under you within a mile. Let us take him back, and you take Juan Sanchez' *grulla* . . . he has the long wind, as Juan says."

"I'd be grateful," he said. He hated to ask, but he did. "Have you got extra supplies? Beans?"

"Take what you will need."

"Suppose our friends from the post drop in for some more palaver?"

"I will cover for you."

He got up and walked to his bedroll, thrown on the blanket with his possessions and got out his war bag and a razor. Even with hot water shaving was difficult and painful, and he left the ragged mustache. She sat and watched him until he had finished and thought, but he is young, perhaps not thirty yet, and remembered Richards saying once that all Ranger captains were chosen young.

There were not many captains in a service which was not army and not militia, irregulars unique among armed law forces. The service had come into being years before Texas joined the Union, and up until two years ago it had looked as if the Rangers might be history, done and past. They had been disbanded in 1870 to make way for a State Police Force, and for the next three years Texas had lived with an organization so brutal, murderous, and oppressive that an outraged citizenry had demanded an end to it. The Rangers had been back in business for two years with telling effect: one special force operated on the Rio Grande and one, the Frontier Battalion, had crossed the Llano Estacado to control the Comanches on the western border.

And the young captains were men of resourcefulness, self-discipline, integrity, and courage. If Bonaventure was among the select she knew that it was because he had proved himself in some manner similar to that in which she now offered to assist him.

When she saw he had finished, she rose and went to find Esteban. He was stretched out beside the sleeping Juan Porrumba, lying awake on one elbow. He got up when he saw her.

"Esteban, the captain wishes to go on before us. You saw his horse. Unsaddle him and put him out with Ebano. He will take Juan's *grulla*."

"At this moment?" Esteban said.

"Time is important to him. See that he has what supplies he needs."

She stood looking out into the starry darkness, seeing the looming mounted shape of Sanchez huddled under his serape, near the rope corral, the black bulk of Ebano staked nearby. There was still a sweetness in the night, the sweet clarity of desert, blooming for so short a time, which is like no other sweetness in the world, and of a substance which brushes tangibly against the skin and is drawn light and pure into the lungs. When the gray-blue horse was brought she went to watch Bonaventure saddle and arrange his equipment: the bedroll containing his tarp, saddlebags, canteen, Winchester in the saddle boot, .44 strapped high, so that the butt was near his waist. They did not speak, but she knew he watched her, raising his eyes to her now and again and smiling in the slow pleasant way he had.

What an odd lovely little thing she was, he thought: quite odd, but not mysterious, detached but not hostile, reserved but not indifferent. That she was at war not only with herself but with the whole world, or at least with a few of that same world's accepted concepts, was written plain, or she would not be championing Rojo. And that little battle within, that would be the natural bent for independence, for freedom of the spirit, pitted against the inflexible strictures of caste. Maybe it was just that she was Mexican, and he had been brought up in a household where French was the everyday language and worship of flowers more important than worship of God and the Englishman who had been his father not important at all because he had not been married to the dazzling Creole girl who bore his child. That too was a way of life in the

New Orleans which had reared him, as different a way of life, and now as far removed, as that of Tres Reyes would be to him, and yet it had played its share in shaping him as the life at Tres Reyes had shaped her. Did the way of life shape, or did it warp?

He wondered if he could come to love this girl. Without ever trying.

"You didn't play tonight," he said finally. His legs were weak and he tried not to let her see that he was leaning against the horse.

"Play?" she said.

"The guitar. I would have liked a little music to settle me down." He made a terrific effort when he mounted, because the minute he put his foot in the stirrup his leg began to shake as if the bones were going to melt. When he was in the saddle he looked down at her. "Thanks again, Miss Dominguez. When I come back up, I'll be stopping to see your father, I expect."

She had come to stand close to the horse, close to the tip of his worn boot. "Captain, how did you know I smoke? How do you know I play the guitar?"

"Just carelessness, I guess," he said.

"Carelessness?"

"My offering you a smoke, I mean. Without thinking. The guitar was lying there alongside you, so I expected it was yours."

He could see she was not satisfied. Her eyes were withdrawn; they looked to him exactly as they had looked the first time he had met her. And as she had done that first time, she gave him her hand. "Good luck to you, Captain."

"You too," he said. When he leaned to take her hand the saddle leather creaked, a worn, comfortable sound, so homely and taken for granted that he did not hear it. "Have a safe trip home."

"There is the finest music of all," she said, smiling.

"Music?" He felt that the tips of her fingers were callused.

"The saddle sings to you."

"So it does." He no more wanted to leave than he wanted to die. "I didn't notice."

Esteban came up. "So now you are prepared. *Buena suerte, Capitán*."

131

"Same to you, Esteban."

"And do not rob any banks or kill anyone this time," Esteban said.

"I'll do my best." He turned the horse and thought, My God, this horse will have the three crowns of Tres Reyes somewhere on its hide and the next thing I'll get picked up for is horse stealing. But it didn't matter. Because when he had done what he had come to do, both he and horse would be going back to Tres Reyes and for the first time he hated to see the day come.

On the same night of April sixth the big herd was on bed ground west of San Antonio.

For Ben Richards, riding the buttermilk horse beside the chuck wagon, the trip into town for a final provision check and supply had been an unwelcome distraction, a diversion he might have looked forward to in a month's time, but which was now a break in the routine he was working desperately to establish.

It would not be long, another few days, before that routine would evolve naturally, but laying the groundwork was his first responsibility. Already the herd was setting up its own travel order: the leaders were taking the fore and would keep it, the drags were tailing the line and would continue to do so, every cow had picked its traveling partner, the rotation of guard watches, swing, point, and drag riders, established. He had been half-tempted to send Uremáy on with the herd and catch up again that night, but something instinctive told him to hold where he was. Too, he had a hunch there might be word from Todd Allenby, and he didn't want to chance missing it.

It didn't matter one way or the other, though . . . if you started a herd out a bare ten miles from Antone, you still stopped in when you got there, as if it was going to be the last chance you'd ever have to say howdy to somebody didn't belong to your own trail crew.

The letter from Allenby was short and to the point: *Hello, old rod*, he wrote. *They are looking to raise the flag at Fort Benton for you early September. I got a buyer for your remuda if you want to unload it when you reach the Judith Basin. In the meantime, don't stint. If you need more horses you got a solid gold credit letter, and you can always draft on me. Live like you are accustomed to and don't hold back on your out of pocket expenses. I got so damn much money this year I am climbing up walls thinking of ways to get rid of it. All U.S. Govt. too, so I figure its good. If it aint, I plan to quit cows. I will look for you in Dodge. Allenby.*

So Antone was behind him, and nothing between him and Dodge but the desolate miles and a herd that tallied out at forty-five hundred plus a hundred and fifty extras to take care of losses, and one large snuffy foot-dragging red steer named Rojo.

He looked over at Bill Sykes, driving the chuck wagon. Sykes, like a lot of cookies, talked to himself, and not just when he was alone either. He didn't care who was around. He had been acquired by accident on the last day of March, one day before the drive started. He had pulled up in the courtyard the middle of the morning and asked if they needed a cook. They didn't need one, any Mexican could cook, but the vaqueros were taken with the idea of hot Yankee bread and bacon. Sykes looked glum and crusty, which meant he was probably all right with a frying pan. He had driven two years for Lon Davis, and this year Davis hadn't bothered to let him know he was folding up like a swivel dude opera hat. Richards asked him how he was with beans. Sykes told him he could cook beans that would fly a tired point rider across the Colorado, horse and all, without once touching water. Richards hired him.

But it was the men of Tres Reyes got tested, not Sykes. The first day out was hell, as it always was, with a scant fifteen miles put behind them and a mile and a half of cows stretched out trying to find their places. When they went into camps that night Sykes came out with a sheet of biscuits that looked like nothing Richards had ever seen, except in his own mother's kitchen. They had a shape for one thing, and they were a browny-gold color for another. Sykes waited, pot-bellied in his floury white apron.

"These biscuits has quite a nice density," Shiloh said.

"You ain't got to eat 'em," Sykes said.

"Yes I has. I either got to eat 'em or starve," Shiloh said.

"I don't give a hang which," Sykes said.

133

Shiloh's eyes went off into the distance. They were innocent, vacuous.

"Which is it goin' to be?" Sykes said.

"Leave him be, he's trying to make up his mind," Corrigan said.

"I don't aim to influence him one way or the other," Sykes said.

After a moment Shiloh raised his hand and spat something into his palm. He held it up to the light and looked at it, squint-eyed. It was a tooth. Richards knew it was a pivot tooth, but he watched anyway.

"I expect your influence with me is just about what the little boy shot at. That is, nothin', Cookie. This here is my tooth. You have busted my goddang tooth with your goddang biscuit."

"You are off the reservation," Sykes said.

"I might be that, thanks all the same," Shiloh said. "Also I will be toothless before I git halfway mark to the Cimarron. If you would care to join me, it would be my pleasure to see you are holdin' a tooth or two, all of 'em, if you want."

Sykes turned away. "Starve then, you vinegar-livered brush buster. You can rustle your own chuck from here on in. I wouldn't fry you a piece of saddle leather you got down on your knees and begged me."

Shiloh was still contemplating the tooth. He never raised his voice or his eyes. "Sykes, I lay you I can crack a rock with this here biscuit."

He seemed to be under Sykes' skin now. "I lay you I could crack the same rock with your four-sided head if it 'tweren't rotten as a gourd."

Shiloh considered this also. "You want to bet like that, I will lay you I can crack *your* head with this here biscuit. At twenty feet."

"You'll come beggin'," Sykes said. "You will beg me for a biscuit before you're finished."

Richards stood up. "Hold fire, game's over. Shiloh, eat that biscuit."

"I got to?" Shiloh said. He sighed and put the tooth back in

134

and ate the biscuit. He chewed hard and swallowed convulsively and nobody took their eyes off him.

Sykes was grinning. When he turned to Richards he said, "Obliged to you, Captain Ben."

"For what?" Richards said.

"For straddlin' my side of the fence," Sykes said.

"I never straddle fences," Richards said. "The only thing you get out of fence straddling is a sore crotch. Look, Sykes, if we could of fired these biscuits off in Hood's Battalion, we could of killed every Union man in Texas."

Sykes stood there a minute, before the sour grin broke over his face. "I had my fun. Better'n most times, too." He went to the Dutch oven and took out another sheet of biscuits. "I always do this first night out, new outfit and all. It does me proud to see a good strong look of disappointment on a man's face when he bites into one a them biscuits." The fresh sheet went around. "These here I pump the air into," Sykes said.

Whatever he had pumped into them, they tasted like they looked, which was plenty good enough for Richards.

"It don't do for a hand to git on his uppers with me," Sykes said. "I never like to see a hand spoiled. I always pass around a hot worrisome batch so when the hot trouble-free batch comes up they can tell the difference."

Shiloh rose and went to shake Sykes' hand. "I'm your friend," he said. "For life. Anytime you are in danger or anything, call on me."

Richards knew a man could make biscuits like Sykes could would never be in danger. He swallowed the last of his coffee and stood up. When he did, Uremáy also rose and went to him.

"A good sign, this man Sykes. No trouble tonight, Ben."

"He had it on me too, I got to admit," Richards said. "You weren't fooled, were you?"

"Of a certainty," Uremáy said.

Richards had the feeling he wasn't anything of the kind but he didn't say so. When he grabbed up Portero, Uremáy too mounted and went out with him. Where the night guard was riding, six men passing one another clockwise and counterclockwise around the herd, there was a low sound of singing, not the music to which

135

Richards was accustomed, but the soft-pitched voices of vaqueros singing old love songs and maybe dreaming of anything but cows.

"I don't know many Mexican songs," Richards said.

"Ben," Uremáy said. He hesitated. "You drive yourself too hard."

"You tell me a way not to and I'll listen. For a while anyway I got to do it myself."

"You cannot do it all," Uremáy said.

"I don't reckon I can. Right now I got to try. Listen, old *segundo*, see Frankie gets relieved for chuck and tell him he's doin' fine with the remuda, will you?"

"It is not your watch," Uremáy said patiently.

"Every watch is my watch. Quit arguin' or I'll bust you to night-hawk and put Frankie in that saddle."

Uremáy did not smile. "Try to take sleep tonight, Ben."

"I got all winter to sleep," Richards said.

EIGHT

On the thirteenth of April Richards came to grips with the first major battle of the drive: water.

Spring was advancing rapidly. Grass, rolling with flowers, was coming on well, and there was plenty of it. But the drought of the preceding summer pointed to a water shortage ahead. Creeks which in season should be running full were dry. Waterholes were depressions in the earth, bottoms black with muck or caked and cracked. A good rain could send flash floods roaring down the arroyos and that could be a problem also, but it would mean water.

Before dawn on the fourteenth he got ready for a long scout.

He pulled out shortly after the herd had been thrown off bedground, in the first dawn. Sykes and the chuck wagon, Hedges and the calf wagon, Frankie and the remuda were preparing to move ahead. The only water he was certain of was at Indian Lakes, and he wanted to see what lay beyond. He was out of camps while the drag riders were still chousing up the tail end of the herd, past the swing men flanking it, past the point riders guiding the lead. He scouted fifty miles that day with the buttermilk and a roan spare, carrying nothing but water and jerky.

The trail here was seventy-five yards wide at some points, paralleled and joined by small local trails. Millions of hoofs traveling northward had etched it legible as a stage road, and nothing grew in the packed broad path. Richards took it.

When he came back to camps it was near midnight, close to the time the whole herd would rise as one mass from the bedground, turn to change its position, and lie down again. There were six men riding tonight and Uremáy had thrown another man on the remuda with Frankie. The herd looked quiet. He tied both horses to the wheel of the chuck wagon, being allowed this liberty by Sykes, walked over the off-watch sleeping two by two, and saw Sykes was awake, looking up at him. Sykes never seemed to need much sleep, or if he did he too had learned to do without it. The coffeepot was always on; if it hadn't been, Sykes wouldn't have lasted two days. Tomorrow's beans were cooking, but there were enough of today's left for Richards, and Sykes rolled out silently and began to heat up biscuits and what the poppers called fried chicken which was floured fried bacon, and opened a tin of apricots. While Richards ate, both Uremáy and Shiloh got up and came to sit near him, but neither spoke until he had finished.

Richards wiped his mouth on the back of his hand. His eyes were deep-sunk and his face beginning to go gaunt with fatigue. Three days' growth of beard stubbled his jaw. A fine gray dust covered him from boots to hat. When he spoke, it was to Shiloh. "I'm almost sorry Frankie was so damned eager to show me what a nighthawk he was. It was a mistake."

"Too late," Shiloh said. "I mean, if you are thinkin' that me and Frankie ought to swap jobs, I tell you now I ain't took with the idea."

Richards shook his head. "This is Frankie's herd too, and he ought to know how it looks."

"How does it look, Ben?" Uremáy said.

"Worse than I figured," Richards said. They spoke quietly, not to disturb the sleeping vaqueros. Sykes stood leaning against the lowered tail of the wagon, listening. "The lakes are full, we've got no problem there. Beyond that there's a stretch I don't want to think about. Sixty miles of it, maybe a little more. And I cut sign of something at the lakes today." He motioned to Sykes. "Give me a splinter, Bill."

Sykes leaned over and drew a small stick out of the bundle of wood in the hide cradle under the wagon, where the cook fuel was carried. They moved closer while Richards drew in the dirt. "Here's the lakes, you know how they lie, about a mile apart. The other side, I picked up sign of three herds."

"Three before us," Uremáy said.

"Well, I didn't aim to be first up. Never figure that. If there's twelve herds ahead of you, maybe grass'll be short when you come through. If there's five or six keepin' to the trail you know there's grass and water where you'll need 'em." He pushed his hat up and a thin shower of dust sifted slowly down on the back of his hide jacket. "One herd went straight through. The other two turned west once they passed the lakes."

"What you reckon it means?" Shiloh said.

"It could mean two things. Either the herds turned west were local stock bein' ranged out to new graze, or they got word there wasn't any water ahead. Maybe somebody from the herd went straight through got word to 'em. I don't like it, either way."

"What is it we will do, then?" Uremáy said.

"It would take me two days in the saddle to find out if the herds turned west were local stock. In two days we could be half-way through the dry stretch." He looked at Uremáy. "The weather," he said softly. "The goddam Texas weather. Last spring it rained every other day and the Indians raised hell with the small herds and we had a blizzard in April. Then we get a decent spring to trail in, and the summer before's got to be twice as dry as it ever is and water's scarcer than teeth in a *paisano*." He handed the stick up to Sykes and Sykes carefully replaced it in the cradle. "I been through that stretch before, and I made it. I reckon I can make it now."

"That is four days without water, Ben," Uremáy said.

"You got a better idea, Tiburcio?"

Uremáy shook his head. "When one cannot go back, one can only go forward."

"We could go west like them other herds," Shiloh said.

139

"We could, if we knew how come they went west. I don't aim to run square into two or three thousand of somebody else's cows just put out to pasture and spend a week cuttin' our own cows out of 'em again. We're goin' on." He turned. "Who's on relief?"

Uremáy rose and went to wake the one-to-three-thirty watch. Richards looked at Shiloh. "You want to tell Frankie how it stands? He can do what he wants?"

"With four men?" Shiloh said.

"He can do what he wants," Richards repeated.

He went and got his bedroll out of the chuck wagon. "Go back to bed, Bill. They can find the coffee, I expect."

He pulled off his boots and jacket and was barely on his back when he saw Frankie come in on the blocky little cowhorse he favored. Frankie came over and hunkered down by him.

"Make it fast, Frankie," he said. "I expect to be dead in two minutes."

"I just wanted to tell you wherever Tres Reyes cows can go M Bar L cows can go," Frankie said. "I'm goin' on with you."

For all he knew Frankie might have hunkered there what was left of the dark. The weariness of the days, the nights, hit him in the back like the blow of a sledge hammer, and he didn't know another thing until the first gray light was breaking up the sky and he rolled out again.

The advance of the herd reached Indian Lakes the following morning, and by ten o'clock the whole herd had been watered. The seven lakes lay in natural rock-bottomed reservoirs. Richards had seen them down a foot or two, but he had never known them to go dry. He let the herd take its time and he didn't push to get it moving again, but it was in his mind that he was still going to get fifteen miles out of it today. Sykes filled two extra ten-gallon water kegs and every canteen in camps. They went on, finding good grazing and making the fifteen miles well watered and fed.

But he threw them off bedground at four in the morning the following day. In the darkness they grazed forward, taking the moisture from the wet grass before the sun could dry it out. Richards held the remuda back with the herd, and for Frankie, who slept during the day in the calf wagon or under the chuck wagon, there would be no sleep unless somebody gave him a few hours' relief.

There was a period, before daybreak, when there was a light moist-smelling wind moving in over them. The vaqueros called to one another, and to Richards, but the cows didn't lift their heads to it. For a time Richards thought it might mean rain, but when he saw the herd ignore it he knew it was a weather freak with nothing in it but empty promise.

The sun came up all of a sudden, rapidly, and yet when it had risen and moved up the sky, it seemed to hang there, poised and still, yellow as fire and glaring hot. The nooning burst upon them with the intensity of summer, windless, with the spring balm gone out of it and the pulsing heat of a season far advanced in its place. The vaqueros stripped to their cottons. Every man riding had cloth over his nose and mouth, soaked with the precious stuff of the canteens. Another freak: first the hint of rain and now a sun burning down like it was July instead of April.

The drag men always had their faces covered, subject as they were to the worst work of the drive. At the tail end, with the full dust of the moving herd on them, they spent the day whipping up the dragging cows. Every cow in the herd had its position to move in, and the drags always remained drags, no matter how hard you tried to chouse them up into the main body of the herd. Sometimes a few sorefoots would lag back with the drags, but as soon as their feet healed they would head for their old position and nobody could pry them out of it. But the drags stayed where they were, dragging. Richards wouldn't let any hand ride drag more than a day at a time. Their eyes were ruined by nightfall, along with their dispositions. The swing men were better off, each with several hundred yards to guard along the main body of the herd, keeping their eyes open for drifters. The point men had it best of all, setting the advance and keeping the lead cows pointed forward. Today the remuda was trailing right along with the herd and taking to it as if they did it this way every day.

Two cows dropped calves in the middle of the burning morning and Richards cursed and turned them over to Hedges and the calf wagon. He hated trailing she stuff. If there were ranches around you could give the calves away. The cow might carry on some, but her milk would dry up and she wasn't any problem. But when you were trailing empty country you didn't have any choice but to shoot the calf, and the crews hated that too. The only alternative was a calf wagon and that was trouble. The McLeans took the trouble; Tres Reyes liked to trail steers and avoid it.

Shortly after noon Richards slowed the herd to a standstill for an hour's rest, but it seemed bewildered by the change in the routine it had now come to accept, and attempted to mill. The swing riders straightened it out and they went on. Frankie had relief horses without being told and when Richards took his fresh mount the boy said, "You're goin' to be doin' this again before sundown, Ben," and Richards only nodded grimly and went back to the left flank, putting himself between remuda and herd.

The heat grew more intense in the afternoon. Richards tried for the second time to rest the herd, and for the second time it refused to rest. Uremáy went back with the drags, stripped to cottons, nothing but his eyes showing between the shield of his hatbrim and the gray mask of cloth over his face. Richards rode with the point men. They were fighting to keep the lead steers to a walk. It was a hard fight and they won it at sundown, after changing horses four times.

But by sundown the herd was lowing and restless, thirst written in wide eyes, moving tails, tossing heads.

The men ate standing, ready to jump to saddle. Sykes filled canteens from the keg and clattered pans and was ill tempered. He had miles to make to a point called The Divide, and he moved out while it was still daylight. Richards saddled Portero and the men picked up their night horses, chosen for eyes that saw in darkness as if it were daylight, sure-footed, built to go without sleep. Again he held the remuda back.

The sun was barely gone out of the sky when the moon rose full, throwing light white as midmorning and shadows twice their length. Richards kept the herd grazing, into the moonlight toward The Divide. An hour out, they could see Sykes' fire, a triangular point sprung from the black horizon of land, pale against the clear arching shell of sky. He had a good meal for them and he dipped into the canned fruit, knowing how good the sweet liquid in the cans would taste.

The grass was still holding and the ground sloped a little, making a first-class bedground. But when the time came, only half the herd bedded. The other half stood clustered in ragged bunches, still restless and lowing.

It was a bad time, a dangerous time. Richards was everywhere, doubling the watches, rousing the relief after a bare hour's sleep. The herd was bedded in triple the amount of space it usually took, but there were those small dangerous knots of steers, moving, protesting, thirsty, refusing to bed. The vaqueros sang and joked and called, trying to set the atmosphere right again, working every minute to make the herd see that nothing was changed, nothing different, and that they would come to water as they always came to water.

There was no sleep that night for Richards, Uremáy, or Sykes. Sykes had coffee and beans for whoever wanted them whenever they wanted them. Hedges had taken the remuda. Frankie was lying close to dead in the chuck wagon, not turning a hair even when the mules hollered into the night. Sykes almost drove off with him an hour before daybreak, when the herd moved out again.

The sun rose as hot and single-minded as it had the day before. There had not been enough water to completely fill the canteens, and they trailed out on a bare mesa as dry and sparse-grown as desert. Wherever they looked, there were the dead-white bleaching bones of herds which had not made it to water. The unnatural heat expanded and sucked back upon itself and expanded again, like a gas building to the point of bursting.

By noon there was a vast ominous thing in the still dry air. The vaqueros sweated silently on sweating horses, back and forth, up and down the line, but always forward. The herd was strung out for nearly three miles, sullen, lowing, tongues hanging. It would not graze or lie down or take rest, and Richards held it to a gait as slow and easy as possible to spare it the exertion of a routine pace.

In that nooning Rojo took the lead of the herd.

For days he had hung back with the drags, moving when he was pushed, but never changing his position. He had accepted his own kind indifferently, and he had accepted man as long as man took

143

him to graze and water. A man on foot would be another matter, but men on foot did not go near longhorns. Always they were mounted, always they loomed higher and larger than the longhorn, and this too Rojo accepted. But it was nothing more than acceptance, nothing bigger than weary tolerance. In the middle of this second waterless day he managed to move three miles up the strung out column, until he was walking behind and slightly to the left of the first steer in the herd. Corrigan, riding point, spotted him and yelled back down the line to the swing rider nearest him and the word went to the drag riders and up the other flank and Richards rode up to see if it was true.

He passed the big steer and saw that its tongue was not out or its eyes sinking yet. The lead steers had moved out, away from the spread of the great horns. If there was no suffering to be seen in Rojo, neither was there patience or the overt acceptance he had shown. It was something more: an endurance, a purpose.

In the early afternoon Sykes rode to meet them with the bad news. The creek they had figured on, or in Richards' case not figured on, was a trickle in the sand. Richards, face gone almost skeletal, sat in the blinding abnormal heat and told himself he had known this and tried to shake off the surging disappointment which bordered on despair.

"Is there enough for the horses?" he said.

Sykes was down to trousers and a long underwear shirt, gray and greasy with sweat. He looked as if he might grow skinny, his flesh falling to flab, right under Richards' eyes. "Maybe for the horses," he said. "Whoever's come through has tried to dig some wells in the creek bed. It might work."

"It's got to work," Richards said.

He rode back to the herd and called Uremáy and Shiloh and Frankie in and told them.

"We're goin' to lose the horses," Frankie said.

Richards looked at him and saw how the boy's face had grown thin and tired, but that the eyes were steady in it.

"We ain't goin' to lose the horses. We got to hold the herd here. That's the first thing. And we got to dig wells in the creek. Somebody's done it before us, so there must be water lyin' in that bed."

"Ben, how far from this creek, do you think, to water?" Uremáy said.

And Richards said, saying it quickly, so that it would be over and done, "Another twenty miles, maybe a little over."

Frankie said, "Hawk for me, Shiloh."

"I don't know who I'm ridin' for any more," Shiloh said.

"You're ridin' for me," Frankie said, "and I been gittin' all kinds of sleep in the chuck wagon. If I'm supposed to be takin' care of this remuda I at least got the right to dig a well or so for it."

Give him that, Richards thought. Give him that, he's as much beat out as the rest of us. "Go dig, Frankie," he said.

Uremáy's sweat-soaked dust-caked neckerchief was hanging around his throat. "How are we to hold the herd, Ben? They will not take rest."

"We got to do it," Richards said. "Look, Tiburcio, I'm goin' to stay with the herd. I want you to scout this creek, five miles west. Sykes will take it five miles east. Maybe, just maybe, we'll hit water, but we can't take it any farther. There's no time. Put six men on the wells and let Frankie boss it. Like he says, they're his horses now."

Somehow they held the herd. The lowing was constant, a tortured sound which hurt the ears, and cut at the heart. The cows fought to turn, looking back across the miles to water. Twice Richards rode to the dry creek to look over the digging. They filled the barrels first. But it all depended on the horses now, and if they could be watered to the eyeballs, Richards still thought he could get the herd through. He sat mounted on the wall of the bank watching Frankie. Naked to the waist, blind with sweat, hair in his eyes, shoveling like a madman, the boy did not even drink himself when the water rose. The night horses were taken down first, as fast as the water came in. Then, a few at a time, the whole remuda was led to the wells.

By nightfall men and horses had been provided for, but there was no water for the herd. Both Uremáy and Sykes had come back from a useless search. The creek was dry for miles.

Nobody got to sleep. The herd refused to lie down. Again the dense ominous thing came in the air, like storm clouds towering.

At midnight the herd began to mill. One by one they took it up, until they were moving in sulky obstinate circles, slowly at first, then quickening the pace, moving so close that horn clacked on horn, something they usually avoided.

Richards fell asleep in the saddle. It was only a moment, a dark, fuzzy moment when his head fell forward and the snap of it jarred him awake and he thought that he had slept for a long time until the hollowness in his body reminded him where he was, that he had not eaten, that he had not slept. There was a stiffening in his arms, as if his muscles had turned to wood. He saw the milling block of the herd under a moon only slightly sliced away from full and rode into the first rider he saw and said, "Break it up, break it now," and put Portero into a gallop.

They spent the remainder of the night pushing through the frantic herd at all the speed they could make, breaking up the mills, racing into them and finding themselves slowed by the force of the massed steers and grinding through on the other side and starting all over again.

By morning they had drifted over a mile off bedground. The sun came up again as it had risen for two days, searing, relentless. The vaqueros knelt and prayed aloud for rain.

The horses were fresh, but no horse, no man, was equal to the herd when it finally turned, and it was Rojo who turned it.

They had crossed the creek, where the wells had already been drunk dry or spread the last of themselves into the sand again. It was the hottest day they had known, and the herd was wild, feverish. It strung out longer and thinner, moaning, tongues lolling, heads lowered, eyes shriveling. When it checked and milled again there was no breaking it.

Richards was riding point. When Rojo turned, he flailed with his hat at the big steer. Rojo kept moving. He grabbed the rope off his saddle and slapped at the steer's head, but it didn't work. When Rojo swung the whole lead swung. Richards shouted down the line. Around the herd men flapped rope and yelled and cursed and whipped with their hats.

Rojo hit the buttermilk sidewise, not brushing him, but walking directly against him, pinning Richards' leg for a moment. When he looked down he saw the big steer was near-blind.

In that one reading of the unseeing eyes, he knew the herd was going blind, and in its blindness and torture it was headed back to the only water it could remember.

He stopped slapping rope and sat and watched the herd file away. It would travel day and night to get back to Indian Lakes.

They did not try to turn the herd, or to point it. The cows knew where they were going and how to get there. Rojo had turned them and they were following by instinct, heads down and eyes close to sightless, but feeling and smelling the familiar bulk of their own kind around them, and moving with it.

At the creek they dug wells for the second time and for the second time watered the horses. Richards selected six men, including Corrigan and himself, to ride with the herd. All they would have to do was stay on its flanks, pushing the drifters back. The rest of the crew changed mounts and pushed off for the lakes, to be there when the herd came in. Wagons and remuda trailed between herd and crew. Uremáy went on to the lakes without protest. The lack of sleep, the strain of the constant alert had hurt him.

Richards saw Frankie briefly when he changed horses. He knew he shouldn't have said it, but he was bone-tired and defeated and sick about the herd's eyes. "I thought you said M Bar L cows could go wherever Tres Reyes cows could go."

Frankie grinned, but it wasn't easy, it wasn't right. It was the kind of grin meant to stick under the hide, like the needles off a fishhook cactus. "I thought you said you could git 'em through."

"It was your steer turned 'em," Richards said.

Frankie said, "I reckon that's on account of he's got more sense than some I could name."

Richards rode on. There was an urgency about the herd now, but not a cow milled or pushed or ran. They just kept walking doggedly, carried maybe not so much by any individual thought of water as by what the rest of the herd was doing.

By late afternoon the herd was strung out a full six miles. Richards knew they couldn't check the drift now, even if the whole crew had ridden swing. There would be nothing to do but set up camps at the lakes and gather in the drifters later.

The crew at the lakes had had a good night's sleep when the first of the herd staggered in, grouped twenty and thirty to a unit. By its steady, constant travel, including the nights, not stopping to graze or rest, they had cut the time back close to half, coming into the lakes in the middle of the afternoon of the second day since they crossed the dry creekbed.

Rojo was first into the water. Richards watched him enter it, still not hurrying. But for the first time he made a sound. He stood in water nearly to his withers and began a low moaning, yet he did not drink. Behind and around him cows straggled into the lakes. The air was thick with their lowing. But for a long time they did not drink. Sometimes half an hour went by before a muzzle dipped. They stood as deep in the water as they could get, as if they would soak the wetness into flesh, muscle, sinew, bone, through the dry dusty hide. They were moaning and blind, and when they drank it was very lightly, as if they refused the water they could not see.

By nightfall a little over thirty-five hundred head had reached the lakes. Once they had drunk they came out of the water and rested and returned to drink again. Not until they had repeated this three times did they begin at last to graze. Richards had been three days and two nights without sleep, save for what he could catch in the saddle, yet it was a relief that lifted half his weariness when he saw the herd take to graze. It was acting normal again, and when he saw it go to grass he knew its sight was returning.

Sometimes when he had waked in the saddle he thought it was Glass under him, and it was a little while before his fogged mind told him that it was Jonah's little night horse. The horse was better than Jonah had thought, as clear-footed and alert as Glass had been, not just as big and powerful. Maybe Portero's size itself made him more agile; maybe one man could get out of a horse something more than another man. As trail boss he had first choice on the remuda. The buttermilk was the best of the lot, and everybody had their own mount string and nobody got on the prod when the trail boss picked the cream, that was expected. He was glad for Portero now; he wouldn't have swapped for another, and inside he thanked Jonah.

He slept all night, not even turning over, while Uremáy and

the fresh crew held the herd and got set to head out for the drifters. But he was awake at sunup and the first thing he did was strip and take himself a swim and shave. Sykes had put out a good breakfast, and Richards had three cups of strong black coffee. Then he called in Frankie and Shiloh and the vaqueros who weren't watching or hunting strays.

"We're goin' to lay over here a couple of days," he told them. "The grass is good and we all need the rest. There ain't a doubt in my mind now those two herds I cut sign of turned west on account of water. The herd went straight through was the one dug wells in that creek, before we got there. They must of got word back to the lakes."

"You think they made it, Ben?" Shiloh said.

"I don't know. If they did, God was with 'em, and they would've been blind as bats and near dead as you can get. If it was a small herd they might of kept 'em pointed. I hope they got through."

"How do we know what's west?" Frankie said. He too was shaved and clean and he didn't seem to have any chip on his shoulder.

"I know roughly what's west," Richards said. "The country's open and there's creeks. A long time between 'em, but creeks."

"Dry, maybe," Frankie said.

"Dry, maybe. But I got a hunch if they are, those two herds'd be holed up here at the lakes, like we are. Sooner or later we'll pick up the trail again, probly before we hit the Colorado. We won't know till we take a look." He glanced at Frankie, and when he did something came up in him with a rising insistence and again he heard Uremáy's voice. Careful? The kid thought he was a curly wolf, but he had always thought that, and he was doing what he was told to do and doing it right. That proved something. That proved a lot. Like Jonah had said: a hair or two of responsibility. But he cut Frankie in on the deal too.

"You got anything you want to say, Frankie?"

Frankie shook his head. "I'm satisfied we ain't got any choice. I wouldn't try to keep the trail with this bunch now if they told me I was comin' out in Dodge City when I got to the other end. But you better tell your point men to keep an eye on my steer, on account of it looks like he's a natural-born leader."

149

"It sure does," Richards said. "And I'll tell you something else: he's the only steer I ever saw come up out of the drags and want to be first to point his horns. Like you said, he's got sense, and maybe he ain't even done more than tap the source."

It was still very warm, but the oppressive heat had dropped off. By suppertime Uremáy was in with the drifters, and Richards joined him to make the count. They had an accurate tab on four thousand and twenty-one. It left six hundred and twenty-nine to account for.

The count was usually made with a stone, tossed from hand to hand for every ten, but Richards used the rawhide string with a series of knots in it that the Mexicans used. He expected to be under count, and it wasn't until he'd insisted on a second check that he accepted the fact that the herd was sixteen over.

He rode across to Uremáy. "Whose drifters have we picked up, Tiburcio?"

"It is the Double Slash B," Uremáy said.

"Bob Barwell's outfit. All sixteen his brand, or are we under count?"

"Ben, I tell you that every Tres Reyes cow and every M Bar L cow is here with us. The sixteen are not ours. Is it your wish that we cut them out for you?"

"Hell no," Richards said. "It's just I wonder if that was Barwell's outfit tried to make it through without water, or if he turned off west and lost these drifters here at the lakes. We'll take 'em and risk gettin' shot for cow stealin'. If Barwell's ahead of us maybe we'll make contact before the Double Slash B reaches where it's headed."

He looked over a couple of bob-eared cows branded with a big B cut by two long vertical slashes, and rode back to camps. He figured to lay doggo today and eat and sleep and maybe play a little cards. Tomorrow he would put in a full day's scout ahead and get the lay of the country to the west. Even if he didn't hit water, the herd would be sloshing when it moved out. The blindness was gone, the grass was holding, and it could take a two-day drive without any real trouble. And another thing he wanted to see to: even if it was done on a scrap of paper no bigger than a mossyhorn's ear, with a pencil wouldn't do more than scratch, he would post word at Indian Lakes that there was no water ahead, and any trail boss thought he could make sixty miles without his herd wanting to wet its whistle was welcome to it.

NINE

Cayetana sat on the wide sill of the window in the Señora's room, which looked down into the courtyard, back against one frame and feet braced against the other. It had rained in the night. The morning was warm and clear, with sun yellow as honey, so thick it seemed piled in drifts along the blue-white walls. Where shadow lay on the wall there were changing patterns of lapis lazuli like reflection of wet gleaming sky.

Roses were budding, below. The leaves of the lime trees looked hard and polished. She could see the women bent at their washing in the *acequias*, the irrigation ditches, and the laundry spread on the bushes to dry. Horses moved on the edge of her vision, heads down to the sap-green grass. The brasada had leafed and there were waxy blossoms on the prickly pear. The one restive note was the water released on the flange of the fountain, falling back upon itself and striking the blue and yellow and terra-cotta Spanish tiles.

The Señora was propped in bed upon two pillows, surrounded by scattered articles which included a box of papers, a silver rosary, a breakfast tray with empty dishes, a newspaper, and a looking glass. She did not turn her head or look up from the study of a parchment spread out on her lap, upon which she made a notation now and then with a small pencil held in her left hand. But she said, "Caye, I wish you would not sit like that. When you fall out upon the tiles, there will be no putting you back together."

"Yes, Mamacita," Cayetana said. "Only I can't see out if I turn." She swung around and put her feet on the floor, but remained seated on the sill. "What are you reading?"

The Señora raised her eyes. "This? A plat of the McLean ranch."

"We aren't going to acquire it, are we?" the girl said.

"Don't be languid, Caye, it does not become you. If you mean reacquire, no. I was merely surmising . . . now that the ranch belongs to Avis and Frank. If Jonah left a will. The deed. I wonder that Avis wants to stay. She has family, in Arkansas, I believe."

"I think she married Jonah to get away from her family," Cayetana said. Her head was turned away; she still watched what lay below.

The Señora put down the pencil and pushed the map away. She saw the girl's reflection in the wide mirror on the far wall. "Caye, you are going to fall out of the window. Please have the consideration and good grace not to do it before my eyes. And I wish you would not repeat gossip."

Cayetana looked around, surprised. "Oh, was it gossip? I didn't know. It was just something I thought."

The Señora was smiling, not the downdrawn cynical acceptance smile, but with amusement and fondness. "What a silly child you are, Caye. Come and sit by me. I feel so much better today. I believe I will sit in the sun and stay down for dinner."

Cayetana came to sit on the edge of the bed. "Do you, Mamacita? I'm happy. I could drive you a bit this afternoon if you like."

"That would be too much," the Señora said. "I find the barouche uncomfortable. Where did your father say he was going today? He came and kissed me and drank most of my chocolate and muttered something and went away."

"I don't know," the girl said. She was looking down at her

153

hands. The Señora regarded her intently. Cayetana always knew where her father was. Eight times out of ten she was with him. All winter she had gone out with him in every kind of weather, and now that the weather was pleasant, she had taken to staying about the house as if it were a last refuge. The Señora sighed: she and her daughter had never been close. Something was changed with the girl, something which she, from her point of removal, could see more clearly than if she shared a closer relationship. She was too wise to question directly. She had gone over and over it in her mind, asking when, asking where, and with help from the little Guadalupe in the corner and the crucified Christ over her bed, it had been sent to her. The when of the change had been the hour of the girl's return from Seville. The where must have been Seville itself. The Señora returned day in and day out to the soliciting of information from Guadalupe and from *El Señor*. She was very patient and very devout and so did not despair. Sooner or later she would know. She did not pursue the subject of don Ramón's whereabouts.

"And as to the McLean ranch, your father turned full title to that land over to Jonah McLean's older brother, Albert, when you were seven years old. It was because of what Albert did for me, you know."

Cayetana nodded. In her mind's eye she could see all of Tres Reyes, thousands of acres of it laid out east and west and south like an unfolded fan held upside down, and a northwest portion which stuck up in the shape of a finger. But the big northern tract which had once been part of Tres Reyes now belonged to the McLeans, given to a man totally down on his luck, because Ramón Dominguez believed that that man had saved the Señora's life.

"Let me brush your hair, Mamacita," Cayetana said. "Put on something bright if you are going out, the red shawl."

The Señora said dryly, "Does the king come today? Anyway, I don't think you can lift me, Caye." She was so pleased with the girl's request that she had to turn her head away. Cayetana moved her easily, folding back the quilt, lifting and turning her mother's small half-withered body and maneuvering it into the rawhide chair which stood beside the bed. Usually Feliciano did this, when Soledad came to brush the Señora's hair.

Cayetana said, "If I push the chair up to the window you can see them washing."

"I have never found much to entertain me in observing the washing of the laundry, Caye," the Señora said.

Cayetana laughed. "Really, Mamacita, you are feeling better, aren't you?" She pushed the chair to the window and the Señora took the warmth of the sun upon her and closed her eyes and held up her face to it. She felt Cayetana begin to remove the pins from her hair. It was still beautiful hair, only beginning to go gray, heavy and quite coarse. The girl's hair, when she bent into the sun, was so black it contained an essence of dark silky blue; she thought that the only thing she coveted was the Señora's thick red-gold hair, knowing how it would have been in youth, like the sky at sundown. But then, nothing else of the Señora had been bequeathed to her either, and one could not spend one's time wishing for something not to be had. She brushed until the Señora's hair fell crisply over the back of the chair and nearly to the floor.

The warmth upon her, the free falling of her hair, the soothing stroke of the brush relaxed the Señora until she could barely keep up her head to the brushing. In the frame of the window her white face, the skin firm but etched with fine hard lines, the defiant chin tipped high, the blue eyes closed, she might have been an offering, a sacrifice to the sun itself. She said in a low, sleepy voice, "When I was younger than you this hair of mine drove me to a great sin, Caye."

Cayetana had pins in her mouth and so could not smile. Her mother's entire existence was a series of sins and omissions.

"I took it down once, for your father," the Señora said in the same sleepy voice.

Cayetana removed the pins from her mouth and put them on the arm of the chair. "Took it down, Mamacita? But why?"

"Because he asked me to. And we were not yet married." She gave a long sigh, which, with her guard down, came out a sigh of pleasure. "Have I shocked you by telling you this, Caye?"

155

"I'm sorry," Cayetana said, "but you haven't. Not at all, Mamacita."

"No, I suppose not. Young people today . . ." Her voice trailed off. She tipped her head farther back, as if her neck could not support it. "Remember something, Caye. Times change. You cannot know what the change of time is, you are too young. Only when you look back will you see that the time you are living in is not the same as the time you look back upon. But values do not change."

"Values, Mamacita?" She hesitated. "Are you speaking of things like honesty? Like courage?"

"Those. I was thinking primarily of moralities. As with the hair. I do not mind at all that you should go about with your hair flying before any man on Tres Reyes. But I should mind very much if you did it in the presence of a man you loved."

The hands on her head were still, the voice behind her quiet. "Would you, Mamacita?"

"Very much," the Señora said. "So with me, with your father. It was wicked of him, but worse for me, and yet I had done it, and what was I to do when it was done?"

"Fly to confession," Cayetana said, and knew as she said it that she had destroyed the moment, the hour, the rapport, torn it apart because of that inherent childlike tendency to say the wrong thing at the wrong time. Her mother's head snapped away from her as if she had been stung.

"Come here, where I can see you, Cayetana."

She went, standing in the sun before her mother.

"Fly to confession, you say. Yes. That is true. Not one day of my life passes but that I sin. Are you so blameless, so pure, that you stand alone, without need of unburdening your soul? Asking pardon? There has not been a Mass said in this house since Father Berrades left us, but I have not lost touch with God, nor, to my knowledge, has any woman on Tres Reyes. I do not know what God you pray to, or what Virgin intercedes for you, but I know that it is not Guadalupe, that it is some overdressed, overburdened Virgin you brought home with you, and whom I have never heard of or looked to."

"Who spies upon me?" Cayetana said, standing, breathing as if

156

it hurt, the brush still in her hand. "Feliciano, with his fox's face and his bandit's heart? What does it matter what Virgin I pray to? She was a gift to me and she hears me."

Prudence overpowered the Señora's anger. Her mouth was still tight, but her voice was normal again. "A gift, Caye. From whom?"

After a long time the girl said, "I could tell you that it was a gift from Aunt Luisa. But that would not be true. To anyone else I would lie. I would lie to my father, to spare him, but I will not lie to you."

The Señora took a deep breath. "I am not to be spared, then, is that it?"

"I had to choose. You are stronger than my father, much stronger. Whatever was taken from your body has gone into your head. If you wished to, Mamacita, you could make power. Great power. I did not always know that you are the strong one. I thought it was Father who was strong. For the world to see, Father is like a big white light, a pillar of courage. For himself, and for me, this is not so. It is only the strong, the powerful, who can take what must be spared the weak."

The Señora's eyes were closed; her nostrils flared a little. "Tell me, Caye."

"I have nothing to tell you," the girl said.

"You lie to me now," the Señora said.

"No, I do not lie, because I have never at any time agreed to tell you anything."

"There is something your father knows."

"Deludes himself he knows."

The Señora turned her head slowly. Her eyes held the girl's. "There is something Tiburcio Uremáy knows."

Cayetana leaned forward, bracing herself on the arms of her mother's chair. "There is something nobody knows, Mamacita. Nobody but God and I. Yes, there are things which happened, which happened around and about me, and they are known, but what is inside, what the heart knows, no, that belongs where it is, and it cannot be told anyway, because there are no words." She stood erect and turned away and heard her mother's voice, with anguish in it now.

157

"Caye, before God, you know what I went through, you know what my life was . . . before your father. I would never let a child of mine . . ."

"It is too late now, Mamacita," Cayetana said matter-of-factly. "Much too late. Shall I finish with your hair or would you like me to call Soledad?"

"Do as you like," the Señora said.

"I would like to finish it myself," Cayetana said steadily.

When her mother did not answer, she returned and picked up the comb and began to separate the Señora's hair into braiding strands.

"Caye," the Señora said, after a time, carefully. "You might find me partisan."

Cayetana smiled, fingers weaving the long braid. "Am I then an enemy camp?"

"Are you not?" the Señora said.

"Now who is being silly." She ended the thick braid and began to loop it on the crown of the Señora's head. When she had finished she inserted the pins and came around to face her mother again. "What dress? And the red shawl, because you are so pretty in it."

The Señora looked up at her. "I have never been pretty. I have never minded. Although I think I mind that you were born beautiful. No one would have thought it to see you that day. You were so small and ugly, the color of flour paste. If I had that day back, that day when you came to us, how many things I would do differently. How many things." Her eyes held the girl's, searching. "And you, Caye?"

Cayetana shook her head. "Nothing. I would do nothing differently."

"Then you are wholly satisfied with your lot," the Señora said.

"Not at all. But I am learning how to wait. I have a good teacher in you, my *madre*. Now, which dress?"

When she had helped the Señora into her clothing and found the red shawl, she went to the door and called Feliciano. He stood at the far end of the corridor, but that was to allay suspicion. She knew he had been outside the door. The Señora was taken down the stairs, exclaimed over by the house *mozas*, and wheeled into the courtyard when Feliciano brought down her chair. There she sat, half in sun, half in shade, watching the finches and listening to the music of the water.

When Cayetana came out she brought more chocolate, and the Señora noted there were two cups. Cayetana sat and drank with her, but when she was finished she said, "Would you like to see the white mare, Mamacita? She tamed like a cat. Esteban thinks she has been ridden before."

"Isn't she with the *manada?*" the Señora said.

"I could go and get her. Anyway, I should love to ride her in if Esteban says I may."

"It would please me to see her," the Señora said. She watched the girl turn the corner of the house and said to Feliciano, "Leave me, Feliciano, I do not need you now."

She heard him go back into the house. Then she closed her eyes again, thinking. Could it be possible that she, who was so closely in touch with all that transpired on Tres Reyes, not only within the household, but down to the last bean in the field, could have lost touch with her daughter, and worse, with her husband? She was sure of it now. What Cayetana had told her was that Ramón knew something she did not know; more, that he had acted in some way upon this knowledge; and most, that he had not acted with courage. Perhaps the word was not courage, but strength. Her Ramón not strong, and without courage? It was unthinkable. Cayetana was mad. Yet she knew something else now. Cayetana loved her. She could say what she wished about not sparing the strong. Whatever had been kept back from her had been kept back because Cayetana loved her. For a long time she had not been sure of this, and now she knew. It was a great deal to know, to be offered, on such a magnificent morning. She closed her eyes and thanked God for it, but thought immediately, again, of herself.

Had she not been crippled, it would be different. How could one be a mother, a companion, to her child, when she could not ride, could not accompany, could not even move freely. If this crippled body were whole, then she might have retained her youth. She was thirty when Cayetana was born. She was fifty now. Yet she was small, active, alert, and she would have kept her body so.

159

A crime, a crime that she should be as she was, and a crime which she herself had committed. She knew how long she would suffer for that, when her soul left her body, and she was prepared. By the very crime, had she cut off her daughter from her?

It was this awakening which sickened her. From the day the child was born she had sworn to give her every advantage she had not had, vowed that this child must be free and understood and allowed to live its own life. On the face of it, physically, she had accomplished this. But what of the mind? What of the heart?

A girl came and took away the chocolate cups. The fingers of the Señora's good hand worked nervously on the arm of the chair. It was horrifying to have a knowledge come too late.

She herself had made only one major mistake in her life, and it was a blunder beyond measure in the society, the era, in which she moved. She had fallen in love with Ramón Dominguez, and for this there was no justification in the eyes of the widowed father who had come close to killing her with the weight of his love. So primed, unleashed briefly from the hold of a possessive martinet, she had thrown herself without inhibition into a world she scarcely knew and found there was another kind of love and that it had been denied her through the paternal assertion that it did not really exist. In Mexico City, accompanying the widowed father on a business trip, there was suddenly in her life, like an explosion, the dashing young *hacendado* who was not afraid to take firm hold upon her chains and set her free.

Her father had not been entirely concerned with the amassing of funds during this brief and impassioned time. He heard out the report of the hireling who followed his daughter day and night. It did not matter that the man was wealthy in his own right. It did not matter that he was half-Spanish and had been educated in Seville. He was a Mexican, an Indian, and if she persisted, she would never see a cent of the fortune she was to receive. But she knew. She knew. The Archangel Gabriel might come to claim her, and the end would be the same. She allowed herself to be taken home.

She did not weep. She waited. She prayed unceasingly that he might die, and three days following her most earnest petition, still building his fortune, he was dead at his desk of heart failure.

160

A week after the probate of his will she transferred a quarter of a million dollars to Mexico City and fled to Ramón Dominguez and precipitated a social scandal. She never went back.

If the union had not been a total success, it was her fault, she knew. She spent hours on her knees, and after ten years of marriage she bore a child, not the son she had burned uncounted candles for, but a tiny girl as passive and sluggish as the backwaters of the Midwestern waterways she remembered. The hours upon her knees became days, days of begging forgiveness that she had prayed for her father's death. Who had looked for such a prayer to be answered, unequivocally and without penance or self-denial? The Roman Catholic Mary of her childhood was replaced by the blue-robed Guadalupe. She lived, still, in the shadow of Guadalupe, with whom she was at ease, and who was, she was certain, more forgiving. She felt almost conspiratorial with Guadalupe at times. That was how well she knew her.

She had raised the little passive child also in the shadow of Guadalupe; a devout child, a good child. They were indulgent with her, she and Ramón. Why not? Often, their eyes meeting over the child's head, his eyes would say to hers, never, never as it was for you, and her own eyes would answer him, never.

No, it was not enough. The Señora's hand clenched into a fist. What of the girl's future? There were a total of five wealthy Mexicans and an American in San Antonio and a young Frenchman with possibilities in San Francisco. She knew what was to be known about them all. And knew too that the choosing was not to be hers, or Ramón's, as it had not been her father's. A convent, then? For Cayetana? That thought had made her smile many times. Then again, did one enter a convent when one prayed to what appeared to be a heathen virgin? Was there such a thing as a heathen virgin?

She watched Cayetana coming back with the white mare, riding slowly, with Esteban at her side. Yes, the mare was beautiful and was made twice as beautiful with the girl, her daughter, upon her back. She admired the mare and said, "Why do you not keep her for your own, Caye?"

"I should like her," Cayetana said. "But Father didn't offer."

"Well, let us surprise Father, then," the Señora said. She looked up at Esteban and winked one eye.

Esteban grinned. The doña Alicia was a lively one, *muy vivo* indeed, when she wanted to be. "She will be perfect for the Señorita with a little more work," he said. The intrigue against the *patrón* appealed to him and he wished to be part of it. "I will work the mare myself, Señora," he said.

"And we know that when you are finished with a horse no one can go farther," the Señora said.

"That is true, doña," Esteban returned gravely.

Cayetana dismounted and turned the mare over to him. He hoped that he might make contact with the *patrón* this very morning, that he might say innocently, "The doña Alicia has decided the little white mare must go to the Señorita Cayetana." Then he would observe every nuance of the *patrón's* reaction, and it would be discussed down to the finest point among the men, when they gathered in the evening.

Cayetana was sitting cross-legged at her mother's feet. "How do you feel now, Mamacita, not too tired?"

"The sun has made me listless," the Señora said.

"Do you think Ben . . . Tiburcio . . . will send word from Abilene?"

"They have never failed to do so. They can hardly have reached Abilene yet."

Cayetana turned to watch Esteban vault from his own saddle onto the white mare. "He is very good-looking, isn't he, Mamacita?"

"Richards? Surely you do not mean Tiburcio?"

"Of course not, I meant Esteban. He looks so soulful when he passes Rosa Benítez. I think we will have a marriage between them."

"That would be nice," the Señora said. "I wish you would think more consecutive thoughts before you speak them, however." Without knowing it, her hand had clenched again. She could write Enrique, she thought. Ramón's brother. He would know. She would rather die than write Luisa, his wife. Nothing open, of course, no straightforward inquiry. She would say only that Cayetana was perhaps sorry she had cut short her visit, she seemed

162

so apathetic these days. (True, the winter had seemed long.) The state of her own health was greatly improved, so much so that she was able to accept . . . and digest . . . much that had been kept from her in consideration of her condition. Yet it was possible that Enrique and Luisa knew nothing. She felt the bite of her own nails, in the palm of her hand.

She knew she could never bring herself to send such a letter.

Because she was a woman, and more, the mother of the girl, she brought herself without difficulty to the conclusion that the base of the trouble was a man. Because her world was closed to a man she could not envision, she decided that the man was Daniél, Enrique's and Luisa's son, Cayetana's cousin. Because of what she herself had been subjected to, it was a simple matter to deduct that Enrique and Luisa had cut the affair off, not so much on consanguineous grounds as what they would consider the misfortune of Cayetana's mixed bloodlines.

Immediately, sitting in the spring sun, she hated them both.

She unfolded her hand and put it out, upon Cayetana's head. She was aware that her touch was not gentle, as she meant it to be, but angry, protective. She was confused. It was too much to know all at once, too much, to feel the heart softened by its perception of love, and choked hard again by anger. The hypocrites in Seville: Enrique with his fond but formal letters, speaking always of Daniél, the son, and knowing her own daughter would be cut to the bone when those letters were read aloud . . .

"What's the matter, Mamacita?" Cayetana said.

The Señora took her hand away. "Dust in your hair, Caye. Why do you not put something on your head?"

She rose obediently. The Señora said, "Cayetana, if I seem always to dwell upon your faults it is only partially because you have so many. It is also because I love you."

She felt the girl had halted, just behind her. Cayetana said, "And if I do not complain, Mamacita, it is only because it is the same with me."

The Señora's smile was faint, downdrawn. "I would like to be alone for a time, now," she said.

When she heard the door close she raised her good hand and pressed it, hard, against herself. There was an insistent, grinding pain in her breast. The pain never lasted long, but she knew it was her heart. And one day, one fine day, the strain would be too much. She was ready for it in the sense that she had made her peace with the world around her and the world which was to come; she looked forward with joy to the day she might say to Guadalupe, having served her time for the passions of the mortal flesh, I have come to serve *you*, at last. She was not sad, but she did not wish to die in the spring, or at the dinner table. She wished to die in her own bed, or like this, sitting where Ramón would ride in and find her. She put her head back against the chair and tried to remember what it had been like to be young, to be free, to be wild with eagerness for the future. It would not come to her, except as a faint, glowing warmth, without intensity. The pain in her breast walled it off, so that she could think of nothing but the pain. She fought it because it was her nature to fight, she was in no way passive. It interested and amused her to think that she, who had been the most passive of children during her formative years, had, once emancipated, gone to the other extreme. Now she fought the failing heart silently and alone, prolonging her torment as a kind of penance.

The theory of physical penance, pain as an atonement, had once engrossed her. Yet when she made the experiment it had not turned out a penance, but a martyrdom. She closed her eyes against the pain and saw again, upon her darkened lids, the line camp a day's journey to the west.

Ramón had been gone two days and was expected to return by nightfall of the following day. It was not that she found herself unable to await his return with patience, it was only that she felt the need to spend a long-pent energy, and to surprise him in the bargain. Cayetana was nearly seven, and she had no qualms about leaving her with the women of the house. With Uremáy at hand all was secure. But she told Uremáy nothing. The old don, the father-in-law, had been in his grave for ten years, but she would also have told him nothing. The cook, Lupe's mother, knew only that the Señora was going to the line camp to meet the *patrón* and assumed that everyone, including the *patrón*, knew it as well as she did.

She put food, water, blankets, a change of clothing and a rifle into an old wagon used to bring in calves, and left the house at sunup.

She had been to the camp before and knew the way perfectly. There were three men on duty, bringing in cows and guarding horses moved out to fresh pasture. Ramón had gone out with a supply crew which serviced the line camps.

In the late afternoon, six or seven miles from her destination, she came down off a mesa cut on one side by a high bluff strewn with boulders. The line camp lay in sight, a small adobe building with corrals near it. When the rear of the wagon lifted, she lifted with it, and for a moment felt herself in space before the seat came up under her again. She heard the bump of the wheel as it struck rock; the wagon lurched as the same wheel wove. When the horses bolted, it tore the lines out of her hands. In another forty feet the wheel was off and the wagon turned neatly and quickly and went over the bluff.

She felt it coming when the rear end of the wagon sagged, and stood upright. There was never a doubt in her mind, later, that she could have thrown herself clear, that there had been time to jump, on the off side. She did not remember being frightened; it seemed to her that her mind was unusually sharp, and she was afterward able to recall in great detail what she had seen and felt. Whatever held her where she was was neither perversity nor determination, or did reason enter it. She simply knew that she must go with the wagon and she went with it.

There was not even the sensation of falling. There was only a pain so vast that she screamed with it until she thought she had burned out her throat. When she made herself stop, the screaming went on, and she managed to turn her head enough to see that it was one of the horses, gut-torn, bones protruding from both front legs. The other was dead. She lay on her right, with the side of the wagon on her from shoulder to hip. Her left hand was free; the right was twisted under her. The wagon was a heap of kindling, yet with her free hand she could not budge the great weight crushing flesh, muscle, nerve. Now that she had moved her head she found it impossible to move it back, and after a time she realized that the unnatural position of her head was more agonizing than the pain of her smashed body.

The sun was directly upon her and would remain so until it went down. The dust which had blasted into the air when the wagon fell was still settling, thick and dry, and she lay in it and thought about thirst. Thirst was not with her yet, but it would be. When she closed her eyes two blinding yellow spots moved up and down, inside her lids, little mock burning suns. She found that if she rolled her eyeballs upward the twin suns moved upward also, but they dropped immediately out of sight, under her lids.

"But I did not mean to die," she said aloud. The voice was a whisper, but it sounded to her as if someone had shouted, and she was impatient to turn her head, to tell whoever had shouted near her, come and help me out of this, can't you see I cannot move. No, not to die. Only to suffer a little, a small cut perhaps, or a sprained wrist. Not to die. She wished to laugh, and could not move enough even to do this.

At sundown, when she wanted to die but would not yet pray for it, a man named Albert McLean, who carried nothing in his pockets but holes and owned nothing but a slab-sided horse, found the wheel lying on the edge of the bluff and looked over.

She was not conscious then, and he believed she was dead. To test it, he shot the horse. When she did not respond he stood for a full minute looking down at her and making up his mind. His indecisive eye caught sight of what appeared to be a food basket, and he had not eaten in some time. It shifted to strewn blankets and a good rifle, and he had not owned either in months.

When he looked back at the woman he saw that her eyes were open and that she was watching him. He saw too that she was dying and that it did not matter what he did.

He knelt and lifted her head and ran water between her dry gray lips. When she tried to drink, her convulsive swallowing made fresh anguish in her. His eyes went to the rifle.

"Who are you, lady?" he said.

He had to put his ear to her mouth to hear her, but he understood. He began to drag the wagon, bit by bit, board by board, chunk by splinter, up on top of the bluff, on the track where the wheel lay. He had no matches; he had a fire drill. When it was full dark, he lit the pile and went back to do what he hated most to do, move the heavy section of wagon off her, because he needed

166

it to feed the fire. Other than that he would not have touched her.

Her eyes, following him, told him she knew, she understood. Straddling her, he got the wagonside up and off in a quick stroke, heaving so hard he threw it completely over. When he had put it on the fire he went and collected the blankets and covered her and sat beside her until they came up from the line camp.

Afterward, he knew that if he had had money and had wagered it on this woman's chances, he would have lost it. Weeks later, many weeks later, he had land and he had a few cows to start him. He sent north for his younger brother Jonah and he thought often of what he had almost thrown away for the sake of a rifle, and when he wished to torment himself he wondered if Alice Graves Dawes Dominguez, in her heart, blessed or cursed him for what he had done.

The line camp was still there, still in use. When she thought of it, she saw it always as it had looked that day, from the mesa.

Soledad had come out of the house with a woven blanket to cover the Señora's knees. "I am not asleep, Soledad," she said.

"But your eyes are closed, Señora," the girl said.

The Señora opened one eye and looked at her. "Soledad, I have often seen you close your eyes when you are not sleeping. Always, when Lupe is angry. You stand with your eyes closed as if you are to be struck down."

"Yes, Señora," the girl said.

"But thank you for the blanket. Will there soon be luncheon?"

"Soon, Señora," Soledad said. She went away.

The Señora had taken her hand from her breast the moment she had heard the girl's straw slippers on the tile. It would not do for anyone to know of the pain. Not even Ramón. And Cayetana never.

It occurred to her that time was very important now, and she did not know how much time was left. No one knew, of course, but when the odds were counted, hers did not appear favorable. And how long would it take to settle this matter of Cayetana's future, with or without the disgraceful coward of a cousin? This time she must have, this time she would do penance for forever, if only it was granted to her.

167

She called Feliciano. When he came she said, "The *capilla*, Feliciano. And quickly."

She would not speak to Ramón. She would discuss it with Guadalupe.

It was dim, cool, in the chapel. Incense flowed over her like balm. Feliciano wheeled her to her accustomed place beneath the altar. She whispered to him. He lit three candles for her and retired to the rear, where he first genuflected and then seated himself on a low stool.

After a long time the Señora placed her hand to her breast and discovered that the insistent pain had vanished. She accepted the sign as an extension of her time and instantly began to consider what appropriate self-denial she might make in exchange. She and Guadalupe bargained so well that they seldom disappointed one another.

Feliciano remained on his stool. He looked not at Guadalupe, but at the back of the Señora's head, or what he could see of it. He was diverted that she came into the chapel obviously on a rush call from some unknown source and not in her accustomed black, but with that flashy red shawl around her. Over the incense there was a drifting aroma from the kitchen, something hot and sweet which made him shift his position and look at last beyond the red shawl, and raise his eyes and pray, please Guadalupe, grant what she wishes, for I die of hunger, please Guadalupe, hurry Guadalupe.

"Feliciano," said the Señora, satisfied, expansive, as he wheeled her through the gates, "do you find time to pray?"

"Continually, Señora," Feliciano said.

TEN

When Richards took the herd out of Indian Lakes, he continued to bear west for several days. There was water in scattered creeks and holes, and they made only one dry drive, thirty miles, without it. Then they struck a local trail which turned north, paralleling the old trail. A hundred miles out of the lakes they came again into the old trail and then to the cattle town of Mason, where they resupplied and the crew took turns wetting down the dust of the drive.

The first sight of hills, blue and shadowy, came to them when they reached the chain of mountains which rose at the headwaters of the Concho. The country was rocky and barren, a big tawny land with muscles in it, warped and eroded by wind. It was May and the grass was good, stretching out to the Llano Estacado, the Staked Plains lying west, and into the northern Panhandle. The season of the heel fly, which bit the cows about the ankles and laid its eggs under the skin, was over, and the herd responded to freedom from the stinging punishment by settling down steadily to the long trek north.

Rojo was still in the lead when they crossed the Colorado. Richards held the herd up for a couple of hours, wanting to cross at the nooning, when the sun was hottest overhead and there would be no danger of it being in the cows' eyes. A cow wouldn't water where it couldn't see the opposite bank, and watering a herd was a hard operation anyway. You couldn't just let it pile into the water, muddying it up and pushing the leaders clear to the other side: you had to do it slowly, letting the cows spread out along the bank and keeping them upstream as they came in, so every cow got clean water. The Colorado was running swiftly but the crossing was easy, and the herd grazed forward into well-grassed, hilly country.

Richards doubled guards and threw an extra man on the remuda. The hills beyond the Colorado had been heavy cow thief territory for years, and cow thieves who had been at it so long knew all the tricks in the book and came up with new ones to keep abreast of the times. The easiest was stampeding a herd. Whatever they could pick up out of a stampede was raced in to have its brands burned over and its ear bobs re-cut. If they had to, they would cut off an ear clean to the head to erase an ear bob. If a man was slick enough he could make out he was rep-man for any number of brands, out to intercept drifters in other herds. He could forge identification, so that he could cut out brands held by other trail drivers, like the Double Slash B's Richards had picked up.

Abilene, Texas, was the last outpost of civilization until Point Supply, Oklahoma, and there was some question about just how civilized that was. Richards made a decision he knew he was going to be cursed for in two tongues: he and Sykes would go into Abilene, but the crew was staying with the herd.

Sykes stood with the tail of the wagon down, checking supplies in the compartmented chuckbox, pulling out drawers and slamming them shut again. There was a forty-five gallon water barrel. Stored around it was bacon in hundred-pound lots, coffee, flour, meal, beans, salt, brown sugar, lard, molasses, jerky, and air tights, canned goods. There was room in the wagon for bedrolls and slickers, extra water barrels, shovels, branding irons, horseshoes, spare wagon parts, patent medicines, pothooks, the crew's tin chuck equipment, and what the hands called do-funnies, the use-less personal items they had collected over a lifetime, and which the vaqueros carried more efficiently in saddle pouches. A cook had to be good at lashing down everything which could move and shift. When he let down the wagon tail for his work table, not a hand, including the trail boss, could touch it, and nobody ever took so much as a pinch of salt or got to enter the wagon except the nighthawk, who often slept in it when the sun was high.

"You ain't agonna let 'em go to town," Sykes said sourly to Richards, "I'm agoin' to git some eggs for 'em." He cocked an eye at the morning sky. "I'm agoin' to fry eggs if the wind don't blow up a dust before sundown or she don't rain into the frypan. And one of these days, they're due for pie."

"Don't put no henfruit in my pie," Shiloh said. "I ain't partial to henfruit pie. Plain old apple'll do me."

"Coffee," Sykes said.

"Coffee pie? My God, Sallie, you'll have me so poor around the equator I won't be fit to do more'n fold over on my git-up end. Remember now, Sykes, apple."

Sykes didn't answer.

Shiloh got up and dusted off his pants. "Talkin' to you is like barkin' at a knot," he told Sykes. "Ben, would you bring me back some makin's? I now and then need a smoke to keep my mind off the chuck in this outfit."

"Sure," Richards said. Shiloh picked up his horse and went out.

"Don't bother me none," Sykes said. "I know he'd die for me."

While Sykes stocked up, Richards went into a saloon and had a beer and wrote two letters. For Ramón Dominguez it was a fac-tual account of their progress, but he told it in detail, and sent his respects to the house. Something nagged at him when he fin-ished, and he finally added a postscript: *tell Cayetana I hope it is going well there.* Then he crossed out the first two words so black and thick they couldn't be read at all, and sealed it up, be-cause there was nothing he could say or do now. The letter to Avis was brief: he was all right and Frankie was all right and the herd was doing fine and he hoped she was giving some thought to what they had talked about. He opened and closed it without endearment in any form, knowing that if he had got such a letter from her, he would have been able to read between the lines. When he was done he bought cigarette makings, and out of his own pocket, cigars and whiskey for the crew, and hung around picking up what information he could until Sykes got there. That was how he learned that Tres Reyes was the tenth herd through Abilene that spring.

They crossed the Clear Fork of the Brazos and the days became showery. He knew it would be raining heavily to the west, for the small streams which sprang from headwaters in the Llano Estacado were running high and swollen. There was plenty of water now, and the grass as good as he had ever seen it. The herd was putting on flesh with it and was in fine condition. The wet was bearable, but heavy rains depressed both men and animals. There was no pleasure in riding in it, huddled under the fishskin slickers, putting the herd through the dirty swirling creeks, keeping your eye out for floodground and bogs where a steer could sink to its belly and take men and rope and horses to pull it free.

Some miles south of the Brazos they turned northwest, in order to hit the Round Timber ford. A day out, scouting ahead, Richards overtook two herds, one of seventeen hundred head up from the Gulf Coast, and a small drive of yearlings under the man who owned them. Lane Weatherell had bossed several outfits in his time, and Richards knew him. The larger herd had vaqueros with it and bore a big blotched brand of the type the poppers identified as Map of Mexico. The yearlings were locals going out to fresh graze.

"By God, Richards, I ain't seen you in many a long year. Who you roddin' for now?" Weatherell said.

Richards told him. Weatherell was a big man, running to paunch, with a blunt wind-bitten face. "I expected by this time you might of settled down to your own spread. How long you been there?"

"Two seasons," Richards said. "We went into Nebraska last spring. I'm headed into Fort Benton with a shipment for Todd Allenby."

"Well, I'll let you in on something," Weatherell said. He was squatted on his boot heels, smoking. "There's four, five herds ahead of you, tryin' to git across the Brazos. It's rained heavy, and that old river's sure foggin' it to git where she's goin'. You cross at the ford, you goin' to have a long wait. That old lady river'll sure give you hell's own time, you try to force her now. I reckon you're just goin' to have to hang back and take her at her own time, after them other herds git over. If you ain't in a hurry, she'll git around to layin' down for you."

"I don't reckon I can wait around that long," Richards said. "We'll look for another crossing. Anyway, I don't aim to throw my outfit anywhere near those herds piled up waitin' to cross. I don't expect they'd take kindly to havin' their graze shorted by my cows. They got there first, it's all theirs."

"They got enough trouble," Weatherell said, "poor damn Mexykins. Got a lead steer down there so snaky I'd of shot him first day out." He grinned. "Don't need a leader, do you?"

"I got one," Richards said.

"Sure, I suppose old Dominguez is one of them with a big critter wearin' a bell on his dewlap and comin' and goin' with the seasons."

Richards shook his head. "Right now we got a steer leadin' us and you can't even read his brand. Ever hear of Rojo?"

Weatherell got to his feet. "You ain't tryin' to make out he's leadin' your herd, are you, Richards?"

"We picked him up right before we trailed. He came up out of my drags and took the lead and he's never let go since. I ain't sayin' he's content. Matter of fact, I ain't sure he knows there's any cows with him. He acts to me like he reckons he's out on his own. I ain't got a cow nor a man wants to git within reach of his horns, and if you think eight feet ain't a long ways, you measure it out."

"Why, what are you goin' to do with the old red?" Weatherell said.

"Drop him at Dodge. He killed a man this spring."

"That's too bad, Ben," Weatherell said slowly. "Yet I kind of hate to see the old king go. You boys down in the brush country goin' to be kind of lonesome with nothin' like him to chase."

"I wouldn't worry any," Richards said. "If there ain't a steer ten feet at the withers with a spread of horn goes fifteen, the boys'll make one up. Say, how you goin' to get those yearlings over?"

"I'm turnin' west here, Richards. I won't cross the old lady when she's in the mood she's in. I'm glad I seen you, though. Wasn't so busy gittin' my own spread underway here, I would of dropped down to see how the rich folks live."

"Anytime," Richards said.

"Good luck to you, Richards. Wish I could help you out some, but I'm shorthanded. You tell Allenby he needs some good two year olds to winter over next season, I'm his man."

The following day Richards pulled Manuel Vega out of the swing and sent him upriver to search for a possible crossing. Uremáy held the herd where it was, not wanting to chance mixing with the herds waiting for the Brazos to fall. Frankie had not come in for breakfast. He had lost three horses out of the remuda during the night and was out trying to pick them up. Richards rode downriver.

Ten miles below the ford, he came into the mouth of a creek which cut off from the Brazos. He sat and looked at it for a long time, trying to judge the currents, watching to see how much debris was being carried. The Brazos was wide, muddy, and running very full, but it was not too swift at this point, as if the creek had drained off some of its force. It was a warm overcast day. He took off his boots and his gun belt and bundled them inside his stripped-off shirt and lay some rocks over the bundle. Then he put the roan horse called Plácido down the slope and into the water.

It was shallow when he entered it, and it seemed to him that Plácido was going to walk straight across. Then, halfway over, the river took them and Plácido was swimming steadily and without strain. Richards estimated about sixty yards of swimming water, before the horse had his feet under him again. The lead bank was easy, but the opposite bank was cut abruptly, and the passage up it was not as wide as he wished it had been. He figured his drift. The current was going to take the herd downstream. That meant he would have to put it in a good hundred yards upstream.

He went back to the lead bank and sat and let his socks dry for a time before he dismounted and put on his boots again. He appraised the far bank. That undercut could be a problem: get the cows bunched up under it and they could drown before a man could lift a rope to help them.

A man could drown here. Ten miles above, at the ford, one of his vaqueros had drowned last season, horse and all. He sat Plácido, looking at the Brazos. But that wasn't to do with the river, with a horse that didn't want to swim, that was to do with the men of Tres Reyes moving out without Cayetana Dominguez there to give them luck. When he looked at the river he hoped the luck she had given them this year was holding.

He took his time going back to camps. Cayetana coming into his mind like that had disturbed him. It had been a long time since he had had a chance to do any thinking; until they had crossed the heaviest complex of rivers he would continue to ride the bobtail watch from eight to ten-thirty, along with the guard. By the time he got to bed everybody else had turned in. He missed the talk around the fire at night, and he missed being able to chew with Uremáy when he felt like it, and he thought now that once they delivered the M Bar L's and got out of Dodge it would go easier and he would have time for it. Right now, until he got this swollen river crossed, there wasn't time to think about anything but the herd.

He moved the herd downstream and let it graze into nightfall. The weather stayed overcast, and the air was moist and pleasant.

Frankie came in for chuck, having picked up his strays. "One of 'em was yours," he told Corrigan. "The one you rode into the M Bar L on. We'll see how he takes to a hobble tonight."

"'Twon't work," Corrigan said. "I'm popeyed he's been so good. I told him to be good, before we come. You hobble him and you won't believe how many miles he can crowhop before morning."

"I like to see him crowhop this river," McLean said.

"Oh he won't try that," Corrigan said. "He's modest about his abilities. Most likely he just wants to git away from all society."

"Chuck pile!" Sykes hollered. "Son of a bitch stew for all son of a bitches. Anybody that ain't one don't eat tonight."

Nobody talked much while they ate. The vaqueros finished quickly, and smoked and got out worn decks of cards and thumbed them, waiting.

175

"Say, why don't you fellers ever play poker?" Shiloh said, to a small leather-skinned vaquero squatting on his heels.

The vaquero got up and went to put his dirty tin dishes in the wreck tub. "Because," he said, "it has no . . . what is the word? Even Uremáy does not know this word. It does not make the heart race, as does the monte."

"I don't know where you been playin' poker," Shiloh said, "but I'll tell you that the heart don't race unless the blood is boilin', and I sat in on a few hands in my time boiled my blood. You ever decide you want to play a little poker, you fellers, I'll join you." He rolled himself a cigarette. "Anybody don't want to listen can start snorin', but I tell you one time I sat in on a hand in Ogallala you wouldn't of believed. You girls know Ogallala is the prettiest, gentlest little town in the whole cow country." The vaqueros laughed softly. They were looking forward to Ogallala, Nebraska. Ogallala, Nebraska, was as wide-open as any town on the trail, maybe wider, and they dreamed of reaching it. "There ain't nothing in Ogallala," Shiloh said. He looked at the end of his cigarette thoughtfully. "I got to admit you can buy some potables there. What was that one, Ben, gin? Gin, I reckon it was. My God. There is some ladies there also, in Ogallala. I expect you would call them ladies. Games too, whatever's your pleasure. Brace games, so you got to look sharp to see where the deal is comin' from. It ain't much of a town. The only thing you got to make sure of is that your gun don't stick."

The vaqueros were hanging on his words, watching his face. "When I want to hear the history of Ogallala I'll take to school learnin'," Sykes said.

"I got into a game there when I was too green to know better and had just drawed my wages," Shiloh said, ignoring him. "Little bitty man with a thumb missin' was dealin', and there was some characters didn't do a thing while they was playing but graze the ends of their cigars. Quietest game I ever sat in. Only thing I said, myself, was, 'I'm stayin'.'"

"Shoot this quail," Corrigan said. "We all know the end. They cleaned you."

Shiloh looked at him. "Well now, I don't know about that."

"Hell, we've heard this story before: the game was braced and they cleaned you."

"Let me straighten out your thinkin', Corrigan. On the last draw, when that kitty was towered up so she'd make your eyes bug out and I was down to my last peso, you'd never guess what I was holdin'. You care to take a guess?"

"Your hat," Corrigan said.

"I would of bet that too if anybody'd wanted it. Get this now, get it straight: three aces, girls, and the prettiest pair of kings you ever seen."

"How much did you win?" McLean said.

"Well, actually, I didn't win nothing," Shiloh said. "The cigar eater on my left was holdin' a straight flush. He chewed up that whole cigar, inch by inch, while he was gatherin' in my money. That's how come I ride for you now. That's the way it goes, though, ain't it? Life is just one big poker hand, any way you deal it. I advise you strong not to play no cards in Ogallala." He looked up at Sykes suddenly, through the smoke of his cigarette. "Say, Sykes, what is that, what you got there?"

Sykes passed down the pies. The beat-up eggwhites he had spread on top had peaked up like snow.

"Calf slobbers," Shiloh said. "Ain't that hell, though? Here he's got to go and make a perfec'ly decent-lookin' pie and then let one of them calves slobber on it. If Hedges don't keep a better eye on them calves . . . I wanted apple."

"You'll git apple, too," Sykes said. "First apple I find I am goin' to stick in your mouth and try out the fat in your head and roast it like a prime hog. The reason I put this here light stuff on top is to keep you afloat tomorrow so's you don't sink like a rock."

"Well, that's good of you," Shiloh said. "I take it all back, on account of you lookin' out for me like that."

Richards finished and jerked his head at Frankie and stood up. They got their mounts and rode over to where the remuda was strung out, a good distance from the herd. He had had little chance to talk to the boy. Now he said, "How's it goin' for you, Frankie?"

177

"I ain't got any complaints," McLean said. "Only I expect to grow out of nighthawkin'."

"Figurin' on playin' *segundo* next season?" Richards said, smiling a little.

"*Segundo*, hell. I figure to be drivin' my own herd next time out. You didn't expect I aimed to throw in with you again, did you?"

Richards brought the horse up and leaned on the horn, watching McLean. It was not something he had reflected on, it was only that somewhere in the back of his mind was the thought that next year he would maybe not be trailing Tres Reyes', but M Bar L's.

"Christ," McLean said evenly, "you done enough carryin' on about our throwin' in with you, Ben. I don't reckon I'd ever do it again. I wouldn't of done it this year, it hadn't been you're hollerin' and Pa's dyin'. That put me between a rock and a hard place."

Richards said quietly, "It did, didn't it, Frankie. I'm sorry about it. I reckon I should of had you ridin' with the herd and learning what you could instead of nursin' horses."

"I learned plenty from Pa," McLean said. "You know I only had one thing in my mind anyhow, and that was deliverin' the herd and gettin' Rojo off the range. I still aim to do that. Then I aim to git as drunk as I can without fallin' down dead, and then I aim to go home."

Richards said, "You wouldn't consider goin' on to Fort Benton?"

McLean looked at him. "You mean deliver my herd and take your remuda on into Montana?"

"The money's good, Frankie. I can use you and Shiloh."

After a minute McLean said, "You want to buy my lead steer, Ben?"

"Buy Rojo?"

"Naw, that was a joke. Rojo ain't for sale, except to the market. I was just figurin' he could take your herd right to delivery point and keep on goin' until he come out in whatever's on the other end of the world. That's the way he travels, looks like." He stared down at the ground, and Richards saw that he was frowning.

178

"It'd be a long summer, Ben. I ain't certain I like leavin' Avis that long."

He felt the same but he could not say so. "Turn it over, Frankie. See what Shiloh thinks."

McLean looked up at him. "I'll let you know in Dodge," he said.

"That's good enough. Keep your eyes open tonight, Frankie, will you, you got to take the remuda over first tomorrow."

"Stay off me, Ben," McLean said on an intake of breath. "Off. You figure because I lost three horses last night I ain't keepin' up with you?"

"I never said that, Frankie," Richards said, surprised. "There ain't a nighthawk ever lived didn't have some horses get out once in a while." He leaned forward again, looking at the boy squarely. "I'm not on you, Frankie. I never have been. Why is it I sooner or later get around to sayin' something to you makes you kick like a bay steer? You know me now, or anyway you'd ought to, and I think I know you, but then I get to figurin' somehow I don't act smart around you. I ain't on the prod for you. You try me, though, by God, I'll say that. Nobody fights anybody in this outfit. Not while I'm runnin' it. That goes for you and me too. All I expect of you is you act human and do your job. And I don't aim to hear how right you are and how wrong everybody else is."

McLean was flushed with anger. "You won't hear nothin' from me, preacher," he said. "And you won't see me hawkin' your remuda into Montana, either."

"Have it how you want it," Richards said, and turned away.

He circled the herd. Everything looked quiet but he decided to take bobtail guard anyway, if for no other reason than to try and ride out his disgust. What in hell was he letting himself in for, wanting to marry Avis and take over the care and feeding of an orphan calf who was having so much trouble learning to suck for himself. It looked to him as if just leading into the subject with Frankie might call for more than words. It got so you didn't even want to say the time of day to him, for fear you'd grabbed hold of the branding iron by the hot end.

And he knew it would take a more patient man than he was to stick it out on the M Bar L with Frankie McLean.

179

If there could be one sentence said, one small opportune time to clear the air, and then know that it was over and done, it would solve it all. But he kept his mind off that, and he never forgot the sound of Uremáy's voice that afternoon on the river. If such a moment came it would come when it was least expected and in some manner you had never given a thought to, and maybe it would be the wrong moment to be sitting on your gun hand.

Every man not on watch helped Sykes and Hedges get off for Round Timber ferry in the morning. The chuck was lashed down tight and the mules harnessed before Sykes could lift a hand. He didn't thank them, but he expressed the opinion that they wanted to be sure he was back by chucktime that night, on the other side of the Brazos. He rolled out as if the wheels would fly off, and they yelled good luck to him and good-by Little Mary after Hedges and the calf wagon, and went to work.

They crossed the remuda first, so the cows could see how easy it was, and would follow. The weather was still warm and overcast. Richards had not let the herd water before crossing. He stationed twelve men at the cut bank on the far side of the river. Their job was to keep both horses and herd moving up the narrow passageway and not let them pile up at the mouth. Stripped to underwear, Levis, and hats, and riding the best swimmers in their mount strings, the crew put the herd over.

When Richards put Plácido into the Brazos on the right point, he was neck and neck with Rojo. The big outlaw went into the water looking neither to left nor right. When they struck the halfway mark, horse and steer began to swim. Rojo came up on the opposite bank without effort and moved up the passage, followed by the lead of the herd.

The vaqueros at the bank kept them moving freely, up and through. Richards lost count of how many times he crossed and recrossed, always taking the right point. Once in a while a cow on the flank drifted into the current and the swing men pushed it back into the herd. The river had not visibly fallen in the night and was still running strong and at full crest. But the crossing went without trouble, and he did not lose a cow.

The herd watered under the cut bank and spread over several

thousand acres to graze. Under the gray sky their moving colors stood out strong and vigorous: brown, brindle, dun, red, slate, cream, bay, black, yellow, grayblue, speckled, streaked, splotched, solid, and no two alike. Along the river M Bar L bulls bellowed and resented; cows were coming in heat as they tended to do when they were driven. Rojo looked them over as if they were all his and moved back to water, sinking first one horn and then the other in the wet red mud and tossing it on the tight-curled hair of his forehead. Steers, singly and in clumps, followed him. Horses which had swum the river uncounted times were watered, grazed, and taken back into the remuda.

By afternoon Richards got the herd gathered and began to move to bedground a mile and a half from the river. He was riding with the gather when Uremáy found him. The *segundo* was mounted on a big sorrel he recognized as being long on wind, and Uremáy tended to favor him when he had riding to do.

"No wagons," Uremáy said, taking off his big straw hat and resettling it. "They do not come, Ben."

Sykes and Hedges should have been in by now. Richards didn't know what had held them up, but he did know he was going to have a long-faced crew if there wasn't any chuck. "What do you think?" he asked Uremáy.

"I go to ride back, Ben," Uremáy said. He held his arm straight out, pointing. "You see how it is here, the land is good, the grass is good. But farther on, where the eye does not see, it is very broken, very rough. Many arroyos. We must go away from them, before we pick up the trail again, or there will be much trouble with the legs of these *vacas*. I believe maybe the wagons have trouble."

"Take a look, then," Richards said. "But it's gettin' on to nightfall. Maybe you better trail a night horse if the country's bad."

"I will do that, Ben. Tell my poor men to rope themselves tightly about the waist and they will endure."

Very late, the sun came, breaking through a dark wall of cloud just before it dropped. Richards watched the wall turn gold along its edges, then red as blood, then purple, as the sun passed behind it. The herd was grazing on its bedground, liking to lie where it had found good grass. By full dark it was the crew milling and stomping discontentedly.

It was after nine when a vaquero picked up the points of light which were the lanterns on the chuck wagon. The crew cheered, and half a dozen of them rode out to guide Sykes in, unharness the mules, and build up the fire.

"My granny, what a country," Sykes said, getting into his apron and letting down the work table. "We floated across this dang-fool river like we was a couple of clouds, Hedges and me, and started up to find you and run right into hell with the hide off. Why 'tain't nothing but cracks in the earth two miles deep and half a mile acrost. There we was wandering around from one table to another, tryin' to find enough of a chain of 'em to git through and we'd cross one or two and come to a bluff near the size of that gap up in Arizona Territory. As it was, Little Mary 'n' me had to dip into a few. 'Twasn't so bad goin' down, but it was tough crust climbin' out. Wasn't for old Tiburcio, I reckon we'd still of been hoppin' around out there all anti-godlin when the last trump blows. Anybody git accustomed to bein' without me?"

"I'm so weak I ain't been able to lick my upper lip," Shiloh said.

Sykes went to work. Richards looked up Hedges and questioned him about the herds still waiting to cross at the ferry.

"Four of 'em," Hedges told him. "I reckon they'll either sit where they are and wait for the Brazos to drop, or try what you tried. We told 'em you was crossin' at the creek mouth. Looks like you foxed 'em, boss. They say there's another herd ahead of you, somewheres up the line."

In the morning Richards reconnoitered, checking water and graze, meeting Sykes and sending him on to pick the noon campsite. He kept his eye open now for drifters out of other herds and several times chased off range cattle that might have got mixed in with his own. The Wichita lay ahead, and he figured it was going to be in the same condition as the Brazos. If it was, there might be more herds laying up to cross, and he wanted to get as far ahead as he could. He rode most of the day with the drags, breathing the dust of the herd, eyes so grainy and scratched he could hardly lower his lids over them by nightfall.

The second day out from the Brazos a heavy rain started at dawn. They rode hunched and miserable under their oilskin fish. The herd was troublesome, wanting to drift, as cows often did in a rain. Sykes raised the canvas fly which sheltered his work table and cursed at his reluctant fire. By nightfall the rain had slacked off, but it still fell steadily. The herd refused to bed and Richards doubled the guard.

The morning was clear and cool, and they picked up the main trail again. Riding ahead, Richards ran into a local rancher and two Mexicans driving horses, and learned what he wanted to know.

The Wichita had been so bad not a cow had crossed it in a week. But it was falling now, and in a day or so it might be forded. There were two herds had waited a couple of days and then turned off to try and find a crossing. One herd was still waiting it out.

He laid up the herd about four miles from the Wichita, throwing it off the trail a mile and a half, where it bedded quietly. In the morning he'd have a look at the river and figure what he was going to do. He listened to the running interchange between Shiloh and Sykes at chuck, and then managed to get an hour's sleep before he went out with the eight-thirty watch.

He liked watching with the vaqueros, mainly because he liked the way they sang to the herd. Sometimes it was downright comical when the Mexicans were riding and Shiloh and Corrigan were riding, the kind of sound they produced. Mexicans liked to sing anytime, and they sang to herds because gringos sang to herds. Like the gringos, they sang soothingly and softly, but the mixture of the sorrowful Spanish and the harsh Yankee could be funny to hear. Nobody knew why cows liked to be sung to, but they did. Some men said it was because the singing covered up other night sounds that might spook them into stampeding, but Richards felt it was just they liked knowing the same human beings who saw they had plenty of water and grass were taking care of them in the nighttime too.

He circled, listening to the low Spanish voices and hearing the noises a satisfied herd made: a creaking of bones and joints, a shifting and rustling as it bedded firm and comfortable, a chewing, a sighing, a snuffling. Accustoming to the dark, his eyes picked up shapes and silhouettes: a steer on the edge of bedground with a twisted down-drooping horn, the watch riders moving slowly through the night. He could see the flare of the fire, where the crew would be playing cards and telling stories, most of which were true. He let Portero's steady pace take him and thought how it would be on the Nueces now, with the wild turkeys out and mustang grapes clustering, blackbirds settling in to pick ticks off the cows, and grasshoppers skittering up under you. And the land green and golden, or black and thorny, depending on where you happened to be, and the time of the year a pain that made your very blood hurt. The pictures he made himself put Avis under his skin like needles, so that he had to hold himself down and where he was, because the way he was beginning to feel he could take the herd across the Wichita tonight and run it so fast it would be crossing the Yellowstone in the morning.

Some sound brought him up sharp, head thrown back. It was a popping sound, like a string of firecrackers had gone off somewhere up the line, toward the river. It took him a little longer to believe it than it should have, but that was because he didn't want to believe it. It was gunfire he heard.

Under and over it there was another sound, like a bunch of Indians were stomping on drums. He held Portero and listened a bare second more, and then he knew what it was and then it was too late. It would have been too late anyway. Against the sky there was a mass rising of horns as the cows lifted their heads to listen. Richards took air into his lungs and shouted it toward camps. "All hands and the cook! All hands and the cook!"

He only got to shout it twice, because the cows were on their feet in a flash, not getting to their knees first like a domestic cow with watery bloodlines did, but rising in one springing motion. For a bare second they maintained their interested, listening position. The pop of the gunfire was closer, and so was the steady drumming on the earth. There was some hollering on his left and he knew the crew was coming, but by then the herd was running.

Richards cut for the lead, looking to find Rojo, knowing by

now that Rojo was going to be first off no matter what set him to it. When he found him on the right point, Richards pushed him, trying to turn him and work him out of the way of what was coming. That was all that was in his mind: to get the herd turned and out of the way.

They were caught blind. The thunder shook the earth and the thunder was cows running. The herd which had been waiting above them to cross the Wichita stampeded into them and they were taken up in it like snow flying in a norther.

There was nothing to do but try to stay on the point of the panicked herd and attempt to swing it. The whole trust of every hand was in his horse and his horse alone, it didn't matter what his own instinct might tell him. The night horses kept them out of holes and gullies, while they tried to keep up with the herd, cussing and singing the same songs they sang on watch, only loud and drawn-out now, and trying to swing the lead. But the herd was caught up in the insane rush of the herd which had swept down on it.

They could not stop it unless they could get the lead milling, until the circle grew and spread and the whole mass was circling on itself. The danger to the riders was not from the herd but from the terrain, the drops and bluffs that only a good night horse could save a man from. But there was danger to the herd. No trail boss liked to mark up his losses, the weak runners who would go down with broken legs, the pile-ups under the banks, the drifters never recovered, the cows who ran to exhaustion and the flesh loss if they got to enjoying a good run whenever your back was turned. Trying to check Spanish longhorns running was what he dreaded most and fought hardest.

It was a long time before Richards realized what had happened. The Tres Reyes herd was so fresh it had outrun the lead of the original stampede. Maybe a steer didn't get much fresher than Rojo, when he had his paunch full of water and green grass, because there wasn't going to be any stopping him tonight.

It was the country itself which finally swung them. They came up on the banks of a creek, and although Rojo turned aside, the lead of the mass behind him rushed into it and found itself swimming. The creek was deep. It slowed the mass and brought it to a halt.

They sat where they were until first light. Richards had his eye on Rojo, grazing calmly as if nothing had happened, with his head turned away. When Uremáy rode up he was smiling faintly. He said, "We have a great many of these animals, now, do we not?"

"If there was a dog around, I'd kick him," Richards said. "You know what they say, Tiburcio: if you can get through the first two weeks on the trail without a stampede, you don't have to look for one any further. Godalmighty. Now we got cows scattered from here to hell and gone, and mixed up with somebody else's cows like fly specks on a hotel wall."

"It is the Double Slash B," Uremáy said. "Your friend. Now we will give him back his cows."

"Now," Richards said, "we'll be a lifetime just cuttin' 'em out."

"Have faith, *amigo*, the days pass swiftly," Uremáy said. "And that one." He pointed at Rojo. "So tranquil, so unconcerned. Well, it was not his doing. Nor ours, either. And our good Sykes brings up the wagon and sees to the coffee. Then shall I put these indolent vaqueros to work?"

"The quicker the better," Richards said, glum. "I reckon I better go look up the Double Slash B."

He found Barwell's straw boss back up the trail, a thin man with a great beak of a nose, looking as disconsolate as Richards felt. Richards said, "Ben Richards, Tres Reyes. You look like you'd been pulled through a knothole in a fence."

"I was," the other said. "Sideways, too. Len Grossett, Double Slash B."

"Sure. I know Barwell. We been trailin' sixteen of your cows we picked up at Indian Lakes. I was hopin' I'd run into you, but I didn't look to do it like this, exactly."

"Seems like you got considerable more than sixteen of ours now," Grossett said. "We turned off at the lakes on account of that dry stretch. Sayin' I'm sorry don't get the work done, but it ain't a lie anyways. I sure as hell didn't reckon to start runnin' half the herds on the Wichita last night, much less my own."

Richards didn't ask him what had happened. Sometimes nothing a man could see or hear would start a herd off. An electrical storm was the worst starter, but then again it might be some fool thing like hammering back your gun when they didn't particularly want to hear it hammered, or a horse stamping his foot at the wrong time, or the cook dropping a tin pan where an echo happened to carry. Grossett volunteered the information.

"It was buff'lo," he said. "I seen 'em late yestiddy afternoon, about a dozen of 'em. I chased 'em off all right in the daylight, but I reckon soon as it got dark they nosed up to my cows to see what's goin' on. Curious critters, buff'los. Next thing my guard bulges up on 'em and they run for it and every Double Slash B is off and flyin'."

Richards said wearily, "It happens. How many cows you got?"

"Eighteen hundred," Grossett said. "I'll bring up my outfit and we'll start cuttin'."

An hour later Richards rode in and gulped coffee and picked up his tally strings. Two hours later they were still cutting, and he gave the strings to Shiloh and rode out with Uremáy and Vega to see to the drifters being brought in. He didn't hold anything against Grossett, even though it was a damnfool thing to begin firing guns when a herd started and usually only scared it twice as bad; but it was another aching, weary delay, and there was nothing like it to get you to feeling you ought to quit cows.

It took them three and a half hours to cut the herds apart, and before both he and Grossett were satisfied with the tally. "I reckon I ought to let your outfit go on acrost," Grossett said morosely.

"Hell no," Richards said. "You were there first. If you can cross the Wichita by noon, I figure to make it before nightfall."

"I aim to stay out of your way," Grossett said.

"You got that tail end to, Grossett." Richards' voice was dry. "I aim to stay out of yours."

The Double Slash B's were moving out. "Watch out fer them buff'lo," Grossett said.

Richards looked around for Uremáy. He thought Uremáy might be trying to catch some sleep somewhere, now that the herd was back together, but he couldn't locate him. He was so dragged out himself that he figured if he found Uremáy sleeping anywhere he would be liable to lie down alongside him and never wake up again, and he didn't even want to think the word, sleep, because the word all by itself had a power in it. Sykes told him Uremáy had lost the small woven saddlebag he carried, while he was out looking for drifters. He and Vega were retracing their steps. Richards had some more coffee to prop his eyes open, but when Uremáy didn't show, he picked up the buttermilk from the remuda and told Shiloh to point the herd and drifted off to take a look.

Along with everything else, he worried about Uremáy. Uremáy drove himself hard and he was tough, but the strain was beginning to tell. Or anyway it told when a hard time like last night came up. Bad river crossings, storms, stampedes, drought, were all part of the cow game, and Uremáy had spent a lot of his life playing it. There wasn't much sense in him wearing himself down to the marrow right at the point he was about to lay down his hand. Yet when he found Uremáy he wondered just how ready to quit his *segundo* really was. He rode up on Uremáy in a group of small trees, catching him in the act of dismounting. He was about to speak but something checked him. Uremáy's and Vega's horses were nose to nose, and Vega was still in the saddle. He raised his eyes and saw Richards and opened his mouth and then closed it again. Uremáy was moving slowly, not as if he was old, or stiff, but with great deliberation. He did not, obviously, know that Richards was there.

With the same deliberation he walked to Vega and reached up and took him by the belt. "*Cochina*," he said in a low, quiet voice. "*Chacal*. Sow. Jackal. I spit in the milk of your mother."

Vega took his foot out of the stirrup and made to kick. Uremáy elbowed the foot aside as if it was an insect come to bother at him. He hauled Vega out of the saddle and Vega fell flat on his back and made no move to rise.

Richards didn't interfere. Whatever was going on was Uremáy's business, but it was in his mind that Uremáy could still work Vega over badly, unless Vega made a jump for his gun. He put his hand on the butt of the .44, just in case, and said, "Need any help, Tiburcio?"

Uremáy stood upright, but he didn't take his eyes off Vega.

"Ah, Ben. I am glad you have come. It saves me much. Would you, as a kindness, dismiss this man, from my sight, and from the crews of Tres Reyes. Otherwise, I will kill him." He stepped aside.

Richards looked down at Vega. "You heard him, Manuel. Pick up your gear and light your shucks. Move on."

Vega got to his feet. His eyes were hot, but he was smiling. "My horse?"

"Take him. You took him before, and the brand on him wasn't yours then, either."

Vega spit at Uremáy's feet, mounted, and rode out.

Uremáy was leaning face first against his horse, with his hat pushed back. The woven bag was hanging from the saddle horn.

Richards said, "I see you located your pouch."

He looked up. "That whoreson finds it for me. I have now lost my wind, as it turns out."

"You care to tell me about it?" Richards said.

Uremáy pulled himself up into the saddle, but it was not deliberate now, it was slow and stiff. "Someday. Someday when you and I have taken the *vacas* across this river, we will sit down together and have a little talk. We will speak of the Manuel Vegas of this world, among other matters."

"I ain't particularly sorry to see him go," Richards said. "I never did like how he twisted Rojo's tail that day."

Uremáy fell in by him. "And now he has twisted Tiburcio Uremáy's tail, and this animal is not a steer, but a bull, and he can use his horns, eh?"

"You'd ought to watch it," Richards said. "Your horns are gettin' kind of splintery."

"That is true," Uremáy said. "But observe how an old bull uses them, even then. Now, you and I, Ben, let us take the little cows for a swim."

"And we'll be one day closer to Fort Benton, is that it?"

"No, we will be one day nearer Tres Reyes. Where else would I wish to be? Where else would you wish to be?"

"I kind of like it there," Richards said, grinning.

"It is good to hear you say this, Ben," Uremáy said, not looking at him. "It is good if a man is happy in the place where he must stay. Where his freedom is, where his heart is, there is his country, no? And a man must stay in his country, no?"

"No," Richards said. "Sometimes it doesn't work that way. Bein' I know you so damn well, Tiburcio, you give me the feelin' you're workin' on something besides gettin' this herd to Fort Benton."

Uremáy shrugged. "I bear watching at all times," he said.

ELEVEN

The detail was out of Fort Supply, a handful of jaded cavalry with a sergeant at their head. They came up on the drive on the divide between the Salt and North forks of the Red River. Richards had picked up their dust on morning reconnaissance, and thought it might be Indians. They were getting into Indian country. He sat for a long time, watching, not overconcerned because he knew from the size of the dust cloud that there was not a great number of horsemen. But he felt better when he saw it was cavalry.

The Wichita lay behind. They had crossed fifty feet of swimming water with no trouble, except that they had to float the wagons over. There was plenty of timber and an equal amount of complaint: brush country poppers had never hankered to be axmen. They blistered their hands cutting and trimming trees, lashed them together, tied the guide ropes to their saddle horns, and took the chuck wagon over with Sykes in the driver's seat shouting orders to them and cussing them as substitutes for the mules. Then they rafted the calf wagon across. Between the

Wichita and the Pease the country was open and the grass still holding. The Pease was down, but it had fallen only recently. The banks were piled with debris, and trees along the bottom were marked with high water line. The Red was three days' drive ahead, and Richards, scouting it a day out, found it low.

The Red was one of the worst of the lot, and every trail boss dreaded crossing it. There were graves, covered over with rock cairns, on both banks. It had been high. Now it was so shallow it was cut into channels, with sand bars lying up out of it. The red bluffs were still wet-black where the water had risen, and deposits of grainy red earth covered everything like coffee grounds. It was not like crossing a river at all, and there was still plenty of water for the herd.

The country beyond was rich with the season, and open, as lonesome a country as there was and looking as if man had never touched foot to it. Antelope, curious, approached the herd and got shot for chuck for their pains. There were buffalo in sight, big old bulls standing hump-shouldered against the fair sky, rumbling out of the way and standing again, herding their cows and calves. The ground was a packed mass of buffalo trails, paralleling and crossing one another, and cut deep.

The trail, narrowing to the divide between the Red's Salt and North forks, sloped upward into a gently rising tableland, and at its apex they looked into a vast green plain, darkened where wind swept the grass, and luminous with flowers. Creeks were everywhere, bordered with big timber and running cold and clear. It was in the divide that the cavalry detail intercepted them.

The detail had apparently been out a long time and had done some riding. The troopers were unshaven and grimy, collars open to show their underwear and uniforms looking as if they had been hung out in a dust storm. The sergeant, an Irishman named Carney, hadn't been young in several years, a professional Army type Richards had seen many times: probably a better and more experienced leader than his officers, but without the education, financial means, or position to make it any further, unless everybody around him dropped dead all at once and he found himself promoted of necessity. He didn't shake Richards' hand, and he acted as suspicious of the drive as drives acted suspicious of Army.

It was not a routine patrol. Carney looked them all over and shook his head. "Well, you got one advantage," he told Richards. "How many men, fifteen, twenty? That's a hell of a lot of cows you're carryin'. I'd say you got weight of numbers with you, anyways." He looked back down the divide, where the wagons and remuda waited on the green plain.

Carney was not a big man, but his face was jowly and full and he seemed to sweat a lot. "All I know's what I'm told. Couple of small herds come into Fort Supply and says they been har*assed* by 'em. Wanted half the herd for lettin' 'em go through their land, that kind of thing."

"Comanche?" Richards said.

"Or Kiowa." Carney looked at him and shook his heavy head. "It don't make no difference. They all got a taste for beef."

"I expect you're on the lookout for 'em," Shiloh said.

Carney said, "They don't put theirselves out where we can see 'em, if they can git around it. Like I said, they was small herds was bothered . . . wouldn't of made a good third of yours. I see you got a heap of horse. They might be interested there, too." He looked at Richards levelly. "I don't want you to git any wrong idees. I ain't an escort. I'm out to keep Indians off and warn any of you trail drivers I run across. That's all I can do."

Uremáy said, "One would believe, when these Indians make trouble, you would help to make the way safe for us."

"One would believe so, grandpa," Carney said. "But what I do is what I'm ordered. And you ain't govermint business, you're private business."

"If we ever get to Fort Benton, these'll be government cows," Richards said. "We're grateful for the warning, anyway."

"I ain't finished," Carney said. "What I'm supposed to advise you, is go back south of the Red again."

"I'm headin' north," Richards said.

"I ain't blind," Carney said. "But if you go back and out through the Panhandle and then hit north you'll come into the road to Fort Elliot. They ain't offerin' escort either, but you might duck trouble that way."

"I didn't look for escort," Richards said quietly. "And I'm headed north."

Carney shrugged. "It's your herd. Neck, too."

"I'm obliged," Richards said. "Do you know anything about the Double Slash B outfit? They were a day or so ahead of us."

"Turned off, sensible," Carney said.

"Thanks, Sergeant," Richards said.

"Good luck," Carney said. "You might need it." He raised his hand to the detail and they pulled out, down the trail.

"My God," Shiloh said. "I wouldn't be in the Army if there was no work left for a man in life but lay down and cash in his chips. Well, I always felt Comanches was worthless as a four-card flush, and their dispositions ain't much to brag about, either. But by dang, I just as soon risk 'em as back up for 'em."

"Comanches I do not like, also," Uremáy said. "Nor do Comanches like me."

"Is that a fact?" Shiloh said. "I reckon what you're sayin' is that Mexicans don't take to Indians and Indians don't take to Mexicans. Don't you feel put out, Tiburcio. There's off times Comanches don't even care for other Comanches."

Uremáy looked questioningly at Richards. Richards said, "Put another man on the remuda and hold it with us. That goes for Sykes too. We'll just keep on like we been doin'. I been as far north as the Yellowstone, and one way or another I aim to see what it looks like beyond her."

"Army," Shiloh said. "Army. What in hell good are they, anyways? Come out and warn you and fog off in the other direction and let you go on to be massacreed."

Richards had no intention of backing off and he had no intention of giving up more than a couple of cows as pacifiers; he didn't feel stubborn about it, but he did feel it was trail crews giving in and acting scared that got the Comanche to getting bolder and nastier about what they called their rights. He would keep on the lookout sharp as he could, and take every precaution he could think of, but he wasn't going to go tailing it into some Army post to stay out of their way.

He did not scout as far ahead of the drive as he was accustomed to doing, but kept it within easy reaching distance. They made camps wherever the noon happened to find them, and usually there was water and wood, and if there was no wood there were plenty of prairie pancakes, buffalo chips. He had given up a cow or two to Indians before. It was a serious matter, giving up a cow, or having an Indian steal one, serious to drive crews because of the principle of the thing; most times, it wasn't their cow to give. They took buffalo calves and antelope when they could, but buffalo calves and antelope weren't contracted for and didn't belong to anybody, although the Indians figured they were all theirs.

He had had real Indian trouble only once, and that was in Arizona Territory with Apaches who ran off the remuda and killed four of his crew, and he decided not to look for trouble now. If it looked for him he would be ready, but he knew there wasn't any way to predict how it would go, simply because you never could outguess an Indian. A Comanche might start out mean as a stallion and end up mild as a sheep or the other way around, and while he was making up his mind which he wanted to be that particular day he could be anything in between.

Forty miles beyond the Red he was beginning to feel nothing was going to happen. He tried not to let himself feel like that because it was when your guard was down after a period of strained watchfulness that you got taken advantage of. He kept up a doubled nightwatch and he still wouldn't let the wagons and remuda precede the herd. He noted the lack of buffalo and game animals now, and how silent the country was without them, and knew that this was what besieged men meant when they recounted that moment when it was too quiet: the Indians had scared off all the game and birds.

He was riding point when Shiloh came in from the lead looking sober and jerking his head off to one side as if he was trying to loosen up a crick in his neck. Richards knew, right away.

He rode ahead with Shiloh. "How many?" he said.

"Take a look," Shiloh said. "I quit countin' at fifteen."

They were waiting strung out across the way, a small band of them in fringed leggings and blankets, some of them bare to the waist, with feathers drooping out of their skinned-back braided hair. "Get Uremáy," Richards said, and Shiloh went back, making dust. Richards took the buttermilk ahead at a slow walk; he didn't raise a hand or say anything, and before he reached them one of them cut out of the center of the band and started to meet him, keeping his horse at the same walk, and Richards figured it was whatever chief they were out under. He pulled the buttermilk in and let the chief do the coming, looking them over and counting one more than Shiloh had counted, and seeing that most of them had guns of one vintage or another in addition to bows, and lances decorated with colored feathers.

The chief wasn't old, squat and blocky like most Comanche, and like most Comanche the whites of his eyes were a peculiar color, more yellow than white and heavily veined. Like he had the jaunders and some busted blood vessels to go with it, Richards thought. When the chief raised his hand, he raised his, straight up, palm out, because it was the only greeting they all understood.

"Savvy English?" Richards said. "*Americano*. Gringo."

The Comanche looked at him for a long time before he answered. "*Hablo español.*"

Richards nodded. "*Un momento, amigo.*"

They sat there, looking at each other and not speaking, until Uremáy came up with Shiloh. "He says he speaks Spanish," Richards said. "I reckon my Tex-Mex'll do, but if there's any fine points to go over you can sharpen 'em up for me." He didn't take his eyes off the Comanche, but he said to Shiloh, "Drift the herd off the trail. Do it slow and keep 'em in tight. Take the remuda with 'em. Tell every popper be ready to jump."

The Comanche was talking. He had a good command of Spanish but he spoke it haltingly. Behind him the little band spread out across the trail shifted and wavered, not holding in their mounts. The sun flashed off the barrels of rifles, held cradled in arms braceleted in rawhide. Wind ruffled the brilliant dyed feathers of the lances.

"He wishes to smoke," Uremáy said.

They dismounted. Richards had wanted to get it over with fast, but if they wanted to smoke he could see it wasn't going to go that way. When they had squatted and lighted up, the Comanche rolled his yellow-whited eyes at Richards and told him they were hungry and they wanted *wohaw*.

All the plains Indians called beef *wohaw*, a made-up word

they had fashioned out of hearing the early freighters yelling *whoa* and *haw* to their teams. Out of the corner of his eye, Richards could see the herd being drifted off to the left and the vaqueros riding it tight. He knew the Comanche had been busy with their eyes too, counting the herd and the horses and the number of men. The Indian ponies stamped and snorted. Richards smoked a cigarette he didn't want because his mouth was dry and tossed his makings over to the chief. The chief, maybe misunderstanding and maybe not, picked them up and tucked them inside his blanket. Richards wanted to grin but he didn't let himself; he hadn't meant either tobacco or papers as anything but a gift of the moment.

He made out most of it, but he let Uremáy translate. The Comanche were a hungry people in these times. They were a peace-loving people, a people of good nature, who let the white men use their land to drive their *wohaw*. The white man made much money from this, but the Comanche was given nothing in return for the use of his land. The white man was using up the grass and driving off what buffalo he did not kill. The Comanche was hungry.

Richards told him directly. He was not obligated or obliged in any way to give out so much as a hoof or a tail. He didn't understand the peace-loving business, either. They had met some soldiers had told them the Comanche were acting warlike with some smaller herds up around Fort Supply. It didn't mean much if you were peace loving on the outside and thinking war on the inside.

The Comanche considered this for a long time. He was in no hurry, and he hunkered on his heels, looking first at Richards and then at the ground, measuring what he was going to say. When he said it, it was a declaration that he was not responsible for what other chiefs allowed their men to do. The fact remained that he had fifty people in his encampment, many of whom were women and children, and they were hungry.

"These cows don't belong to me," Richards told him. "They belong to the United States Government, and they're for some other hungry Indians. Blackfoot."

The Comanche's yellow eyes were dark with contempt.

"The Blackfoot stay on the reservation and the U. S. Government gives them beef," Richards said.

The Comanche leaned over and spat on the ground.

"But I don't like to see women and children go hungry," Richards said. "I'll give you two cows."

The Comanche digested this in silence. Then he held up his hand so that Richards could count fingers and thumb. "*Cinco*," he said.

Richards shook his head. "Two. I offered two."

Again the Comanche held up his hand.

Uremáy leaned to Richards. "Compromise, Ben. You offer two, he wishes five. Give him three."

"Three," Richards told the Comanche. "Three and no more. That'll feed you and you can make some jerky besides."

The expressionless face he looked into turned aside, in acceptance. Then the eyes swung back. "Horses," he said.

Richards stood up. The Comanche saw the severe set of his face. "This smoke's over. No horses." He held the Comanche's stare with his own. "And you get word to your people, wherever they are. You got three cows from me, and that's all you're getting. Make sure they understand that."

The Comanche looked satisfied, but Richards didn't know why he should, since he had asked five cows, and horses, and wasn't getting what he asked. "They will know," he said. "But I do not speak for my brothers, the Kiowa." He turned away.

"Wait a minute," Richards said. "Kiowa? Where are the Kiowa?"

The Comanche stood where he was, but he jerked his head around and looked at Richards. "My brothers the Kiowa are ahead. I do not speak for them."

"How many?" Richards said.

The Comanche's mouth pulled upward, raggedly, in a trace of a smile. Richards could see the gleam of his teeth. "Many," he said softly.

"I asked you how many."

Still smiling, the Comanche held up both hands. Then he lowered and raised them again. When he had done it ten times, he said, "Twice that," and this time Richards let him go.

They cut out three lame steers from the drag and the Comanche went away with them, the feathers fluttering, the rifle barrels picking up the light. When they had gone a short way they began to yell, racing their ponies and putting the steers into a run.

Richards stayed where he was, biting at the inside of his lip and thinking. Two hundred Kiowa. The thought was enough to give a man nightmares. A bunch of Comanche was bad enough, but he had settled with them now, and he had made no settlement with the Kiowa. Then he thought, what difference did it make? Two hundred crows taking flight all at the same time could bowl you over if you happened to get in their way. He wondered if Carney knew about the Kiowa. Probably not, or he would have said so. Just a big peaceful encampment, on the lookout for *wohaw*. But it would be kind of pitiful odds if Carney's detail came up on them and tried to shoo them off.

He had made up his mind not to go back and he was going to hold to it. He was going to go sideways, instead. At noon camps he called McLean in and told him, and Uremáy. They were going to have to look for something other than the regular ford of the Salt Fork.

When they broke camps he pointed the herd west, off the trail. He had both Shiloh and Corrigan on scout, not out of sight and within easy distance of the herd, so they could tail it back if they had to. He let some of the crew in on the news about the Kiowa: McLean, Corrigan, Hedges, and Sykes. Shiloh and Uremáy knew, but Uremáy could be counted on: the vaqueros weren't to know. Indian fighting was a large portion of the Mexican's history, and he had accepted his portion reluctantly. Even so, as Richards pointed out to Uremáy, if they ran into two hundred Kiowa, it wouldn't be much of a fight.

They crossed the Salt Fork just before dark, after following a well-defined buffalo trail five miles west of the ford. They were all a little jumpy, he guessed, except Sykes, who was carrying on like a three-ring circus. When things were running smooth Sykes was full of bile, but just let it simmer to the idea of a showdown and he took on like he was getting ready for a ladies' quilting bee. Richards hoped they weren't communicating the jumps to the vaqueros; as it was, the vaqueros were not only unsuspecting but were bragging about how Tres Reyes had put it over on the Comanche. By now they had it down to fifty Comanche who had only got one cow, and that a dragging cripple. By the time they got home, where they'd really have an audience, the Comanche would have been seventy-five in number and not got anything.

Richards was jumpy himself, and it was well after midnight before he had any urge to sleep. Even after the urge came he lay awake, feeling a little heavy because he had drunk too much coffee. He tried to think about Avis, about how she had looked, and felt, and nothing would come to him except the way the Comanche had smiled, the pulled-up lip and the gleam of the teeth. He slept and dreamed of it. An hour or two later, waking, he sat up. He could smell rain, and when he looked up at the sky he saw that a thick layer of cloud had covered it over and was moving fast to black out the stars that still showed.

The morning came gray, still full of the smell of rain, with great sweeping dense gray clouds that were fringed black on the edges and which seemed to overtake and tower over and fly under one another. He kept the herd pointed west, through a country of small sloping hills and good water. A few days west and then a turn north again ought to put them out of range of the Kiowa encampment.

When the rain came it was a downpour that flooded the low spots in minutes, a cold stinging rain. Yet Richards was glad for it. "A real goosedrownder," Shiloh said, trying to roll a cigarette. "The best goosedrownder I ever saw," Richards agreed. "And it's washin' out our tracks better than a scrub brush." "Don't thank me," Shiloh said, throwing the soggy cigarette down in disgust.

The rain lasted several hours and went away, rushing clouds and all, making way for a watery sun, but it came back in the middle of the night and fell as if it was making up for lost time. The cows were restless and kept getting up and lying down again; they tended not to lie out apart from one another so each had plenty of room, facing in all directions, but to gather together and face away from the rain. The misery was general and McLean contributed to it at breakfast by asking Richards if he had any idea where they were.

It made him sore, but he held it back and said matter-of-factly that he reckoned he knew his left foot from his right, and that they were due to cross the North Fork of the Red when they turned north.

"I say we're out in the Panhandle," McLean said. There was nothing defiant or smart about him, or even conjecturing; his voice was almost loose with indifference.

Richards saw Shiloh look up and the shifting eyes of the vaqueros, coming around to him questioning. "Quit talkin' like the Panhandle was the middle of the Pacific Ocean," he told McLean. "I expect I can still tell east from west."

McLean was grinning. "The sun comes up in the east and goes down in the west, don't it?" he said. "Or is it the other way around?"

Shiloh sighed. "No law says I got to listen, Frankie," he said. Richards ignored them both and finished his meal deliberately. But he rode out to the remuda ahead of McLean and sent Hedges in for chuck and so was waiting for McLean when McLean got there.

"I ain't set for an argument," McLean said when he saw him.

"Same here," Richards said grimly. "I never am. People know me well tell me there's one thing they can always count on with me: I'm peaceable as a new-dropped calf unless I am, as the sayin' goes, provoked out of my endurance."

"I didn't aim to do that, either," McLean said.

"No? What did you aim to do?"

"I aimed to ask a question and the only answer I got was some cross-footed directions about east from west. You can tell me now if you don't want to upend the crew. Are we lost, Ben?"

After a minute Richards said, "Do you know what a Kiowa is?"

"Don't joke me, Ben."

"That's the last thing in my mind. Will you give me an answer, straight. Do you know what a Kiowa is?"

"It's an Indian, or so I was told."

"You were told right," Richards said. "You want to add anything more from your great store of knowledge?"

"I don't know what you're gettin' at," McLean said.

"I reckon I forgot a long time ago how it feels to be as wild and woolly and full of fleas as you are," Richards said. "Even when I was your age, if somebody said two hundred Kiowa to me, I kind of stopped and thought about it. If it'll help your state of mind any, maybe you ought to know a Kiowa is something more than an Indian. He's the only Indian, outside of an Apache or a Comanche, that I don't care to bark my shins on if I got a choice. I'd just as soon figure a starvin' wolf or a sore sidewinder for my best friend. When a man doesn't have a steady line of work and regular meals like a popper or a plow-chasin' farmer, he gets to feelin' kind of nasty. Since Kiowa don't have any cattle except what they can steal, and wouldn't stoop to plantin' corn, their temper usually ain't the best. Now if you feel so strong that I got you lost somewhere in the Panhandle, you and Shiloh can cut out the M Bar L's this morning and strike northeast. I wouldn't waste a word to try and stop you."

McLean sat there, staring at him.

"And another thing," Richards said. "You're the first man with his lights turned up day and night I ever let stay in an outfit of mine. You'll be the last, too. You know what they do with hands like you, Frankie? They stretch you belly down over a log and whip hell out of you with a pair of leather leggings. It smarts enough so a man either gets some sense in his head and quiets down, or he takes a freight." Richards leaned on the horn; the rain ran off his hands and dripped down the buttermilk's withers. Then he made a mistake, and he knew while he was doing it that he was making a mistake. "You haven't made any trouble in this outfit, Frankie, except for me, and you were hot to make it for me long before you ever threw in with me. Whatever your reasons are, if you could kind of talk about 'em with me maybe it would clear this thing up once and for all, and you and me could start actin' like I expect people were meant to act: that is, decent to one another." Because it had come in his mind all of a sudden that McLean might have things to chew over that he, Richards, couldn't even begin to guess, and that he had nobody left to talk to about them.

"Don't get soft in the head on me," McLean said. His voice was sober, low pitched. "When I got any problems I work 'em out for myself. You been around old lady Dominguez too long.

I ain't got any confessions, and if I did, you don't look much like a *padre* to me. Anyway, you talk too much."

"I keep hopin'," Richards said, "that one of these days a word or two might get to you."

"Words are cheap," McLean said suddenly, raising his hand, pushing back the wet dark lock of hair, settling his hat over it.

"That's where you're wrong," Richards said. "Words ain't cheap. Sometimes they cost a man a lot. The only thing doesn't cost a man anything is to be mean and down, because that's the easiest way. That's what makes you cheap, Frankie."

He took his breath in sharp and short, so that it made a little whistling sound. "I'd ought to kill you for that, Ben."

"Maybe you ought to, but you won't," Richards said. "On account of I don't think you got the guts for it."

"Are you sayin' I'm a coward?"

"Take it however you want it. I expect I could call you out on the face of the threat you just made, but I don't aim to. Much as I like the odds on my side, it wouldn't be a fair enough match. And if you killed me, I don't expect it would make you any less cheap or any less mean, maybe more so, so I would of died for nothing." He smiled with conscious irony. "Nobody wants to die for nothing, I reckon. I won't forget you threatened me, Frankie."

The boy was staring at him, eyes suddenly feverish with something more than fury. He broke out incoherently. "Ben, for Chrissakes, I didn't mean that. You know I didn't mean it. Sometimes I think I must be crazy. I didn't want to come with you, I didn't want to be drivin' cattle, it all come at the wrong time, and sometimes I go kind of out of my head thinkin' about it and not knowin' what to do or what's goin' to happen, like I can't make up my mind whether . . ." He stopped, hacking it off short. Richards' face was neither puzzled nor severe, but patient, carved in an attitude of waiting. Having burst out in some inner ordeal, the boy now chopped it off as effectively as if he had been throttled. He saw something so close to gentleness underlying the hardcut cast of Richards' face that it came near frightening him. He did not want gentleness, but he needed it. He did not want understanding, but he needed this also. He did not want to speak, and yet to speak would have cut him free. He did not know how to approach or to accept gentleness, understanding, release.

"Ben, I didn't mean what I said. I swear to God. Will you forget it?"

"I'll forget it," Richards lied. So, Tiburcio Uremáy, we work closer and closer to the colors and shapes of your dream. His suspicion that something was eating holes in Frankie was now confirmed, but unless the boy was willing to talk about it, it didn't make any new rules for the game. McLean was holding out his hand, into the rain. "Ben, I'll try, I swear I'll try. I won't open my mouth except to say howdy. That's the truth."

"Sure," Richards said. He had heard McLean's promises before. But he leaned over and took the boy's hand and felt that it was shaking.

"I'll be kind of glad to get to Dodge," McLean said. His voice sounded shaky too.

"I expect I feel the same," Richards said.

The herd was moving out. Richards rode up on the right point, so preoccupied he didn't even look up when he passed up the swing. He would be gladder than McLean could ever surmise to reach Dodge and drop the M Bar L's, although he would be sorry to lose Shiloh and Corrigan. And Rojo. He spoke to the big steer when he reached the point, before he trailed out ahead of him. Rojo knew his name now, or anyway he knew there was a word and that it was always addressed to him, and sometimes he responded to it, flicking his tail high or swinging the massive spread of horn when he turned his head. He slogged steadily into the rain this morning and did not acknowledge Richards' presence or the word he had come to recognize. The herd was sullen, and so were the vaqueros: McLean had planted it in their minds Richards had got them lost. He figured the only member of the outfit wouldn't be happy about reaching Dodge was Rojo, and he felt, as he had felt before, not a pity but a *simpático* with the big *ladino*. You didn't humiliate a splendid brute like this with pity, no, but neither were you without feeling for him. Sometimes he wondered if Rojo remembered Jonah, or anyway remembered the man, and the horse, he had killed. There were moments his eyes looked long with memory.

The rain went on for two solid days, softening the ground and making the grass spring and glisten. You could almost see it growing. By the third day the crew was so wretched nobody was talking to anybody. Richards too was withdrawn and silent, barking orders when he gave them at all, but it wasn't just the rain, it was a hundred things hammering at his skull and pulling his thoughts. He had a few bad dreams when he slept and some even worse ones when he was awake, and he knew what a fool he was to have figured he was going to have a long summer to think about Avis in his off hours and take pleasure in his own misery. Now he found himself thinking not only about Avis, but about Cayetana and what had become to him in his present state of mind, the rest of those loco Mexicans, not to mention McLean and his revealing outburst. He kept as far from McLean as he could, because he figured if McLean wanted to talk to him McLean knew where he was.

There was sun at last, on the day he pointed them north again, and then east, toward Fort Supply. He knew they had cut successfully around the Kiowa threat, and that the rain which had near drowned them was a blessing. It had lasted just long enough to wipe out their traces before the ground began to get springy and hold water-filled footprints a coyote could have bogged in. The sun, with the world wet and gleaming, and the knowledge that they were headed back for the trail, made an immediate change in the crew. It didn't take them long to get back to normal again. As sullen and resentful as the herd had been and despite the fact that Richards was getting twenty miles a day out of it, it had taken on weight with all that fresh wet graze. But Richards began to trail behind the herd, and he sent Uremáy far out on the point, and it was for a purpose. The earth was so wet now that there would be no dust to warn of approach. Dust was a very good thing, in its way: it always told you somebody was coming, and Richards liked to be forewarned. Until the sun dried things out they were going to have to keep a sharp watch.

They felt they were safe by the time Uremáy pointed out the thick timberline which marked the North Fork of the Red. They had been nine days off the trail, and unless the Kiowa had figured their every move and were running ahead to anticipate them, the danger was over. He was out three lame cows, and he considered himself lucky.

Sykes had antelope ribs and steaks for chuck that night. Everybody was feeling so good they didn't even want to listen to Sykes and Shiloh hound each other, or play cards. It was enough just to lie back and look at the sky starred over and think about how clean the air felt after being washed and how secure life was when you had your belly full and a fire to warm you and a dry bedroll to get into when you couldn't prop your lids up any more. Richards went off to find Uremáy after chuck and found him lying apart, by himself, leaning on one elbow and smoking.

"You care if company comes?" Richards said.

"I would resent it," Uremáy said. "But as it is you . . ."

Richards dropped down on a corner of Uremáy's heavy woven poncho. "Looks like you wanted to be by yourself," he said.

"Listen, my gringo," Uremáy said. "In the event it is not known to you, all men are by themselves. Alone. There are times when other men around him are nothing more than a buzzing of flies." He settled himself and stubbed out his cigarette. "If you look from where you sit, you will see that a fire and the men around it are of much greater interest and importance than they are when you are with them. Everything is red and black and gray, with the great blackness around it. The movement becomes unreal, as if one had some control over it. As one might jerk the strings of puppets. Only the fire is real to me. So, Ben. How many miles to Dodge City?"

"About three hundred," Richards said.

"And then we will be at the halfway mark of our journey."

"Not exactly," Richards said. "Trail crews always like to think Dodge is halfway mark to wherever they're goin', unless it's Dodge itself, and then it's halfway home."

"Something is on your mind tonight, Ben?" Uremáy said.

"I seem to have something on my mind about ninety percent of the time and nothing but a big blank the other ten," Richards said. He wondered if he ought to tell Uremáy about McLean. He decided he wouldn't. Not about the threat, about the rest. But it wasn't really something between him and Frankie; he wasn't sure it was anything Frankie had wanted to share even with him, and he would probably be off the reservation if he talked about it. Minding other people's business only got you in over your head. On the other hand, if you minded your own exclusively, you got to feeling both repressed and depressed, man's nature being what it was. Men ought to be dignified and self-contained, instead of gregarious and egotistical. To put it plain, man ought to be something more than snoopy as an old coyote. It was funny how he didn't seem to feel right unless he was saddled with a dead horse a lot of the time. Maybe he just hadn't managed to adjust to his environment and never would. Richards felt kind of snoopy.

"We could cut into that ninety percent," he said. "If it ain't too personal to talk about, I mean."

"Such as?" Uremáy said softly.

"I was just wonderin' where Manuel Vega is tonight."

"In hell, I trust," Uremáy said, lying back and looking up at the sky. "You wish to know why I felt it necessary to pull him from his saddle and break his neck in so doing if it was at all possible. I make no secret of it. As you may remember, I hired Vega and Mendez one day when I was feeling generous with the *patrón's* moneybags. My heart is always open and bleeding for my countrymen. Such a misfortune. So. It is all of the simplest nature. This most dismal specimen of humanity, my countryman, looks too long where he should not look and thinks thoughts he should not think, and one day when we are out searching for my lost possessions he voices his thoughts." Uremáy cleared his throat. "I do not believe that he is the first man to have such thoughts, or that he will be the last, but such a man must learn not to voice his thoughts to me. I have a capacity for listening. This too can be a curse, believe me, *amigo*. So when this Vega, this pig among men, this *cabrone*, tells me his thoughts, I listen. What do I hear? I hear his innermost desires, impossible as they may be, and as his innermost desires cannot be carried to a conclusion by himself alone, he must of necessity have a companion for them. When the companion is La Morena Flor, then I feel I must kill this man, not so much for what he thinks, but that he dares say it aloud to me."

Richards looked down at him. He was lying prone, looking up at the sky, with his voice soft as a woman's, and no hint apparent of the lengths his rage could take him to. "You mean he said something about Cayetana? About him and Cayetana?"

"That is very good thinking on your part, my gringo. Be forewarned. Think what you wish, but be careful what you say to me."

Richards couldn't help smiling. Uremáy was an old bear, all right, but the talk brought up something that had been in the back of his mind ever since the night he had given Uremáy Cayetana's letter. It was something you couldn't even ask your own father, but nevertheless the thought was there. He said, "I'd give a lot to know how it's goin' at Tres Reyes."

"I would give all my teeth," Uremáy said. "And consume nothing but tequila until the day of my death." Then he said, as if to himself, "*Jesús, María, y Santa María de Guadalupe*." He turned his head and looked at Richards. "By the time we have returned to Tres Reyes, it will perhaps be resolved. I hope only that it is resolved for the good."

"And by the good, you mean in Cayetana's favor, I reckon," Richards said.

"The longer you stay with me the wiser you become," Uremáy said. "Distance is the plague of mankind. If man could fly, as the swallow, what would life be like then?"

"Twice as mixed up as it is now," Richards said.

"You may be right. But how many problems would be solved, how quickly. Do you know that you are a strange one, Ben? Either you rein yourself so tightly that there is no danger of your ever breaking free, or else you are without curiosity."

"Wrong on both counts," Richards said.

"Do you not lie awake at night explaining to yourself, and rejecting all your explanations as to the nature of the letter you found?"

"No, I don't lie awake," Richards said, smiling again. "I wonder now and then, but I learned early that wondering about something you got no way of knowing the outcome of doesn't get you across the creek."

Uremáy said, "Why did you do what you did, for her?"

"I don't know," Richards said after a time. "I reckon the whole thing kind of, well, plugged me. I never saw a woman come so close to faintin' right in front of me before. And then too, sometimes when I'm around her I figure somebody ought to do something so she doesn't have to carry that sadness with her like she does."

"So you see this?" Uremáy said.

"It's plain out," Richards said.

"No, it is not. The *patrón* does not see it. This is not because he is a fool, but because he is involved with his own affairs."

"I would of expected Cayetana was his affair. What about the Señora?"

"The Señora sees everything and knows everything. No, believes she knows everything. Behind the closed door of that room there are conspiracies which would put governments to shame. A great woman, the Señora. An admirable woman. If she could walk, God in His mercy knows what might befall us all." He crossed himself. "Now, Ben, whether or not you know it, you are drawn into Tres Reyes, and you must ask yourself if you will ever be free of it again. Or if you wish to be."

Richards said wryly, "Just because I happened to pick up that letter?"

"The single reason."

"It would of been found anyway. When the boys went down to bury that dead steer. They couldn't of missed it."

"Ah, but the *patrón* and I missed it," Uremáy said reasonably. "It was meant that you find it. This I believe." He closed his eyes. "Tell me what you see on Tres Reyes," he said. "Tell me what you think of the people of the big house, from day to day."

Richards began to roll a cigarette. "What do I see? Well, I see the Señora now and again, and she's a smart one. And so set in her ways I don't reckon she'd move for a prairie fire. I see Dominguez busy as a bumbler makin' honey, or I reckon in this case money, but square. I see the little daughter bein' cut off from everything but what she can make up to amuse herself at, when she ought to be havin' the time of her life, and unhappy about it. Or anyway unhappy about something." He lit up and looked at Uremáy. "And I see a *peon* boss doesn't miss a trick and probly knows more than all three of 'em put together about what the other one's thinkin'."

209

After a long time Uremáy nodded slowly, in assent. "And is that all you see of me?"

"No. I see too that however close the father and the daughter are, when the chips are down it ain't the father she goes to. It's the *peon* boss."

"And what are your thoughts on this?" Uremáy said.

Richards turned, watching him levelly. "I reckon you know what I think. But seein' how you treat people think their thoughts out loud to you, I wouldn't open my mouth for money."

Uremáy was smiling. "You believe that I am the father of La Morena Flor. I tell you that I am not, but that I wish I were. Does this satisfy you?"

"It clears up a point," Richards said. It was what he had been thinking about not two minutes before.

"It is a great pity, truthfully," Uremáy said. "I would have made her a splendid father. No. I have no children . . . well, that is not entirely true. None that I may claim, let us say. Natividad's fault, not mine. The poor woman wore out her knees, praying. She and the Señora, praying for the same gift. I believe the worn out knees may have hindered rather than assisted. Now, as to you. You wish to marry the *rubia* widow, do you not? But you are curious, more curious than the *patrón*, even, about La Morena Flor."

"A man's always curious about a beautiful woman, when he doesn't know much about her," Richards said.

"Let me advise you, *amigo*. No matter how much you think you know of a woman, there is always something to be learned. This is also true of horses. But it is as I said: you are bound to Tres Reyes now, by the simple acts of finding a letter and delivering a letter. Because of this, perhaps, you are entitled to know what went before, and I am the only man who can tell you. Yet, only if you wish to know."

"I reckon I would like to know," Richards said. But what was in him now was something more than curiosity. He had a feeling of depression, lying heavy in him, as if he had heard something as sad and incomprehensible as the song Cayetana had sung in the courtyard. Something he maybe wouldn't understand, and that would make it all the sadder. And a warning leaped in his brain, like a signal: he was not bound, no matter what Uremáy said, and he wanted no part of anything which might strengthen the tie at the very time he considered breaking it.

"It is a long story, my *gringo*," Uremáy said. "It is a long story because many things happened, and I cannot tell it all to you at one time. What my own eyes did not see was told to me by La Morena Flor, and what was not told to me my heart knew. I wonder only if I can tell you what it was like, that time in the old country, after the winter was done and the spring came and there were red poppies in the grass. Pastures such as you will see only in your own northland here, Ben, so that the poppies looked like blood spilled in the green and all the clouds appeared to slide down the hills, so fast they moved. I do not know if I can tell you how the air smelled, the country air where the black bulls lifted their heads, and the smell of the city, of spice and oil and flowers and dust and sunlight and churches, the smell of Seville in the spring. Well enough, then. It will be difficult to say this, but let us begin."

TWELVE

The man on the straw pallet was dried out with fever. The dryness was in the drawn skin of him, in the cracked lips and lusterless hair. The lids of his closed eyes were thin and parched. His breathing was shallow.

The heat was very bad. Bonaventure sat on a three-legged stool, against the wall. There was some coolness in the adobe. His head was tipped back and he breathed through his mouth. The sheen of sweat began at his hairline and ran down across his breastbone, where his shirt was open. At the foot of the pallet, Pedro Lozano, standing, had also opened his shirt, the light-blue cotton of the Rurales. He wore a wide belt with a pistol on it. He was a small lithe man with quick delicate wrists and a long mouth like a slash, and good teeth. He watched the unconscious man.

After a time he said in Spanish, "He opens his eyes now and again."

"Unh," Bonaventure said, not moving, not changing his position against the wall.

"Do you think he is awake, Aaron, when he does that?" Lozano said.

"Unhhh," Bonaventure said again, drawing it out this time. He was staring at the join where ceiling and wall met, on the opposite side of the room. The heat was all over him, like a pressure, crawling.

"Listen," Lozano said. "When he opens his eyes, as he does, speak to him."

"No use," Bonaventure said. He sat up slowly and scratched at himself, at the crawling sweat.

The woman came from the other room with water. Bonaventure looked at the *olla*. "Beer?" he said to the woman. She shook her head and went away.

Lozano wrung out a cloth and put it on the unconscious man's head. Instantly the prone body writhed away from the touch, as if it had been fire laid upon him. Bonaventure said, "No water's going to help him now."

"Perhaps it will bring down the fever," Lozano said. He continued to press with the wet cloth, and the body stopped twisting and turning and lay still again. Lozano poured water from the *olla* into a clay dish and soaked the cloth and wrung it out again, and looked at Bonaventure. "Try, now, Aaron. Try when he opens his eyes."

"All right," Bonaventure said, almost indifferently. He kicked his hat out of the way, where it was lying on the floor, and went to bend over the man. The eyes were wide open, staring up at him, and he knew they saw nothing. "Buster," he said. He stopped and scratched himself. "Can you hear me, Buster?" There was not a flicker in the upturned eyes; they were pale and hard as marble. "Buster, I hate to be the one to tell you, but you aren't going to make it. Can't you try and say something, while you still have time."

The eyes closed.

"It's no good, Pedro. What a hell of a cut of bad luck. Nothing but bad luck since I crossed the river."

Lozano looked at him, a quick, appraising look. "And some good, I should say, or you would still be trying to pry the bars out of Morisco's jail. Nor do I call it bad luck that our paths have crossed. Though I do not seem to be doing you a service here, with this."

Bonaventure picked up the *olla* but he only took a sip. The water tasted like the clay of the jar, red, earthy, stale. He put it down again. He wanted beer. "There's got to be a *cantina* in this place," he said. He got up and went through the curtain which hung between the two rooms and told the woman again. "*Cerveza.*" Again she shook her head, looking suspicious. He gave her some money and told her to go and get some. Her hand closed over the money, but the look did not leave her stolid face. She would have to be paid more, for the stabling and care of horses, for food, for drink, for allowing a man to die in her house, and she would have done none of these things if she had not been frightened of the Rurale uniform. When he went back, Lozano was drinking from the *olla*.

"Don't drink it," Bonaventure said. "I would lay odds whatever Buster's got he got from water."

Lozano drank. "You forget I am Mexican," he said when he had lowered the jar.

Bonaventure slumped against the wall. The effort of rising, walking, speaking to the woman, had exhausted him; he found himself staring at nothing in a stupor induced mainly by the heat but in part by frustration at the turn things had taken. It still seemed to him absolutely right and natural that he would have found Lozano, even in a place as big as Coahuila. He had half-expected to find him, just as he had expected he would find Buster sooner or later, only Buster was dying, so he guessed he had found him later, as late as you could get. Lozano was up around the border from time to time, in demand because he spoke excellent English. Mexicans and Texians still didn't think much of one another, and there were misunderstandings and murderings and thefts and captures which took an interpreter who could do something more than horse around with the bastard border lingo. Lozano ought to be an officer . . . he was the kind would have looked good years ago carrying a sword and wearing a plume in his hat, Bonaventure thought. But he guessed Lozano didn't much care about that kind of thing.

He had crossed from Nuevo León into Coahuila, following a

214

hunch more than anything else, and he finally struck a village where, yes, there had been a gringo, many weeks ago, many. They remembered him because he had stayed two days with the Roviras, trying to heal a gall on his horse, and he had bought a mule and paid in gold. Gold, Señor, true gold. He had ridden south when he left.

Many weeks ago. Still, Bonaventure took his time. Time was nothing in this country. Time was for people who were packed and crowded into cities and towns, where the black smoke of the new era, the new age of industry, thickened the air and houses sat one on top of the other. Time was not for this vast place of sand and brown hills and rivers and stones, of pockets of grass and trees laced along watercourses, of sky so huge there was no way of telling where it began and where it ended, of harsh sun and sandstorm, of quick rain coming in purple cloud moving down mountain passes, and red plateaus thick with pine and red rock, and wild timbered mountains where clouds hung below the trees and drifted into bottomless gorges, and sun-baked dun-colored villages lying under stark-crossed church towers and buzzards drifting on dark wings. Time had left no footprint here. There was a word for time, but the word had an echo of emptiness, like the country.

At every pueblo he asked. He asked children playing, old men, farmers working the stony soil of the arroyos, women making tortillas on the flat of their arms, wives grinding corn in stone *metates*, woodcutters coming down with their loaded mules, water carriers walking beside burros loaded with white clay jars. No one remembered, and they would remember a gringo. Then he knew Buster had been avoiding villages where he would be remembered. Buster had talked a lot about Mexico City, about how he was going to get there one day. The Rangers he bunked with believed him: Buster was foolhardy brave and did things on dares and when he said he was going to do a thing he did it. Buster had apparently cut down through Coahuila, traveling southwest, and then turned south to Zacatecas. But only because it would be harder to trace him that way; anybody else would just head south from Nuevo León.

Buster wasn't just anybody as far as Company B could see.

215

In the middle of a late May afternoon he learned from a village father that a Rurale troop had passed through that morning, heading northeast. Juan Sanchez' *grulla* had had an easy time of it so far, pulling green grass and eating cracked corn when Bonaventure could get it, and not lacking for water and never having to lose the wind Juan Sanchez boasted of. Bonaventure tested the *grulla's* long wind, turning him back and overtaking the tough, hard-riding Rurale troop at nightfall. There was a lieutenant named Garzas in command, and there was Pedro Lozano. The little Mexican sergeant threw both arms around him and it was kind of like coming home after you had been drifting around looking to find one. He told the lieutenant about Morisco, and the lieutenant shook his head and said some uncomplimentary things about local militia, and he told the lieutenant about Buster and the lieutenant frowned and said that it was an American matter, of course, but this (also of course) was the soil of Mexico, Old Mexico, his Mexico, and it seemed to him that the Rurales had some jurisdiction in the affair. When he headed south again Lozano was with him.

It went easier right away. He felt a greater freedom in the pueblos, when he let Lozano do the talking. He might have been Mexican himself, except for the Texian rig, but he wouldn't get rid of it. Part of him had to stay Texian, and most of him had to stay Ranger, he didn't have any control over that. But let the blue Rurale uniform come into sight and people ran into doorways that didn't have any doors, women and children clustering, while the men stood in the sun and waited, and answered the questions. No, Señor. No gringo. And Bonaventure knew they were not lying, that they would not lie to Lozano as they might have lied to him.

A woodcutter told them. He had been in the mountains, he and his sons and grandsons, two young men and three *chicos*. They returned to their village with a string of six burros, patient under the lengths of trimmed wood cradled on either side. The wood smelled fresh and resinous, the cut ends creamy white. They had passed through Huarabachi, where the old man had a sister, a small pueblo, Señores, not even a church, and very poor. There was a gringo there; the whole village talked of it. He was with a woman whose husband was away working for a *hacendado* far south, and he had offered the woman money.

Huarabachi was a clump of buildings set under the shelter of a brown mesa, some adobe, some nothing more than brush *jacals*. There was water running by it and willow and cottonwood lining the steep banks. A wind sprang up as they forded, clacking old seed pods against one another and swirling dust up off the mesa. When they rode up the track between the houses the blowing earth gusted into them, so that the horses gaited on the bias, swinging from it. Grainy, like salt, it forced its way through the lips and grated between the teeth and crusted at the moisture of the eyes.

Children darted and were called back and men came, caution stamping their faces. Lean dogs ran snapping at the hoofs. Lozano shouted into the spiraling dust. *"Hay un hombre Americano, aquí. Un gringo."* It was statement, not question. An old man with sunken eyes and a trembling gray stubbled chin raised his arm and pointed down the street.

The house had no doorway, only a tattered sun-bleached curtain which bellied inward. It was the last house in the line, set somewhat apart, with a crude corral off to one side. There were a horse and a mule in the corral. A raunchy spotted dog slept on a pile of stacked wood.

No expression showed in the women's eyes. They moved from Lozano's face to his uniform, flickered over Bonaventure, and returned to hold Lozano's. She did not speak, drawing aside the curtain. Lozano went to tie the horses to the corral rail. When he entered, Bonaventure was standing in the second of the two bare rooms hung with saints and gourds and chili peppers, looking at the man on the pallet.

The woman turned away. She said in a flat voice, *"El muerte es en esta casa."*

"Talk to her," Bonaventure said. "Find out." He was kneeling by the prone man. Lozano and the woman went into the other room. Outside the wind howled, driving around corners. The hot stillness of the room held the sour smell of oil, the dry smell of chili and corn and the beaten earth of the floor. It was as if the oil was trapped in the airlessness.

Bonaventure checked breathing, pulse, and pulled back the lids. No movement of eye followed his passing hand.

Lozano came back. "He's been here a week. She says her husband is gone, and he offered her money to care for him and the string until he could go on his way again. She says he has not eaten in four days."

Bonaventure, stooping, straightened, squatting on his heels. The woman had said it: death is in this house. Buster, you damn fool, you crazy damn fool. And you didn't make it to Mexico City. It seems, in all this time, you could have made it to Mexico City and back again.

"She says he was not riding south, but north," Lozano said softly. Bonaventure glanced up at him but he didn't say anything. Then he tried saying Buster a few times, but he knew there wasn't going to be any answer.

Lozano went to work, raising the unconscious man and stripping away the filthy shirt. Only when the water touched him did the man stir; the eyes opened and closed, opened and closed, the cracked lips fell apart. Then nothing. Once or twice he opened his eyes for a long period. The lids moved over them slowly, blinking.

The woman came with beer, in a clay jar. She was a thin woman, young and straight and hard, looking pure Indian. Bonaventure drank beer too quickly and felt it swell his belly and the gas of it come up in his throat. It made him sweat more. The sound of the wind made him sweat.

At sundown he stood in the doorway, with the curtain pulled back. There was no fragment of cloud. On the mesa the dust still veiled up and the sky looked rusty through it. The first star was enormous and very white on a field still touched with the pearly luminescence of daylight. When the wind died, a cold like the cold of snow began to move down, blade-sharp in the dry air, in the blue shadows. The mesa was suddenly white rock with a queer heavy strata of jet black, like onyx, zigzagged through it in a wide vein. The village was quiet and the stars lay over the black and white mesa which sheltered it, and he could see mountains dark against the greenblue line of color on the horizon. The black oblongs and rectangles of doorways bloomed yellow, throwing slanting lines of light on the ground, outside. Inside, the woman set out food: beans hot with chili and a strong gristly meat that might have been goat. Bonaventure sent her for more beer and watched the man on the pallet.

Buster, old man, how much longer? How much longer? Buster, I wish you could tell me, I wish you could say it.

The women came with the beer and stubs of candles. Bonaventure could hear the dying man breathing. He had not been aware of this until now. Lozano also noted it and bent to look into the still face and found nothing more or less than was there before and sat to finish his meal.

"You know what I would like," Bonaventure said. "Among a lot of things, I mean. I would like Morisco to stop me on the way back. So I could hold up the money and show him. He was interested in the money, when he thought I robbed the bank. Only I would want you with me when I did it."

Lozano did not smile. "There will be no Morisco there."

"I wouldn't want to see him in trouble," Bonaventure said.

"No?" Lozano looked up grimly. "Lieutenant Garzas will see that he has trouble."

"Militia have a hard enough time of it."

Lozano shook his head. "I sometimes wonder at you, my friend. What kind of man are you? You do many things it would be hard for other men to do, or you would not be a Ranger captain. I see you are very tough and very just. But I see also that there is a softness in you . . . no, I do not wish to offend you, Aaron. You come into this big country of mine, and it can be a hostile country, but you do not think of this, no, you think only of this man who has deserted your ranks, and you will stay on his trail until you find him if it spends ten years. But, on the other hand, you do not wish Morisco's head brought to you in a sack. You have pain at the thought that you must return and confront Ramón Dominguez with this evidence, and I do not know if it is because you do not wish to face Ramón Dominguez or if it is because the little daughter is in your mind. Or both."

"Both, maybe," Bonaventure said. "You ever see her, Pedro?"

"No, but I have heard. And if you think what I believe you

219

think, you would do well to quit the Rangers and take this money and set yourself up as a wealthy suitor."

"On fifteen hundred dollars?" Bonaventure said. "On Ramón Dominguez' own fifteen hundred dollars?"

Lozano was still grim. "And we will never know how much more."

"Not much more," Bonaventure said.

"No? Why not?"

"Because where could Buster spend it? And I don't reckon even a man like Richards would be worth more than a couple of thousand to Dominguez."

"This Richards. I never saw him. He worked herds down here, when he was young, with the brothers Torres. You know him?"

"We've met," Bonaventure said. "I know him by reputation more than anything else. Not that there's much to know about him. We checked into all that. His family moved from the Connecticut Valley to Indiana, and then to Texas when he was around eight or nine. So I expect you could call him a native Texian. He fought with Hood and got hurt early and that was the end of it. He's fought with, and against, your people too, Pedro. I expect we all have, at one time or another. And all the rest is trailing those damn cows, and you can look at it two ways: either it's a poor beginning and a poor middle and a poor ending, or maybe it's to his credit he lives as he wants to, with no attachments. Take your choice."

"And in all this, no woman?" Lozano said softly, dubiously.

"A woman was the trouble, in Galveston. Four months in jail, and then he was tried and acquitted. Maybe he was skittish for a while afterward, I don't know, but he didn't cut over the border or anything . . . he just went on like he always had and ended up at Tres Reyes, and I expect that's some kind of reward for being square in this world."

Lozano looked down and watched Buster Lyons dying. "And this man, also, his trouble is a woman."

Bonaventure drank some more beer. "If it hadn't been for a woman, he might have died here all by himself, is that it?"

Lozano was shaking his head. "*Pobrecito.* If he had kept his tongue in his mouth, where it belonged. And now you will never know what passed between him and Ramón Dominguez, unless Dominguez will tell you."

"I think I will tell *him*," Bonaventure said slowly. "Because I think I know. And when I tell him what I think I know, he will tell me. Even if he denies it, he will tell me, there are ways in which he will tell me."

"Yes," Lozano said. "The sign of the shifting eye. The sign of too much protest. The sign of the lie, where one traps himself. What is wrong with this man Dominguez, Aaron?"

"He has always had the best there is. He believes you can buy anything with money."

"Indeed. And this last . . . is it not the truth?"

"It's the truth. Look, you can even buy a Texas Ranger. A Texas Ranger enlists for a year and draws two dollars a day and furnishes his own horse and doesn't even have a flag to ride under. But Buster is the only Ranger I ever knew was bought. Not only bought, but arranged the buying himself."

"But how?" Lozano said. "If Richards was clear . . ."

Bonaventure closed his eyes. "Richards was clear, Buster was smart, Dominguez was stampeded. The details need working out, but I expect I can see how it was done. And Richards never knew it or needed to know it, or anyway that's what I believe about him."

"And once Buster had arranged these details, he made his mistake, no?"

"Not no. Yes. He told a woman and the woman wanted to go with him and when he went with only the promise to send for her she knew he was lying and came to me."

"This woman. Some *puta* of the town."

Bonaventure seemed to be thinking. Then he said, "As a matter of fact, the respectable wife of a respectable merchant in San Antonio. A whore has a kind of code, I expect . . . cross her and she figures that's the way the luck is running and goes on looking for another chance. But it's dangerous to confide in a respectable woman. Because when it doesn't go her way any more she'll sacrifice anything, even her good name, to get square."

Lozano gave a grunting laugh. "You are saying that respectable ladies are dangerous, then, Aaron, and sick with vengeance."

"When they're sore at you," Bonaventure said, scratching his head. "She was sore at Buster."

Lozano said, "But you have pity for Buster, do you not?"

Bonaventure glanced at the still figure in the corner. "I don't know. Now. In the beginning I was spitting nails. The Rangers is my life, or the biggest share of it. What hurts them hurts me. Then after I thought it over it interested me some . . . Buster always interested me, in the sense that he was a little crazy. I expect I don't much like seeing him die like this. But sorry for him?"

"To die like this," Lozano repeated. "With a fire that consumes him and fifteen hundred dollars he will never enjoy hidden in the nose bag of a spent horse. Why do you think he was riding north, Aaron? Do you think he planned to return?"

"I don't ever expect to know," Bonaventure said. "He had all the time he needed, to get where he was going. He didn't go. Maybe he was sick for a long time. Maybe he had time to think."

"And when you write your report," Lozano said, "this is what you will say: that he was returning."

Bonaventure shot him a long look. "It appears so, doesn't it?" He got to his feet. The cold was coming into the room now, routing the trapped heat of the day. He took his own clean shirt and blanket and went to Lyons. When he raised him, Lyons' eyes opened again and the cracked lips parted. There was for the first time a thing which might have been recognition, or a level of it, in the marbled eyes. Bonaventure reached out for the *olla* and it was beer, but he poured a little into the palm of his hand and dripped it over the parched mouth. The head turned away from it and then turned back, seeking. Lozano came with the water. And Bonaventure leaned into the foul stale breath and heard the first words, not spoken, but pushed up out of the throat, the collapsing lungs.

"Bon— Don't want . . . die."

"We won't let you die, Buster," Bonaventure said.

The eyes closed again. Bonaventure passed his hand across the mouth and felt nothing and bent his ear to find the heart beat and there was none. He looked up at Lozano.

Lozano crossed himself. He whispered it. "Do not tell her, until the morning. She will not want a dead man in the house."

"Will they let us bury him here?"

Lozano shook his head. "It is *campo santo*, holy ground. They will not want him."

Bonaventure was standing. "On the way back, then. Because we'll sure never get him home."

"Home?" Lozano said. "Yes, you pity. Now I will risk offending you, Aaron. There is nothing more to be done. We will sleep."

He spread his blankets on the floor. Bonaventure took his blanket back from Lyons' pallet, but he didn't lie down. He sat on the stool again, pulling the blanket around him. Lozano blew out the candles. After a time, he snored.

He sat staring into the darkness. There was no window in the room, and the dark was furry black, a strange uncomfortable black. No light showed under the curtain between the rooms; the woman too had gone to bed. He liked hearing Lozano snore. He was not certain he could have stayed in this black furry room, with no sound but his own breathing; even in the dark a man liked to open his eyes and see some essence of light, to know that light was there and that more would come. What was your name again, Buster? . . . a name you didn't like and wouldn't use, Barent or Boynton, something with a B, that boiled down. It will be on your record: Private Barent-or-Boynton Lyons, enlisted Company B, let's see, 1874, early, under Captain Aaron Lightbourne Bonaventure, in the city of San Antonio in the State of Texas. Died Coahuila, in the Republic of Mexico, whatever the date is, June . . . is it June? . . . 1875. And in between did some things to be remembered for. Shot some Comanche and captured some. Was with me when we took that road agent, Judge his name was, a funny name for a road agent. Made a one-man charge on some Mexican cow thieves were holed up where they couldn't be got at, and scared them so bad they gave up. To be remembered for. Bilked a man out of money, a little blackmail to get yourself some easy living and found dying was easier. And quicker. And cheaper. Swore an oath and lived by it long as you could, and deserted Company B. Something to be remembered for.

He slept. In the darkness the stars were rushing toward the

morning, and while there was no morning in the room when he woke, he knew it was at hand. There was light now, a thin crack of it showing under the curtain. He was stiff, his back felt as if it had broken clean in two, across the middle. He gripped it in both hands and said "God" between his teeth. Lozano was awake, stirring. *I would sell my soul for coffee.* He did not speak to Lozano. He pushed through the curtain and saw the woman crouched at a small fire built upon the dirt floor, near the doorway, so that the air pulled out the smoke. *"Buenos días,"* he said. *"¿Café, Señora? ¿Chocolate?"* The stolid face turned up to him, the head moved negatively. He staggered around the fire and out into the coldest part of the night, the time before dawn. Two days here and no coffee to be found. What a country, my God, what a country. He stood leaning against the crazy-cut timbers of the corral, holding the small of his back. Whatever was happening in the sky, where the night went away, had thrust the mesa up black, as if it had been layered on the grayness. He liked the cold, it felt clean. Overhead stars were scattered and fading. He saw the light come, not in the east, from its source, but in the west, where it arched to touch first white and then pink on the mountain peaks. Suddenly he could find no more stars. A rooster crowed and a cow bawled. The light washed down the mountains and the top of the mesa began to burn silver. In the corral the mule got to its feet.

He went inside again. The woman had beans for him. Lozano came out and they looked at each other, silent. He had slept in that room, with Lozano, and with a dead man. Lozano had snored, but the dead man did not make a sound in the furry dark. Lozano told the woman. A small fear showed in her eyes, flicking fast, when she crossed herself.

"Let's get out of here," Bonaventure said. He went into the other room, to do what had to be done.

Lozano came in. "Will you pay her with the gold?" he said, standing, watching.

"I'll have to, U.S. coin's no good to her. I'll make it up. I expect Texas owes her something."

"Aaron, leave her the horse. It will mean more to her than the money. We will take the mule, he is in better condition."

"And what will the husband think, when he comes home and finds his woman with gold, and a horse?"

"He will think good fortune has descended upon his house in great measure," Lozano said.

Bonaventure stood up. Lyons' body was wrapped, stiff, in the old blanket. He went and picked up his war bag and Winchester and handed them to Lozano. Lozano had put on his big gray hat and the crossed bandoliers of cartridges. "Tell her to burn this straw," Bonaventure said. From Lyons' *morral* he took two five-dollar gold pieces. He stood holding them in his hand, staring at them, tossing them a few inches into the air and hearing them clink together when they struck his palm. When Lozano came in from saddling, Bonaventure handed him the ten dollars.

"We are short of beans," Lozano said, looking at the gold as Bonaventure had done. "Perhaps she will give us some."

"I don't want beans," Bonaventure said wearily. "I want bacon and bread and coffee. And we need a shovel."

"I have the shovel. The handle is broken," Lozano said. "So I shall pay now, with the gold of Tres Reyes."

Bonaventure put the strap of the *morral* over his arm and stooped to lift the wrapped body, swinging it up and over his shoulder. When he came out the woman stood waiting, looking at him, with no change of expression. But she said, "*¿Es verdad, Señor? ¿El caballo?*"

"*Verdad*," he told her. "*Gracias, Señora, mil gracias.*"

You don't weigh anything, Buster. You wasted away to nothing, the heaviest part about you was that gold.

When he lowered Lyons' body across the mule the brim of his hat flapped up and stayed up, in the first wind. Dust came around the corner of the corral in a lifting burst, graying the shaking leaves of a single tree. They put their heads down, swinging the horses away from it.

"Sun," Lozano said, squinting at the running pale light at his feet.

"Wind," Bonaventure said.

They mounted. The *morral* was wrapped in Bonaventure's rolled blanket. Lozano led the mule, burdened with Lyons' body, the bent, broken shovel, the *aparejos* with beans and tortillas.

225

"There is no help for it," Lozano said. "We must take water from the river."

At the creek they let the horses and the mule water. Bonaventure went down among the salt cedars and filled the canteens. The wind was cut off here, under the banks, but when he returned it struck him with force, tearing at his hat, blowing the stinging sand into his face. He took off his scarf and lashed his hat on with it, tying the ends under his chin. Lozano had tightened the chin straps of his gray *sombrero*. The wind seemed to come from all directions, and Bonaventure glanced up at the mesa and saw the earth belly and sail, a fine drift of it shifting off and blowing to powder. He rode head down, cursing, feeling the grit collect in the creases and hollows of his skin.

By the nooning they had outrun wind and dust and come to a dry creek in the foothills. The hoofs flicked stones. Ahead there was a pass through the high hills, sunlight pouring down it. They went up, into the pass, and from its height looked down into desert and mountains circling brown and cracked with arroyos, blue where the direct light had not yet touched.

"Here," Bonaventure said.

Lozano tied the horses and unroped the shovel, but Bonaventure took it. "Then I will take my turn," Lozano said.

Bonaventure didn't let him. It had rained in the heights but the earth was hard. He needed a pick. He stripped out of his shirt, soaking sweat, and wound his scarf around his hand, and when it was finished it was too shallow, but it was all there was. He lifted the blanketed body and set it in and saw that Lyons wasn't going to straighten out, but would lie there with a great concave curve in his midsection from hanging over the mule, and shoveled the dirt back. Lozano began to carry rocks. When the dirt had been shoveled, Bonaventure sat for a while, knees up, staring at the earth between his boots. Then he got up and went for rocks. When they were done, Lozano crossed himself, and after a while Bonaventure did the same.

They rode down out of the pass. The country looked big enough, far enough, to see to the Bravo. But it was a long way ahead, a lot of miles. A lot of miles, a lot of days, a lot of nights, since he had lain in that wash, watching an outlaw steer, watching a woman, waiting to cross the river.

"There," Lozano said, swinging his arm.

He had to look a long time, to find it. He brushed at the sand which had collected in the corners of his eyes. He licked sand from his dry lips. Then he picked up a glinting in the still, hot air: the glint of a metal bell in a church tower. He could see the tower and a second, its twin. But the pueblo around it was the color of the earth, the color of Mexico. Beyond, there was a blurred line of green, where trees would be, and water. They came down into the flatland, riding together, Lozano leading the mule.

"This country," Bonaventure said.

Lozano smiled crookedly, showing his fine white teeth. "Have a care, Aaron. My country."

"I was only about to say it seems to me always to be . . . well, to be waiting for something."

Lozano glanced at him, still smiling. "My poor patient country, waiting. Always waiting."

"But for what?" Bonaventure said.

"¡Huy! For something great and good to happen to it."

"Is that it? I don't expect it will ever get ruined, then, will it?"

"If you mean will we ever be as zealous, as industrious, as . . . venturesome, as *Tejians*, perhaps not."

Bonaventure saw the crooked smile had not gone away and that it was bitter now. "Do you still hate us, Pedro?"

"You are my friend," Lozano said.

After a moment Bonaventure said, "I am honored."

"We are two people, Aaron."

"It will change."

Lozano shook his head. "There will be changes. But in the heart of my country, the living, bleeding heart, no."

"Only the waiting, eh?" Bonaventure said.

"The waiting is as old as my people. They would not know what to do without it."

"I'm grateful to you for what you did, Pedro."

"It was little. And we saw each other."

"You'll cross the river again."

227

"No doubt. Your border towns draw me, with their little lusts. And one day I shall go to this ranch of the Three Kings and look upon this man Dominguez. And his daughter. But it will be far behind your seeing of them, Aaron."

"Maybe not." Bonaventure shifted in the saddle. "Maybe not. I have to make a decision before I get back."

"Upon what matter?"

"On whether I ought to face Dominguez with this now, or wait until Richards gets back from his trail drive."

"Aaron . . . I did not ask you before. It is not my concern. Is it known among the Rangers? About the money?"

Bonaventure shook his head. "No. Nobody knows but you and me. And Dominguez. And the woman who knifed Buster. All Company B will ever know is that Lyons deserted the ranks."

"And this Richards. Will he stay with a man who has bought him, if he knows the truth?"

Bonaventure drew a long breath. "I don't know that. How could I know?"

"Then you may be driving him from his work, his position, if you tell him."

"Yes," Bonaventure said. "That is what I will have to decide."

"I see water now," Lozano said. "There, beyond the green. We shall rest there, Aaron, and eat well in the village, and in the morning we will go north and one day we will come to the river."

There was smoke standing straight up in the windless air. The horses lifted their heads, smelling water. They took their time, crossing to the brown pueblo under the twin towers.

THIRTEEN

Richards rode down the slope and took in the look of the river with weariness pulling him slump-shouldered in the saddle. After a time, shaking his head, he said aloud, "Well, they ain't boggin' any further, anyway." He raised his voice. "Shiloh."

Shiloh came up out of the river, making his third crossing. "Ain't that hell's own business, though?" he said.

"Could be worse. Hellish part is the time it's goin' to take us to get 'em out. Just keep 'em movin' fast as you can and we'll worry about the boggers later. Any word from Uremáy?"

"You can see his spread-out, from the far side," Shiloh said. The horse turned with him, knowing its work, and went back into the river on the flank. Shiloh's yell came drifting up the bank, over the bawling of the cows. "Hoo, damn you, hooooo, fog it there, cows, or you be settin' till doomsday."

Richards counted twenty-three cows bogged to the belly in the quicksand. They stood lowing, while the herd, moving fast, worked around them. Several hundred yards upstream Uremáy, with the smaller split of the herd, was having the same trouble.

229

They had divided the herd hoping that one or the other of the crossings might prove easier, and so that the sheer weight of numbers wouldn't roil the quicksand and get it sucking all in one place.

The Washita had given them no trouble. It was deep and the banks were slick and they skidded into it, but they had hit it at a time when it had calmed down from high water. Richards was feeling good about the crossings, but when he saw the condition of the South Canadian he knew he had been feeling good too soon. The water was very low, not more than a foot of it, but a cautious test on Plácido told him that what lay under it was a bottomless ooze that only speed would get them through. They would have to push the herd in a few at a time, on the run, and hope for the best.

Normally the herd went to a river thirsty, but Richards decided this was one time there would have to be an exception. Any cow which hit the water and stopped for a drink would be stuck where it stopped. There was a creek two miles south of the river. They watered the herd and split it, and by mid-morning the advance was put into the South Canadian running. There was no turning back, although they made a try at it, bawling and complaining. As long as they picked up their hoofs they were all right, but if they hesitated they were trapped.

The heaviest steers sank first. From the bank, Richards saw Rojo bog halfway across, the great spread of his horns raised high in the sunlight and his voice belling.

In the beginning, feeling the shifting sand take them, they fought. But once held they ceased to struggle. They sank to their bellies, when their own dispersed weight stopped them. If the river had not been so low they would have drowned. The horses moved quickly, knowing the danger, but they gave out rapidly under the strain and had to be changed often.

Richards thought they would never stop coming. In bunches of a hundred they rushed across, leaving the big ones bogged. When things went well, he forgot the size of the herd. When there was trouble it seemed to him he was bossing every longhorn in the world. Moving upriver, he found four M Bar L bulls trapped along with ten or twelve steers and cows, and a shot horse out of

Uremáy's mount. It had fallen and broken a leg trying to get out of the mire. It was the first horse they had lost.

A vaquero named Díaz came up to him when the last of Uremáy's split was crossed. "Señor Ben, we must take rest. You know what it will be, getting these sons from the mud."

Richards shook his head. "No time, little brother. We're goin' to be haulin' hide till dark as it is." He raised his hand to Uremáy. Uremáy's face told how he felt for the lost horse. "Luck, Tiburcio. Stay in touch with me." He went back down to his own crew, seeing the herd spread out across the river, but not grazing because it was still nervous from the crossing.

Sykes and Hedges had gone downriver to try to find a safe ford for the wagons. If they got stuck they were on their own. Until the boggers were out, Richards couldn't spare a man. He put three vaqueros with his split of the crossed herd and pulled his crew back to the bank.

"Ropes and hobbles," he told them. "Shiloh, let's see what you and me can do with the old red."

Shiloh said, "I ain't thump hearted with anticipation."

"Anyway he can't kick you," Richards said. "Let's go."

They peeled out of everything but pants and went into the water, into the treacherous soft suck of the bottom, while the horses waited riderless. Richards came up along Rojo's left flank, putting his hand out on the red hide and slapping it lightly. "You behave, now, old *ladino*. We'll see what we can do for you." He backed off and slipped the knot in his heavy work rope and backed some more, judging what it was going to take to lay the rope over the horns. He settled it on the first cast and drew it tight and saw the massive head swing to him and the killing rage in the wet black eyes. *You blame fool critter, I'm only tryin' to lend you a hand.* He waded out with the rope and hitched it to the saddle horn of the big pulling horse called Pieface. Men converged on the single rope, cinching their own ropes to it and then to their saddle horns. Richards slid back into the river, hearing Shiloh's soft, dumfounded voice.

"My Christ, Ben, I can't even lift his tail. Give me a hand, will you?"

It took both of them to pull Rojo's tail up out of the bog. When

231

it was free they coiled it up on his rump and tied it with a hobble rope. Richards signaled Corrigan and when Corrigan reached him, stationed him at the left rear leg. Shiloh and a vaquero began to push at Rojo, trying to rock him, while Richards and Corrigan burrowed in the mud at rear and front legs. In under the horn, while Rojo bawled his protest, Richards could feel himself go to the ankles in the pulling ooze. But he was a man, he was light, and he could work back out. His hands went deeper and deeper, trying to get the foreleg free; he held the rope between his teeth, while the sticky bottom roiled and swirled around his arms. He felt the hoof at last, and the clove of it, and let the rope fall out of his teeth and kneed it down, feeling the stinging salt of his sweat in his eyes, and worked the rope through the clove of the hoof. He doubled the leg and snubbed it short and kept pulling the quicksand away with arms and hands aching, until Corrigan grunted at him and he knew the rear leg was snubbed. Then he yelled at Shiloh, and pushing, pulling, they threw the outraged red steer on his left side and went to work the right legs free and snub them.

When it was done they staggered up out of the mud and into their saddles. The work rope had six ropes on it, and six horses ready to pull. He drew Pieface in tight with his knees and barked "now" and the horses strained off at as much speed as they could get up.

Rojo came up out of the quicksand, legs snubbed, tail coiled, savage in his fury. They skidded him up the bank and on dry ground. "Get those ropes off, and then lean forward and shove," Richards warned. He drifted his work rope off the horns and saw the dismounted crew scatter to saddles. Rojo flashed to his feet. Richards had barely put the horse to moving before the steer charged him.

The horse outran him. Richards grinned to himself, leading Rojo, thinking the *ladino* was maybe humiliated more than anything else. Around him the crew cheered and raced, trying to draw Rojo, but Rojo had fastened on Richards and nothing swayed him off. Richards ran him a while, kind of enjoying it, leading him away from the herd, but pretty soon it came to him that rather than being beat out from his time in the quicksand, Rojo was keeping up with him and showing no sign of slowing down. The red's endurance raised his admiration, but he was feeling beat out himself, and there were still more cows in the mud than he liked to think about. He drew Pieface up and backed him into a tight fit of grouped trees and watched Rojo come to a grinding halt. Stopped cold, the red lowered his head and began to slash at the earth with first one horn and then the other. Stones flew. Then, warily, looking as if he was thinking every step of it, he circled the snug little grove, never taking his eyes off man and horse. Richards knew a small chilling moment of total aloneness, when Rojo crossed at his back. There was no entry for the horns; Richards' feet were touching wood on either side of Pieface.

Rojo came around again. Still eying Richards he made a violent cut at the nearest tree, sinking a horn in the trunk and shaking so that the whole tree looked to tear out.

Then he withdrew. He stood and looked at Richards for what seemed a full minute. He turned and began to walk off, back to the herd. When Richards passed him on the return, he was grazing, calm and indifferent, and did not lift his head.

Shiloh was back in the river. "Meant it, didn't he?" he grunted when Richards came in with the work rope. "I'm glad you was forkin' a saddle, and not on your bootheels. You looked kind of silly ridin' around out there just about mother naked with that big old steer tryin' to get his horn in your gizzard."

Richards handed him the work rope. "Let's see how you do, ranahan."

Shiloh's steer didn't chase far, but it chased. Most of the bogged steers were so mad at being stuck and roped and dragged that they were ready to take it out on the first horse, the first man, within charging distance. Richards could remember the time a big black had bowled over the chuck wagon and got a horn in one of the mules.

By late afternoon the crew was coming up out of the river stooping. They were all experienced at working boggers, but they didn't do it often enough. Grimacing under the prod of his own aching back, Richards thought what life would be like without a horse. A cowman spent his whole life in the saddle, not even walking from bunkhouse to breakfast if he could help it. A whole way of life built around a horse, and it wasn't until you had to get down on the balls of your feet and use a few muscles you seldom used, or anyway seldom used in the way they were being used now, that you thought about it. It was always a good moment when you climbed back into the saddle and felt the pull of the horse against the work rope, the bogged steer.

Near sundown, rolling a cigarette, forcing himself to take a break, he began to worry they wouldn't get all the boggers out by dark. If it was a good light night, not even necessarily a moon, they could continue to work. But a clouded-over sky would put an end to it until morning and also come up with another threat. The last thing he wanted to see now was rain: the river, flooding, would drown the boggers in less time than it took to cinch a saddle. He threw down his cigarette, looking with distrust at a sky innocently fair and tranquil, and went back to work.

Uremáy fared better. His boggers were out and choused into the split and the split was being drifted down on the main herd when the *peon* boss rode in. Richards still had eight boggers but with Uremáy's crew to lend a hand it looked as if they would get them all out by dark.

Sykes came up in the nick of time, just when Shiloh was complaining that his backbone and his belly button were shaking hands. They had drawn the calf wagon over by loosing the mules, driving them across, and roping to them. They unloaded everything in the chuck wagon. With the pull of the mules and the chuck wagon snubbed up to the calf wagon, they had pulled it over. And then crossed with the equipment, little by little, and refitted again.

"I would like to be in Congress," Sykes said, dropping the tail of the wagon. "I would like to be in Congress just one term. One term is all I ask. I would see there was a ford and a bridge on every river from the Ree-o Grandy to the Teton. I would oversee 'em personal."

"Make them bridges good and wide," Corrigan said. "So we got plenty of room to cross a herd."

"I do not care about your damn herd," Sykes said. "I am thinkin' of my wagon. I am thinkin' of poor Hedges here, with his box full of spoilt-rotten weanlings have not yet learned how to walk they are so weakkneed from bein' drug on wheels. I am thinkin' of my mules."

"You just lost my vote, Sallie," Shiloh said.

"Well boys," Richards said, "it doesn't matter now. We're almost into Oklahoma and making better time of it than I figured to make. I looked for bog on the Washita, and even back on the Red, but this Canadian girl almost put one over on me. Let's hope the North Fork's not waitin' to play us any tricks, and before you know it we'll be in Oklahoma with the old Cimarron under our belts and Dodge just layin' there lookin' for us with the welcome mat out."

"Aymen," Shiloh said, removing his hat.

Dodge. Good-by M Bar L's. Good-by McLean, most unpredictable of neighbors and nighthawks. Dodge. Hot water and a clean shirt and whiskey and Todd Allenby. And mail. Maybe mail. Maybe a letter that could set you up so nothing that lay ahead could make any difference, and nothing too big to take on singlehanded.

He looked down at Uremáy, sitting some feet from the fire and rolling his first after-dinner cigarette. "*Tengo consado*," he said.

"*Si. Tambien, compadrito*. There is an ache in the back which is new to me. The bulls. Mother of God. With more than tails to weigh them down, I tell you. Vaqueros are not what they were, in my time."

"No?" Richards said.

"Nothing is as it was in my time, however. All was better then. Seat yourself, gringo. I will say this: when don Ramón and I went out, when we took the trail together, no misfortune stood in our way. Even the country is not as it was."

"Just too lucky to talk about, weren't you?" Richards said.

Uremáy thought a moment. Then he said, "No. We were younger. It is all the same as it was then. A man forgets."

"I don't reckon you forget much," Richards said.

"As it is with all men, I remember only what I wish to remember," Uremáy said. He looked at Richards soberly. "Do you sleep, or do you spend an hour with me?"

"How's the state of your health?"

"Hard work clears the head," Uremáy said. "I have only to cast back upon what I have already told you. Yes. The ship. Did I say this: that when I have stood upon the shore, at the gulf, and in my Mexico, I wished for nothing more than to be upon that sea, free of the land. Free. And when I was upon that sea I wished for no more but to feel the earth under my feet and the dust of it in my nose. And my poor Natividad, lying moaning, with no thought in her mind but to die. And La Morena Flor, when there was a storm and the seas came high as the ship itself, rolling past like green mountains with snow upon their peaks. Somehow she stood upon that deck and watched, with her eyes wide and the salt of the sea flying over her, and it was as if the devil had come to her. She would say to me, 'I am frightened, Tiburcio, I am frightened.' And would not move from where she stood. Well enough, then. She was frightened. I feared many things that whole long time we were at sea. Five weeks of it. And such a ship, and at last the weather so fine we hardly knew what to do with ourselves. If I had had a horse. Yes, a horse would have been the thing. I could not have gone far with him, true, but it would not have been so strange, that little life we lived upon the water."

"What kind of a ship?" Richards said.

"A merchantman, small and very pretty she was. Don Enrique had made all the arrangements. The little ship came from Cádiz with sherry and almonds. A nice cargo, no? Some of it went ashore at New Orleans, and the rest at Galveston. They kept aboard enough for us, which made many things less important than they might otherwise have been. It is why I say to you, if man might fly. Consider the days simply crossing Texas, consider the days simply crossing that sea. And at my age." He was silent, considering, and Richards considered also. It would have been strange, and a great thing too for this man, born a *peon* and bred to the *peon* soil, with a heritage of the sorrows of Mexico and no idea of the size of the world or the seas which surrounded it. Or maybe it was the land surrounded the seas, he wasn't sure, since he didn't have much of an idea of any of it himself. All he knew was the world was a big place, bigger even than Tiburcio Uremáy could tell him.

236

"That year," Uremáy said. "I am thinking back to where you must have been. Yes, with the Selvo herd. We set forth in July, and you came to Tres Reyes in October, no? And when we returned the following spring, you had long since taken the herd to Nebraska and did not return until nearly the ending of summer. So, you were walking cows north, as is your occupation, and at the same time we were out upon the seas. And do you know, when I got down from the ship I could not walk. No. I rolled about as if I had spent the entire month in the *cantina*. But it is all worth it, my friend, for what am I greeted with, at Cádiz? I am greeted with a horse. From the private stables of don Enrique Dominguez. And a very fine carriage, of course. With perhaps too many corners and carvings upon it to suit the *mozos* who must keep it bright. And a mounted guard, with guns, in the event there are *bandidos*." He laughed. "I, to be saved from *bandidos*, who have lived much of my life with *bandidos* in the very country where *bandidos* spawn. Well. We saw no *bandidos*, and inside myself I laughed at my little Spanish brothers. Did I tell you this, Ben?"

"That you laughed? No, you didn't tell me that."

"But I did. As I had forgotten how to walk I was relieved in my soul to see the horse, even though his teeth were not of the best."

"You hadn't forgot how to ride?" Richards said.

"I? I forget such a thing? Well, then, this is how the *peon* boss of Tres Reyes and his homesick Natividad, and La Morena Flor came at last, in the ending of the summer two years ago, to the city of Seville . . ."

He did not hold out his hand to her, but bowed, a tall gangling boy in black, with white at his throat and ears which stood out and forward, too large for the narrow, crooked featured face. She had put out her hand to him, turning it sideways in a frank involuntary gesture. Now she withdrew it, disconcerted. He had a merry face: as if he sensed her discomfiture he held out his hand, but it was too late, and she, in the little comedy of manners, found herself bending lightly toward him, bowing as he had done. Daniél."

237

"And Cousin 'Tonia," Aunt Luisa was saying.

They embraced briefly and drew apart. Antonia Dominguez was three years older, plump and very plain, although the large limpid eyes were striking. There was restraint in her greeting. But Uncle Enrique had a hug for her, and it was like being home so closely did he resemble his brother Ramón. The progenitive strength and vigor of the old don had overcome the milder genetic offerings of both wives, Spanish and Indian. The half brothers might have been twins, except that Ramón, six years younger, had worn better. Enrique was running to flesh, and so gray he was near white. He was clean shaven, but the big face, the big shock-haired head might have been Ramón's. "*Bienvenida, bienvenida*, Cayetana. Why you are pure Dominguez," he said, and she knew then that they had looked for something of the American mother in her and were perhaps pleased not to see it.

Aunt Luisa also was comfortably fleshed and had been prettier in youth than her daughter. She moved quickly, like a small round bird hopping, but her eyes were languid and the soft flesh of her face was slack.

But how white they are, Cayetana thought, *and how strange, in this country of sun*. An odd green yellow white which spoke of uncounted hours indoors, all of them but Enrique, who was ruddy and sunburned. She felt suddenly isolated, alone among strangers whose mouths said welcome but who stared at her. It was Daniél with his merry face and swift smile who put her at ease.

"Uncle Ramón is reticent, Cayetana. He does not tell us what a beautiful cousin he sends us."

She thanked him, watching him gravely and steadily. But his relaxed homely narrow face made her smile at last. She felt close to him the moment he made her smile, as if they shared some bond, some secret. She put her hand on Uremáy's arm. "This is Tiburcio, who has watched over Tres Reyes since long before I was born. And Natividad. Now they watch over me."

Uremáy, learning from the young Dominguez, bowed to the women. He held out his hand to Enrique, pleased at the resemblance to his *patrón*. "I am your servant, don Enrique."

"You are my guest." Don Enrique's voice was loud, much

238

louder than the *patrón's*. But his eyes were soft. "Old man, it is forty-five years since I have seen my brother. He came to us at fifteen and spent five years in this house. We will have much to speak of, you and I."

Luisa clapped her hands, but she fell wide of the peremptory tone she strove for. "Not at this moment, Enrique. This child must be worn to the bone. We shall rest, through the heat. Now, Cayetana, you and 'Tonia shall go to your room and become the dearest of friends. Señora Uremáy . . ." She looked into Natividad's sick suspicious eyes, saw with dismay the impassive Indian set of the woman, and glanced away. "The servants will take you to your quarters. I trust you will find every comfort."

Antonia's hand was on her arm; she could feel its warmth and moisture through her sleeve. "Come, I will show you the way."

Sleep was far from her mind. The arrival, the fulfillment of dream, the coming at last to the city in the sun, had built a pressure of excitement in her, so that she felt she might float away with it. She wished to see, to do everything now, immediately; to take upon herself on the instant all that the new life would have to offer, and to return in kind, on the instant, all of herself that she would give to it. Impatience made her ache, and the knowledge that a whole year lay before her did nothing to diminish it. Aboard ship, she had been sick with longing for Tres Reyes, yet in the last days she had given it only passing and indifferent thought. She missed no one of her people. She was free, knowing that the word meant many things, and that there are times when one must be free even of the things that are loved most.

Don Enrique Dominguez' town house was in the Barrio Santa Cruz, the old section which had been the Jewish quarter in the time of the Moors. Down crooked winding complexes of narrow streets and through glistening squares hung with blossom and marked with the Holy Cross, the high walls shut off the world of the city. The ordinary double wooden gate which looked as if it might open into a stable gave instead upon an enclosed patio of polished tile and fountain, of hanging geranium and vining rose and rough barked palm. The house was bluewhite with carved terra-cotta friezes over windows faced with outcurving iron bars and

239

backed by shutters on the interior. The roof sloped orange tiles with little patches of green lichen sprouting between them.

Inside it was dim and rather musty, from the servants' quarters in the rear to the second story, under the crooked tiles. The dimness came not alone from the shutting out of light, but from the dark ponderous furnishings, the walls of gray-blue tapestry pricked with gold thread, the shadowy patterns of the dusky rugs. Yet the thick sirupy heat was in the thick-walled old house and the thick sunlight sifted between the cracks of the drawn shutters.

"This is only our town house, of course," Antonia was saying. Her voice was high and sweet, a little hesitating. She was seated before her mirror in a loose flowered robe which disclosed her full throat. But her eyes were on the mirror, watching Cayetana seated on the bed with the contents of a small straw basket spread around her. The room was quite large, with a long shuttered balcony and two wide beds. There were paintings on the walls, an Adoration and saints, and some of country scenes. "We came back early because you were coming, but the summer's been so long I didn't mind at all."

"Will we be staying here, then?" Cayetana said.

"We will go back and forth . . . Father's interest is at the farm. We have splendid horses. And of course we will go to Las Pasturas. That's his main concern, now that he's purchased a share of it."

Cayetana looked up, meeting the older girl's eyes in the mirror. "None of this seems real to me, 'Tonia. All the things and places and people Uncle Enrique's written of. I wanted to see it all myself, for such a long time, and now I can't believe I'm here."

Antonia turned on the cushioned stool, facing her. "We want you to be happy, Cayetana." Again her voice was hesitating. "I suppose you know how we live here . . . I mean that it will be different from what you are accustomed to. Uncle Ramón indicates that you have lived a much . . . much freer life than we are used to."

"Freer?" She said the word which had been in her mind earlier, when she had thought of herself as free now.

"We do not go about much," Antonia said, "when we are living in the city. On Sundays and holidays, of course, but other than that . . ." She lowered her head, not looking at Cayetana. "There are studies . . . lessons."

"But I've had all that," Cayetana said. "With Father Berrades."

Antonia was shaking her head, slowly. "Here we learn dancing, music, sewing. Things of the household, you understand. I am to tutor you in the social refinements." Now she looked up and there was a flush in her round cheeks. "Forgive me, Cayetana. We know, of course, that your mother is a woman of wealth and breeding, but your father has asked particularly that you be instructed in the art of manners."

Cayetana sat looking at her. "I didn't know I was lacking in them," she said hopelessly. A coldness came up in her, drying her hands and touching her heart. What Antonia was telling her was that she would be a prisoner in this house, trapped by the mores of another race, a new society. The thought troubled her, but she would not allow Antonia to see it. Surely where there was entrance to a house there was exit. "Perhaps I could teach you and Daniél English, and then it would be a fair exchange," she said. "I suppose I've done everything wrong, ever since I got here."

"Well," Antonia said, "you shouldn't have held out your hand to Daniél as you did. I see you are naturally grave, which is much in your favor. We laugh in this house all we please, but when you are laughing with a gentleman you must be certain to do it from behind your fan. Otherwise, it's considered . . . vulgar." The flush came up higher in her cheeks. "And we don't go into the sun without protection, because . . . well, you see how dark you are."

"I was born with this color, cousin," Cayetana said cheerfully. "A fourth of me's Indian, just like Natividad. I doubt we'll be able to do a thing about it. I do hope I'm not going to be a burden to you, 'Tonia. I don't want to interrupt your life in any way if I can help it."

The older girl raised her head. They looked at each other. "You are very generous, Cayetana. I didn't mean to imply my life was a great . . . social success. It isn't. Neither Daniél nor I were given more than passing graces. As you can see." Her voice was wry. "With Daniél it does not matter, he is a man. But I think it will be difficult for you, for a time. In a sense, you have the power to make it difficult for me. Perhaps the less you tell me of your way of life the better it will be. I am dissatisfied with myself as it is." She turned again, to look at her own reflection, tilting her head this way and that as if she searched out the vantage point for her most perfect image. "Does it occur to you that while you are here perhaps a very good alliance may be arranged for you?"

The room was so still Cayetana could hear her heart beating, quick now, and uneven. She was stricken. "Who says this?"

"Why . . . it must have been in your father's mind."

"Did he tell this to Uncle Enrique?"

Antonia shook her head. "I don't think so. But I know that . . ."

Cayetana interrupted her. "I'm certain not. Father would have talked to me if it were true. Not that I have any objection at all to loving someone, you understand. There's nothing I would like better."

Antonia was looking at her with interest now, her head perfectly still and her eyes fastened to the mirror.

"I think that loving someone would be the most wonderful thing that could happen to me. You know how Father and Mother met and married, in spite of every opposition. Or at least I like to think of it that way."

Antonia cleared her throat. She was blushing clear to her neck. "How old are you now, Cayetana, just turned eighteen? Please don't put any notions in my head, they've all been quite successfully suppressed. And you mustn't feel as you do, it's not allowed." She turned again on the stool. "Except when one's lying awake in the dark. An alliance doesn't necessarily mean loving someone, you know."

"Never," Cayetana said. "I would never marry someone I didn't love. No one could force me to do that. Or . . ."

"Or what?" Antonia said, staring at her in amazement.

"Or force me not to love someone I did love," Cayetana said.

The older girl was disconsolate, but she was smiling a little. "Whatever will we do with you, Cayetana, if you persist in these ideas? I see you are going to make my life difficult after all. I had so hoped you weren't." She rose, still smiling. "Sleep now.

242

When the heat of the day is gone perhaps Father can be persuaded to give us a carriage ride to the cathedral." She went to her bed, nearest the wall, crossed herself before the hanging crucifix, and lay down, raising an arm across her face. Small beads of sweat shone in the indentation between her chin and lower lip.

Cayetana went to the shuttered window. She opened it a crack, slowly, and looked out. The little balcony had tiles for a floor, and there were bright pots of greenery on its iron railing. She slipped through and stood on the tiles, feeling the sun shining hot in a sky as blue and depthless as that of her own country. Only not so large, for it was all cut up by the heads of the ragged palms, the blocky squares of the shoulders of buildings, the slanted tiled roofs. The cathedral tower soared like bronze lace, so slender it seemed to drift against the sapphire arc, its minarets like pointed caps of brown lace. She looked into another courtyard below her, beyond the wall. It was the rear patio of the house across the way, and there was washing strung to dry and orange trees with glossy leaves and two cats stretched in the shade.

Seville was empty, asleep, and dreaming under the bright Andaluz sky. She leaned against the railing, aware of a stillness in which no birds sang, almost afraid to breathe in case the small sound might start up a clatter of hoofs, rolling of wheels, slamming of doors, shouting of children, calling of voices. She closed her eyes against the brightness and a lone sound came to her: the humming of bees in a whole city of cascading flowers blanketing white walls.

She went back into the room, closing the shutter. Antonia had not moved. She took off her serge basque and put on a white shirt, cut like a man's with narrow sleeves and a high collar. She went out of the room and into the hallway and down to the courtyard. When she entered she saw Daniél stretched under a sweet jasmine eating an apple.

He leaped to his feet when he saw her. "What a nice surprise, little cousin. Couldn't you sleep?"

"I didn't try. I think I'm much too excited."

His tall gangling figure moved lopsidedly, bringing her a chair; he seemed to walk at a slant. "Would you like an apple?" he said, holding out his own half-eaten fruit to her.

243

"Nothing, thank you, Daniél. It's cool, isn't it? Why don't you all sleep out here?"

His smile became laughter, open, pleased. "That's the most sensible suggestion to come from this house in three centuries. Don't broach it to your Aunt Luisa, though. It bothers her enough that I lie here in the afternoons." He sat down at her feet, on the tile, and took a huge bite from his apple. "I don't tell her, of course, but sometimes I gallop all about the city at this hour. I should explain: gallop afoot. That's the most pleasure there is, peering into the windows of the shops and deciding what I'd like to buy when the shutters are opened and drinking a little glass of something now and then."

Then Daniél was free. Or was it only freer? She tested him. "It sounds wonderful. I should like to go along, one day."

"Would you? Truly?" He threw his apple into the air and caught it again in an excess of good spirit. "We will, then. The city's no good except for reading and talking bulls and politics and going to Mass. I'm nearly through with my studies, you see, and I've not got much to do but watch the ladies pass. Even so, they scarcely notice me. In the country one can always go and feed the chickens, although I don't much like chickens."

"I don't either," she said. "They always pick me."

And they looked at each other suddenly sober, feeling the mystery of kinship beyond blood.

"Daniél." She leaned to him. She owed him an apology, and it was best to make it now, while they were alone. "I am sorry I tried to shake your hand today. I didn't know I wasn't supposed to."

He looked up at her, and then down at her hand, where it lay on the edge of the chair. "What a fool I was not to take it," he said. "But then, I am always too late with too little." He grinned. "'Tonia's been tutoring you already, I see."

"Not at all. 'Tonia's very helpful . . ."

His eyes were keen and bright. "Loyalty, among many virtues, cousin?"

"Oh, I don't like that word, virtue," she said. But she was laughing, delighted with him. "It sounds so . . ."

"Smelling of incense," he finished. "We mustn't laugh so loudly, we'll have the whole house up and ashout."

She covered her mouth with her hand. "And I have forgotten too that I am not to laugh when I am with a gentleman, except from behind my fan. But I haven't a fan."

Daniél leaned back on his hands, shouting with laughter. "Why, Cayetana, you're a breath of something clean and wonderful in this house." He sat upright, staring at her. "New blood. Poor 'Tonia. I shall take care of you. At least I shall try to take care of you. Do they call you always Cayetana?"

"At home I am Caye."

"And to the old man, Uremáy, you are the brown flower."

"Ay, do not listen to Tiburcio. He thinks he is my mother."

His head was on one side, considering. "He names you well, I think. I am glad you have come, Caye. We will have good times together, when no one's looking. I'm not at all brave, though, it's only fair to warn you. Mother raises her hand and 'Tonia her eyes, and I'm withered to ash. But when we're alone I'll be brave. I'll ride farther and harder than ever before when we get to the country, and I'll topple a bull for you at Las Pasturas. That's a promise. A hard one to make, too, for I don't feel at home with the bulls."

"Antonia says your father has bought an interest in Las Pasturas. Is it near Seville?"

"At Jerez de la Frontera. That is the real bull country. At Las Pasturas is one of the oldest strains in Spain. Much liked by the public for their nobleness. But not liked by the matadors, for they are too big. You'll see for yourself. If the weather's good, the real trials will come early in February and the best bulls chosen for the fair. The season is not good now . . . only a few corridas for the charities. But the little trials go on, for those who like to keep their hand in and see the majesty of the Pasturas strain."

"And you will topple one of these great bulls," she said smiling, "for me?"

"I did not say a great bull." He pulled at the wings of his black waistcoat with dignity. "A calf, perhaps, a very small calf."

She was half-amused, half-regretful. "Daniél, I won't hold you to that promise."

"But you must," he said. "You see, in all my life, I have never kept a promise, and this one I mean to keep. Only don't remind

245

me of it, if you please. I've been such an ass as to make it that I couldn't possibly forget." He got to his feet and stood looking down at her. His elbows made sharp angles in the bend of his coat sleeves. "D'you like books? I have some books, one on the Las Pasturas bulls. I'll show them to you." He started across the courtyard, stopped, and returned to her. "Would you mind holding my apple? You have bulls, on your ranch, haven't you?"

"Bulls with great horns. Something like yours, I expect, since they came from yours, long ago."

"And you sell them for meat. Oh well, ours too, when the mules have dragged them out of the ring. It seems strange, doesn't it, when you think of it."

"What does?"

"Why, that here are these great bulls of ours, and they are good for nothing but to be fought. If we did not fight them, might as well let the breed die out. Still, as long as your longhorn cattle survive, in America, the blood of the fighting bull will survive. That's rather nice to know." He started away and returned a second time. "You must forgive me if I speak so much of the bulls. But I will inherit my father's interest one day, and I must know what I am about."

"Perhaps you will inherit it all?" Cayetana said.

"That will not come to pass. Las Pasturas has been in the Quesada family for generations. Now the old don is feeble." He spread his hands. "To be honest, senile. But the older son has sons of his own, and the young don will come to the same day." His eyes moved upward, as if he beseeched. "If he lives long enough, for as I see it now, his end will be with the bulls."

"The younger son is a matador?" Cayetana said.

"Angel? No, not a matador, never. The Dos Santos y Quesada do not breed foot fighters. Matadors are bred in the back alleys of Seville and Córdoba and Ronda. Angel works from a horse, he is a *rejoneador*. Well, never mind, you will know them all, and look over the strain I shall inherit as well. Here, I may as well finish that on the way." He leaned over and claimed his apple and went off with it.

Cayetana leaned back in her chair. The odor of roses trapped between the walls in the warm stillness was almost overpowering.

The sound of the water in the fountain made a small coolness. After a time, aware that she was not alone, she turned and saw Uremáy standing at the side of the house, come from the servants' quarters, and watching her with a slight smile spreading his gray mustaches. When she saw him, she rose, although he was coming to meet her.

"Tiburcio. Come and talk to me. Are you comfortable?"

"Very fine, all of it," Uremáy said. "I did not wish to disturb you, when you talked with the young don. You should be resting, little one."

"And you should not? How is Natividad now?"

He looked away from her. "It will pass. It is only the strangeness. Give her a day and she will be chattering with those women in the kitchen as if she were at Tres Reyes."

"But she does not weep?" Cayetana said, concerned.

"Well. A small tear," Uremáy said. "Ay, such a sausage as I just had, small flower. It made me think of heaven, and now I fear that I have eaten it so fast that it will shortly make me think of hell. Is there anything you wish?"

"Nothing, Tiburcio. We are going to look at books, Daniél and I. The strain of bulls he will inherit."

"Inherit?" Uremáy said. "Holy Mother. I would like to take him up the trail to Kansas, one day, and we shall see what he thinks of inheriting bulls. God be with the young man, however. Now. I must ask, as we are here, we have arrived. Are you happy?"

"I am happy," she said, putting her hand on his arm. "Have no fears for me, Tiburcio."

"All my fears are for you," he said. "Or consider what don Ramón would plan for me." He drew his finger across his throat. "When you need me, you have only to think, where is that man, and I will know what man and come."

He went back to the kitchen. She turned her chair, so that the sun fell over her shoulder and sat facing the house. Her eyes found the upper window. Somewhere beyond it, Antonia still slept. A small furrow drew her brows together. It seemed there would be a cross to bear, in the midst of light and gardens, but surely the art of manners was a small cross; her strength would rise to it. She lowered her head and saw Daniél coming across the courtyard. He held three great books in his outstretched arms. A pair of small spectacles with gold rims teetered on the bridge of his nose. The apple, eaten to the core, was perched on the books. His long legs bent at the knee as if they were on springs.

"Let me help you," she said, reaching up to take the books.

When he bent to her, the spectacles slid to the end of his nose, and the apple core rolled off and fell in a potted cypress, and they were motionless, holding the books between them, and smiling at each other in the afternoon sunlight.

FOURTEEN

"Go in there?" Shiloh said. "Me? So they can gawp at me, is all. I don't look to be gawped at by the Army. It is gittin' to be so this whole danged country is boilin' to the lid with 'em. What good are they, anyways?"

"You said that before," Richards said.

"What am I sposed to believe, I am met by a piddling clump of them fellers in blue, tellin' me to watch out for my hair and then aimin' to send me right into the middle of a couple thousand Kiowa?"

"It was me aimin' to send you there," Richards said.

Shiloh looked at him. "I'm goin' to air my lungs about that one day too, Ben. I reckoned to see first off if you can manage to git me to the freight pens at Dodge. If you can do that, then I'm free of you and won't have no more worries. *Adiós*. Hug and kiss the Army for me."

"A freight pen would be a good place for you to repose in," Sykes said. "I am tickled to death you ain't comin'."

"I'll tighten my belt, till you catch up. How much supplies you think Fort Supply'll supply? I'll tell you what Fort Supply'll supply: a hot eye and a cold word. I reckon I could make one bean do me all the way to Dodge, if I had to buy off the Army."

Sykes cursed his mules, to start them up. When they had turned off the trail to enter Fort Supply, he shook his head and looked at Richards. "I never had a man at my chuck felt so strong about me as that boy does. There's times I could bust right down and cry."

"Yes?" Richards said. "Well, hang on till we see if we can get some flour out of the post sutler. Then you can cry like hell if you're of a mind."

The herd, with Uremáy on the right point, would cross the North Fork of the Canadian before Richards and Sykes caught up with it again. The river was quiet and looked to provide an easy crossing. There wasn't a man in the crew particularly wanted to stop at Fort Supply, Oklahoma. Mexicans and U.S. troops had nothing but mistrust for one another. And if Texians felt an admiration for the soldiers who manned the plains outposts it was grudging. For one thing, they were not used to military code but to civil law as enforced by the Rangers; for another, they were not quick to forget that ten years earlier they had been engaged in a war for secession, against Federal forces. But Sykes was short on flour, and Richards wanted to check into the fort to see if they knew about the Kiowa encampment and find out whether there was any news from Carney's patrol.

Uremáy had scouted the North Fork himself. The bottom was firm. There would be no repeat of the quicksand trouble on the South Fork. The mid-June weather was clear, hot, pleasant, with a few showers now and then to wet down the dust and cool things off. He had never seen the grass better, and riding point, ahead and to the right of Rojo, he found himself studying grass, plain, ordinary, green grass, and feeling a soft, sorrowful nostalgia while he studied it.

This would be his last trail drive. It was not that he was so old, sixty was not so old. Nor did he feel that his strength had diminished appreciably. It was not the quick eager burning strength of his youth, but a quiet slow power, which he must spread out and conserve and expend with care, to make it last him the time he needed it. But trail driving was work for young men, young strong men who did not need to spread out their strength and could call it to hand at a moment's notice. For many years he had bossed the Dominguez herds, north, east, south, but he had never been as far north as Montana, and it was good that he should see this, make this long journey, when it was to be his last.

A gift to him, he knew. The position he had held for so long, the work he had planned and overseen, this was now Richards' heritage. A man would be a fool to reject such a heritage. Yet Richards was a gringo, he had not been born to Tres Reyes, and perhaps it was asking, expecting too much that he should feel the same pull and potency of the place. He, Uremáy, would oversee the field work and the horses and have time to sit in the sun if he wished, and it was in him that Richards was not merely a replacement, but something more. He felt that Richards belonged there now.

He had the dark fatalism of the Indian, and the old, crowding superstitions. He looked for signs at all times, and when there were none, consciously or unconsciously he made them for himself. The only aspects of Richards' life which he knew were surface aspects: the old trouble with the law, which might have broken a lesser man, or, more probably, worked some unfortunate change for the worse; the business with the young widow . . . a woman who, he felt with certainty, could look out for her own interests; the spoiled troubled boy, basically a sound boy, but without the disciplines which were essential to the whole man, the decent man, who pointed the vital difference between men and stripped it naked, and perceptible. These were the only extraneous meaningful facets of Richards' life which were known to him. But of greater importance, he knew that somewhere along the way Richards had acquired the human decencies, the restraints, the ability to laugh at himself without which man was no more than a dull defenseless absurd deluded fool. A quiet man; yes, there was the key: to make no display of anguishes and afflictions, to be steadfast in the right but to admit the wrong, to stand up to adversity with composure and yet fall upon the sacrificial altar of mortal passion, to know how to command yet submit with patience. How fundamental these things were, and how rare.

Sixty years, Uremáy thought. I have lived sixty years, and don

Ramón the same. And we come to the end of our summer, denied the sons who would have made us secure. One small woman, one small child, is all that stands between us and the future, living and dead. Richards must stay at Tres Reyes. Otherwise what was to become of it?

His eyes closed, shutting out the bright-bladed glimmer of the grass. He could see sunlight red through his closed lids. *Dolorosa, Dolorosa*, Virgin of Sorrows, forgive me, that I lay open the heart of my beloved *niña* for the eyes of others, for eyes other than mine, and thine. *Cristo de la Salud*, Christ of the Bullfighters, destroy that evil which caused me to kill a man in my dreams. Virgin of the Macarena, hold thy hand over Angel Quesada, for I have wronged him, and make it not come to pass that my dream of his death sends him to it. Guadalupe, Mother of Mexico, turn thy face upon this man Richards, unbeliever though he may be, for he is the man, he is my man, and he may yet be yours. *Nuestra Señora*, let him return to Tres Reyes, for it is my country, my country . . .

"Hey, Tiburcio, you all right?"

He jerked his head up and saw Corrigan had come around the point and was looking at him intently, with concern.

"You seemed like you was about to fall out of the saddle," Corrigan said.

"I was praying," Uremáy said.

Corrigan grinned, taking it for a joke. But Uremáy's face looked so taut and strained he had thought the old man might be having a fit of some kind. "You sure you're all right?" he said.

Uremáy sighed. "If all was well I would not be praying, since it is not man's nature to pray when all is well with him."

Uremáy wasn't joking him after all. He crossed the lead again and went back to the left point and had no sooner got there than Uremáy shouted to him. "*Despacio, despacio*. There is the river. Slow these sons."

They wheeled and went down the swing, slowing the herd to spread it out for the crossing. When Uremáy came back up the other flank he saw that Rojo had moved out and was going very slowly to the river, his head high on his thrown-back neck, as if he lingered at the smell of water, in no haste to reach its source. He sat looking at the red steer. He said to himself, I did not think we would bring you to this, Rojo. Your trust makes a wound in me. Drink deep, old *ladino*, for when you have crossed this water, and the Cimarron, and come to the Arkansas it will be the last water you will ever cross.

Richards and Sykes came in that night when they were setting up camps. There had been no further word from Allenby, which made Richards sure he had arrived in Dodge on schedule and was waiting for them. Carney's weary patrol was being relieved, and the commandant had every intention of keeping his details out until the last of the trail herds had moved up from Texas. They knew about the Kiowa. Carney had sent in a dispatch rider requesting instructions as to what to do about the big encampment, but the Indians had solved the problem for him by folding up and moving out. They had gone due west, and Richards had it pretty well figured that they had been traveling ahead of the Kiowa two days at the most. He had to close his eyes when he thought about it, and he didn't have the heart to mention it, even to Uremáy.

According to the officers at Camp Supply there were more cows in Dodge City than had ever been gathered there before, and trail crews camped all around it. In three years' time Dodge was replacing Abilene and Wichita as the biggest trail town in the cow market, and there was a mayor up there was already talking about it being the capital of the state.

"Hell, if it gits that big it'll be worthless," Shiloh said. "They won't let cows in. There'll be all kinds of laws about how you can't trail a cow past the governor's mansion, and by dang, I bet you the governor's mansion'll be on the same street as the stock pens and the track arunnin' right next to the outhouse."

"My God," Sykes said. "Outhouse? How often do you think the governor goes to the outhouse?"

"Why, I expect he goes the normal amount of times just like anybody else," Shiloh said. "On account of he's governor don't make him . . ."

"You dang fool," Sykes said. "There won't *be* no outhouse. There will be a place *inside*, with marble on the floor and silver on the faucets and most likely a gold chain to pull 'er by."

"Say, you're right," Shiloh said. "I never thought of that." He shook his head. "Ain't a doubt we won't be allowed to run a cow past. All it would take would be some old renegade like Rojo to go foggin' up the steps and onto that marble floor you're speakin' of. Why, it'd be the end of the cattle industry. I got to say a few words to this mayor, when I git to Dodge. Civic pride's one thing, but he's carryin' it too far."

Richards scouted the Cimarron early in the afternoon and decided to bring the herd across by nightfall and make camps on the far side. The Cimarron could be rough; he had seen it wild as any river he had ever crossed, but the fine June weather and the end of the heavy spring rains had taken the kinks out of it. The water looked to be running fast, but without treacherous currents, and when he tested it he found there wasn't more than twenty yards of swimming water.

He pointed the herd slightly upstream, to keep the sun out of their eyes. By nightfall they were spread out on the far bank, off the trail a mile or so, and grazing on a fresh bedground. It was the easiest crossing they had made, and like Uremáy, he was beginning to invent signs for himself. He was too honest not to admit that outside pressures, the responsibility of the M Bar L's, the nuisance of the bulls, which fought with one another when and where they got the chance, the cows dropping calves, had kind of cramped his style. They were irritations which had had to be put up with because he had made a dead man a promise. Now the end was in sight; he had done what he said he would do and his conscience was clear, although when he stopped and thought about it he realized that the clarity of his own conscience was not so important any more. What mattered now was that he had carried out his end, and that he would now be shut of McLean for the rest of the summer. He looked forward to the only responsibility he had really contracted for: the delivery of the Tres Reyes herd, and he sensed a new independence in being free of a score of annoyances, doing what he was paid to do, no more and no less. Too, he had had a peculiar feeling in him for the past few days, an actual physical working, as if his gut was churning. It wasn't exactly an attack of nerves, but it could pass for one. It was the consideration of the letter from Avis he was looking for,

for one thing; for another, there was a wandering of his mind that was new to him, and the wandering kept taking him back south, to the Nueces country, and it was because of Uremáy that his mind had got into this habit. It wasn't the kind of habit he liked to cultivate, mind wandering; it spoke of old age about to dry-gulch you, or worse, your brain making to rot, but he didn't know a thing he could do about it as long as Uremáy kept passing out fragments of a story that had to do with him picking up a letter. A couple of times he thought it would be a lot easier if he and Uremáy could just sit down under a tree somewhere, where there was shade and some water running and maybe a bottle of whiskey at hand, and he could listen and ask some questions and it would all come out straight and clear in his mind. But it couldn't be any other way than the way Uremáy was doing it, and because of that he spent more time thinking about it than he maybe would have done if he'd heard it all at once. He looked forward to what Uremáy told him, and yet he knew the thing he looked forward to most, the thing that had got him in such an uproar inside, was seeing if there was a letter waiting for him. The only thing he could remember he had ever looked forward to as much was the year he was ten and had been told he might, just might, find himself with a rifle for Christmas. As it had turned out, his sisters had got the whey-faced little dollies they were all fired up about, but that morning had been the bitterest disappointment of his youth. The rifle hadn't arrived, and even though it eventually got there it was two weeks after Christmas and all the gloss was rubbed off his anticipation.

Although maybe it hadn't been a total loss. Maybe that was the year he had begun to learn there wasn't a weapon made would fight fate.

He thought he might as well let Uremáy talk to him some more, and maybe it would take his mind off his nerves. The first watch was out, and along about time for the guard change he left off checking with Sykes on a supply list that seemed ten miles long, and figuring up how he was going to rotate the crew so everybody got a good crack at Dodge and couldn't voice any complaints when they left it behind. He had just turned away from the wagon when he heard a clattering sound.

255

The crew, playing cards and smoking around the fire, looked up, intent and listening. It had sounded like the rattle of a tin pan, out in the dark somewhere. Before he could get it straight in his mind it came again, only this time it wasn't a single sound, but the sound a tin pan might make if somebody took a couple of swipes at it with a stick, and then it went clanking along, rolling over and over, across the rocks.

There was a sharp shout from the darkness, and he made for Portero. Out of the circle of firelight he crashed into a man, running, and did not stop and they cursed one another and went on. In the dim starlight he saw the moving shapes ahead and even as he swung into the saddle knew there was nothing to be done. The herd was on its feet and running north as if Sykes had spooked it off banging every pan in the chuck wagon.

They are going to run right into Dodge City, Richards thought. Christ, they are going to turn every herd waiting to get into the pens, and there will be a sum total of a hundred thousand head running wild all over Kansas and Oklahoma and maybe clear into Wyoming for all I know. He thought, fleetingly, of them racing into the governor's mansion as Shiloh had predicted. It was a damn good thing there wasn't one to run into. He gave Portero his head and let the horse take him to the point. Corrigan and two vaqueros were there already, and he could hear Corrigan's voice over the running hoofs, high-pitched and drawn out in a kind of wail that sounded something like an owl being strangled. The rest of the crew was on the move and racing for the lead. Something wet flicked him across the mouth and he raised his hand and wiped off a gob of foam that had blown back on him, maybe from Portero, maybe from the running mass of the herd. One more river to cross, and at the rate they were going, they were going to cross it tonight.

It did not last long, not like the stampede back on the Wichita, which had kept them in the saddle till the creek had stopped them. This time the crew turned them, working on the point until two or three of the lead were trying to swing, and then two or three more, turning to mill. For one everlasting and very bad moment Richards found himself within an inch of Rojo's horn, while he pushed and goaded; then the horn swung away as the

256

red steer pulled to the left and turned. They quieted almost as easily as they had got up and begun to run and by the time they were circled the whole crew, Sykes included, was riding around the enormous mill and calling violent curses in tones of warm endearment and knowing there wasn't going to be any sleep because even when they got the herd straightened out it was going to take all of them to keep it on bedground. As tired out as a cow could get, it would be nerved up to run again if any man so much as creaked a jaw, yawning.

Before dawn Sykes went back for the wagons. The herd had been left where it came to a stop, and it had been jumpy the rest of the night. When Richards finally came in for breakfast, McLean was in, sitting cross-legged, with a cup of coffee in his hand. When he saw Richards he picked up something on the ground beside him and held it up wordlessly. It was a big strip of tin, like a good-sized can had maybe been flattened out, and it was still new and shiny though it was dented up some.

Richards stood holding it, looking at it. It didn't make any sense to him, and then he began to remember: the sound that had come out of the night, just before the herd got up and began to go.

"You know that horse of Corrigan's," McLean said. "The one with the wanders. I didn't hobble him last night."

Richards only looked at him.

"I reckon I got careless, bein' so close to Dodge and all."

Richards didn't acknowledge the admission, or the apology, whichever it was.

"That horse slipped out on me," McLean said. "By the time I noticed it and went for him, he was headin' for camps. Looks like he wasn't content just steppin' on this thing, he must of played around out there kickin' it like a kid with a stone. That's what set the herd off, Ben."

Richards put the hunk of tin down and ran his hand over his face. "I could use some coffee," he said.

"I'm awful sorry, Ben. I expect you could call it my fault."

Holding to his promise, Richards thought. "Hell," he said. "I reckon if you want to stretch a point, you could call it the

257

Spaniards' fault for bringin' horses into this country in the first place." He took a bitter swallow from the cup Sykes handed him. "Let's go pick up the drifters," he said.

Uremáy was riding alone, down through a flat piece of country where some small white daisylike flowers looked as if they had sprung out of the rock. The sun was moving up the sky slowly, taking off the dawn chill, but there was still dew in the grass. He had been in twice with drifters, accompanied by two of the vaqueros, but on this third trip out he rode alone. Not that he was no longer searching; rather, the search had become a matter of increasing importance to him. He did not know if it had been generally noted, but he did not think it had been, or there would be conjecture among the crew: Rojo was missing.

Now, Richards knows this, he thought. He picked his way carefully, noticing the small flowers, just the color, so white, just the size, so small, for La Morena Flor's dark head. Richards knows Rojo is gone because Richards knows now the position of every steer in the herd. Well, that was an exaggeration, surely, but there was a great deal of truth in it nevertheless. For one thing, if a steer didn't find its traveling partner right away it was prone to make a fuss, and go to searching until the pair was reunited. Also, one became accustomed to seeing the big blue with the twisted horn in one place, always, or the splotched yellow with the black lobo streak moving along in its own familiar position, or the old black with a wall eye trailing with the drags. He had never had the feel for this spotting of the trail order, but Richards did. Richards knew Rojo was gone just as surely as he knew which end of himself to put his boots on.

Uremáy found himself chuckling, a little clucking sound that came up in his throat and felt comfortable there. Could it be that after all this time Rojo was making a bid for freedom. Could it be that, having assumed the lead of the herd, in partnership with Richards so to speak, he had taken it into his head to break the partnership. And so close to the end of the trail, or at least his end of it. It did not seem to him possible that Rojo, having secured the position of command, independent but tractable, would break away now. For what reason? He had had his chance:

no better chance than the night he had led the stampede on the Wichita, led it so superbly that he had outrun the entire Double Slash B outfit and when he was finally stopped surveyed the damage he had wrought with indifference, and returned to be fed and led and watered as man directed.

He sobered, picking his way higher up into the rocks, where he could get a look at the country around him. Little Mother forgive him, but was it in the very mind of this outlaw that the end of the journey had come, that nothing lay ahead for him but the prison of the pens, the terror of the boxcar and the rolling wheels, the final meeting with death? The old superstition flooded him, cold and wet, like water running in his veins. He was close to the supernatural concept of the animal as capable of many things which man, the highest order of animal, could neither attempt nor understand. The coyote, for instance; the coyote did things which were more than human, horribly so, and the same with the panther and the wolf and the snake. Horrible indeed, not to know if such an animal crossing one's path was what he seemed, or a devil disguised, come down from the high places.

He was impatient with himself. He had been away from all that too long, much too long; he had felt no real terror of devils since he was a child, although he did not doubt that they existed. To think otherwise would be to lay himself open to their insidious visitations. He shuddered suddenly. What if some devil had been with them all this time, cased cunningly in the rough red hide of the *ladino* steer?

It was not true because he did not believe it. When he did not believe a thing it was not true, and when he did believe a thing it was God's word. A very simple and workable philosophy. The red steer was only that: a red steer which had had a small time of glory and become, now, a part of the tradition of Tres Reyes, legend in the cowcamps, and nothing more.

Yes, something more. From the height of the rock he looked down into a small valley, well grassed and protected. Something more. A thing of great potential danger, which had carried death upon its horns and which must now discharge its debt. Rojo was grazing quietly below him, head down, standing upon his head, as the gringo crews said. He seemed to Uremáy larger than he had ever looked, filled out on good grass. Mother of God, those horns. If a man was to make the sign of the cross it was at sight of those horns he should make it.

There was a narrow exit at the end of the pocket, running crookedly out through the rocks and into the clear. Just wide enough, perhaps, for the horns. There was no thought in Uremáy's mind that he could bring Rojo in alone. He was a long way from the herd, farther than he had gone on his two previous searches. But the pocket was so secluded, the graze so fine, that he knew he could return with three or four men and find the red steer still busy with the long wet grass which had not been touched until he touched it. He sat watching the slim red legs moving slowly in the grass. Then he put the horse forward, down out of the rock.

Not until a hoof struck stone and he saw Rojo raise his head did he sting the horse into a run. The only sound which came from him was a low grunt, an animal sound, but he reached up and took off his huge straw hat and swung it, flailing the air. Startled, Rojo threw up his horns and turned to face him, and the grunt became a word and he shouted it, over and over, still swinging his hat, with his knees pressed sweating, turned in, against the flesh of the horse.

"¡Vaya! ¡Vaya! ¡Vaya!"

He could not have counted the times he said it. For a while he thought he would crash head on into the red steer. He was so close he seemed to see a calmness in the black liquid eyes, and yet even as he noted it the old wild light that he remembered sprang into them, the old wildness was in the tossing head.

Rojo spun, in wet spangled grass to his fetlocks. Then he was moving, the great bulk of him slamming forward on the slender racing legs, up through the cut in the rocks, and the horns cleared it and he was gone.

Uremáy sat the horse panting, as if he had come a great distance, as if he had done a thing which had taken all his power. He could feel his legs trembling, where they bent to the horse, and sweat leaking hotly, under his arms, in the palms of his hands, beading his upper lip.

The horse put its head down, pulling strongly at the sweet high grass. It was a long time before Uremáy picked up the reins and started back to the herd.

McLean was sitting on a rock with his legs stretched straight out before him and his broad blocky shoulders hunched. His hat was off, letting the black lock of hair down low on his head. He had not eaten much, but he hadn't got up to empty his plate and put it in the wreck bucket. Rolling a cigarette, his face was morose.

Three steers gone out of the herd, and one of them had to be Rojo. Maybe he was getting paid back for letting Corrigan's horse slip out of the remuda and kick that strip of tin around and start the herd running. Maybe. Maybe you did get paid back in this life, after all, and he was overhasty to go around thinking it was bunk. I earned it, he thought. He felt neither angry nor bitter, but empty, as if something had flushed him and taken out his insides in the flushing.

Nobody wanted to talk to him about it and that was all right with him. He had made a promise to Ben Richards and he meant to keep it, and if somebody had the gall to ride him, or even offer sympathy, it would be hard going to keep his mouth shut. He looked over at the crew, around the fire. Richards had made the mistake of getting up to fill his coffee cup, and ramrod or not, he had to fill up for anybody held out their cups to him. He came over with two cups and handed one to McLean.

"Thanks," McLean said.

Richards was uneasy, but it didn't show. His face had its severe cast, and he didn't look at the boy. He said, "You know, I reckon Avis was right."

McLean nodded. "If you mean about wantin' to shoot that red steer, we should of done it the day Shiloh and me took him. Now we'll never git the chance."

Richards hunkered down, on his bootheels. "One thing, there won't be any other trail crew pickin' him up and bringin' him in. He got kind of used to lettin' us take care of him, but he was too smart too long. I would be willin' to bet it all came back to him the minute he got his nose in the wind again."

McLean didn't say anything.

261

"Listen, Frankie," Richards said. "Maybe it doesn't help much, but you know you're the only man in that red steer's whole lifetime managed to get a rope on him and put him on the trail?"

"And lost him one river short of Dodge City," McLean said. His voice wasn't bitter either, but there wasn't any expression in it. "Here I was thinkin' that if Pa could by any chance look down and see me, he'd know I'd made up a lot of things to him, and maybe be proud."

"I expect he would be, anyway," Richards said. He liked what the boy had said, but it surprised him too. In a way he felt the loss; or perhaps what he missed was the kick of having Rojo leading his herd. But in another sense there was a compassion in him, both for the red steer and for McLean. A couple of wild orphans fighting each other was what it had boiled down to, and one of them had had to win. He could think back to the times he had been close to Rojo, beginning with the day the outlaw had burst out of the brush to confront him, and ending with the moment the deadly horn had near touched him when he tried to turn the point of the stampede. Well, it was over. He, none of them, would ever see the red steer again. But someday, some year, the news would drift south about him: he had been seen in Nebraska, in Oklahoma, in Kansas, in Wyoming, and pretty soon he would be more a ghost than anything else, the stuff of which myth was made, and he would be able to put in his own word about it because he was the only man in the business could say, that red steer led my herd to Dodge in '75.

He stood up. "I'm pullin' out around noon tomorrow, goin' into Dodge. See if Allenby's there yet. Uremáy can bring the herd across the Arkansas. Come along. I'll put Hedges on the remuda and Díaz or somebody on the calf wagon, and you and me'll get this load of hay off our heads and be lookin' like roses by the time the herd gets in."

For the first time McLean looked up at him. When he met the boy's eyes Richards thought, Goddam, now I've done it, now I've set him off for sure. McLean's brows were drawn together, under the black forelock; one hand was clenched so hard around the tin cup the bones of the knuckles stood out white. But he said, "That's obligin' of you, Ben. I expect I would like that."

Richards had been holding his breath. When he let it out it sounded to him like an explosion, but McLean didn't seem to notice. "I'll pass out the orders. You be ready after noon chuck."

"Sure," McLean said. His brows were still drawn, watching Richards walk back to the crew. Richards didn't have to do that. Richards didn't have to be so damned kind to him, or whatever it was he was being. He reached over and picked up his plate and got to his feet. He thought about what he had said to Richards: I'd ought to kill you. He thought about his horses, and how he had stayed with them and done the best he could with them and let his steer walk in the lead of the herd. For the first time in his life, the first time he could remember, he had been checked short, and he didn't know whether it was Richards or whether it was Rojo had done it; he only knew he had to grit his teeth to keep from letting his face crack apart when he had to go to the wagon and show himself and stand on his own feet, just like any other man, and act like it didn't matter.

Todd Allenby had run to weight since Richards had last seen him. He was prosperous looking, there was a gold watch chain draped across his paunch, and he had on a white collar and a gold stickpin with what appeared to be a diamond in it. He wore striped trousers and a black coat with tails and his boots were shined and there was a cigar clamped between his teeth. Only the hat showed its years, a good gray hat creased into shape from long wear. His arm felt heavy across Richards' shoulder; he wasn't a tall man and yet it would not be hard to feel dwarfed when you were around him.

The voice was booming, pleasant, coming from around the cigar. "Old rod, I am glad to see you. I got three more herds out on the trail somewheres, and you are the first in. I get to buy you a drink for that. You are makin' good time. While I got it in mind, they are movin' the Blackfoot over to Beaver Creek this fall, but Fort Benton's still your delivery point. Did you have a good trip?"

"Not bad," Richards said noncommittally. "I'll take you up on that drink. This is Frankie McLean of the M Bar L. He trailed some cows up with me."

Allenby's grip was a crusher, but it was real, there was nothing put on about it. "Seems like I run into your pa a couple of times, McLean. Jonah gettin' too old to boss things now, eh? Turnin' it over to the younger generation."

"Jonah died last spring," Richards said. "This kid told me he aimed to be the best nighthawk I ever had, and he just about made it, too."

"Say, I'm sorry about your pa," Allenby said. He pushed his hat up, showing a thatch of black hair salted with gray. The light struck off the ring on his little finger. His pale cool eyes were wide spaced in the handsome ruddy heavy-featured face. "This your first trip to Dodge?"

"Yes," McLean said. He was still unlimbering his fingers from Allenby's shake. Then he said, "Sir."

Richards was looking around. "Dodge doesn't seem much different from last year, when we passed through. What I'd heard, I was beginning to think it was bulging up like Chicago."

"Might come to it," Allenby said. "Must be thirty-five, forty herds out there right now, not counting what's passed through. We'll put Abilene out of business yet. What's the condition of your herd, Ben?"

"Prime, just like you ordered." Richards' voice was laconic. "What's the condition of the market?"

"Couldn't be better," Allenby said.

"You look like it, Todd."

Allenby took the cigar out of his mouth and hooked a thumb through his watch chain. "Listen, nurse, there is money to be made in cows, and don't you forget it. Sure, I'm set. I'm a government contractin' agent, and I don't do it for nothing. And I got two more herds comin' into the Chicago market that's paying off for me and nobody else." He flicked the ash from his cigar. "I got married, early in the spring. Don't know as I told you. Young widow lady from Louisiana."

"Congratulations," Richards said. "I had a feeling you were old enough by now." That diamond, or whatever it was, in Allenby's stickpin reminded him of something. Three diamonds, three diamond tears on the cheek of a glittering golden Virgin.

"Let me tell you," Allenby said, sententious, "a fine woman

264

is hard come by in this damn country, and I never intended to settle for nothing else. None of these painted cats for me."

Frankie was restless, shifting his feet and looking off down the street, squinting against sun and dust. They stood under a wooden porch roof on Front Street, which passed as the business district. They were in the north end of the town, where the hotels, the stores, the theaters and the higher class gambling houses were set up. The Santa Fe track ran north of this section, and his eye picked up the raw lumber of the cattle pens along it. He had seen the smoke of trains, standing straight up in the windless air, when he was still ten miles south of Dodge. Front Street was dried up and full of holes and there were wagons and cowhands going up and down it. Once in a while he caught the drab and somehow out-of-place bell of a woman's skirts brushing the crooked boards that fronted the buildings. Men looked purposeful but relaxed too, coming either to the end of their drives or laying over to get the trail out of their systems before they had to move on. Looking up and down he read signs and repeated them to himself automatically, moving his lips with the reading: The Alamo Saloon, Comique Theatre, Tom Sherman's Dance Hall, the Dodge House. South of the tracks, it was pretty run down, all cheap boardinghouses and saloons, and the women Allenby had referred to as painted cats.

"I'm stayin' at the Dodge House," Allenby was saying. "We'll have a drink there and then you boys can do whatever you want to do. Get cleaned up, and we'll have a first-class meal. On me, though, that's got to be understood right where we're standin'. If you need cash on your letter of credit, I got it for you. You expect to pass out a few pesos so your boys can have some fun, don't you?"

Richards kept his tone light, but something was happening to his hands. It was as if he couldn't keep them steady any more. "First I got to check into the Wright House and see if there's any mail."

"Their whiskey's as good as anybody's," Allenby said. "Speakin' of checkin', you better do the same with that hunk of metal you're carryin' on your hip. Both of you. You want to go into the south end of town that's your business and you can carry your hardware. But north end, no guns. That's the law now."

Richards looked at him for a minute. Then he looked at McLean. The boy didn't seem to have heard; he was still staring off down the street. "You got to check your gun, Frankie," Richards said.

McLean turned his head. "Sure," he said indifferently.

They walked up Front Street toward the Wright House. Allenby's hand moved fast, touching the brim of his hat to one man or another, and once removing the hat altogether, bowing, stepping aside, when a woman with two small children passed. In spite of his rough-hewn vigor there was a courtliness, a courtesy about him which might have been ludicrous in another man. He never lost the train of his conversation, even when he was touching his hat or standing aside on the tilting boards.

"This town mushroomed when the railroad came in three years ago. Booming now, booming. Twenty-five men got killed here the first year, every last one of 'em corpse and ca'tridge affairs. That ain't countin' the fifty or so got shot at and lived to talk about it. It's been hell's own time, I can tell you. Tried to get Wild Bill Hickok to come in, but he's the law in Abilene these days. Leastways they're makin' a try at it . . . this new mayor, Hoover, he's set up a city council, and we got a county sheriff, name of Bassett. That's how come you got to pass your hardware over the counter now."

"Nothing wrong with that," Richards said. "Can they make it stick?"

"If you mean is there any danger of your gettin' shot in Dodge these days, the answer is absolutely. Any time, but mostly when the sun goes down. No, there's times and there's men it won't stick with, but it's better'n lettin' every hootowl and gunslinger and drunk in to do as he damn pleases with whatever he's carryin'. Say, you got no idea, Ben: there's four hotels in this town now, and a couple of theayters, six or seven dance halls, and more saloons than you could shake a stick at. Why, they figure there's twelve hundred cowhands all lightin' on this street durin' the trail season. And that ain't countin' the freighters and the Army and the buff'lo hunters."

They turned into the Wright House. Richards went directly to the desk. He wished, for the moment, that both Allenby and McLean would go somewhere else. But Allenby evidently knew everybody in town. He called the desk clerk by his first name and introduced them and finally drifted off to talk cows with two Midwestern buyers standing in the dining-room doorway.

Richards had both hands on the desk, pressed flat, as if the pressure would steady them. "I do have mail for you, Mr. Richards," the clerk said. He was an interminable time producing it, looking over the single letter front and back, as if he could read it through the envelope. Richards knew, even before he put out his hand for it: he had already seen the russet splotch which marked Dominguez' seal.

It was just like Christmas morning after all. He could feel discouragement begin to smolder in him, curling at the edges of him as if he had been dropped square into the center of a fire, small enough so he could get out of it without too much trouble, but scorched nevertheless, hurt all the same. It was what came of putting too much faith in something. He could still hear her voice: whereabouts should I send it, Ben? And his own: Dodge City. But I'd get it for sure at Fort Benton. She had promised and he believed her, and there would be a letter at Fort Benton, but Fort Benton was so far away that it might as well have been the end of the world. He thought suddenly, viciously, it might as well be the other side of the damn ocean, it might as well be Seville, Spain.

He broke Dominguez' seal. He only half-heard the clerk's voice.

"You are Frank McLean, of the M Bar L? I have a letter for you, if you'll wait just a minute. All righty, young man, here we are."

He glanced up and saw Frankie turning the letter over in his hands and looking unnaturally sober, and then he saw the boy rip into it and heard his voice and it too was sober. "It's from Avis," he said.

The little fire he had been dropped into was burning hotter, there was fresh fuel thrown on it. He stood leaning against the desk, holding Dominguez' unopened letter and fighting resentment, envy. He felt if he spoke he would snarl.

"What's she say?" It wasn't a snarl, it was thick in his throat.

McLean had turned his back, square. When he finished reading the letter he folded it up and put it in the pocket of his shirt, under his leather vest. Then he turned around and his face was still solemn, but it had a look of self-consciousness, of caution. "She says everything's fine. She's got a Mexican family camped out and they're doin' the chores and bringin' in wood. Says she's been over to Tres Reyes and they're all well there and askin' for us."

Richards stood looking at him. "Is that all?"

"Well . . . she says the flowers is good this year and she is sorry we ain't there to see 'em." Spots of color, like wine, stood out on his cheekbones. "The bluebonnets never been better, she says."

The bluebonnets never been better. There was something funny, and terrible, in the prosaic disclosure. But he clutched at the straw, just when he was about to go down for the third time. She had used the word, we. She was sorry we weren't there. The cold solace of it crept over him and he picked his way out of the fire and wondered if whiskey was any good for where he was burned.

Allenby had already gone to the bar. Richards had a drink and was on his second when he realized he had not read Dominguez' letter. Well, it didn't matter, he had more time than he liked to think about, to read it. He arranged to meet Allenby later and went to the desk and checked in. He and McLean had to split a room. The clerk was apologetic, but they could surely see that rooms were at a premium this time of year. He handed in his gun to the clerk and McLean did the same. He didn't feel any lighter without it, but he felt strange. Because of Ramón Dominguez he had made the mistake of taking it off, out of respect, and because of Uremáy he had made the mistake of putting it on again, out of superstition. He was a little lightheaded now, and he figured it was the whiskey and he ought to quit while he was ahead. He would get cleaned up and his hair cut and have some dinner with Allenby. Then he would go down to the livery stable and pick up the buttermilk, head back for camps, and let all the crew but a six-man watch come into town. After that he could maybe help McLean finish up his business. There would be no trouble getting rid of the herd: Dodge was full of buyers in boots and big soft hats and half-dude clothing. Anyway, they wouldn't cut the M Bar L's out until the following day.

McLean went off on his own. Normally Richards would have suspected him of heading for the nearest saloon, but this time he knew otherwise: he was off to be by himself, to read and reread that letter, until the edges began to fray and he could recite it by heart. Not because it was from Avis, maybe, but because it was a letter and all his. It could have been a three-word dun saying Pay your bill, and he would have acted just the same about it.

He bought a white shirt that was stiff as a piece of planking. After that he let a barber get to work on him and had a bath in the rear of the tonsorial parlor. On the way back he bought a hat, gray, like Allenby's. When he went into the Wright House he almost didn't get past the bar; then he thought maybe Frankie was off having a few, and he ought to keep his mind in shape and the wheels turning. But when he went up, McLean was in the room, shaved and barbered and all the rest of it, lying back on the bed without his shirt on yet and the pillow bunched up under him at an angle so it looked as if his neck was broken.

He lay there and watched Richards try on the hat.

"Lucky I got my hair cut first," Richards said. "This damn thing would of slid right down over my eyes, like a blindered horse."

McLean said, "Say, Ben." He sat up, hunched forward now on the edge of the bed. "I got to ask you something, and I don't rightly know where to begin."

"The beginning's always a good place to begin," Richards said. He took the hat off and set it on the fake-mahogany chiffonier.

"You and me has had some words now and again," McLean said. "That's how come it's hard for me to say it."

"Let's forget about all that," Richards said. He turned around, seeing the boy was looking down at the floor between his socks, seeing the long thick swell of muscle in the naked brown shoulders.

"Well, you know you asked me once did I want to go on to Montana with you, after I dumped the herd. I reckon I would

269

like to go along." He looked up and met Richards' eyes. "If you still want me."

After a minute Richards said, "I kind of recall you said you didn't want to leave Avis that long. I didn't figure at the time you were just usin' it for excuse."

They watched each other. McLean said, "I wasn't. But it looks now like she'll make out all right for the rest of the summer. I reckoned maybe Mr. Allenby could take care of my money for me until we got to Fort Benton, either bank it for me somewheres or hand it over at the end of the drive."

Richards was silent for a long time. Then he said, "I made you that offer in good faith, Frankie. It still stands. I'll have to let Corrigan and Hedges go, but they won't have any trouble pickin' up work."

The boy had got up and was standing at the window, looking out. Sunlight made little green patches on the dark surface of his smooth young skin. The back of his head, the dark hair cut short, was somehow new, vulnerable. Richards didn't want to look at it.

"I'd like to go on with you, Ben."

Richards turned away, and saw his own drawn tired face, with the skin dried taut and the fine tracery of lines spreading and did not want to look at that either and said bluntly, "Why?"

McLean said, "Because I would like to pay up for a lot of things. Sayin' I wish they hadn't happened don't take away they did. I reckon all the time you had it figured I was goin' to get my comeuppance. And maybe I did, back on the Cimarron. I ain't sayin' I can't use the money, I can, but that ain't as important now as tryin' to work off what I owe you."

"Back on the Cimarron? You talkin' about Rojo, about Rojo gettin' away from you, Frankie?"

McLean nodded, shortly, once. And Richards thought, No, I don't aim to have him along, sulling and moaning every step of the way, and working himself into the kind of man his pa used to be every time you made mention of that red steer. But when McLean came away from the window he didn't appear to be sulling. His eyes were clear and steady; the corners of his mouth looked as if they were ready to turn up, instead of down. And

Richards knew one thing: his relationship to and with McLean had to change, and this was the first opportunity that had come down the road.

"You're on, Frankie, like I told you. You and Shiloh both. Now what do you say we go meet Todd. After that we better get out to camps for a while, and then if you want to we can round up some buyers. I reckon Todd can find you a good deal in no time . . . tell 'em come out tomorrow after we cut out the M Bar L's, and they can look 'em over."

They were leaving the room when Richards said, "Say, you better tell your boys, Frankie. No shootin' on the street and no forkin' their saddles into any saloons. Everybody's on their own hook, so they ought to know the rules. I mean it now, I don't want to see my boys in any trouble." He stuck the key in the lock and turned it. "I expect you aim to head into the south end, after dark."

McLean fell into step with him. "Naw," he said. "I reckon not. I'll wander around and have me a drink or two, but I don't figure to go near them places."

Richards went down in a mild state of shock. He didn't say anything, but he was thinking it: all it had taken for this boy to get beat out was a savvy *ladino* steer? By damn, Rojo, it didn't break my heart you forgot to show up on the Cimarron, now I wish to God you'd done it a long time ago.

FIFTEEN

"You know the little thing my people say?" Uremáy said. "About Jesús Pequinas' ox?"

"Sure," Richards said. "I heard that from the time I was a kid. Whenever they wanted to know something nobody was sure of they'd ask when Pequinas' ox was goin' to get to market."

Uremáy nodded. "Let me tell you, *amigo*, this saying has its twin in the city of Seville. Or did when I was there. Although it was not an ox they asked for, no, it was the King."

"The King?" Richards said. "Had he gone someplace?"

"*Compadrito*, he had indeed gone someplace, as you say. I heard it forty times a day, within the house and upon the streets. 'Any word of the King?' It became so that when I passed Morena Flor she would whisper to me, so that no one could hear, 'Any word of the King?' and I would answer, 'God alone knows, Señorita.' Well, this King . . . Carlos his name was, Carlos Maria de los Delores, of Bourbon, he was fleet of foot as Ebano. We did not know it, of course, but the government of Spain had fallen and in the north country there were many battles fought.

Carlos, *pobrecito*, had fled the country with the rest of these Bourbons. I will say for him that he attempted, now and then, to return. In fact, when we were upon the sea, in the summer, he went himself to lead a battle near the city of Bilbao."

Richards was rolling a cigarette. "You mean you got there right in the middle of a war?"

"True. We did. And the strange part of this is that even with the government fallen, the whole of Andaluz remained as it was, as it must have been a hundred years before, and as I believe it is at this very moment, untouched, with the sun smiling upon it. The war came south to Valencia, but it did not stay. It was not like my Mexico, not like the days of Juárez, may his soul be at rest . . . you know I am Zapotec as Juárez was? All that transpired in Seville was the asking of that single question, with the face serious as the face of God . . . Any word of the King? . . . and then on to the horses and bulls, the sausages and *manzanilla*."

"So she . . . you weren't in any danger."

After a long time Uremáy said, "She was in great danger. Because the wars of the heart are more than the wars of kings. But who is to know these things? Let me tell you. When the summer season was over there was a grand affair at that house in the Barrio Santa Cruz. We had gone back and forth to the farm all that was left of the summer . . . *ay*, such horses, Ben . . . young Ibarra would have torn out his heart to see them. It was a pleasant time and Natividad was easier in her mind, and then appeared this flock of the *muy rico*, the well named, to greet La Morena Flor. As it then developed, the Dos Santos y Quesadas owned the house next door, to the left of us, and two days before this affair the servants came and opened it and hung the bedding to air and made all preparation to receive the owners, although as it turned out only don Julián and the old don appeared, and the old don was too weak in the legs to do more than sit in his chair the whole time. Such a coming and going of carriages in the light of the torches, until far into the night. I, of course, did not participate, but I saw much on my errands of the evening, and I was a proud man that night, and at peace in myself also, seeing her so beautiful, and as I thought, so happy . . ."

273

She had long ago forgotten the names, and the faces had become a blur. How many faces, how many voices, how many questions. So many who wished to know if it was true there were wild Indians still abroad in America, if she had seen them, if she had known anyone who had been scalped, if she indeed spoke the English tongue, if it was true the Mexican Army was forming to march upon Texas, if the longhorn cattle were as brave and formidable as the old fighting strain from which they had sprung.

Daniél was at her side, all elbows and knees and his hair curling damp and tight on his brow like the curly forelock of a maverick steer. Enrique and Luisa maneuvered among the guests. Antonia moved like a sleepwalker, towing in her wake a bandy-legged man with big strong features and waxen flesh whose head was too large for his body. The mellow subdued light of the candles masked the desperation in her eyes.

"Little cousin," Daniél said, "don Julián Quesada. At last, Juliano, I thought you had not come."

He bowed over her hand, a tall man, very straight, light-haired, but with skin dark as her own. "So you are Cayetana. Forgive me for the use of your name, but I have heard it so often. There is an alliance of our families, through Las Pasturas, so you are one of us."

He had not released her hand. She liked him at once, though he was older than she had imagined him. "My wife, doña Mercedes, sends her regrets . . . one of the children has a flux. Nothing serious, but you know the concern of mothers for their little ones. Any word of the King, Daniél?"

"God alone knows," Daniél said absently. His eyes were all over the room. "Where's Angel?"

"Somewhere between here and Toledo, I suspect. He should have left a week ago, but he's evidently been detained." He was watching Cayetana, smiling. "So, have they told you, you come to Las Pasturas next month? No? There will be a *tienta*, a trial, now that the weather's cooler. What's the matter, Daniél, you're white as bread."

"It's nothing," Daniél muttered. Curse Julián. He had been trying to forget the *tienta* and his promise to Cayetana along with it. When Julián Quesada had excused himself he took out a huge

274

handkerchief and wiped his sweating hands upon it as if it were a towel. He caught his sister's glance. She made a wild gesture at him, fanning herself rapidly and showing her teeth in a forced, rigid smile. "'Tonia says you aren't using your fan properly," he said, turning his eyes straight ahead and nodding at an old woman on a cane who seemed about to fall forward with the weight of her bosom.

"I can't speak through it," Cayetana said. "I sound like a cow mooing."

They looked at each other and laughed. "I like him," she said. "Don Julián."

"He is the real heart of Las Pasturas. I think Angel only cares about his horses."

"His horses?"

"Trained horses. He does it himself, for the *rejoneo*. Horses worth more than any bull ever bred, worth more than . . . well, perhaps a whole herd of your longhorns. A small herd, anyway. There are only a few stallions in the world for this breeding, and maybe one out of two hundred horses can be trained."

"Trained? You mean to perform tricks?"

"Heavens, cousin, more than tricks. Trained to outthink the bulls is what it comes to. It's not at all like the Portuguese *rejoneo* . . . the Portuguese are so busy shaving the bull's horns and sheathing them that they've forgotten how to kill, so that all it is with them is an exhibition of horsemanship. It's more than that with us, but you don't see it much any more. It's strictly a game for the *caballero*, to keep his hand in, and it's only worth seeing if it's perfect. That's why it isn't popular, as it was in the old days. But it will be again, we'll come back to it. It takes years to train a horse and more, to teach him not to fear the bull. Because he fears it by instinct. So you see what a horse must be, for this work. Angel can perform every act with a bull a foot fighter can, and without a cape, with only the horse to take him out of it."

She slid her hand through his arm, feeling his thin flesh. He had told her a great deal about himself. She knew now what he wished he was, what he longed to be, and how artlessly he had opened the door to his world of private illusion.

275

It was not until the evening was over that the self-knowledge came to her. The meaning of the reception, the ordeal it had been, left her almost ill with distaste.

It was nearly dawn. She stood at the window with a single shutter drawn back, breathing the fresh chill air and watching the stars snuff out like candles in the gray awakening of the sky, the cathedral tower ghostly, a gloomy spire like the point of a spear, transfixed in the colorless leavings of the night. Antonia was in bed, with a wet cloth over her forehead and her hair spread out upon the pillow. Antonia had already carefully, gently, pointed out the small failures and omissions of the evening, but she had also been lavish in her praise. Cayetana had conducted herself well: it was that natural decorous gravity, and the way her face blossomed when she smiled at last. Not a man there hadn't been stunned by her, there was no question; all the time Julián Quesada had stood talking to Uncle Enrique he hadn't been able to take his eyes off her. The white mantilla had been so right, the black would have been much too somber.

She listened dutifully. But the high comb and the weight of lace were heavy on her head. She had not liked any part of this, after all. If she had conducted herself well, as Antonia admitted, it was only because such conduct was basically innate, and not, as Antonia believed, acquired. Now, inside herself, she shrank from the memory of hands which touched and lingered, eyes which probed and caressed. It had been appalling when all was said and done; the enormity and intimacy of the contact had been an outrage, a stripping away of every shred of her privacy, the price she must pay because these people wished to be generous and loving. A wave of homesickness for Tres Reyes crested in her, so burdening her with tears that she put her head down against the rim of the shutter. Why was she so unreasonable, so ungrateful, simply because she did not wish to be touched or looked at or discussed, why? *Why, except that what it comes to in the end is that they've stood me up like a slave in the market place, that is why. They are pimps.* There was a term she had heard that the trail men used. Blacksmithing, they called it. Aunt Luisa and Uncle Enrique were blacksmithing this night. She wished to smile at the thought and could not. She had been brought here and made

276

prisoner in this beautiful city, trapped behind the white walls and bound with a hundred boresome daily tasks in the name of learning, and now they placed her upon display and were perhaps this very moment lying awake, venturing suppositions on the highest bidder.

Even Daniél. He had let her come with him one afternoon, and once they were upon the street, in the siesta hour, he had not, after all, been inspired to do something adventurous, unorthodox, but had taken her to sit for an hour in the dark dusty-smelling church of Santa María La Blanca, which lay at the northern end of the Santa Cruz quarter.

She felt that the lack was in herself. For the first time she knew how shy she truly was, and yet how restive at the strictures life imposed. A paradox. Nothing would change it. Revolt was unthinkable, she was too compliant, too submissive. She closed her eyes and wished that she might look down and find her foot booted and lifted to Ebano's stirrup, the good taut leather against her, and the long day ahead to go where she wished, be what she wished, to look across and see her father or Uremáy beside her. Or to find no one beside her. To be totally wholly stark alone.

She heard the rustle of the sheets and was guilty. " 'Tonia, I'm sorry your head aches."

The girl's voice was muffled, but not with sleep. "It will go away."

She closed the shutter and crossed the room and reached up to take the lace from her head, from the foot-high silver comb. The tears were gone and the evening was very real to her again and she said the wrong thing because it came so easily to her. "I thought him charming . . . your friend Menéndez. Have you known him long?"

Antonia's eyes were wide open, under the damp cloth. "Forever. I wish he were thinner. And his head . . . he is all out of proportion."

"It would seem there are many fish in this sea of Seville, 'Tonia."

Antonia was silent. Then she said, "Guzman Menéndez is the only fish my father has managed to net for me in five years. He will not let him go."

Cayetana knew she was weeping. The weeping was silent and

277

awful. She went and sat beside the older girl and after a time Antonia put out her hand and Cayetana clasped it. She could feel how cold her own fingers were, how comfortless.

It was monstrous. But she had learned something of herself tonight. Guadalupe, if you watch over me here, answer me this: Why do people want to know so much of themselves? Now I think I can see myself in Daniél. We are alike, he and I. Passive and frightened, the two of us. He will never break free. And I do not want to let myself become as he is. . . .

There was a scattered burst of applause and laughter. Along the little pavilion where the women sat, Julián Quesada's youngest son, a boy of four, came marching, dressed in gray country clothes with his little belly swelling his cumberbund. Under his arm was a shortened *garrocha*, the heavy stick used to upset the bulls. When he heard the applause he looked up into the pavilion. A pink carnation fell at his feet. He bowed, picked it up, tucked it into his belt, and went on his way. He had seen the blossom not an hour before, in his own mother's hair, and he was not deluded.

Under the awning the women chattered and waited. Aunt Luisa leaning forward pigeon-breasted, her mouth pursed out like a little beak. Doña Mercedes Quesada, small and dimpled, younger than Julián, and warmly cordial. Antonia straight and proper in a blue velvet riding skirt and frogged jacket, with a small round velvet beret tilted over one eye. Cayetana, denied her own riding clothes and boots, which her aunt thought shocking, stiff in long skirts and draped shawl, bareheaded and resentful of the sheltering roof which shut out the sun. Around them were clustered wives, daughters, cousins, and children's nurses of the neighborhood. Lined below the pavilion were the men of Las Pasturas and their guests who had come to participate in the *tienta*, men in country clothes and Sevillano or Córdoban hats, a sprinkling of house servants, the field hands who lived and worked with the bulls, spectators from Jerez who had managed to find a way into the *ganaderia*, the ranch.

It had taken the Dominguez, by carriage and horse, two days to travel the forty miles from Seville to Jerez. Uremáy was with them but Natividad had not come, having found kinship and content with the kitchen servants. They were to stay three weeks. But they had both left and arrived later than planned, and the carriage had taken them directly out to the fields. Only Enrique and Daniél had gone to the house, to change clothing and see to the horses. They had bypassed the town of Jerez, although Cayetana could see it, set off to her right, with a brown stone church rising, and skirting it, the buildings Daniél said were wine factories, standing square under dusty trees and surrounded by acres, miles, of vineyards. The fields of twisted olive trees had given way to great meadows springing with lush grass, greener than any green she had ever seen. There were broken hills thrusting in the distance, under a wide sky which shaded from pale cerulean along the horizon to deep clear autumnal blue at the height of its arc. They rode from sunlight into the shade of flying cloud shadow and into the sun again. Venerable trees rose in fields starred with late yellow bloom and watered by the Guadalete and the Guadalquivir, the river of life. The sea was only a few miles distant, and the air sparkled with it, a clear clean silvery air which still bore something of the languorous sensuous summer in it. The rolling hills, verdant as in spring, lifted and sloped, folded and clefted, under the flying clouds. Horses and bulls spread in dark drifts across the rich plain. They had come to a country of fresh open vistas, primitive vigor, end-less sunshine.

A small portion of the Las Pasturas herd was clumped together near the stream which cut the field. They were two year olds. Already the *peones* had gone in, wearing the colors of the *ganaderia*, shirts striped blue and white and flat white caps, moving with an old acquaintanceship among their charges, ready to cut out bulls for the trial. The main *tientas* were held in the spring of the year, but a few exhibitions were given in the fall. It was more than sport, more than spectacle. Out of the test would come the young bulls for the ring. Some, upset by the long beechwood *garrocha*, would run when they had regained their feet. But some would rise and charge and take the small light point of the testing lance and charge again. They would be separated from the little cowardly bulls which ran, and for two or three years they would live on the best the land had to offer.

She knew what to expect, what she had come to see. She had

absorbed Daniél's enthusiastic lectures and pared them down into the significant facts. What was to come was no different, in essence, from much she had known and heard of in Mexico, and yet there were differences: there was a joyous air of fiesta about the country, a virile air, a virile people, and there was an easy professionalism. The scale of it was grander, and more profound. And because she alone was prepared, she was not surprised when Antonia, beside her, suddenly gave a shriek and put her hand over her mouth.

"Oh no," she said. "Daniél!"

Cayetana watched the ungainly boy move out across the field, mounted, with the *garrocha* under his right arm. He seemed to lose some of his awkwardness in the saddle, but he looked dejected and he held the *garrocha* at a bad angle.

"It's quite all right, Julián's with him," Mercedes said soothingly, but she too looked surprised. She reached up and tugged at Aunt Luisa's arm, for Aunt Luisa had stood up, her mouth open, but unable to speak. "It's nothing, Luisa, nothing, he should learn, he should have done it years ago . . ." She looked across at Cayetana, but the girl was turned from her; she saw only the calm profile and the grave regard.

The *peones* had cut out a bull and driven it off from the herd. From the pavilion it looked small, but Cayetana knew how it would look to Daniél: the cathedral-size bull he insisted was bred at Las Pasturas. But he was on the move, spurring the horse forward after the animal, with Julián six horse lengths behind him. The little bull was not graceful, but neither was he lumbering, and it was very fine to watch, with the two men, lances ready, steadily gaining upon him across the long green field, under the white patches of cloud.

Daniél came up behind the bull, the lance tipped straight out from under his arm, and a little downward. Her mouth was dry, watching, as she knew his must be. It was not a thing of skill but of grim determination with him. The end of the *garrocha* struck the bull in the rump, too low. It was the weight of the horse which felled the animal, rather than strength or dexterity on Daniél's part. The bull went down and rolled over and got to its feet again. But Daniél had checked the horse beyond him, and the little bull picked up his feet and charged furiously. Before he could reach Daniél, Julián had maneuvered his horse into the path and was waiting with the light *pica* lance. The bull struck the lance hard and Julián held him off with it, letting him push and go away.

Four times the little bull came to the lance, as angry as when he had first charged, and on the fourth rush Julián spared him, turning his horse out of the way and riding back toward the pavilion with Daniél at his side. There was clapping and shouting and the little boy was jumping up and down calling in a high clear voice. "Oh he was brave, he was brave, and he wanted to kill you, Daniél."

Daniél was flushed to the ears. He looked up eagerly, searching for Cayetana, smiling, seeing that she was biting at her lower lip. *But I have nothing to give him, not even a flower.* He hooked his heel in the stirrup, dismounting, and she stood up and took the yellow shawl from her shoulders and called his name and threw it to him.

The men in front of the pavilion turned to look, and to applaud. What had got into Enrique Dominguez' bookish son this day? The old don Quesada, white haired, with trembling hands and legs, called out to Daniél, but Daniél did not hear him. "Caution, *escolar*, or she will have you in the bull ring of the Maestranza."

She was still standing, with her hand on the rough wooden railing. A man below her had turned, tall in the black *trajes corto*, the tight short jacket and white shirt, the flaring ornate chaps, the pushed back Córdoban hat. He was a younger Julián, but the mouth was thin and wide, the nose more aquiline, the eyes a dark brilliant gray, and the eyes never left her. For a long time they looked at each other, unsmiling, unmoving, speaking without words, rapt, intent, dreaming. She saw the sudden white flash of his teeth, as if they were clenched. Then Daniél's face, pale now and covered with sweat and triumph, seemed to fly up before her. He passed her the shawl. "I am proud, Daniél," she said in a low voice. When she looked again Angel Quesada had turned away.

She sank back. Aunt Luisa was having a spell, occasioned by her only son's temerity. Her life was so arranged, so serene, that the unaccustomed always descended upon her as if she had been struck down by a plague. Mercedes was bent over her, fanning her, while she lay back with a hand at her breast, and her eyes closed. Antonia was concerned but impatient, and at last Mercedes turned, her eyes full of laughter, and called to the little boy. He came galloping up, straddling the *garrocha* as if he rode a horse. She sent him for the carriage which waited at the edge of the field, and he led it back still at a gallop and solicitous hands, Enrique's not among them, removed Aunt Luisa to the house with Mercedes in attendance.

Cayetana could sense more than impatience in Antonia. There was a thing which might have been animosity in the rigid set of her body. But she was silent, staring at the back of Angel Quesada's head, the not quite fair hair above the white line of the collar. After a moment Antonia said, "Caye, this is disgraceful. You should go to the house with Mother." Her eyes were fastened on the field, where the horsemen were grouping and the *peones* riding to the herd. "How dare you *look* at a man like that. And he is no better. Mother of God, if Mercedes had seen you I would have died of mortification."

Cayetana turned to her, astonished.

"You should know something, and if Daniél hasn't bothered to tell you, I shall. Angel Quesada's been pledged since he was sixteen, to a daughter of the nobility, in Toledo."

There was silence between them. Then Cayetana whispered, "Why hasn't he married her?"

Exasperated, Antonia too was whispering. "I will not talk about it any more. Please don't spoil the day."

She would not apologize, to Antonia or to anyone else. What was there to be sorry for, if two people had looked at each other with honesty and without shame, and in so doing, told each other that for both of them, nothing would be the same again.

"How do your studies go?" he said.

"My studies? The study of lace point is making me mindless. I like Daniél's histories, though, I've learned a new word out of them. Seraglio."

They were sitting in the grass along the stream, under the green hills. A quarter of a mile away Daniél was walking bent-shouldered, head down, leading his horse, staring at the ground. She felt herself again, in her own clothing and boots, which had shocked no one at the *ganaderia*. He was hatless; there were tawny streaks in his hair where the sun had burned it.

"Tell me about seraglios."

"You know they exist. The Moors are gone from Spain but the seraglios are not. I'm part of Uncle Enrique's."

He was laughing and she knew he was laughing at her, but it did not matter. "No seraglios in Mexico?"

"Not at Tres Reyes. I live in Texas, by the way, not Mexico. Shall I tell you what I have seen of Seville, in the month I have been here? We climb into the carriage first, like a flock of hens, all clucking and rustling." She counted on her fingers. "The cathedral. All the churches, in fact. The tower of gold. The tower of silver. The Alcazar. The University. The court of oranges. The bull ring. Oh, and the El Grecos and the Murillos and the Velázquez', but not enough of them."

"Christ save us, but that seems a lot, all in a month," he said. "What else would you like to see?"

"The city. I want to walk in it. I want to go up the Street of the Serpents with no voice calling me back. I want to cross the bridge into the Triana quarter."

"But they won't let you out of the seraglio."

She shook her head.

"Do you always do as you're told, then?"

"Always. They tell me to pray and I do so. They tell me to play my guitar and I play. They tell me to sing and I sing. Well, I don't really sing." She was looking down at her hands, clasped on her knees. "The singing master said I was beyond hope. They brought in the gipsy from Triana, Cachango, and I was terrified of him and now I am singing *flamenca* because I have a voice like an echo in the bottom of a well.

He was stretched out in the grass, staring up at the sky. "Not like that. Like wind in the pastures." He turned his head, looking down the line of the field. "What in the name of God is Daniél doing?"

"Oh, he's taking up botany. I expect he's looking for specimens. Rocks, too, he's got enough to dam the Guadalquivir."

"Good," he said. "I hope he finds something never found before and has to go another five miles to do it. Don't his enthusiasms tire you?"

"Not always. You are his greatest enthusiasm, you know."

"Don't remind me. I'm fond of Daniél, and life's difficult enough."

"It must be, for you."

"Why only for me?"

"Because . . . it seems that people fall into a pattern and live, from one day to the next. But you must drill and train and practice, to live. Why aren't you arrogant?"

"I am. Supremely. Vain. Demanding, all the rest of it. Did Daniél lead you to believe I was an aescetic recluse?" He raised on his elbows; the brilliant gray eyes were faintly wary. There was a streak of the rough-grained, a provincial toughness, in him. He cultivated it because he knew women liked it, although he was not as profligate as his position, his profession, his money and his time permitted. When the brilliance and wariness left his eyes, a somber irony darkened them. Under the vital alert good humor of the Andalucían, the vast talent for indulgence, there was the dark abstruse current, also purely Andalucían, of esoteric despairs and premonitory disasters; the dreary specter of some dismal fatalistic birthright which was ominous, even sinister, a sense of the futile and resigned.

He rolled over in the grass and reached up and touched her arm, lightly; there was a litheness in fingers and wrist which was almost delicate, the hand and wrist of a horseman, and under the silky flexibility the strength and temper of forged steel. It was not the first time he had touched her, in the past week. There was a fever in him, he was dry and burned with it. The fair wind coming fresh from the sea seemed to him arid and stifling. An alien urgency marked the hours of his days, and the nights; he no longer felt remote, a shade superior to ordinary men. Every innocuous contact they had initiated had hurled itself like a boulder, under the weights and stresses of the relationship, to further crush the thin and crumbling edge of inhibition and restraint. In them both there was the need to be swept away by the storm of their own, and each other's seething, stunning emotion. They spoke and

284

fell silent, as if they waited. They waited as if they knew no way to bridge the tide which carried them, broad, potent, swelling, outwardly tranquil, but sucking and swirling with undertow in the depths of itself. The inconsequential was upon their tongues, but they would remember the gliding glances, the words drifting low and lost when the breath was caught and held, the touch both mysterious and perceptive, the senses exposed to, shaped by, a new and ardent design. The old familiar perspectives were changed: the very color and substance of sunlight, grass, sky were altered, and yet in what manner neither of them could have said.

Daniél had disappeared following the bend of the stream. She waited, imprisoned, more captive than she had ever been in the house in Seville.

"You can guess all the worst of me, now, Caye, and whatever good there is. All but one thing."

"Maybe I don't want to know, how can I tell? . . . don't make me listen!" Her hand had slid into his; she was suffocating with dread. Her love for him was blind and utterly trusting, and she asked nothing in return. She had put Antonia's warning out of her mind with an effort which had cost her all her strength, and she did not want to hear the same words from him.

It was not what he would have told her. Exactly one hour after the *tienta* he had wanted to tell her that he loved her, but she would not give him the opportunity. Her responses were unpredictable, and he had spent twenty-six years surrounded by women whose responses were as stable and ordered as the routine of their days. "Why won't you let me say it?"

But she was silent, moving her head in a slow, negative gesture.

She was not playing games with him, he knew; she would not have known how to begin, she was too ingenuous, and too considerate. He could sense her susceptivity to him, and yet he knew, *Maria Purísima*, that all such certainty was frail myth. "I am coming to Seville in December," he said. "Do I wait that long?"

"We have two more weeks here," she said gravely.

"You say that as though it marked the end of the world."

Her fingers were working in his, not quite nervous. "How should I have said it?"

"As if it were the beginning."

"December is far away, Angel. So is Seville for me, now."

"Good. On the last count, anyway. I want to believe I've made it so. Father likes to spend the winter in the cafés and Julián's getting good at it too. It's the fate of the aging *ganadero*. But we take a little of the country into the smoke and the talk. Then I must come back, the end of January, to work with the horses."

"When will you fight?" she said.

"The Sunday of the Resurrection. Will you come?"

"Do I have a choice?"

"With your Uncle Enrique, no, you'll come. If it were left to me you could choose for yourself, I've got no seraglio."

"And do you regret it?"

He was not amused. His hand tightened and drew, pulling her off balance and into the grass with him. "Not for a moment. Caye . . ."

"Daniél's coming." She breathed it, half in pained resentment of Daniél and half in gratitude, freeing herself and scrambling to her feet under the shelter of a gray, sunshot oak.

He groaned. "Oh damn Daniél."

"Hush. He loves us. And he is . . . careless."

He sat up, the white smile slashing his face. "The consummate *duenna*. Don't say you've missed him or he'll never leave us again."

They mounted and rode slowly to meet him and turned homeward.

The main house of Las Pasturas was whitewashed and rambling. It had been added to at random and was comfortable and informal. The courtyard, within its eight-foot walls, was hard beaten earth; it had no tiles, for horses came constantly into it. There were blue and white majolica jars of aguave on either side of the door, and the door itself was dark and thick, with great hinges and brass studs. Within, the rooms of the lower story opened casually into one another from the central rectangle of the entrance hall, so that it took a stranger time to get his bearings. As the *cuartels*, the programs of the bullfight adorned the walls of the great *bodegas* of Jerez, wine country since the time of the Romans, so the aged casks of *fino*, amontillado, aguardiente, were to be found at the *ganaderia*. From the entry to the enormous family room, the walls were hung with the emblems and apparatus of the profession: the heads of bulls which had acquitted themselves nobly in the ring; posters and paintings and *cuartels*; vara lances, and banderillas in frills of red and blue and yellow paper; ornamental bridles and spurs; *rejones*, the lances of the castigation and the death; the little banderillas bearing red roses; metal pins with the blue and white ribbons of the *divisa* of Las Pasturas, which were set in the bull's back as he came into the ring; big raw silk working capes of gold and magenta; swords and daggers and scarlet serge fighting capes; *impressarios*' contracts in black frames and striped Andaluz serapes; silver horse trappings with pendant half-moons, gems, medallions, stars.

When they rode in, a *peon* was leading two horses out to the stables. "More guests," Daniél said. "This house will fly open at the seams, Angel."

His arms were around Cayetana, helping her to dismount. "This great house," he said, under his breath, "and too small for us." For a moment she hung quivering against him; the ground swelled beneath her like sea.

When they entered the big room Guzman Menéndez, of the bandy legs, rose to greet her. His florid face was that of a huge predatory cat, crouched to its prey, eyes gleaming and anticipatory. She turned and saw Antonia's still white face, and knew that her cousin's future had been sealed.

"So then there was the wedding," Uremáy said. "Ay God, I have never been drunker. For days, it now seems to me. An occasion like the ascending of a saint, there were so many candles, so many little boys in white, with the voices of angels. And that was how the Señorita Antonia came to leave the house in Barrio Santa Cruz. La Morena Flor was lonesome without her, but she was closer, of course, to the young don than to his sister. For myself, I made of it a tragedy, and yet, God be my witness, not a month from the time the Señorita became Señora Menéndez a change took place in her. Her eye was brighter, her step was quicker, her voice was livelier. She bloomed, like the rose." He sighed. "Which proves what I have always suspected, that a woman is better off with any man than with no man at all. La Morena Flor, of course, would not agree with me."

"Well," Richards said, "what about this bastard with the horses?"

Uremáy looked at him. "It is not natural, the way in which you share my feelings, Benjamín. Well, on the seventh day of December the Dos Santos y Quesadas, the old don and don Angel and don Julián and doña Mercedes, and the little ones and what seemed to me an entire pueblo of servants, arrived at the house next door. They came on this day as it is the time when every living soul in the city of Seville gathers in the Plaza del Triunfo at midnight. There is a shrine there, called the Immaculada, to mark a great earthquake which occurred long ago in Portugal. There was throwing of flowers and singing and chanting. I did not, myself, quite understand why one should observe the occasion of an earthquake in another country, or any earthquake at all, but I never missed my chance to enjoy life as it came to me, even if it was of a religious nature. The religion there was as it is here, nobody but the women paid any attention to the priests, and with the exception of a funeral, everything churchly ended in fiesta no matter how it had begun. So, I went to the shrine, and I stationed myself behind my Morena Flor, in the event that she should need me, and while I did so a terrible truth was made known to me. I do not know if it came from heaven, but I suspect it did not. I suspect it came only from looking upon Morena Flor's face, and seeing in it that she did not need me any more. She had only need of him. He was with her that night, or with the family, and when I looked at him I began to hate him as I have never hated before in my life, Christ absolve me. Do you know what I am saying?"

"I reckon so," Richards said, looking stonily into the fire.

"It is hard, not to be needed when you have become used to being needed. The purpose seems to go from things. Until the end of January there was a coming and going from one house to another. There was a double iron gate in the wall, opening upon the courtyards. Every day those two were together, an hour here, ten minutes there." He leaned over and spat upon the ground. "The blindness of mankind is one of life's mysteries. The foolish aunt and uncle, encouraging this one and that one, persons to whom my Señorita gave not a second glance. Not one eye in either of those houses, not one but mine, saw what was happening. I do not think they were ever alone, unless it was some chance meeting in a passage or an empty room. But I tell you that as discreet, as careful as they were, I knew what was taking place. The longest weeks of my lifetime: they were not lovers, not then, and I wondered what could be in Morena Flor's mind when she thought of that woman he had been promised to for ten years." He laughed harshly. "Ten years. And so far from each other they could barely have kept an acquaintanceship."

"Couldn't he of got out of it?" Richards said. "There wasn't any law he had to marry her, was there?"

"Negotiate for his release from this woman? Not easy. It was not only her name, the political and social advantages. There was his position to consider also, the certain fascination of his way of life. Understand, he did not do what he did for money, money was the last consideration. No. He was heir to a fine farm which raised fine bulls, and now and again he was under some compulsion to show the *afición* not only how good were the bulls, but how good was the heir himself. This is no small fame, my gringo. And who was I to point out the evils and errors? I sat with my mouth closed and drank more than was good for me and waited for the world to crash in upon us all."

"And it did, I expect," Richards said.

"Not until the spring came, and Holy Week and the fair were upon us. I breathed again through the last of the winter, when he had gone back to Las Pasturas, but I believe I knew that I was breathing as if there would be no air left in the city when he returned." He twisted on the woven blanket and tried to see Richards' face in the dying glow of the fire. "Do I make you unquiet in your soul, *amigo*? If I do, perhaps it would help if you would think of this as an old adventure of an aging man. A part of the history of Tiburcio Uremáy. All men are eager to tell their histories, to anyone who will listen. Do you know now why La Morena Flor sorrows?"

Richards rose and picked up the coffeepot from the fire. "I

know some. You want a cup? But that letter I found . . . you ain't sayin' it was from him, from this Quesada?"

"Coffee, no, my nerves jangle and hum like the wires of the telegraph, in San Antonio. The letter . . . another day. It is time for the guard change." Uremáy reached into an inner pocket of his coat. "As you mention letters at this moment, here is the *patrón's*. What did you make of it?"

Richards turned, the cup in his hand. "Nothing. I thought it was pretty usual. Was there something in it I was supposed to see and didn't?"

"No. Only the reference to the little widow . . . that she was well."

Richards drank the coffee off in one draught, scalding himself in the process. When he had put down the cup he said, "I have been told twice, by Frank McLean and by Ramón Dominguez . . . and I reckon it came straight from Avis . . . that she ain't been eaten by a bear. That's good enough for me."

"Where do you go, Ben?" Uremáy said, looking up, startled at Richards' grim tone.

"I aim to mount this guard," Richards said. "Who in hell could get a good night's sleep after listenin' to you." He paused, seeing only the faint shine of Uremáy's eye, the broad cheekbones standing out copper in the shadowed face. "About that King . . . did they ever get word of him?"

"I say now as I said then: God alone knows," Uremáy said.

Richards went around the fire and put the toe of his boot under Shiloh's behind, rousing him. Uremáy called to him, softly, across the darkness. "*Compadrito*, it is beyond midnight. You cannot go without sleep for the rest of your days."

"No?" Richards said. "Well, like a steer, I can still try."

SIXTEEN

Beyond the Solomon River a great flat tableland stretched northward a hundred miles. The certain fresh balm with which June had tempered the atmosphere went quickly as the summer moved toward its zenith. The earth began to look dry and burned; a hot pressuring stillness was heavy in the air.

They were making twenty miles a day and sometimes more. The days were sixteen hours long, with the herd on the trail before daylight. Often, on the wide plateau, it would rise and graze forward before Sykes had sounded chuck call. It would be two or three miles ahead when the crew reached it. Dodge City had come and gone, and they still spoke of it and the good time Todd Allenby had showed them as if it had never really happened, as if they had spent all their days and would spend what was left of their days drifting north on the sunbaked plains of Kansas.

They had crossed the Big Boggy, turning west to avoid the fertile farm lands of the Solomon Valley. Big Boggy was, nine times out of ten, a terror to both trail crews and herds, and there were times during the season when they lay up for days, waiting to cross. It was only sixty feet wide, but it had its caprices: some places the shallow water was dead still, except for a slight riffling current. A few feet from the still water there would be a whirling pool in which a horse could sink out of sight. They hit it at a good time; it was down, but heavy June rains had been at work in the high country of its headwaters, and within another three or four days it would be overflowing its treacherous banks. As it was, they mired a few cattle, but the bottom was thin as gruel, and no match for the quicksands of the Canadian. They would have felt better about the crossing if it had not been for the picked-over and decomposed bodies of cows from a herd ahead, which had mired, drowned, and washed ashore. The rotten stench of the dead flesh was in their nostrils until they left Big Boggy behind.

Richards was up on the point. He felt heavyheaded and a little queasy, which was what came of keeping yourself fagged enough to drop right off when you hit the bedroll, and then not being able to do it when you got there. He was still not quite used to finding Rojo missing from the lead and there were times, overtaking the herd in the first daylight, when he half-expected to see the great span of horns standing out against the summer sky. He saw little of McLean, busy with the remuda, but when he did, neither of them mentioned the lost *ladino*.

McLean had sold the calf wagon in Dodge and felt profited by the deal, since the thing stood to be replaced before long anyway. And as Richards had known it would, the drive was going easier and more efficiently, with the cows and bulls and calves gone. He had quit fretting about the letter, or the lack of it, just as he expected the novelty of getting one had worn off for McLean by now. You couldn't keep fretting over something you didn't have; you could only keep expecting you were going to have it some other time. He was riding thinking what a deceptive, unjoyous thing hope was when all was said and done because once it had pulled the wool over your eyes and you were outright disgusted with it, didn't it show up again, big as life and promising to come across with all it had denied and more besides, when Shiloh came up out of the swing and fell in with him.

"Sleepin' out?" Shiloh said.

"My eyes closed?" Richards said.

Shiloh looked at him. "Not closed, exactly. Droopy."

"If I was asleep, do you care?" Richards said.

"Deep in my heart, yes," Shiloh said. "It beats all what a man misses when his eyes is closed. Look there."

Richards looked, where Shiloh pointed. Ahead was a grove of shade trees, leaves turning silver like the leaves of the cottonwood, and reflecting the silver-blue color of the still water which lay beneath them. It was a mirage. There was a shimmering ethereal beauty in it, and it looked as if they could ride straight to it, and dismount under those trees and kneel to the clean sweet water. It stayed with them for a long time.

After that they saw several each day, sometimes many miles away, often close enough to touch. At times, from the drag, the whole lead of the herd would look to be gargantuan, steers, men, horses and all, looming up into the sky. Richards liked the combination of the trees and water most. He never fully lost the notion that one day he would catch up with it, and it would be real.

There had been a scarcity of wood all across the west Kansas plains. Sykes had cooked over cow chips and every man in the crew had got out of the saddle a hundred times a day to pick up a twig here and a branch there, to transfer to the cradle under the chuck wagon. But when they crossed the Nebraska border and approached the Republican, wood became plentiful again and the mirages vanished.

The Republican gave them no trouble, and after the herd had been crossed a couple of hours before sundown and were grazing forward to bedground, Richards went over the trail situation with Uremáy. He knew this country; the condition of the rivers ahead was vital, for between the Stinking Water and the South Platt there was a stretch of forty miles, a two-day drive, without water.

July had come in hot and clear, without any rain to speak of, and rain was needed. But there wasn't a soul for miles around to ask the condition of the rivers. They might be low and they might be raging. Within ten miles of the Stinking Water, Uremáy was instructed to hold the herd, and Richards went out on scout at dawn, trailing two mounts out of his string.

He did not return until close to midnight two days later. He had ridden nearly ninety miles, out and back, and had sighted Ogallala on the far side of the South Platt. Both rivers were low, and the stretch between was dry as an old bone.

"You got as far as Ogallala?" Shiloh said to him at breakfast.

"Not to Ogallala," Richards said, already knowing what he was getting at. "Just to the Platt."

"You mean you got that far and quit?" Shiloh said, breaking a biscuit thoughtfully. "The things I am expected to swallow." He looked up at Sykes. "I don't mean the biscuits, the biscuits is topgrain, as usual. I mean the big augur here, settin' lookin' me straight in the eye and tellin' me he got to the Platt and didn't rattle his hocks gettin' across it. He ain't got much of an opinion of what is under my skull. You can see what he thinks of me. I bet he don't believe I could drive nails in a snowbank. If it wasn't I was nearly there myself I reckon I would froth up into a real sod-pawin' mood about it."

"Before you start," Richards said, "take all that stuff you claim is under your skull and kindly direct it to a dry drive. After that you can worry about gettin' to Ogallala."

Shiloh stood up and flung out his coffee grounds. "All hell wouldn't keep me from it," he said. "And if I got to go forty miles without nothing extra to cool my gullet, I surely aim to fill up more'n my canteen when I git there."

Ogallala lay in the valley of the South Platt. When the herd at last came lowing and thirsty to water, the day was dead and gone, and across the river lights were beginning to spring up and flicker in the summer dusk. Like signals, Richards thought. If he didn't let them cross tonight they would never forget it, and they would hate his guts.

They had made the dry drive by deliberately watering the herd at noon and pushing it off right afterward, and they kept moving until well after dark. The night was quiet, but by mid-morning of the following day the herd was beginning to make noises which showed its discomfort. At noon they changed horses and McLean went on with the remuda; the horses would be fresh and well-watered when the crew reached the Platt. They goaded the herd on fast, alert for milling or the attempt to turn back, but they got through and the big-horned heads went up and the voices bawled out when the smell of water came to the parched nostrils. Now they were on bedground, and Richards got ready to cross the river and see if Allenby was in from Dodge.

He came back an hour later with the news that Allenby was expected the following day. He had felt a little desperate because he was short of cash, but when he told Albert Coleman at the Lucky Dollar Dance Hall, Coleman didn't take more than a flying glance at his letter of credit: he went into the office and came out and handed Richards five hundred dollars and told him not to forget who his friends were.

He left six men with the herd. There would be a two-day layover, and the crew would all get their chance, but he had Sykes pick out eight black beans and thirteen gray ones and they drew them and he took his chance along with the rest of them. There was no question about Sykes; he would be going in the following morning to stock up and he didn't care one way or the other. Uremáy drew a black bean and so did McLean. McLean only lifted his shoulders and turned away.

He gave them each thirty dollars and they took off their boots and rode for the river. "Adíos, cows," Shiloh said. "See you in the morning, if I am able to focus my eyes." He rode ahead, into the dark water, and his voice drifted back to Richards, bringing up the rear. "Oh go-o-o tell the news to my gray headed muuuthur-r-r, Go tell the news to my sister so fay-u-ur . . ." When they had crossed Richards said, "You want to come with me, Shiloh?"

"You aimin' to play a little cards?" Shiloh said.

"No," Richards said.

"I never seen you dance."

"You won't see it tonight, either."

"You feel the need of female companionship?"

"I saw the last female I want to see for a while when we dumped those M Bar L cows," Richards said.

"Say, too bad there ain't a church in this town, you would have a huckydummy time of it. Thanks anyway, Ben, but if I stick with you I can see that all I will git in Ogallala is a haircut."

"Stay out of trouble," Richards said, but he said it as a joke. Shiloh would be the last man in the crew to lose his bearings.

He regretted Allenby hadn't arrived, and after he got cleaned up and had a beer he began to feel as aimless and unpreoccupied as he had in the days when he was drifting. There was some difference though, because while he was out in the middle of nowhere, just like he used to be, there was something waiting for him when it was all over. One way or the other, yes or no, but something. Hell, I'm going back to camps, he told himself. I'm going to buy Al Coleman a drink with his own money, and then I am going home."

Coleman had gone out on an errand and they didn't know when he would be back. Richards wandered around and watched some cards being played and had two or three drinks and bought a bottle to take back to camps with him and sat down at a table and nursed his glass. The town was as noisy as any he could ever recall being in. They whooped and called and galloped out on the street. He forgot how men sounded, after the long empty silences of the trail. Their laughter was soaring and gusty and they banged with their fists when they wanted to drive home a point, and they shouted when they talked. There were six or eight women in the place, and with the exception of two who had seen better days he placed them all under twenty, meager bodied and bright eyed. One of them coughed a lot, and it bothered him. The hell with all this. He could buy Coleman a drink tomorrow.

"Well hello, cowboy. I was afraid you'd quit the trail and I wasn't ever goin' to see you again."

He looked up, disliking the term she had used to identify him, and said, "Hello, Carrie. How are you?"

She was short and fleshy, in a red dress. There were a few undisguised gray hairs showing, but the rest of her was all red paint and white powder, and the black ribbon around her throat only pointed up the low cut of her neckline. She was worn and tired; there was no powder made which could conceal the dark rings under the eyes. She might have been pretty once, but it was hard to tell, since she had maybe started in this game every bit as early as the young girls he had seen circulating.

"You look great, Richards," she said.

"You don't do so bad yourself."

"For an old girl, you mean?" She laughed, and it was genuine.

"I didn't mean that. Don't put words in my mouth," he said. He picked up his glass and dumped the whole shot into him and wondered why he did it.

"I wouldn't dream of it, dear," she said. "The less you say the better it is. I always kind of liked you because you did instead of said. How long's it been . . . three, four years anyway. You ain't changed much." She looked up at a passing man in need of a shave and said, "I'm roped for tonight, Ed." Richards knew Ed had said something or done something he'd neither heard nor seen. When he had passed, she leaned forward. "You better ask me to sit down and have a drink, Richards, so I don't look like I'm floatin' loose."

"All right. Sit down. I'll buy you a drink."

She sat with her elbow on the table, chin in hand, watching him while he struggled to catch the bartender's eye. When the drink came he looked at it narrowly.

"Kind of weak-lookin' whiskey you're drinkin' these days, Carrie."

She laughed again. "If you'd had a few more yourself you never would of noticed. It's tea."

There was humor in his voice. "I take it back, there have been some changes. What are you doin' in Ogallala?"

She sipped at the glass and then gave a cocky toss of her head. "Oh, I move around. Or anyway I used to. No more. I own half this place now, Richards. Me and Al Coleman. Goes to show what savin' your money'll do for you."

"Everybody gets up in the world in Ogallala," he said. "Coleman advanced on my credit letter tonight, so I reckon I ought to say *gracias* to you too."

She sipped again, thoughtful. "Is it true you're bossin' for that big Mex outfit down on the Nueces? The Three Kings, ain't it?"

"You keep up with things, don't you, Carrie?"

"I got to, in my business."

"I reckon so," he said. "Have another cup of tea?"

"Not so loud," she said, laughing again. "Look, Richards, I got the nicest little place you ever saw, upstairs. Red plush from one end to the other . . ."

He was shaking his head, and he felt kind of mournful about it. If anybody had asked him what was the hardest thing a man had to do in this life, the downright ugliest toughest, he would have said that it was saying no to a woman when she had her mind set on yes. "I can't, Carrie."

"You mean you ain't stayin' over?"

"I got some cows to nurse."

"Sure," she said mocking. "You always stampede into a cow-town and ride right out the other end, don't you? What is it, Richards, a woman?"

He was silent.

"Oh come *on*. Where do you expect I been all these years? You think there's a woman anywhere in cow country don't know what her man's doin' when he hits Ogallala? I thought you and me was friends. It's been a long time."

"I'm not stayin', Carrie."

Her eyes narrowed. Then she lifted the fleshy shoulders in an exaggerated shrug. "It's a free country," she said.

He pulled the cork out of the bottle and had another drink, without even thinking about it, except to think that he wanted it. She was sitting tight, as if she had no intention of getting up and moving off, even though she knew that was what he wanted. "You ought to tell Aunt Carrie all about it. The part she don't know, that is," she said.

He could feel the whiskey. "What does that mean?"

"I listen to men talk most of the night, dear. I know that greaser spread's got a perfec'ly delicious little daughter just about ripe to fall off the tree. What a setup for you, after all these years."

He was not angry, but anguished. Anger would have been better, quicker, cleaner, and he would have understood it. More, so would she. His mouth twisted. "You're wrong, for once, Carrie. It ain't what you think."

"No? My, the sad songs I get to listen to." She stood up. "When did you saddle such a high horse?"

"Carrie, for Christ's sake, are you mad at me!"

Her eyes were still narrowed. "Me? Mad at you? If you ain't the conceitedest man I ever run up against." Her head swung away and her eyes went over the room. "Is that sandy-haired one out of your outfit?"

He turned around and saw that Shiloh was standing at the end of the bar. He hadn't seen him come in and he wished he hadn't seen him now. "Leave him alone," he said. "He's just a kid."

"Well now, you all had to be kids before you got to be big boys, didn't you?" Her voice was sharp as a knife, mocking again. "So good luck, Richards, I'm glad I seen you. It's too bad those Mex dishes go to seed so fast."

He got to his feet and picked up the bottle. The floor wasn't as firm under him as it should have been. He didn't look at Shiloh again; if Shiloh couldn't take care of himself he deserved her. The whiskey had not lifted his spirits, and he could not recall whether he had had four or five. He felt dull and empty, weighted down with a weight that was cold and dead and unyielding as a bag of sand.

Uremáy looked up and saw him coming back into camps, saw him dismount and walk across to the fire, saw that he was unsteady on his feet, and that his eyes looked hollow and withdrawn. "You return early," Uremáy said, only a little curious.

He stood holding the whiskey bottle by the neck and looking at Uremáy. "Tell me the rest of it," he said.

On a windless shining Palm Sunday, at four o'clock in the afternoon, the first procession of Holy Week moved out from the Street of the Serpents. In the light of flaring candles Nuestra Señora de la Hiniesta rose high above the throngs which lined the streets to see her. Beneath the swaying platform on which she rode the feet of the faithful who supported her worked like the feet of a centipede. There was an insistent roll of drums, accompanying her. Before her moved the Confraternity of her church, robed men in high conical hoods, only their eyes showing in their masked faces. When the dusk began to fall the enormous tapers they carried creased the shadows with springing light. At every block the great platform was lowered and eager hands passed wine to the sweating exhausted men who bore it. By the time the

299

Hiniesta had passed into the cathedral, from which she would return to her own church, the Virgin de la Amargura had begun her annual journey through the streets. The Passion was upon Seville.

She thought of the penitents of Mexico, coming down from their villages to the nearest church, holding their poor candles, a winding serpent of flame in the twilight. She remembered Father Berrades, waiting, at Tres Reyes, while the *gente* came in their clean cottons to light their candles before Guadalupe. There was a pure sweet sorrow in Christ's death. Here, there was disturbing and gloomy grandeur.

The streets were massed. In the wooden stands near the cathedral the Dominguez and Quesada families, seated with conscious reverence, watched the *pasos* enter or emerge. Overhead the bells rang; the slow roll of the drums filled the night. The fringes of the golden palls which sheltered the Virgins shimmered and swung.

The city slept through the spring mornings, but on Wednesday she rose early and went with Uremáy and Natividad to the cathedral. Oppressed with the burden of a steadily mounting emotion which had in it nothing of spiritual ecstasy, she lit what Uremáy considered an extravagance of candles to the Cristo de la Salud, the Christ of the Bullfighters, who would enter the cathedral at sundown. When she had done so she slept until the afternoon, a shallow dreamless sleep from which she rose with weariness and the same sense of oppression. In the stand that night, when the dark fell and the drums rolled, under the black lace of her mantilla where it draped her to the cushions, her fingers were locked hard in Angel's, locked until they were numb. She no longer resented the thrust and push of the crowd for it forced them upon one another, shoulder, thigh, knee. The rhythm of his breathing was in her with the steady pulse of the drums. Around them women in black and white lace ate chestnut pastries dripping honey and cloves and cinnamon and speculated on the identity of the masked penitents. Below, the masses surged into the cobbled street, singing, offering wine, falling silent as the imageries of Christ's Passion approached on the slow moving platforms.

By Thursday the tenor and feel of Holy Week had begun to

change. Good Friday was at hand, and there was an expectancy quivering in the air, as if the city had been brought to the point of explosion. Until six in the morning of Good Friday there would be no respite. The streets were foul with broken glass, paper, rags, slick with spittle and the melted wax of a thousand spilling tapers. When the Confraternities came barefooted in their black and white and purple and gray and green robes, some in chains and shouldering crosses, she thought she could see evil in the hard glitter of the eyes behind the masks, relentlessly searching the streets. There was something baleful in the slow turning of the hooded heads, safe from identity, a malevolence in the working of the hidden mouths offering muffled insolences to the passing women.

Fettered by an uncompromising and scrupulous sanctification which had begun with massive solemnity, the city now hovered on the brink of a convulsive frenzy, prepared to burst its holy bonds.

At three o'clock in the starry morning of Good Friday the Macarena, Virgin of the Bullfighters, came at last to the cathedral. She stood tall and very young under the brocaded golden pall, vested in gold from coronet to train. One slender hand was curved to her breast. On the flawless cheek the jeweled tears appeared to tremble and fall in the glow of the numberless slim tapers which banked the scaffold. Waves of fragrance half-cloying sweet, half-pungent spice, rose from the blankets of orange blossom and white carnation surrounding her. When the platform shivered and swayed upon the human shoulders which carried it, she appeared to quicken and stir. From throat to hem she blazed with the gems of the parish church of the Macarena.

The stands would remain filled until the Christ of Calvary was in procession, after dawn. But the locked hands had devised signs, and they rose. Angel turned and looked at Daniél, behind him, a long sharp look. Passing his father, Daniél leaned to touch him on the arm. "We're cramped, Father. We will walk toward San Lorenzo and wait for the Christ of the Great Power."

Without Daniél it would not have been possible. The throng was crushing, unruly, boisterous but good-natured. The processionals waiting to enter the cathedral had blocked the main streets and made them almost impassable. They gained the walk across from the Giralda, the tower of the cathedral, and turned to look up at the slender ochre spire. In a small area above and around it the sky was luminous in a flush of light, as if the illumination of the tapers had ascended to girdle it in a pale aureole. Suddenly the bells pealed and a cloud of white doves flew from the dark recesses of the tower and soared on the edge of the flushing light. When the bell had ceased, they fluttered back, settling like fragments of drifting snow, only to rise and soar again when the bell broke the upper silences of the night.

They moved on, into the milling crowd. Bottles shattered on the stones and voices called, over the drums. The hooded men of the Confraternities, eerie phantoms, held their flaming tapers as if they threatened with fire. The tension was a stretched chain, waiting to snap and whiplash. Across the Street of the Sun, while the bearers rested their platform, a wild mourning cry arose from a second-story balcony, flooding the street with primitive lament. Against the lighted interior of the room behind, the figure of a young gipsy woman with hair to her hips sprang out above the waiting processional. The drums were silent while the *saeta*, the agonized protest of the gipsy, towered and swelled with the force of the dark broken voice.

It was over. The drums rolled again. The press of the crowd thrust them forward, and Angel flung both arms around her, shielding her with his body. His abrupt words were lost to her, but she was instantly tense with fear. The crowd was out of control around them, carried by its own momentum. A group of gipsy boys the color of their own copperwork had formed a living cable on the edge of the throng and were rocking the whole mass, chanting. Fighting it, almost swept off her feet, she felt his desperation. Then a voice lifted from the human chain. They had recognized Angel and were calling to him, bantering, with a familiarity they would not have dared at any other time: Pick the biggest bull, don Angel. We'll be there cheering for you, on the sunny side. Dedicate the bull to us, don Angel. And a path was cleared for them, deliberately, for a bare second, and they broke free half-running and into a short side street so dark they could barely see one another.

They leaned against the wall, breathing again. She began to shiver, calling up the fermenting violence of the crowd.

"Caye, you're cold."

"No, I'm fine now . . . Oh God, where's Daniél?"

"Have we lost him? What a pity."

"Angel . . ."

"Come," he said, and took her hand and they followed the street and the tension was here too, as if the murky shadows waited to disgorge formless and unknown terrors. They emerged in a small square which received them with a clean sharp delicious stillness. The sound of the drums, the clamor of the cathedral bells was dim and lost and their footsteps made hollow echo in the square.

"Look," she said.

They were outside a shop which sold religious articles. It was shut and dark, but overhead, from the living quarters, a thin light streamed down from the open doors. The little golden Virgin glowed, as if with her own inner light. "Is it the Macarena?" she said.

"Yes, Nuestra Señora de la Esperanza. Caye, she looks like you."

"Don't, that's blasphemous."

"Would you like her? I want you to have her. She's special to me."

"I know," she said. There was a flat resigned finality in her. "I know. And I wish . . . Angel, the time has passed so quickly, the whole year will be gone . . ."

And all the insane nameless repressed passions of the week flared in him and erupted. His voice was rough, savage. "I'm not going to let it go. I'm not going to let you go. I'm going to say it. I want to marry you, I'm mad to have you. I've thrown away the winter, trying to find my way out." And no wariness in him now, only the dark, almost ominous, fatalism. "All the days spent, used, and I can never have them again. And no choice. Only one way. I'm going to take it."

She cried it at him, in pain. "But what of . . ."

In the street, with the light shining down from above, the light with no sound, he took her by the shoulders, without gentleness.

"I'm going to Toledo, as soon as the fair's over. I'm going to break this thing."

"But it isn't fair, it isn't fair to her."

"To me either," he said harshly. "I've never cared about her and I never will and I'm not going to let the Quesadas arbitrate my life." The almost brutal harshness fell away from him; his voice was thick with wonder, with the mystery of what he saw in her. "Christ be with you, Cayetana, I have a great fear for you. You are too innocent. Too good. Too trusting. You haven't a spiteful bone in your body. They will sacrifice you, these bloodkin of yours. You will let yourself be sacrificed. Sacrifice to me, then. Can't you say you love me?"

"Yes. More than anything," she said. "Since the first moment, at Las Pasturas." She was crying. But she was faint with the wildest sweetest oldest joy in the world, burning with a steady upright flame, and purified.

It was a long time before she could speak again. "My father. You will come to Tres Reyes?"

"I'll go anywhere, do anything you wish me to do."

"But you must speak to Uncle Enrique."

"No. He will not listen to me. Julián won't listen. Not until I come back from Toledo. María de los Reyes, what a fool I am. I should have gone in the fall, I should have left the hour I laid eyes on you."

They were clinging together, under the grieving eyes of the Macarena. There was a sharp series of footsteps, running, and they broke apart. The footsteps turned up a side street.

A grayness was beginning in the east when he opened the gate in the wall, next to the house of Enrique Dominguez. There was dew on the tiles of the courtyard, and a cool, unmoving silence in the dark garden, the empty house, in the coming dawn. In the Street of the Sun the gipsies wailed for the Virgin of the Afflictions, and the Christ of the Expiration, on a bed of scarlet carnations, was beginning his final journey over the Guadalquivir, to Triana.

"Little conversations come back to me," Uremáy said. "One here, one there. I was a great deal in the kitchen those days . . . there was a bread they made through Holy Week, all worked with sugar and oil. Well, that is of no matter. The place to learn all things is the place where the servants gather. One can eat an olive or two, or an orange, and listen. There was money changing hands and much talk concerning which matadors were to open the April fair. Possibly Carmona, who was native Sevillano and a great favorite, but getting old. Even Lagartijo, who I was assured was one of the masters, or Cayetano Sanz, but they hoped not because while he did fine things with the cape his swordwork was so bad it spoiled it all. The little gossip. Doña Mercedes thought she was fooling everyone, don Julián in the bargain, but they all knew she was going to have another *niño* . . . except perhaps don Julián. Don Daniél had got lost in the Good Friday crush and broken his spectacles. A beautiful Macarena had come to the Señorita Cayetana from the house of the Quesadas. The Señora Dominguez was out of temper with the little María on the morning of the Resurrection because little María was late with her chocolate. But the reason the little María was late was because she had found the Señorita Cayetana's slippers so stained with dew and earth that she had been trying to dry them in the event they were to be worn to Mass. Are you still *borracho, amigo?*"

"I wasn't drunk," Richards said. "Or anyway I don't reckon I am now."

The untouched bottle sat between them. Uremáy said, "In that event I will have a small drink. I did not think it would do for us both to be leaning sideways into the night, as you were doing. Was there something you wished to say?"

"Is that the end of it? Your works seem to of run down."

"Not at all," Uremáy said. "Permit me to continue. The day Our Lord rose I went to Mass, along with everyone else in the house . . . I remember the day particularly because I believe it was one of the finest days ever to come with the sun. One might say the very air had been touched by magicians. By four in the afternoon the crowds were hurrying up the Paseo de Colón, along the Guadalquivir, carriages, horses, afoot, all in a fiesta mood to get to the Maestranza. That is the bull ring, and a pretty thing it is too. Think of it: bulls and Christ risen, all in the same day. Promptly at five a processional of another sort came out upon that yellow sand. No Virgins at this hour, although I don't doubt there was praying beforehand. Two horsemen with plumes in their hats and behind them don Angel all in gray *trajes corto* and tooled *chaparejos* on a black horse which might have been Evano, then three matadors so heavy with gold and silver I did not see how they walked at all, then more men and horsemen and at last three black mules in red harness, all jingling with bells and looking eager to drag away the bulls. Such a sight, Benjamín. If I had not had this weight upon my heart, and the fumes of too much manzanilla in my head, I think that I myself might have been encouraged to jump into the ring and try my luck. Well, you have seen bulls fought, and you like or dislike it, or perhaps do not care, even as I . . ."

The black horse came across the sand with a high sharp lifting gait, hoofs varnished and crimson silk braided into his mane. The key to the bullpen was thrown down from the president's box; a mounted constable caught it deftly in his plumed hat. One by one the matadors and their *cuadrillas* slipped out to the passageway between the wooden barrier and the stands. Alone in the ring, Angel Quesada put the black horse through an execution of Spanish dressage to a steadily mounting chant of appreciation.

At the far side of the ring he changed to a gray dappled horse which showed its Arab blood in the slender legs and small elegant head. It wore a high Andaluz saddle and heavy metal stirrups. Crossing the sand for the second time, he paused before the president's box. The gray Arab stood upright, balancing upon its hind legs. When it came down again, he took off his hat and made the *brindis*, dedicating the bull.

Daniél was leaning from the box, his face alight. Angel had dedicated to him. A little sweat of pleasure shone on his bony cheeks. Slowly, formally, the horse pranced across the ring until it had reached the *toril*. Then Angel turned him, his back to the door. The horse stood like stone. Only the softly flicking ears betrayed him.

"He's going to cite from the gate," Daniél said.

Oh God, what am I doing here? "Shouldn't he?" she said faintly.

"Usually he waits in the center of the ring until the bull comes out." Daniél's face was serious, his forehead creased; he would

306

appraise and judge seven bulls of Las Pasturas today, in the interest of the *ganaderia*. The trumpets blasted, jarring her. The *toril* gate flew up and the bull slammed out.

It was an enormous *berrendo en castaño*, white, spotted sorrel. She saw Angel take one swift glance over his right shoulder; then horse and bull were off across the sand.

"Cathedral," Daniél muttered, and she knew now what he meant. The red and white bull was a four-year-old, over twelve hundred pounds, massive in chest, withers and hump. The *astifino* horns, wide, thin, curving upward, were a pale graygreen, shading to onyx at the tips, their color disclosing his caste. He was splendid and she did not want to look at him. The gray Arab's long silky tail seemed to flick the bull's muzzle, going away. Then the Arab checked and turned, standing for a mere second, feeling the familiar pressure of knee and bridle, and charged straight at the bull in a fast frontal attack. But the bull too was moving, to intercept the horse, and Angel flashed past the horns and leaning, set the castigation lance into the spotted withers with a single downward stroke. The lance snapped off, leaving the blade in the bull. From it, a small blue and white flag unfurled against the spotted hide.

Daniél was muttering beside her, and now and again Uncle Enrique leaned across her to question his son or point out some facet of the deadly game. She could feel a bright mist in her eyes, like unshed tears. "He's getting more out of that bull than the bull knew it had, and God knows it's a great bull. But he's taking too many risks," Daniél said to her glumly.

She had been holding her breath, without knowing it. The horses were being changed for the third time, at the far side of the ring, while the bull stood watching, not tired, only boiling with a fury that showed in his great humped neck muscle, his lashing tail. The third horse was also black and it launched into a frontal attack as the gray had done. Angel had two banderillas in his right hand now, and he placed them dangerously, slowing at the last possible moment and letting the bull overtake him. But he did not let it pass and he sank the sticks the most difficult way, while the bull was still slightly to the rear of the horse. They did not stand upright in the flesh, but lay flat, hooked only through the hide, as they should have been. There was a roar of approval

307

from the stands. Twice more, with the frontal attack and the half-turn he placed banderillas, once with both hands, the reins clipped to his belt, guiding the black with his knees, the second time leaning into the animal to sink the short sticks called *cortos*.

"His judgment's magnificent today," Daniél said. She heard the banderillas clattering and saw that at last, as she had feared, the bull had overtaken the horse. She wanted to cover her eyes and could not move. Close to the barrier, an indefensible position, Angel swung the horse short, met the bull, and veering obliquely from the saddle, set the little seven-inch banderilla with the rose upon it, and the rose flowered red on the bull's withers. In the plaza they were standing, shouting.

Again the horses were changed, and the fourth was pure white with black stockings and a black strip of silk in his mane. Again the bull stood watching, waiting, his great sides heaving, but his mouth closed, still showing his caste. But his neck muscles were weak now and his head was down, opening the vertebrae to the one small entrance where the steel would cut the aorta and kill instantly.

For the third time bull and horse were running and curving across the sand, the horse offering its exposed side, and the bull flashed by on the flaring edge of Angel's left *chaparejo* and the first of the three *rejones de muerte*, the lances of death, was sweeping downward, a short lance in blue and white frilled paper, with a fourteen-inch head. The white horse deflected and stood, the lance driven home. There had been no blood but the red spreading where the banderillas were placed, but the bull was already dead. There was a single rush of blood from his mouth; the forelegs crumpled at the fetlock, and he went down slowly on the sand with his eyes still open and crashed over upon his side.

The sound in her head was more than applause, it was like the drums of Holy Week. Daniél was up and cheering and the mist cleared and she saw that Angel had swept off his hat and was up in the stirrups, making the formal acknowledgment. He settled and the white horse rose and stood upon his hind legs as the black horse had done, and then leaped high in the air, all four feet off the ground, and it was finished.

"Caye," Daniél said, "are you ill? You look . . ."

She was going to vomit, right here, and disgrace herself and the family.

"Was it the bull?" he said anxiously. "I didn't think you'd mind, he died beautifully, and Angel was never better and if he comes up and finds you didn't like it . . ."

They were all concern and conflicting advices. Enrique had already gone down to the barrier. Daniél must not leave, he would have six bulls yet to judge. But she would not, could not, stay. Uremáy came forward from the rear of the box and quietly settled the matter. He would take her home.

She leaned against him, leaving the noise of the plaza behind. Outside, hundreds who had been unable to secure seats waited for word of what was taking place. When the carriage came, she seemed to recover herself, though her eyes were still sick and distant. "I don't want you to come, Tiburcio," she told him.

He watched her steadily. "I cannot let you go alone, Señorita."

She sensed his formality, and he her rising insistence.

"It does not matter, I wish to be alone."

"I cannot permit it, Señorita."

"I will not have you, Tiburcio."

"And what am I to tell the Señora, when I return to the box?"

"Tell her what you wish, after I am gone."

"Morena Flor," he said, breaking.

And she broke also. "Tiburcio, please. Please."

The carriage came up. He helped her in. They did not speak again. He knew she would send the carriage back. He waited a few minutes, under the dark arches of the outer gates; then he started up again. Angel Quesada was just leaving the box. They met on the stone stairs.

"She has gone home," Uremáy said.

"I know, Daniél told me . . ." He stopped. His face went white, and hard. Uremáy's eyes were like the eyes of the bull, black and raging. "Be careful what you insinuate, old man," he said softly.

"I do not insinuate," Uremáy said. Despite his eyes, his voice was calm. "I know. And it is you who should be careful. If you do anything to harm her . . ."

309

The powerful hand shot out, driving him back against the wall. "What are you to her, *peon?*"

"I was sent to care for her," Uremáy said, still calm. "I see I have made a poor thing of it."

White and grim Angel released him and went on, down the stairs. Uremáy stood against the wall, his heart pounding. He saw Angel ride out, looking neither left nor right, ignoring the clamoring crowd, and when he had gained the top of the stairs he peered out the arch of the wall and saw the horse turn left, back down the Pasao de Colón.

"All the week of the fair," Uremáy said, "I could enjoy no part of it. Not the ladies in their ruffled dresses or the dancing or the horses parading or the livestock show, not even the wine, Christ witness, which will show you how my mind was. I know that he went directly to her when he left the Maestranza, that they were alone for the second time. The rest I could only surmise, seeing how she was the next day. She shone, like the morning star. That fine brute of a bull, and it was the man she sickened for." He shrugged. "No doubt she would have grown used to it. Then she would either have had a hunger for it, or stayed at home and prayed for him. But she rode three days of *feria* with him, behind his saddle, with her skirts spread all around her like the foam on the sea that I remembered, and red poppies in her hair." Uremáy's eyes were morose. "And how else could he have been with me, that afternoon, but the way he was? I took the taste of his triumph out of his mouth for him. No, I would have been the same. You would have. It took me a long time and much thought to see this, so that at the end, when it was too late, I came to know that there was . . . what? . . . a certain rightness in him, for her. I think he dominated her, just as I saw him dominate his bull, and I think she had need of this."

"That sounds mighty peculiar, comin' from you," Richards said.

"Why so? Loving someone does not make us blind to their weaknesses. Well. They found a hundred ways to be alone that green April week . . . the *bailes* to slip away from, the afternoons to hide in the caves of myrtle in the gardens of Delicias Viejas. Daniél was riding with one of the Quesada cousins behind him, a

310

bright girl she was too, and the Señora Menéndez was to have a child, and the old people were off to one grand affair after another and there was fiesta in the air from sunrise until sunrise, so who was to watch them? But I will say that by then all those sightless people in the houses in Santa Cruz were at last getting back their vision. On the fourth day of the fair . . . you remember the stained slippers, of which I told you they gossiped in the kitchen."

"Kind of," Richards said.

"Well, as it turned out, the little María became weary of trying to clean and dry those slippers. Myself, I believe she mentioned it to the Señora in all innocence. Nothing was said to Morena Flor of course, but that evening, when don Julián and doña Mercedes had gone out to dinner at ten o'clock or so, don Enrique crossed his courtyard and entered the gate in the wall which led to the Quesada courtyard. I kept myself awake with a headful of ugly thoughts and a bottle of aguardiente, and so it was I knew he did not return until midnight. I do not think Morena Flor left her room for nearly a week, but whether of her own choice or because she was not permitted to, I cannot say. I never saw don Angel again."

SEVENTEEN

"Do you wish to confess to me, my child?"

"No, Father," she said.

"You have confessed this week?"

"No, Father."

"The week before perhaps?"

"No, Father."

"There is no absolution without confession, my child."

The voice was oily with self-assurance. She raised her eyes at last and looked at him for a long moment. He was a fat scented voluptuary, a friend of the rich; there was an alarming intimacy in his approach and she saw beyond his false solicitude to the avaricious core of the man. He was no grubby mendicant, but a part of that august entourage which moved in the refractions of multicolored light, in the purple gloom of the vaulted arches of the cathedral. The thin care furrowed face of Father Berrades came into her mind.

"I am with you as a kindness to your uncle. And to you, of course. I am fond of the family," he said complacently.

She lowered her eyes and did not look at him again.

"If you do not put your entire trust in me, I cannot help you," he said. The chair creaked under his weight. He glanced about the dark closed room. A thin crack of sunlight edged between the shutters, filled with motes of silvery dust. Antonia's bed and personal possessions had long since been removed, and in the corner the image of the Macarena glowed dimly. "You petition the Macarena's intercession?"

"And Guadalupe, Father," she said.

He dismissed Guadalupe with a sluggish wave of his hand. "So having brought dishonor upon the house of your uncle, you have nothing to say?"

"No, Father."

"You are young to be so cold and unrepentant. Have you no perception of the extent of your sins?"

"Yes, Father."

"This being true, what measures will you take to expiate them?"

"I have asked pardon of my uncle, and of God. I will pray."

"Your voice lacks earnestness. For the sake of your mortal soul I ask that you pray now. I will join with you and then I will hear your confession."

She rose obediently and went to kneel before the Macarena, drawing her scarf over her hair. She was aware that he remained seated, behind her, and she could feel his eyes on the back of her head. *Hail, Mary, full of grace, the Lord is with thee* . . . he is right, why can't I feel anything, as if I were dead. Why did I let it happen, because I loved him is the only reason, and I suppose that in itself is a sin, and Aunt Luisa is having another spell and Daniél avoids me, and I never knew before how wicked and evil I am and now they are sending me home and isn't that punishment enough? Isn't it enough to *know* I have sinned and that I am contrite . . . am I contrite? . . . yes I am filled with contrition and shame and I beg forgiveness, somebody forgive me, even if there is no understanding sometimes there is forgiveness, and I wish it had not been this man, I wish it had been Father Berrades . . ."

She raised her head and looked into the compassionate eyes of the Macarena. The thought of her mother before Guadalupe shocked her; how easy it would be to come to that, after all; a lifetime of unending invocation, an eternal postulant.

She crossed herself and rose.

"I had looked for more protracted atonement," he said. "Are you ready to confess to me now?"

"No, Father."

He sighed. But he was more cynical than curious. "May I ask your reason?"

"I will confess to my own priest, when I have gone home."

"The sword of retribution may descend at any time, upon the unshriven. That is a long time of vulnerability, lady."

"I will chance it," she said.

He stood up. His garb was immaculate and plain, but a huge red stone, like blood, adorned his hand. "You have gentle manners and are courteous, but you offend the Church, through me. Nevertheless, I shall pray for you."

"Thank you, Father."

He went to the door. Then he turned. "I regret that I must ask, but it is your uncle's wish, and as you have not seen fit to spare him it is my duty to do so. You are not with child?"

"No, Father." Her voice was so low he could barely hear it.

"God go with you," he said piously, and left her.

When she thought of prayer, that same image of her mother bore upon her like the cross itself. When the dusk came down she opened the shutters. There were footsteps in the streets, a few first lights. The city would come to life now. Behind the cathedral spire the sky was the color of ice and topaz.

The house was like a tomb. There was still light in the sky when Enrique knocked and entered, but she was glad that they could not see one another.

"There is a ship out from Cádiz, in five days," he said. "The time is short, and we will have to hurry. I will accompany you, of course."

"Uncle Enrique, where is Angel?"

"He left for Toledo, a week ago."

"He sent me no word?"

"Only that he had gone."

"And you will not let me wait, until he comes back?"

"Cayetana . . . may I sit down?" He lowered himself slowly into the chair where the priest had sat. "I wish I had the power to make you understand. Father Alonzo tells me . . . are you unrepentant?"

"Oh no, Uncle Enrique, before God, I swear it!"

"There, do not swear, for I believe you. These difficulties you have got yourself into. . . . As I remember, the first words from your mouth were 'it is not his fault.' I did not deny this then and I will not do so now. There are certain liberties, allowed to us, which are not allowed to women. Angel is no saint, but my heart breaks not only for you but because of what he has done: deceived me, betrayed my confidence. Only because of Julián was I able, today, to mend the breech in our relations with Las Pasturas which might have resulted from this. I do not mean to force the issue upon you, but I do wish to impress on you the gravity of your transgression."

She wept at last, coming to him and kneeling at his feet. "I know this, Uncle, I know it, but if we are married what difference . . ."

"You only bring more wretchedness upon yourself, Cayetana. There is no possibility that he will break his contract. What would he offer in exchange, to a woman who has spent the better part of her girlhood waiting for him and, because of this, removed from all other prospect? Having lost his head he is now on an errand of desperation and nothing more."

"But he does not love her."

"You have much to learn," he said heavily. "To begin, I think you had perhaps not place so much weight upon this word, love, for if you do it will surely bring you to ruin. And try not to cry, it helps nothing."

"Do you forgive him, Uncle Enrique?"

"Him?" He was surprised.

"I couldn't bear it, if there was feeling between you, because of me."

"Time has its own way of easing things. You will find this too, if you will let yourself. Child, we must be practical. I have written a letter, which I entrust to Uremáy, explaining as best I can the

315

circumstances which have come about. There is no reason for anyone but your father to know."

"My *father*?" She drew away from him, in fresh pain. "Oh please, Uncle Enrique, I beg you not to tell my father. If anyone must know, it is my mother."

He was silent for a long minute. When he spoke it was with bleak reproach. "Cayetana, since you were seven years old your mother has been a helpless cripple. Do you not realize that over all these years your father has kept many things from her, anything which might affect her condition. Do you ask of me now that I ignore your father, the head of your household, and burden your mother with something which might well cause her final decline? Child, child, your blindness astonishes me."

"It is you who do not understand. My mother . . ."

"Will be spared, at all cost. When will the young learn to let themselves be guided by their elders? I was proud of you, Cayetana, you were dutiful, as Antonia is. But she has a strength you do not have, and that is perhaps why she is happy and you are not."

She had risen. She said, "I mistrust your word happiness as much as you the word love. I am grateful to you for all you have done for me, Uncle Enrique. And I will not forget what I brought down upon this house. May I ask what you have told Tiburcio?"

He too stood. "I told him that you are homesick. He seemed to understand and accept this."

She was smiling thinly, to herself. Why not have told him the truth, when he already knew it? He was silent, as Indian-stoic as Natividad, and he drank too much, and she could not meet his eyes, seeing in them that he knew.

"Can you be ready by morning, Cayetana?"

"Whenever you wish."

"Then there is nothing more to say. Except, perhaps, that you are very dear to me, to us, and that I take this action only for your own well-being. Someday you will thank me for it."

Since she could not deny this, she remained without answer. When he had gone, a maid came to help her pack, but she sent the girl away with a request only for linen and straw matting with which to wrap the Macarena. At ten o'clock the same maid came with a dinner tray, which she left untouched. Near midnight there was a quiet knock at the closed door but no one entered when she responded. She lighted a candle and went to it, listening with a first fierce hope. Something rustled under her skirt and she bent to the scrap of paper which had been slipped beneath the door. The lone word, *courtyard,* was written in Daniél's scrawl.

She went down an hour later, bitter with the knowledge of how easily she had learned to slip from this house, to the gardens. The night was sticky with the scent of roses and jasmine, the moonlight white and brutal. Without preamble he said, "Caye, if it would help, I'll marry you. I don't mean I shouldn't like to, I should, very much you know."

Her affection for him was touched with sadness. Dear Daniél, the unwitting accomplice, spinning out his small bright reveries, brought now to believe that he would defy his father, bear her away, make it all come right again. "Bless you, Daniél, I only wish it might have been that way."

His serious owlish eyes were fixed upon her. "I wish I'd been some help to you. I don't really believe in hell, that's too much strain on the credulity for me, so I don't think you'll go there, or Angel either, and while I don't want to upset you or try to convert you or anything, I hope you won't spend any time worrying about it . . . I mean, I like to believe good things about God if one has to believe anything about Him at all. What I'm trying to say is that I shouldn't influence you in any way, and if I only had the courage of my convictions and a little more meat on my bones, I would fight Father and the Church and every bull on Las Pasturas, one after the other, but as you already know I will be lowered into my grave still keeping the *ganaderia* books and dreaming of a thousand other possibilities, all of them glorious and none of them feasible. What can I do, for you and for him?"

"Daniél . . . do you think as your father does, that he won't be able to break his contract?"

After a little time Daniél said, "I seldom think as my father does, but I don't know. Angel is very generous, but there's a streak in him ruthless as his own steel. I've always envied him it, it gets him what he wants. What shall I tell him?"

"That I will do nothing until I hear from him."

"Is that all?"

"Daniél, I can't burden you. There is nothing I can tell him that he does not already know."

"Well then." His voice went high and thin, breaking with something close to tears. "What will you do, Caye?"

"I will go home and die a little bit every day, until I know."

The second day out of Cádiz she fell ill with a sickness that had nothing to do with the sea. She lost neither consciousness nor reason, but lay disembodied, floating, a small hollow shell curved round and round upon itself like the chambers of the nautilus, with a separate anguish lodged in each adjoining recess, staring at the beamed ceiling of the rolling cabin with her fist against her mouth, to keep from screaming.

"So it was I said good-by," Uremáy said, "to much that I had looked upon with pleasure. Good-by to the pretty girls walking with their arms locked in the afternoon streets. Good-by to the pitchers of red *sangría*, with slices of melon floating in them. Good-by to the shops and cafés along the Street of the Serpents and the black iron cross which looked as if it had been made of lace, that I passed every day in the Plaza Santa Cruz. Good-by to the twisting streets and the plazas where I sat in the shade and ate fried dough, and that brown river flowing out to sea carrying all Andaluz upon its back. But I felt a great impatience for the return. Back to Tres Reyes. I only asked God why the return should be made in these circumstances, but God did not answer me. It is a way He has. There are evidences of Him all about, yet He does not let me see Him. Being a small man, the smallest in His universe, perhaps, I console myself that He does not bother with me, and yet when I am about something I should not be about, there is no doubt that He singles me out. Well, I have run the wagon off the road, I see. I think you have fixed in your mind now a good portion of my history, as I promised."

"Wait a minute," Richards said.

"I have come to the close. We came home and life began where it had stopped and there has not, to my knowledge, been much change since."

"You mean she never heard anything from any of 'em over there, from him, all this time?"

"Did I say that? No, there were letters, of course. I do not believe that don Enrique ever made mention of facts other than those which directly concerned their day-to-day lives, and what bore upon them. Careful letters, I am sure, since he knew they would be read aloud, to La Morena Flor and the Señora. If you mean were there letters from don Angel, there were three. Two were destroyed, as was one from don Daniél. The third you picked out of a *huisache*, with its outer cover gone, and handed to Morena Flor on the stairway of Tres Reyes."

"My God," Richards said. He turned and looked at Uremáy. "And all the time I somehow knew she never saw it before."

Uremáy said, "It appears that I will have occasion to make my apology to don Angel, before I become too old to remember what I said to him and he to me . . . words I did not wish to repeat, even to you, and which I would rather forget."

"Then he got, how did you say it, out of his contract?"

"He did. There were no details. Only that he had written twice before, that nothing had changed with him, and that if he did not hear from her own hand that she did not wish him to, he expected to take ship in the summer. Her silence he put down to the fact that his earlier letters had gone astray. As indeed they had, it pains me to say."

Richards was still looking at him, his eyes disturbed. "I'm goin' to have a drink now, Tiburcio. Are you sayin' that don Ramón held those letters back from her, never let her know about 'em?"

"Are you making a harsh judgment, *amigo*?"

"You're right, I am," Richards said. "Something that didn't belong to him, something that wasn't his business only in the most roundabout way. That ain't right, Tiburcio. That makes what I thought was a big man look damned little."

"I am forced to agree. However, suppose you put yourself in don Ramón's place for a small time. You have a wife, so disposed so young that she bore you no sons. The hope of your land, your wealth, your very country is in your only issue, in this instance a girl. It is very necessary that you make a proper arrangement for her, one which will see to the continuing of your line. No, do not give me that crooked smile of yours, Ben, you own nothing and you are free to go as you wish, but that is no reason to look down upon men who are not. Now let us say that there is a man who wishes to take this daughter of yours away, to another country, so that she may have sons to insure the continuing of *his* line. And let us say also that this same man has been in such a hurry about it that he has not waited for the usual offices of the priest. The temper of fathers toward young men who have seduced their daughters is too well known for me to speak of."

"You Mexicans are all crazy," Richards said. "All livin' back in the . . . whatever that time was when there wasn't anything bein' learned, the dark ages I guess it was. So if don Ramón felt this way all he had to do was pick out a man just like the Spanish side of the family was tryin' to do and marry her off. And if he didn't want her to marry over there, why were they workin' at it, like you said, with that big stomp and all?"

"There would have been no objection to a man of the city who would return and learn the operation of Tres Reyes. A *caballero* with interests twice the size of Tres Reyes was another question. And as for an immediate marriage, arranged with some *hacendado*, there was one problem even don Ramón could do nothing about: the matter of arriving at market and offering . . . how shall I say it? . . . damaged wares."

"My God," Richards said again. "You're serious."

"When it comes to La Morena Flor I am never anything else. Now, before you think more harsh thoughts about the *patrón*, let me tell you that I believe he will have his score settled if Angel Quesada arrives at Tres Reyes while we go to Montana on this trail which never ends. And I do not doubt he will, he seemed bent upon getting all that he wished from life, even as the *patrón*. Our misfortunes in Seville, as you can perhaps see, drew La Morena Flor and me close together, very close, and if it served to draw her closer to the *patrón*, it was so that he could keep watch upon her."

"If you think you're endearin' Ramón Dominguez to me, you better change your mind, on account of . . ."

"Because of what?" Uremáy said softly.

"Nothing. I was thinkin' of what she said he told her: that

she was the most trusting and innocent or whatever it was, and how he couldn't of been more right if he'd tried for it."

"You do not believe in sin, then, *amigo*?"

"Sure I believe in sin, I've dipped into it myself now and then and expect to stay in good health to do it some more before I'm finished. But I don't reckon a person ought to be made to pay for it and pay for it, I reckon the payment ought to end someplace. I would say that of all of 'em, this Quesada was the only one playin' square after all. Maybe he went about it kind of ass backward, but he wasn't foolin' about tryin' to catch up, was he? You got a way with words, Tiburcio. You had me believin' what a nice kindly happy family they all were, with maybe a few queer ideas, and he was the one should of been pistol-whipped. But somewhere along the line you got twisted up, didn't you? What you've gone and done is made it so I won't ever feel the same about Dominguez again."

"I beg you not to get yourself into such a passion," Uremáy said.

"Why not, to see that little girl treated like that. By God, I am glad to know it was me busted it wide open."

"It was in me that you might be," Uremáy said.

"And you can sit there on that old poncho and tip up that whiskey bottle and say that Ramón Dominguez did what was right, what was decent?"

Uremáy put the bottle down. "*Amigo*, I will tell you the truth before God. It is well that we were ready to move out of Tres Reyes, and that you had done me the honor to ask me to go along as your *segundo*. During that time I searched about here and there and found again my patience and my good sense. If it were not for that, I believe that on the day I discovered what he had done, I would have gone for my machete and struck off his head."

Shiloh came into camps at noon wearing a black hat, which he took off the moment he dismounted, making an unsuccessful attempt to roll the brim. The guard had been relieved and was off to Ogallala. Nobody was around but Richards, the watch with the herd, and Uremáy.

"You think I am just barkin' to hear myself when I talk about

Ogallala," Shiloh said, standing frowning, with the hat between his hands. "But that ain't so. I didn't know you was even in the Lucky Dollar till I seen you go out. You looked to me like walkin' was gittin' to be a lost art. You should of stayed around. That bartender was servin' a free snake with every drink. How do I look?"

"*Malo*," Uremáy said, "*muy malo*."

"I'm sorry I asked, that bein' the case. First I lost all my money in Ogallala, and last night I had to go and lose my . . ."

"Never mind," Richards said, "I don't aim to hear about it."

"Would you do me the good manners to listen? I lost my conk lid."

"Your hat. How in hell did you lose your hat?"

"Danged if I know. I took it off polite-like when that lady come up to me at the bar and I never seen it again. Likely somebody swiped it. Look at this boardy thing. It ain't got no more character than a new-laid egg. Ben, you ought to of seen her room. That lady's, I mean. There was red stuff all over, windows and all. What do you think I ought to do about this hat?"

"Stomp on it," Richards said.

"We could start an *estampede*," Uremáy said. "Only for you. If you ride the point and throw your hat before the *vacas*, it will come up looking as if you had owned it for a hundred years."

"That's too big a price, on top of what the hat cost," Shiloh said. "Especially as I am feelin' as if I had got mashed through a strainer. Say, as we're all among friends here, what in the nation do you suppose is eatin' Frankie?"

Richards said, "That's the last thing I would of called it. First time he's acted like a member of the human race since I can count."

"You always did have hopes for him, didn't you, Ben?"

"I always did."

"He don't act right, bein' he was always changeable as one of them little bugs turns different colors like whatever they happen to be sittin' on. Don't misunderstand me, I always got on good with Frankie, and Jonah too, and Miss Avis . . . all of 'em, even old crazy Sid Lunt, the M Bar L bein' my home away from home and all, and he just don't act like Frankie McLean no more."

"Where is your home, Shiloh?" Uremáy said.

"Oh I ain't had one in years. I never broke the law, though, so I ain't afraid to tell my name, which is *Eugene* Framerson, but my ma begun callin' me Shiloh on account of that was where my pa got killed. She was sentimental about it. Well, anyways, Frankie ain't had more'n two drinks and he says to me that he expects he will be back with Sykes this afternoon. As I am kind of used to the idea of haulin' him out of the local lockup everytime we git anywheres close to what smells like it might be civilized, I am hard put to it to figure him."

"Rojo," Richards said.

Shiloh thought about it. Then he said, "You reckon so? Why if anything, I expect he'd be hornin' the brush about that red steer. He don't look to me like he's touchy about nothin'.'"

"Perhaps that is because he sees that it does no good to become angry at something he can do nothing about," Uremáy said.

"That ain't never stopped him before," Shiloh said. "Whatever it is, I'm in favor of it. If he can keep it up I won't miss Jonah so dang much when I git home again. On the other hand, though, if it was losin' Rojo, I hope that old outlaw goes clear to Canada and don't show his nose again."

"What makes you think that?" Richards said.

"What did I say I was thinkin'?"

"About him showin' his nose."

"Well, he could be headed home. Ain't that right, Tiburcio?"

Uremáy spread his hands. "It has been heard of, but it is not usual."

"What do you think, Ben?" Shiloh said.

"I think I am in camps outside Ogallala, Nebraska, and that ninety percent of this crew is goin' to be ridin' out of here tomorrow morning with nothin' but a head, and that Rojo is havin' himself a high old time somewhere south of Dodge City and that that is the last we are ever goin' to see of him."

"You do take the joy out of a good palaver," Shiloh said. "Say, Frankie was not just airin' his lungs after all, there he is now, with my dear friend Bill Sykes. Well, I am goin' to close my eyes and see if it will puncture this swole head I got before I go on watch. You gentlemen got everything under control, I suppose, and can do without me for a minute or two."

They watched McLean and Sykes coming up from the river, the mules drawing the freshly stocked chuck wagon. Richards was silent, and Uremáy saw how stern his face had become. "You are thinking about that boy?" he said, inclining his head slightly toward McLean and Sykes.

Richards shook his head. "As a matter of fact, I was thinkin' about that day you were all comin' up from the border, with the mustang crew, and she . . . Cayetana rode ahead and ran straight into Rojo. You remember?"

"I remember. She told you this?"

"She told me on account of it was right after Frankie and Shiloh'd seen him, when he'd got Jonah. Why do you think she did that, sat there and they didn't even try to make for cover?"

"You do not know?" Uremáy said.

"I got kind of an idea now, but I don't know as I can say it."

"It was to do with many things," Uremáy said. "She was alone, for one thing. And the sand. There was that animal, with horns which make the horns of the bulls of Las Pasturas seem as sewing needles. There was, perhaps, even a thought in her whose nature I do not wish to examine, for my blood freezes in me with the thought. Is that enough?"

"Plenty," Richards said. The sun was hot on the open plain of the river, but something cold started up his spine, getting colder all the way, until finally he got up and reached around and folded his collar back over his hide vest, so it could find its way out. Maybe he hadn't known the words, but he thought now he could call up the tune.

In a little under a week of leaving Ogallala, the Tres Reyes herd was following the North Platt, in days of warm drizzling late July rain. It was smooth trail country, with small creeks flowing into it. By the time the weather cleared, they found themselves trailing sometimes within feet of the Platt, sometimes with ten miles between the herd and the river. The Platt was wide, and without banks. It was running higher than normal, due to heavy summer rains in the mountains, and Richards kept his eye on it.

It looked to him as if it was going to be a major crossing, if not a troublesome one.

He had had a flying conference with Allenby, got his money, and paid Al Coleman. Allenby's drives had all come into Dodge on time, and he would now ride north, contracting for local cows through Wyoming, and be at Fort Benton in time to receive the Tres Reyes herd.

Three days after they had crossed the Wyoming line they came into the Forty Island ford of the North Platt. Sykes left the outfit, headed for the wagon ferry at Fort Laramie. His sour insistence on meeting them on the other side or letting them starve acted like a goad, but they looked at the river and then at Richards and then at the river again, with a silence that said more than words.

"Starve, then," Sykes said as he set off, cracking his whip over the mules and cursing them, with the wagon lurching as if the wheels would pop off. Richards grinned wryly and dumped his boots and mounted Plácido. Opposite him, in the river, lay two small islands. He walked the horse to the first one, on firm sandy bottom, with the water up to the saddle skirts. But as soon as he stepped off the first bar, Plácido was swimming, in high still-swelling water, but without heavy current. The middle channel was a good hundred yards wide. The horse took it easily and found bottom again fifty yards from the far shore. Richards rode out and stood in the stirrups and waved his hat and saw the remuda stream in off the flat and into the water. When it had reached the first island, Uremáy started the lead of the herd across.

He could not remember when he had seen so many cows swimming such a long distance.

The country beyond the North Platt was as good to look at as it was to trail in, but there was a change in the weather. They were climbing, and the heat of the day seemed concentrated in the hours of the nooning; the clear air chilled quickly, and the nights were cold. Mountains rose on their left, shunting off in a ragged chain. To the right spread a broad wind-rippled plain, marked with local cattle trails.

Three days beyond, the mountains vanished, and the broad plain edged into the rough ridges which signaled the rise of the

Black Hills. They came into an uneven trail which was mainly wagon tracks routed out of the earth, and Richards surmised it led to some mining camp in the area. The wagon trail led on for fifteen miles and they followed it before turning off to cross a dry fork of the Cheyenne.

Richards pointed the herd northwest, toward the Powder River. But the dry Cheyenne crossing had told him something and he was cautious. Summer rains in the mountains were too variable to be relied on, and he confirmed his suspicion with reconnaissance. From the south fork of the Cheyenne it was eighty miles to the Powder, and there wasn't so much as a mud puddle in between.

"Don't you git sick of them long rides?" Shiloh said to him when he got back.

"Only when there's no water," he said.

"You think it might rain?"

"Someday," Richards said. "Someday when we don't need it. We got two things on our side, though. The weather's cooled off and we're comin' into the full moon."

"Pure poetry," Shiloh said. "But it don't git the cows to the Powder."

"That's the spirit," Richards said, "and you hang on to it, on account of it's goin' to be a far stretch before you get any sleep." He looked at the men around the fire, sitting close because the night was cold. "I don't like to mention it, but you all remember Indian Lakes. I expect it'll be some time before you forget it. But this herd's as trail broke now as it'll ever be, and I reckon it's time to find out how far it'll go in a day. We're goin' to hit the south fork of the Cheyenne tomorrow about noon. There's no water runnin', but there's enough pools so we can water to the last inch of dry gut. That's horses, cows, water barrels and canteens, and you boys. In that order, too." He glanced up at Sykes, standing against the wagon tail and picking his teeth with a splinter. "Bill, point out a beef, a good fat one, and we'll butcher it in the morning. I want fresh meat for the boys all the way in."

Sykes nodded. "Steaks for breakfast, dinner, and supper," he said.

326

"Hell, don't ruin 'em," Richards said, "just keep their strength up."

They watered in the holes of the Cheyenne's south fork. By nightfall Sykes had ridden far ahead and McLean went out shortly afterward with the remuda. Richards rode at the point with one of the lanterns from the chuck wagon; at the rear, Díaz rode with the other. When the dark came, they were lighted, but they were needed only as beacons to mark the lead and the drag. They held the cows in tighter than usual, not letting them spread out. The moon came up a hair short of full, and the night burst clear as day around them, with a blue cast to it and long springing shadows and a sharp chill in the air that neither felt nor tasted like the end of July. It was well past midnight before Richards let them go on bedground.

In the morning they moved out early, taking the dew from the grass. The dew was a help, and so was the cool weather; the herd didn't thirst as quickly as it would have in the Midwestern heat. It went to its noon rest quietly enough, and it didn't make trouble when he kept it there through the hottest part of the day. But when it rose to move off again it began to complain. The remuda was with them now, and it was the horses which were his immediate concern. They were weakening quickly; grass without water was no good for range horses, and to spare them he put the crew to eight and ten changes of mount through what was left of the day and into the long moonlit night. In the full light prairie dogs came to stare at them from the edges of their holes. They heard both wolves and coyotes, howling and barking as if the full moon had set them to raving and calling to one another, across the hills and prairies. By midnight the herd was uneasy and only half of it bedded and he doubled the guard. In the morning there was an unusually heavy dew, and he spread them to let them take advantage of it. Then he went off to scout the last ten miles of the stretch and emerged into groves of shivering-leaved plains cottonwoods, and found the water up to Plácido's knees.

The longest dry stretch of the drive was over, and the crew cheered when the herd, tongues hanging, came at last to stand and dip their muzzles in the Powder.

He kept them moving northwest. Once they had crossed the

327

Tongue River, and the Yellowstone, he would be in country he had never seen before. Out of the Powder the trail led into a long valley which sloped gently upward. On the left the first of the Bighorns pointed into a sky like crystal laid over deep water. They were coming into beef range, and while they saw no ranches, they crossed dozens of local trails and two or three times a day came upon local herds turned out to graze. The locals were heavier than the southern cattle, and the range horses they started up were higher and better fleshed. Richards knew that come spring the whole Tres Reyes herd would look as good, wintered over in the colder climate, on thick wet grass.

They crossed the Crazy Woman, an open, clean-running fork of the Powder. The local trails became more numerous, but they all ran in the wrong direction, west to the lower reaches of the Yellowstone. Between the Crazy Woman fork of the Powder and the Tongue the land changed abruptly, pushing up in rugged drifts of hills grassed a foot deep and running fresh water. Richards returned from his last Wyoming scout well satisfied. They were right on the nose as far as trail time went, and the only casualties he could count were three drags to the Comanche, the dead horse out of Uremáy's string, and Rojo. He knew the danger of congratulating himself too soon, but it looked as if they would be going into the Judith Basin with time to spare.

All he had to do was find his way to Fort Benton. It didn't worry him. That letter was going to be there, and if that letter had been sent to hell itself he would have found his way to it and worked around every obstacle that might rear up and try to hold him off while he was doing it. He felt so good now that he let the boys go out and shoot some blacktail grouse that looked as if they might be serving a better purpose in Sykes' frypan than just flushing stupidly in and out of the brush cover.

In the middle of the afternoon they crossed the line, into Montana.

EIGHTEEN

Through the heat of the day the Señora remained in her room with the light curtained off at the window and the door closed. She seldom slept. At night, in the dark, she lay awake for long hours, listening to the silence of the house and making conversation with herself. An hour's sleep would come to her, and then she would awaken again. In the morning Cayetana came to comb her hair and prepare her for the day ahead. One day like another, endless. To the casual eye she might have appeared indolent. Her mind was never still.

She had taken to spending her mornings in the main room of the *casa*, bright with slanted rectangles of light where the sun came in the front casement windows. Not until noon were the shutters closed. She seemed to take a new pleasure in the informal comfort of the big room, heavily furnished, yet light and open with its fresh white walls. Some mornings she read; others she talked with Father Berrades. Directly after lunch Feliciano returned her to her room, where the furniture had been dusted, the floor washed, and the linen changed. They believed that she slept the afternoon away, and she said nothing to disprove it. Dinner was served late, after the house had cooled, and it was rare that she did not go down to join them. By nine o'clock she was in the *capilla*. By ten, she was back in bed.

The household remarked upon this change in the Señora's routine. It amused her that they seemed to find her mornings downstairs, her punctual arrival at meals, signs of improvement, where there could be no improvement. She wondered if they did not know this, or if they encouraged her because they thought she did not know it.

Many of her perspectives had changed since Father Berrades returned. She knew that Guadalupe had sent Father Berrades back to Tres Reyes. Illnesses and marriages and various family disputes called him back over the border. She was not deceived. He was human, and there were times when he simply wished to go home. Often she thought that if it were not for his inherent simplicity, his natural dignity, and what she considered the sometimes erratic workings of his mind, he would be no different from any other poor parish priest of Mexico, often penniless, often slipshod, often ineffectual. In the beginning the Church had found his offices at Tres Reyes somewhat unconventional, but it had recognized Tres Reyes as a pueblo and, taking the generosity of the Dominguez' into its consideration, had allowed him to remain.

His return had settled several matters. For one thing, her heart was sound as an oak. When the slow leaden pain spread through the misshapen cave of her chest and her breathing grew labored, she now believed it only some harmless muscular ache, come to remind her that martyrdom was portion of her lot. The doctors had told her long ago that her heart had been pulled out of place, almost into the right side of her body. They were undoubtedly all liars and fakes. When Berrades came back she theorized that she had missed his presence to such an extent that she had become self-pitying, fastening upon a failing heart as a means to spite him.

The change in the routine of her days also indicated a change in her critical faculties. She felt that she became more abstract with age, as if whatever flame was left within her was pure and cold. Shock was a word whose meaning she no longer knew, a state she no longer recognized. The night of Father Berrades' return, when Feliciano wheeled her from the chapel, she saw that Cayetana had been sitting not three paces behind her, her hands in her lap and a square of blue lace over her head. The moment of surprise pulled her pale eyes wide, and then it was over. Nothing surprised her again.

Earlier, before the heat became so intense, she had almost prayed for some distraction. When Avis came several times and spent the day with her, it fed her dissatisfaction. Awake in the night she made comparisons she wished she did not have to make. Was it some Yankee trait, this cunning strength, this healthy sensible outlook Avis had, and which she felt was characteristic of herself? There were certain softnesses, yes, but they were always on such a practical plane, they were never sentimental. Either Yankees were unsentimental people, by and large, or she had grown too accustomed to the racial apathies of the Mexican. Why did not Cayetana have some of that splendid hard resourcefulness which was so obvious in Avis? The emotional pliancies and quiet containments which had been so tender and admirable in lover and husband, in Ramón, and to which she had been so receptive, she found only annoying in Cayetana. Still, Avis was her only diversion. The second diversion of the summer she considered of an auspicious nature.

The Ranger captain, Aaron Bonaventure, had come to Tres Reyes with a horse he said belonged to them. She knew that this was not the real reason he had come, but she contented herself for the time being with the story that he had run into one of the Tres Reyes mustang crews at a time when his own horse was played out, and had borrowed Juan Sanchez' *grulla*.

At dinner that night she watched him carefully, with the little downdrawn smile. She thought him physically attractive, stalwart, though of undistinguished intellect. The dark hawk features indicated to her vigilance, energy, nerve, authority. He had the manners of a gentleman, and they emerged naturally, they were not something he had studied, and aped. The Creole blood was unfortunate. Creoles were a shiftless lot, in the main. It was as if they had taken into themselves from the moment of birth all the lethargies and torpors and shallow gaieties of that damp airless miasmic Mississippi delta city they so loved. He seemed an exception. She found herself more and more taken with him as the evening progressed; he was temperate, confident, serious but not without humor. But long before dessert she listened with one ear only. With the other she was listening to herself. At last, pretending her undivided interest, she dropped out of the conversation entirely, knowing that quiet attentiveness sparked by a discerning question or two marked a woman firmly and appreciatively in a man's mind.

Reserve, but not this little wall of silence Cayetana maintained. Ramón was genial; Bonaventure had a way of drawing him out. She, herself, was somewhat excited. She had decided that this Ranger captain was a man of great possibility, and she looked at Cayetana and thought, I shall have to do it all myself. She is losing her looks. Does she weigh a hundred pounds? She seemed a child again, coming down this morning on the albino mare. Once, when Cayetana made a small remark, she wanted to cup her ear and shout, do not mumble. Why could the girl not put herself out a little? She was so taken with the project she now entertained that she could barely contain herself until it was time to leave the table and go to discuss it with Guadalupe.

She had expected that they would go to the main room, but as she was wheeled into the chapel she realized that they had instead gone into Ramón's office. That left Cayetana out entirely, and the knowledge vexed her. She sat staring at the altar, debating whether or not to seek Cayetana out, to impose immediate dictates. Dear Heaven, the courtyard full of flowers and we cannot find one that suits us enough to put in our hair, we cannot find more than the merest of smiles, we cannot contribute even one interesting idea to the conversation, we cannot . . . ? She turned her head as far as it would go and lifted her hand and Feliciano rose and left the chapel.

When he returned he came up behind her chair and touched her, once, on the shoulder, and she knew that Cayetana had gone to sit alone in the dark courtyard and was even now perhaps lighting another of those odious cigarettes.

He did not know how to refuse either the brandy or the cigar, so he accepted them. It was bad enough he had been taken into the family like a long-lost son, showed the progress which had taken place since he had been gone, and sat down at the table as if he had come home to stay. My God, how could you dislike a man like Dominguez, or mistrust him? He had already fallen for the Señora. What a way she had with her, and one which, astonishingly enough, evoked no pity: the assured grace, the equanimity, were those of a great lady. To be more precise, if they belonged to a woman playing at being a great lady, she had made a striking success of it. Still, the uneasiness which was in him was not entirely due to the nature of his mission. For weeks he had carried a vision in his mind, and the vision was not as he remembered it. He was not disillusioned, but was tempted to smile inwardly at himself, for he knew now that his preoccupation with it had served only to throw the vision out of proportion. In actuality, the girl looked as if she were perishing of some incurable paralysis, as if she would end as taut and dry as the man who had died in Mexico. The thought made him suspicious and brought to his mind the words she had spoken on the night she had effected his release from Morisco. He had not thought of it in some time, but when he saw her, her face and her voice evoked it: dying by degrees. Yet he could sense no undercurrent of conflict or disorder within the family. You expected, in the presence of a guest, that they would all be on their best behavior, but they appeared to be the kind of people who were on their best behavior at all times.

He leaned to the match Dominguez held out to him, and drew on the cigar. When he had savored the smoke he said, "I expect you know why I'm here, Señor Dominguez."

If there was any change of expression in Dominguez' face, it was in the eyes; for a moment the dark pupils seemed to dilate and contract. Then the look was gone. He said, "I am never certain of anything, Captain Bonaventure."

Don't make it difficult for yourself, Bonaventure thought. "I'm sorry to have to tell you that Barent Lyons died in Coahuila a few weeks ago. I think you knew him as Buster."

Dominguez leaned back slowly in his chair. The hand holding

333

the cigar was steady, but Bonaventure saw him take a long, deep breath. "How is it that you know this?"

"I was with him when he died," Bonaventure said. "And maybe I owe you this much: if it hadn't been for your daughter, I don't expect I would have been. I got picked up by some militia over the border and spent some weeks with 'em I'd as soon forget about. They talked to your daughter and the man running your mustang crew, and if it hadn't been for her, I might still be there."

"A circumstance with which Esteban Ibarra has already acquainted me. Though I did not connect you with Lyons, at the time." The hint of a smile touched his lips. "Now you are going to tell me that Lyons informed you of our transaction before he died."

Bonaventure shook his head. "It would have made it easier, if he'd been able to. All I know is that I have fifteen hundred dollars, gold, I think belongs to you. U.S. currency, denomination of two hundred, one hundred, fifty, and a few fives, probably exchanged and contracted for out of Mexico City. I could check that, if I had to."

"It interests me," Dominguez said, "that you have not already done so."

"I thought you might want to tell me about it," Bonaventure said.

Dominguez was silent. Then he said, "What is to happen to me, if I tell you what you wish to know?"

"To you?" Bonaventure looked at him quietly. "You could start, sir, by just making one simple statement of fact: Lyons blackmailed you."

Dominguez put his hand to his forehead. He seemed to be thinking, and Bonaventure waited quietly, drawing on the cigar but not tasting it any longer. "Lyons came here, in November I believe it was, yes, a year ago last November." He stood up and turned his back to Bonaventure. "And told me something I knew, had known for some time. Richards had been with Tres Reyes a little over a month. What thought is in the head of this Lyons, that he assumes I will take into my home, into my family, a man whose past I know nothing of? He must have known that I knew . . ."

334

"That Richards killed a man in Galveston," Bonaventure said.

"Yes." His voice was impatient. "What secret is this? It is known, it is known everywhere. It is not a matter of women's gossip . . . men respect Ben Richards, they do not sit and discuss his misfortune, they do not use his misfortune against him." He turned to Bonaventure. "I knew it all, before I ever offered my herds and the freedom of my house to Ben Richards. Five years ago he was a younger man. As was I. As were you. He quarreled with a man named Vance. The quarrel was over a woman, this I know also. And he ended it by killing Vance."

"The jury said it was self-defense," Bonaventure said.

"I do not argue with juries. If Richards had come here and told me himself that it was self-defense, I would have accepted his word. Without question. If this man Vance was so unwise as to draw a gun and attempt to shoot Richards in the back . . ."

Bonaventure said, "What were you going to say?"

"Only that I took Richards here because I believed he was the man I needed. He has not disappointed me. He is worth a great deal to me."

Bonaventure said, "About two thousand dollars' worth?"

And Dominguez said, "More. Much more. The price was Lyons', not mine."

"What did he tell you?" Bonaventure said.

"That he, personally, had new evidence against Richards. That he had only to speak and the case would be reopened. For two thousand dollars he was willing to forget this new evidence. He wanted gold because he knew it was negotiable all the way to Mexico City."

"Sir," Bonaventure said, "did you ever hear of double jeopardy?"

"I am not a fool, Captain. Lyons was a man of great self-confidence. And immense stupidity. I knew that he was lying."

The ash fell from Bonaventure's cigar and lay in a neat roll upon the floor. "I beg your pardon?"

Dominguez came back and sat down. He leaned forward, looking at Bonaventure steadily. "Captain, I knew my man. Not Lyons. Richards. I knew how he was tempered. He came to my table, in the presence of my wife and my daughter, with his gun

335

on. He went nowhere without that gun, and a rifle in his saddle scabbard. It may be that he slept with that gun, I do not know. I do know that if you had brought the whole Border Battalion in here to take him it would have cost you dearly. Wait, do not interrupt me, I understand what it is you would say. That he was free, that he had been cleared by due legal process. What does this mean, in Texas?"

"What?" Bonaventure said. "What?"

"Any man who held a grudge against Richards, for whatever reason, could have disposed of him and gone free. Have you forgotten those years of the State Police? Have you forgotten the violence and murder and the law taken into the hands of brigands, not the least of whom *were* the State Police? Let me tell you, Captain, when that man came to me he was wary as a cat stalking and being stalked. A man without home or family, what you people call a drifter. Depressed at the thought of a lost war, with a time in prison, awaiting trial, to weigh upon him, trailing cows all summer because it was what he did well . . . perhaps the only thing he can do, I do not know . . . moving from one ranch to the next. Out of all this, I saw one thing: a man who could be so deeply disturbed by the circumstances which had befallen him, was a man of sound and humble mind."

"Even," Bonaventure said, "if he was prepared, as you think he was, to go to any extreme not to let these old troubles come to a head again."

"Even so. When the horse has had a little taste of the corral, he is ready to run when he finds how sweet the grass is beyond the gate."

"And it was worth . . ."

"It was worth two thousand dollars to me to remove this man Lyons, whom I thought that neither I, nor the Rangers, would ever see again. It was worth it to insure that these deceits and embarrassments did not come within Richards' hearing." He looked past Bonaventure, at the wall. "Because that year, last year, I had a herd worth nearly twenty thousand dollars ready to go to Nebraska."

There was a silence. Bonaventure shook his head. "I'll tell you something, Señor Dominguez: I had some trouble making up my mind as to whether I wanted to come down here and talk to you about this alone, or wait until Richards gets back. I think maybe I made the right decision."

Dominguez held up his hand. "Captain, I beg you to let Richards know no word of this, if you can in conscience do so."

Bonaventure said nothing.

"He would leave me, leave Tres Reyes, at once. He has too much integrity. You see, there was a time, this winter, when he nearly discovered the truth."

"How?" Bonaventure said.

"I had two talks with Lyons, here in this office. When he came the third time it was to . . . to receive the money from me. This door was open, and we entered talking, for there was no one on the lower floor, and I went directly to the safe and stood with the money in my hands, still talking. I do not believe he was here more than five minutes."

"And?" Bonaventure said.

"And when he had left, I discovered that my neighbor, Jonah McLean, was sitting in the rear of this room, there, where the partition is that you see, waiting for me. It was a very bad time."

"I can see it might have been," Bonaventure said. "You mean he heard it all?"

"Not all. But enough. Of course he had felt compelled to rise when we entered, but my own eagerness to finish this matter prevented it. He could not well break in upon us at such a time. He was an honorable man, McLean, and a friend of Richards. But at the end, when he knew he was dying, he used a portion of his knowledge to unsettle Richards' mind, and on that day Richards came to me."

"And you told him . . . ?"

"The only lie I could tell him, and still keep him at Tres Reyes. Now, what is it that you must say to me?"

Bonaventure was shaking his head. "I haven't got anything more to say, don Ramón. I had it pretty well figured out, all but that last, that took me off guard. I'm glad you felt free enough to talk to me about it. And you haven't broken any law." He looked down at the floor and then up again, at Dominguez. "At

337

least, sir, you haven't broken any law that is in my jurisdiction to prosecute."

"And there will be no word of this, to Richards?"

"None from me," Bonaventure said gloomily.

"I am very grateful. It has relieved my mind, somewhat, to speak of it."

"The trouble with relieving your mind," Bonaventure said, "is that the burden kind of sneaks over and rests on mine. This has been an enlightening visit for me, don Ramón, in a lot of ways. I hope I haven't worn out my welcome."

"Not at all," Dominguez said.

"I'd like to come again."

"You are welcome at Tres Reyes at any time," Dominguez said. But his voice was formal now, and remote. "If you have nothing further to discuss with me, shall we join my wife and daughter?"

"I would like that very much, sir," Bonaventure said.

He knew it would be a long time before he came here again.

When Cayetana rode out a way with Bonaventure in the morning, the Señora's gratification took on a hopeful edge. She so regretted his departure that she was afraid she might have been overeffusive in her insistence that he come whenever it was possible. But she was sincere, and the little half-smile on Cayetana's mouth provoked her. Yet Cayetana leaned and kissed her, before they rode out.

"I won't be long, Mamacita."

"Oh take your time, take your time," the Señora said grandly. *God's will be done in spite of you, my girl.*

Two days later Father Berrades came in. When she saw him she felt as if she could rise to her feet. She wanted to go down on her knees and wet his hand with her tears. She did not know how much she had missed him, needed him, until Soledad came running up the stairs, calling, and she looked up from her bed and saw the tall thin figure in the brown Franciscan cassock, the narrow, furrowed face, the dark hair touched at the temples with gray. The tears did not quite overflow, and she looked prepared to censure him.

"Juan Antonio Berrades. I might have died, waiting for you."

338

"Now, Alicia," he said, smiling.

"Are you well, Father? You look tired. How are all your family?"

"A quarrelsome lot, as you know," he said, still smiling. "But all in good health, now. And yours?"

She sighed. "I sometimes feel, these days, as if only God holds us together."

"And is this not enough?" he said. He came to the bed and took her hand. "Alicia, when I hear you speak, it is as if I had never been away. Where is my little Caye?"

"Here," Cayetana said. She had heard Soledad calling and come to stand in her mother's doorway. When he turned to her his eyes grew sharp, questioning. What had happened to her, where was the youth and the blossoming of her face and all the small sweet graces of the fine eyes, the curving mouth? But she had run to him, flinging herself into his arms, and he could feel her tears on his neck. "A fine welcome," he said. "What more could I ask? I come home and everyone weeps to see me."

In the afternoon of the following day, during siesta, Feliciano reported to the Señora. Father Berrades had been with the Señorita Cayetana, in her room, for over an hour.

The Señora lay in her bed, staring at Guadalupe in her corner niche, and flexing the fingers of her good hand.

Berrades and don Ramón had known each other for years, although Berrades was considerably younger. They had an easy relationship which was based upon the exterior life of the ranch. He asked nothing more than that Ramón attend Mass and Ramón was acquiescent. When they talked, in the evenings, over cigars and brandy, it was of the ranch, of history, of old revolutions, of finances. When he talked with the Señora it was of none of these things.

"You enjoy baiting me," she accused him. They were sitting in the big room, in the morning sun.

"I do no such thing, Alicia. But at times you leave yourself open, like a gate in a wall, and I am always tempted to go and close the gate."

"What have I done? I make a simple statement, ask a simple question, and you go off on tangents which have nothing to do with . . ."

He was standing at the window, looking out into the courtyard. "You never make simple statements, Alicia. There is always some purpose behind them, something . . ."

"Ulterior," she suggested, her mouth drawing down in irony.

"Very well, ulterior, if you will have it so." He turned around. "Did you know that loving God too much can be a sin?"

"Is that a canon of the Church, or an opinion? If it is the latter, I will not accept it."

"Why not?" he said.

"Answer my question, first."

"It is an opinion."

"I thought so. One I don't believe you are entitled to. How can one love anything too much? Could I love . . . ah, I see your point, Juan Antonio. Love can be a millstone, is that it? Do you believe that overlove of God could drag me down?"

"I do not believe that wild horses could drag you down. I am only saying that I sometimes wish you were a little more dependent upon yourself and a little less so upon God. You abuse your dependence upon Him."

"No one tells me anything," she said, "except God and Guadalupe."

"How well informed you must be, in that event," he said drily. "Alicia, there are times when I would give much if all my parishioners were as zealous as you, as unquestioning. It would solve many problems. On the other hand, I sometimes find you . . ."

"Dull," she said.

"Never that. Bigoted."

She was not offended. "I would rather be a zealous bigot than a quibbling catechist."

"Are you debating preferential sins?"

"I prefer none, and have too many."

He stabbed a forefinger at her. "And the greatest of these is that you proclaim it as if your sins were better than those of anyone else."

She said bluntly, "I am a rapacious greedy old woman, who loves her husband and her daughter more than God, after all. I have tried to live a Christian life."

"Don't whine," he said.

"A hurt dog whines. You were with Cayetana a long time yesterday."

He came and sat down, opposite her. His eyes were probing but not unfriendly. "You know better than to broach this. If it will help you, I will tell you that she is easier in her mind today than she has been in many months."

"My restraint makes an ugly sickness in me, Father. Sometimes I shout inside to be mean, to be demanding. Last night was the first in a year that Cayetana has gone into the chapel."

He half-laughed. "Well, then, thank God for it."

"I will not ask you any questions."

"*Muy bien.* Then I am spared the necessity of refusing to answer them."

"You are impatient with me."

"Not at all."

"If you were her mother you would understand my feelings."

"That is obtuse, Alicia, and unworthy of you. I am not her mother, I am her priest."

The Señora's hand was clenched into a fist. "I beg your pardon for that remark. Truly I am glad you are back, Juan Antonio. If some order does not come to this house I am sorely tempted to simply go to bed one day and expire."

"Now you are dealing with mortal sin, if I may remind you. At any rate, I have no fear you will carry out such a threat." He was looking at her, smiling. "Alicia, you would have made a splendid actress."

Her head was back against the chair; her eyes were closed. "And you," she said, "a magnificent Jesuit."

At dinner, intent upon his office, he said, "By the way, Ramón, did I see Pablo Aguilár this afternoon?"

Dominguez did not look up from his meal. "He carries the mail from San Antonio these days. I neglected to mention to him that you had returned. He is with the Ibarras, if you wish to see him before morning."

"What mail, Ramón?" the Señora said.

"A note from Captain Bonaventure, thanking us for our hospitality." He looked down the table at the Señora. "Thanking you, most of all. I shall bring it to you later." His voice was

341

fond. How well she was looking, how cheered by Berrades' return. Their little duels bored him, but he knew how much she enjoyed them, and her pleasure was important to him.

"Do you know Captain Bonaventure, Father Berrades? The finest young man I have met in years." She was returning Ramón's fond offering, but her voice was edged, as if she willed him to expand, to add weight to her argument.

Cayetana's fork clattered against her plate. Aguilár in, without her knowing it, when she had looked for him, watched for him, for days. Her father had made a point of receiving the mail himself, but she had been certain of her ability to intercept Aguilár. Her hands began to shake. She felt sick and flushed, with the blood beating in her head, hammering at her skull. She thought the meal would never end. When it was over, she went into the chapel with her mother and Father Berrades.

The little flickering candles lighted nothing but Guadalupe's face and figure, and that only with glancing planes of wan reflection where her robe folded outward. The face was so shadowed she could hardly see it. Her mother was a dark shape some distance ahead, and Father Berrades nearly lost to sight where he knelt under the crucifix. After a time she got up and left the chapel. A crack of light showed beneath the office door. She hesitated, pulled with the need to go to her father, but weak with a terror that overcame her need. She went up to her room. When she lit the candles, the Macarena sprang golden out of the dark.

I have two choices. Nuestra Señora, I wish to take the honorable choice, but that is the most difficult. I am not brave. You cannot make me brave, unless there is some seed of it within me to begin with. I can go into that room, when he has left, and search for myself. Or I can face him. I do not want to face him. Nuestra Señora, help me to face him.

She left the candles burning. When she went down her mother and Father Berrades had gone to the main room, but the light still showed under the office door. She knocked once, apprehensively, opened the door and went in.

Dominguez was seated at his desk. When he heard the door open, he swung around in his chair. "It's you, Caye. Come in."

"I thought there might be something I could do, Father."

342

"You've been at the books, I see." He was smiling, and yet it seemed to her that he appeared agitated. His face was rather flushed. But she knew that her own nervous state was not one from which to draw such conclusions.

"I'm quite well caught up." She sat down, near him, in the chair Richards was accustomed to sitting in. "Might I see Captain Bonaventure's letter?"

He reached into a pigeonhole of the desk and handed it to her. She only glanced at it, and the paper shook in her hand. They spoke to each other in Spanish.

"No word from Tiburcio?"

"Not since Richards' letter from Dodge City," he said.

"Nor from Uncle Enrique?"

He looked up at her. "Nothing, this time. I must get a letter off to him tonight, before Aguilár goes back in the morning. Is there anything you would like to say?"

"Only my love. You might say I think Daniél is a poor correspondent."

She was watching him, dumbly, and it seemed to her that his face reddened again. She had both hands locked together, so hard they hurt. "Father."

"Yes?" he said.

She waited for strength. "Nothing," she said.

He reached over and patted her shoulder absently. "If you did not wish anything in particular, Cayetana, I must get some correspondence attended to."

She rose. He leaned back in his chair, watching her, and she could see clearly now that he was indeed disconcerted. "Caye, you do not look well at all. If it were not so hot, I would suggest that you and your mother get away for a while. I know she cannot stand a long trip, but perhaps a few days in San Antonio. Some new clothes, and a visit with the Sanlucars might cheer you both, eh?"

"Thank you, Father, that's very generous of you. I will think about it."

So I cannot find the courage, even for this. She went back upstairs and blew out the candles and lay down in the dark. She thought she must have slept, but it could only have been for a short

343

time, for she woke to the sound of her mother's chair in the hall, heard her mother's voice, and Father Berrades'. When she heard Berrades call good night to her mother, she got up and went to the door. In the light of the wall sconces he was surprised at the whiteness of her face. Her eyes made him think of a trapped rabbit.

"Father, could I speak to you for a moment?"

"Of course, child. Have you been lying here in the dark?"

"Wait, I will light the lamp." When the light flared in the room she said, "I am ashamed of myself tonight, Father. I thought I had found some courage and then I lost it, at the last moment. I meant to speak to my father."

He sat down. "What about, Cayetana?"

"I have been looking for Aguilár. I thought I could intercept him. What if there was a letter, for me?"

He put his chin in his hand. "You did not speak to your father?"

"I asked him if there was a letter from Uncle Enrique. He said there was not. Then how could I ask if there was anything for me?"

His mouth was compressed, thoughtful. "Cayetana, sooner or later I am going to have to have a talk with your father. I know that you wish it was as soon as possible. I am not looking forward to it. Despite the fact that I have been a member of this household for some years, I will undoubtedly be told to tend to my prayers. The summer is half-done. If don Angel carried out his intention to take ship, do you not think it best to wait?"

"Father . . . Oh God, I spend all my time waiting."

"I know, child, I know. But a little longer. One would think you did not have your whole life before you. Cayetana, would you like me to go down now, and ask him if there was some word?"

"No," she said. "I would like you to give me the strength to go and ask him."

"I cannot do that. You know I cannot do that." He gestured at the Macarena. "If this Lady cannot do it, how can I?"

"You can command me."

"Cayetana." He half-smiled. "I can command you to do nothing you cannot do of your own free will, you know this. Sacrifice a little longer. It will all come right, in the end."

344

She looked at him. "If anyone else said that to me, I should think it hypocrisy."

He took a breath. "It was hypocrisy. Things do not always come right in the end. I am sorry, Cayetana."

"I don't care what words you use," she said, "as long as they comfort me. Sometimes I can no longer be honest with myself. No, don't speak to my father."

When he rose, he stood and looked at her for a long moment. Then he said, "I will say something that is most unhypocritical, Cayetana, something I perhaps should not say, but like you, I prefer to be honest with myself. When I kneel in the chapel these nights, it is you I pray for. And yet I wish to say too that I am glad in my heart that this experience came to you, that you had as much as you had. For I think it is better to know pain and understand it, than never to know it. To be a wolf for a time, rather than a sheep unendingly. Do you know what I am saying?"

"Yes, Father."

"Are you crying, Caye?"

"No, Father."

"Well, there is a small lie I hope you will not forget at confession. Will you remember?"

"I will try, Father."

"If you pray to this dazzling Lady of yours, ask for strength for me. I am the one who will have to thrash this out with your father, for the good of his own soul if for nothing else. I go down to see Aguilár now. Sleep, and see how different this looks by sunlight."

But she did not sleep. She heard Feliciano's *guaraches* slapping down the hall. She heard her father come up, with Father Berrades, and knew it was late, perhaps after midnight. When the house was silent she rose and went out of the room. The wall sconces had been snuffed, and she went downstairs in the dark, forgetting a light. When she reached the gates of the chapel she saw that someone had lit a votive candle. She went in and picked it up. The glass was hot, and she slid it quickly into one of the empty silver holders, knowing that the heat would eventually reach this too. She crossed the hall and went into the office and closed the door behind her.

345

The Señora, having lain awake contentedly for several hours, had finally fallen into a deep sleep. When she opened her eyes, sluggish with the abruptness of the awakening, she thought she had been dreaming. Her brows were drawn together, in the attempt to remember what it was she had dreamed. The dream itself would not come, but there had been an aspect of it which was highly unpleasant. She seldom dreamed, and when she did often resented it. Twice she had dreamed of Guadalupe appearing to her, and once of *El Señor* Himself, but the latter appearance, rather than transporting her, confused her and made her ashamed of her audacity, as if she had had some control over it.

It was not a dream, it was a sound. Trying to put her mind in order, still half-drugged, she suddenly felt her flesh begin to gather and prick. It was as if even that part of her which was dead and without feeling had been lightly touched with needles. She made a tremendous effort to move herself, raise herself, on the pillows. The sound was a scream, somewhere outside her room, and the scream was a word, and she thought the word was father. Father? Ramón. Something had befallen Ramón. Or was it Father Berrades? Was it Cayetana's voice? No, it was *not* father, it was *mother*.

A sweet exultant chill crawled across her twisted shoulders; she knew a moment of total ascendancy, the old battle won, the prize in her hand, but she was choked with dread. *O curse the dark, curse this helpless body of mine*, it was Cayetana, running, and the scream was cold as a dagger of ice in her breast, the same scream which had torn out of her own throat, under the bluff, with her bones splintered and her body destroyed, waiting to die . . .

She reached with her good hand and grasped the post of the bed, dragging herself up, pulling at her own inert weight, until a nauseous sweat burst out upon her and the hideous dull pain began to spread in her chest and the icy dagger skidded sickeningly and sank its point deep into the red straining field of her heart.

NINETEEN

Allenby came into camps in a rig drawn by two matched roans with black stockings and tails, his feet braced on the dashboard and a cigar between his teeth. Beside him was a thin man with a thin, hooked nose, wearing a tall white hat. Behind the rig rode a cavalry detail. A band of Indians, braids swinging against bright draped blankets, trailed in the rear.

"You better put your white shirt on, Ben, here comes the augurs with the money," McLean said. He was making a last check on the remuda, which had been circled into a rope and rawhide corral. He looked a hair worried. All the horses he had seen since he crossed the Wyoming border were so big and well fleshed they made the Texas strings raunchy by comparison. The northern horses had had grain, but they had fattened on rich grass, clear water, and cold weather.

"I have heard," Shiloh said, "that if you take a full-growed Nueces country horse and stick him up here one or two winters, he will not only take on the old tallow, he will actual come to stand another hand high. If that is the case, and I have not merely had my off-leg pulled, what in the nation do you spose would happen if you took one of these corporation-type sugar suckers and put him down in our country a winter or two?"

"I dunno," McLean said. "He would maybe shrink up into a jugheaded puddin' foot."

"I hope you ain't callin' this remuda names," Shiloh said. "It come longer than it ever knowed to, in all its innocence, and done without water and rode half the night and sweated till it frothed and chased after stompedes, and I am feelin' kind of bad about sellin' it and not particular who knows it."

The big man with the hooked nose was named Holiday, and he spent a half-hour with the remuda. He was taciturn; when he had finished his inspection he said bluntly to Richards: "I'll take 'em. Half price on the sorefoots."

"Done," Richards said. "Give my boys time to cut out their private stock and you can have 'em."

Cavalry and Indians were looking the herd over, and Allenby was pushing his way here and there, making notes in a black book he carried, and chewing his cigar from one side of his mouth to the other. When Richards came up he said, "See what a cow'll do in this country? These slabsides of yours started puttin' on flesh the minute they crossed the Powder. Say, that chief with the red blanket over there wants to buy your palomino."

"My what?" Richards said.

"That horse you call a buttermilk. He'll trade you the blanket, a beaded rifle boot with fringe a foot long, and his sister if you want her."

"Thank him kindly," Richards said. "No sale." He jerked his head at Shiloh. "Cut out the buttermilk, Portero, and Plácido for me. And tell the boys not to do any foolish swappin' with these Blackfeet. They still got to get home, and they won't make much time walkin' it."

The fact that Holiday was an independent contractor did not stop the cavalry; they were anxious to help him cut out the sorefoots. "Look at that," Shiloh said. "Army. Here they are supposed to of learned somethin' in the saddle and they don't know no more about cuttin' out a horse than my old auntie. They couldn't cut a litter of kittens out of a barnyard of cats. All they can do with a horse is feed 'em and lead 'em."

The Blackfoot reservation lay a couple of days' drive northwest of Fort Benton, but reserve pasturage was available for the herd, and Indian and government riders would take it from the post to its final delivery. Richards was not sorry to see it go, and it seemed to him that there were a hundred last-minute chores to be disposed of: questions from both Allenby and the Army concerning the trail route he had followed, forms to fill out, vouchers to sign, cows to count, weights to estimate.

They had followed the Tongue River for several days, through a vast land of water and grass. The nights were cold, but the August days were invigorating; the air was winey with the essence of the country's clear cool sweet waters. Immense meadows spread before and around them, running into broad green valleys. Behind, the purple-gray peaks of towering mountains poised as if they had been carved, on an endless sky.

They came on range riders two or three times a week, and while they got some conflicting advice now and then, nobody had managed to point them wrong. The news traveled, in some mysterious way, and range riders were on the lookout for them, wanting to see this big herd that had come nearly three thousand miles, from the far southern border.

They crossed the Rosebud and then the Sweet Grass, several times, where it wound upon itself in its swarded bottoms. There were countless clean creeks to ford, before the country sloped down to the Yellowstone.

On the banks they met buffalo hunters camped in a welter of hides, hides stretched to dry and hides piled in towering bales, waiting for the freight wagons which would take them to the Missouri. Beyond the river the route ascended again, following a tributary of the Yellowstone. Huckleberries were spilling a choice fragrant yield for miles: they were blue fingered and blue tongued for two or three days. The land continued its gentle ascent until it reached the divide which led down to the Musselshell. From its crest, a long range of hills swelled to the left, traced over with the time-worn track of buffalo, elk, antelope, deer. To the right, brought close by the lucent crystalline air, a plateau spired with warped cinnamon buttes stood sentinel.

There were no range riders in this country. Once they had crossed the Musselshell, Richards spent every day in the saddle, riding ahead. The land became rocky and uneven, its divides and valleys spreading due north to the Missouri. Once he met two men panning gold. They seemed to him mistrustful, a little hostile. A day later he crossed paths with another band of buffalo hunters. They told him if he turned due west he would pick up the military road which led to the complex of northern rivers.

A long mountain divide lay before them, cutting between the Missouri and the headwaters of the Musselshell. From its summit they looked into the great valley of the Judith River, green as a sea, and cut by the winding brown path, no bigger to them from the heights than a buffalo trail, which led into Fort Benton.

On the first day of September, across the broad steely band of the Missouri, they saw the United States flag snapping in the wind above the post compound.

The fort dated from 1821, when the first mountain men had brought their keelboats up the Missouri to open the fur trade in the country of the Blackfoot, the Mandan, the Ree, and the Blood. It had been called Fort Benton in the early days of the Missouri Fur Company, and it kept its old name when it became a military post. It lay on a deep inward curve of land between the Missouri and the Teton, and on orders from Allenby the herd was crossed as far as the latter river, not much more than a stream, and spread to graze on the fertile plain between the two bodies of water. The longhorns of Tres Reyes had come to the end of their journey.

"I don't know as I want to hang here too long," Shiloh told Uremáy. "I hear these Blackfeet got some sort of a thing goin' where they poke splinters through their briskets and string themselves up on rawhide till the splinters tears out. I wouldn't want to git caught up in any such doings as that, I can tell you."

"It is very old," Uremáy said. "If you are caught up in this it will not be so bad as it might have been. Were it Mexico, in the ancient times, they might have cut out your living heart. It is all the same worship, made to the sun."

"Well, I hope you will excuse me, then, while I git down on my elbows here and pray for rain. I see these bucks look mighty friendly, like they ought to look, seein' as I have brought them all this good beef, but there ain't no way of tellin', and I'd sure be galled to the end of my days if I had to call out the Army."

"For myself," Uremáy said, "I will be glad to begin the journey home."

Shiloh looked at him, his mild blue eyes pensive. "I reckon you will, Tiburcio. You have spent a lot of days ridin' herd on one critter or another, and now you can say you have been to Montana. I expect you won't never have to leave Tres Reyes again."

Uremáy was looking down at the ground, between his feet. "That is what I wish," he said. "You will see, Shiloh. The hour will come, when you have reached my time in life, when a voice says to you, home, and you are pulled there as strongly as you were pulled away from it, when you were young and the whole world was before you."

"Yes," Shiloh said. "I can see me and Frankie now, in our rocker chairs, out front of the M Bar L, tellin' each other lies about how it used to be. Be quiet, will you, Tiburcio, you give me an itch to git to it. Right now I don't care if I never see another Nueces steer as long as I live. I am goin' down and watch a Blackfoot horse race. You want to come?"

Uremáy shook his head. "I wait for Ben," he said.

"You might have a long pull. I seen him ride out of here on Portero like he was off to flag down the Kansas Pacific before it run over a baby buggy. He didn't even stop for Allenby."

Uremáy looked at him. "I will wait," he said again.

When Shiloh had gone, he sat down and rolled a cigarette. Outside the post there were a few Blackfoot tipis set up, conical shaped, with two forward wings made of hide set out from the tip, and painted with red and yellow and black symbols. The Blackfeet were racing horses on a flat near the river, raising dust where the grass was worn off and making a splash of moving color in their vivid shirts and blankets. Cavalry troopers and a few officers came and went, and the crew was hanging around taking everything in and probably wondering how long it was going to take them to get back to Ogallala. Uremáy sighed. Not long, he was sure of that. Five months on the trail, but they would make it back in a little over two, striking nearly forty miles a day when the going was good, and thirty when it was not. The trip back would be pleasant, he knew, without the responsibility of the herd. The night's sleep would be unbroken, no watches to mount, no stampedes to check, no dry stretch so wide they could not cross it. But he was unsettled. Where had Richards gone, riding out of the post so that even Shiloh remarked on it. Then he thought, I will take our horses, Ben's and mine, and the things which belong to us, and I will make us a little camp away from all this sound and sight of men, and then I can do no more than wait, as I am doing now.

He was asleep when Richards came in. Opening his eyes, he saw Richards unsaddling Portero, hauling the saddle off, a black shape against a black velvety sky flowering with still white stars. There were several fires, including his own, gone low in the night: a few outside the post compound, one or two where the outfit was sleeping, near the chuck wagon. Uremáy raised himself and called softly.

Richards turned around, but he didn't speak. When he had taken care of the horse he came to the fire. Uremáy could see his breath, coming out in a little cloud, like steam.

"I thought perhaps you would not find me," Uremáy said. "You were gone long."

Richards still didn't say anything.

Uremáy sat up and scratched his head and yawned. "You do not feel like speaking, eh?"

"Why?" Richards said. "You got any more of your life history you want to tell me or something?" Then he said, "I didn't mean that, Tiburcio, I'm kind of off my horse."

"Shiloh said you had ridden out as if you were in haste to go somewhere. What is it, Ben?"

"Well," Richards said. "There was this bullet comin' by, and I happened to sort of lean against it, and it got me, right square in the gut."

Uremáy was upright. "You have been shot, *amigo?* Christ's death . . ."

352

"Never mind, old *segundo*, that wasn't what I meant. Go on back to sleep, will you?"

Uremáy was suddenly motionless, speechless. It was as if some dark thing loomed out of the night and touched him, a light, stroking touch, like a brushing of feathers, before it vanished. Richards had leaned to the coals of the fire and lit a cigarette. Uremáy saw his face, brown and hard as earth, in the pink smoldering glow.

"Ben, I do not mean to ask your affairs."

"That's all right," Richards said. "I just wanted to be alone a while. What I mean is I wanted to be alone a while to see if I wanted to go on bein' alone."

Again the dark fear stroked at Uremáy. He pulled his blanket up around his shoulders. "Would you offer me a *cigarillo?*" he said.

"Sure. Have a cigarette?"

"Ben, may I do some service?"

"No," Richards said.

"And if I ask a question?"

"Ask away."

"I said to you once that all men were by themselves. Alone. That there are times it can be no other way. But when you say to me that you wish to be alone, it gives it a different meaning, no?"

"I expect so," Richards said.

"So that if it is that a man wishes to be alone, it is because he has some weight upon him, and I am not sure that at such a time it is well for him to be alone."

"Well, I ain't alone now," Richards said, "on account of you are with me."

"Continue," Uremáy said. "Continue to close yourself to me, to shut me away."

"I ain't doin' that, Tiburcio. Maybe tomorrow I can make it plainer. Right now, no."

"Tomorrow we will start home," Uremáy said. It was a statement, but there was a slow rising interrogation in it.

And Richards said, "All right. That's what you really wanted to ask, wasn't it? Tomorrow we start home. But I ain't goin' all the way with you, Tiburcio."

Uremáy was up on his knees, clutching the blanket around him. "Not going back to Tres Reyes? Ay, God, Ben, what has happened, that in the time between the noon sun and the coming of the day you make this decision? Do you tell me this has been in your mind before this time?"

"It was there," Richards said. "Stuck away as far as I could make it go, but it was there."

"You do not wish to go back?"

Richards said, "No, I would like to go back. Only I can't do it."

There was silence. Then Uremáy said quietly, "Very well. It is as it is, after all. I am an old man, but not so old that I have forgotten the sting of my own pride."

Richards put out his cigarette and lay back on his elbows. "Do you listen as much as you talk?"

"Of a certainty," Uremáy said stiffly.

"Avis McLean is not goin' to do me the honor," Richards said. "She is sittin' back there on the M Bar L waitin' for Frankie to come home."

"¿Como?" Uremáy said.

"That's the truth. It might not sound so, but that's the truth. Does it explain things to you?"

Uremáy had got up and come to squat beside Richards. "Several things. There is no longer any wonder in me that our young wrangler was so filled with wrath, when your path crossed his."

"You think he knew, how it was with me?" Richards said.

"You think not? Hui, Ben, I remember . . ."

"I remember too. You warned me, didn't you? Be careful of the young McLean, you said. Cuidado. So I rode with five beans in the cylinders day and night lookin' everywhere but in the right place, didn't I? Can't you be more goddam specific with these warnings of yours?"

"The portent of a dream is not written to be read, Benjamín, for it takes many shapes. And now our Franco is become a man in his youth, unquarrelsome and sober, because he is about to take upon himself the responsibility of a wife . . ."

"There's more than that. She says it was a hard letter to write to me, and I reckon it was, hard for her to do, I mean, but at least

354

she didn't give me any handouts in the lie department. I expect I can figure now that from the time she climbed out of that wagon and said yes to Jonah it was Frankie she had her eye on. And here she is pullin' two ways, with me tryin' to drag her off at the same time she's tryin' to get some sense into that kid's head. Well, she managed it. She evidently sent him out of the M Bar L chompin' at the bit and then made sure the good news was waitin' for him in Dodge." He sat up. "By God, if I don't have the rottenest luck with women. Have to near get killed and defend myself the only way I knew and hire a lawyer to get me free, over a bitch that wasn't doin' a thing but use me, and now go and act like a fool bull with the she stuff when I long gone ought to of known different."

"And this . . . *this* is why you do not wish to return to Tres Reyes?"

"Tiburcio," Richards said. "I spent a lot of my life alone. I don't know what meaning you want to put to alone this time, but I mean stark alone, just ridin' the country and thinkin' about things or not thinkin' about things, however I happened to be feelin' that day. It was a good kind of life. I ain't sayin' there weren't times I reckoned it would be all right to have something to tie to, there were. Still are. But I know that kind of life, I know it better than anything else. Maybe it looks better to me now, lookin' back at it, than it really was. But I'll tell you: it ain't something I got to strain to make myself go back to."

Inside himself Uremáy felt shrunken and small, cold with a cold which was more than the northern night. "And Tres Reyes," he said. "It is nothing more than one small piece of the many pieces. Forgive me, but did you stay there because it kept you near the Señora McLean?"

Richards shook his head. "No. I hadn't got that bad off, not yet. I stayed there because it meant something to me."

"And now it means nothing to you?"

"Now nothing means much to me, I reckon."

"Forgive me again. You say to me, do I have more stories to tell to you, and if you will permit me, I will tell you one. It will not take long. Do not say to me, yes, I will listen, but only because it is my friend, Tiburcio Uremáy, who tells it to me. Say yes because in your heart you wish to hear it."

Richards felt a sudden bitter smile on his mouth. "Did I say yes?" he said.

"I had every certainty that you would. Listen, when I was younger than you, much younger, *amigo*, when the *patrón* had gone to Seville for his schooling it was, I went into Mexico to spend some time with my father's brother. And what is it that happens to me, poor luckless child that I am, with my songs and my freedom and not much else in my head? In the village of my uncle there is a girl. What else could happen to me, at that age? Never, until Morena Flor, did I see such black hair, so full of blue light you would think the sky had come down to touch it. Such eyes. Such hands, like little brown birds. God alone knows how I suffered. Even had she loved me, I would have suffered, so that you may imagine what I felt when this pearl played her small games with me. A little glance here. A sway of the hip there. Such hips, by the way, did I say that? And what was I to her? Nothing. Not that much." He snapped his fingers softly. "Do you know what it is that I did, with my heart in a thousand pieces?"

"Sure," Richards said. "You went out and looked for Natividad."

"That is another story, and has no bearing upon this. No. What I did was go away to be a *bandido*. Because that was the way to show this girl. That would make her think again of the *valiante* she had turned away."

"How'd you make out?" Richards said.

"Not well. Not well at all. I rode north, south, east, and west, and I could not find any *bandidos*, at that particular time, to join. But like you, I rode alone, through a country so large, so lonely, that one wonders where it begins and ends. I thought I would spend my life thinking of this girl, and sighing. And as I rode I thought less and less of the girl, and began to think of something else. I began to think, I am alone. I am alone in the world. I saw nothing, no other man, no pueblo, not so much as a rabbit running before me. I went across a great desert, and I thought, I remain alone, and one day I looked at the ground and there was a dark shadow riding before me which was not my own, and I raised my head and saw an eagle gliding over me, in the sky, with his wings held perfectly still. And I said to myself, I am no longer alone, there is an eagle in this country, and I went up into the high places, where there were pine trees and red rocks, and I said to myself, now I am alone, and the first day, when I felt my aloneness the most, even there the same shadow passed over me, and I knew that there was no place I could go. Wherever I went, on the land, there was the shadow of the eagle, and when I saw it drifting before me, when I felt it upon my own body, blocking out the sun, I said to myself, how fine it would be to make that shadow on the land, leaving something of myself upon the earth where I passed. I think it was then, for the first time, that I saw my own shadow, and I thought, but I am like the eagle, I too leave my shadow as I go. And I knew that no matter what came to me, what glories and desolations, what joys and sorrows, that same shadow would come drifting, in the mountains and the low places, and I thought that if I were to survive I too must cast my shadow, and that I should like my shadow to be as strong and proud and free as the shadow of the eagle." He stopped; Richards was not looking at him. "I do not know how much shadow I cast, then or now, and I suppose it must be that such a shadow as mine goes into the grave with me. But I know that the eagle's shadow will endure, long after I am dust."

Richards' voice was flat, low. "Any more?"

"Nothing more. Except that I have seen, in my time, many eagles leave their shadow upon the land. Some were young eagles, and their shadows wavered, but they were there. Some were old eagles, and there was a power in them, and they remained constant."

After a while Richards said, "I don't reckon I might make much of a shadow."

"Ben, what is to become of Tres Reyes?"

"When did it become my responsibility to the end of my life? Will you quit talkin' as if I was the only man in the world could trail a herd of cows?"

Uremáy shook his head. "I see it all now, in the eye of my mind. Before another spring Morena Flor will be gone, in spite of the *patrón.* By spring there will be left only three eagles of my knowing: the *patrón*, the Señora, and this lazy Zapotec who speaks to you now. We will not cast much of a shadow either, any more. We will tire quickly and go to roost early. And the day of the *hacendado* will be over. It will never return."

Richards said, "The eye of your mind is a thorn in my side, Tiburcio. And I wish to God you would take your claws out of my soul."

"So be it," Uremáy said. His voice was soft, almost benign. "Go where you will. I have sadness for what has happened, but to walk away from it does not mean that it will not follow. Go where you will."

He went back to his blankets, but he did not sleep. He lay upon his side, in the cold starry night, and saw that Richards did not move, but remained looking into the last of the fire, with his knees drawn up and his arms clasped around them, and when the dawn moved up wet from the rivers of the valley, neither of them had slept and they had not spoken to each other again.

Allenby invited himself to breakfast. He came out in his fancy rig, bringing whiskey and smokes for the whole crew. He would be leaving for Louisiana before the week was out. "I got to get home by Christmas," he told them, "and see if I can't persuade Mrs. Allenby to move out of that unhealthy climate there and into someplace where you can draw a clean breath."

"You mean like Texas," Shiloh said.

"Homesick, I see," Allenby said. "Anytime I want to lay out and dry up like a piece of rawhide, I will move to Texas."

"All right, I'll be there," Shiloh said. "I see our cows is good enough for you, though."

"Good enough in anybody's book, boy. There's just too much of that damn country down there to suit me." He clapped Shiloh on the back.

"No need to drive me to my knees over it," Shiloh said, coughing. "When you git to the Nueces country, look us up. Tiburcio and me, we will be the ones in the rocker chairs."

"McLean," Allenby said, "I have transferred your money to San Antone. There is no use of your ridin' clean back to Texas with it, it is too easy to get rid of that way, either by you or some-body gettin' wind you're carryin' it."

"I'm obliged to you, Mr. Allenby," McLean said.

"You won't know what to do with yourself now the horses are gone."

"No, sir," McLean said.

"Sykes, I expect you got a job every season now, with Tres Reyes. There's men thinks Richards here rods this outfit, but you and me know different, don't we?" He was shaking hands all around. "Say, you Mexykins did all right. Easy on that whiskey now, it's got to last you to Ogallala. Ben."

He was looking at Richards, the cool pale eyes squinted a little, as if the smoke from his cigar had got into them. "If I don't catch sight of you next year, I'm goin' to want to know the reason why. If I can get the wife off her . . . ah . . . get her off the idea of city livin', I got a notion I would like to drop down and make Dominguez' acquaintance. If the market holds, we are goin' to be doin' business together for some time to come. You tell him I said so."

"I'll tell him," Richards said.

"*Adiós*, then, to you all. A safe trip back, and start gatherin' those cows soon as you get there." He was climbing up behind the matched roans. "I'll look to see you all next summer."

They watched Allenby off in the rig. Two officers came out of the post and intercepted him. Shiloh said, "There is the picture for you. What happens to you in the Army is you git to wear a pretty blue uniform in the middle of noplace. Keep your hand in the cow game, though, girls, and you may end up with a out-size turnip in your watch pocket and a gold chain on your boosum. Look over there and let the lesson sink in."

Sykes was rattling off in the chuck wagon. As suddenly as if a bugle had sounded from the post, they were mounted and moving out, McLean still handling the extra mounts. Richards took a last long look behind him, from the saddle of the buttermilk, and saw the far drift of the Tres Reyes herd, grazing on the Teton. *You came a long way, cows, you and me. I don't look to come this far again, maybe, not with your kind under my wing, anyway. And I remember that big steer led you, with his horns held high and too much in his mind for me to figure, because now he is free of you, and free of me too, and I aim to be the same; mostly I aim to be free of me.*

He could recall, returning from Nebraska the year before, the anticipation with which he had looked forward to the return. It had been like going home, back to something which belonged to you, and maybe more important, to which you belonged. He had a family, for the first in a long time. His parents were dead and his sisters married and moved away, and he had found another family. If he had not been taken into it as completely as he might have been, that was his fault, not the fault of the people at Tres Reyes. It was because he would not let himself. It was because he would not be bound. But there were times he wondered if man was meant to be rootless.

They had nearly crossed Wyoming before he approached Mc-Lean, while the boy was stringing his night corral around the horses. When he came up, McLean was making a little whistling sound, not a tune that you could name as such, but an unconcerned, satisfied kind of sound. He looked up from slipping a knot and the whistle trailed off. "Oh, howdy, Ben," he said. His voice was self-conscious.

"I reckon you're glad you got one day less to travel toward home," Richards said.

"That's sure. If we could set the pace goin' out we set comin' back, and had enough cows, we could make two drives a year and look like money."

"Frankie, I'd like to ask you something that ain't any of my business. But your pa made a point of mentionin' it to me, and it's turned up kind of important in my thinkin'. Was he bad in debt?"

"About a thousand dollars," McLean said unhesitatingly.

"He said this drive would pay off, and leave him something over, but at the time he said it he was tryin' hard to influence me."

"You mean to take the herd?"

Richards nodded. "But you'll be able to square it all now, with no trouble."

"Pa was an honest man, Ben, and I don't reckon he ever dreamed of bein' rich. When things got tight for us, I always used to pound at him to go borrow from don Ramón, but he never could see his way clear to do it. My God, it was like havin' a bank right down the road, and he somehow didn't have the nerve to ask for a loan."

"Not nerve," Richards said. "High-minded about it, I expect. There was nothin' wrong with that. He worked hard and he lived honest, like you say, and I only wish he might of had some time this last year when he didn't have to worry about money, when he could of known everything was paid up and he was startin' clean again."

"Rojo beat him, in the end, didn't he?" McLean said. "Beat me too, I reckon."

"I don't know as I'd look at it that way. Things are the way they are, that's all. Rojo didn't know he'd done something he shouldn't of done, and I don't believe he's runnin' free thinkin' about how he put one over on you. Now and again I get an urge to hand you some advice, but I still ain't certain I should. Don't think about Rojo. Your pa spent too many hours out of his life sweatin' that red steer, and I believe even if he'd known what it would lead to, he wouldn't of been any different. I wouldn't want to see you do the same."

"Ben . . . goddamit," McLean said suddenly. "I still git nightmares over that damnfool thing I went and done, said to you. If you could tell me now I made it up to you, on this drive, I don't reckon there would be much more I could ask for."

Richards put his head back and looked up at the sky, where the prairie stars were hanging white. "You made it up. But you didn't do any less than I figured you would. Frankie, before we go any farther, you and me, I want to tell you I never once had too many doubts you'd be good enough to ride the river with, once you made up your mind. The day after your pa was buried I was about to say to you, you be good to Avis, and I couldn't bring myself to it, so I will say it now."

McLean was standing, watching him.

"I don't have any judgments to make one way or the other, on account of it not bein' my place. But you remember what I said."

"How did you know?" McLean said, softly, between his teeth.

"There was a letter here for me. I could say it was just a

friendly word from a neighbor lettin' me know everything was all right back home, but the fact of it is it was to let me know how the land lay."

McLean wasn't looking at him any more. "Then I reckon you know why there was times I wasn't sure I could stay in your company without wantin' to knock you down and kick your teeth in."

"I reckon I do."

"Ben, I'm sorry."

"Nothin' to be sorry for. I wanted to say good luck to you and clear it up between us, since I look to be headin' west once we hit Dodge City."

"You ain't goin' back? Ben, not account of this, not on account of me and Avis?"

Set a good example, as your ma would of said, and do not lie to this boy, Richards thought. "Partly. I don't aim to lay in the sun and sweat if I can find some shade someplace else. But more than that, personal reasons too. I don't know as I could set 'em out where they would make any sense to you."

"Ben . . . damn it, I wish it didn't have to be this way. I feel kind of as if it was my fault, your feelin' like you do."

"Kind of?" He could feel the dour smile pulling at the corner of his mouth. "You keep on the line now, Frankie, because if I hear otherwise, I'm liable to come back and straighten you out the only way I know."

"I reckon you would," McLean said. "It don't seem right, somehow, Ben, none of it. When Pa was alive, it was like I had a sister fussin' over me and givin' me hell and tryin' to make me see all the things I done wrong, and not understandin' that I couldn't be any way but the way I was, on account of her. Now . . ."

"Sure," Richards said. "Just like Christmas morning."

"Like what?"

"Nothing. Something I thought of when I used to be young and fool-headed.

"Where do you aim to go, Ben?"

"Anywhere," Richards said. "Anyplace there's cows. Sometimes I reckon I got born into the wrong breed of animal."

"Ain't there anything I can say might change your mind?"

362

"Not this week," Richards said. His ear was ringing, a funny sound that was half like the clang of a bell, half like a running of surf. "My ear's ringin'," he said, "somebody's talkin' about me." The ringing was like an alarm had been set off, as if something was telling him not to say anything more, not to make any pronouncements he might have to back away from. But he had nothing more to say to the boy, he had said it, and from now on in all they would have to do would be act like friends and neighbors. That shouldn't be hard to do, if the reins were kept tight enough. It was crazy how anything could get as wild inside you as a dream could, rising up big and bright and then laying down of its own accord and ending up no more than a little heap of dust, and you could take the toe of your boot and push it around until it was worked out flat into the earth again, and that was the last of it.

Riding back through some nameless divide, in the morning, he saw a shadow floating in the grass, to his right, and there was a quick surging in him which felt like alarm. When he looked up, he saw it was only a turkey buzzard.

"If there is one thing that I would not wish to be, it is in debt to any man," Uremáy said.

"Well, I have looked over my books, and you don't owe me a thing," Shiloh said.

Díaz was gathering up the cards. "And if a man I know, who sits beside me, does not have a change of fortune, he will soon owe his saddle."

"I draw the line there," Shiloh said. "You can have my money, my shirt, and my hopes for the future, but I draw the line at my saddle. I am sorry my name ain't McLean, as if it was, I'd do nothin' but rake it in with both paws. Couldn't lose tonight, could you, Frankie?"

McLean threw his cards over to Díaz. "My luck's turned, is all."

"I can't stomach a doggy winner," Shiloh said. "Always quittin' while he's ahead."

"Like you say, life is just one big poker hand," McLean was grinning. "And tonight I happened to be holdin' it. Hard luck,

Shiloh, that's one day less you git to sit in that rocker chair you got on the brain these days."

Shiloh gestured at Uremáy. "It's him does that to me. He's got the dangdest headful of notions I ever come across. Say, excuse me all to hell, Tiburcio, you said something a while back and I don't reckon we let you git to finish it. My own self, listenin' to a list of who owes what makes me go to sleep quicker'n a overdose of redeye, but seein' it's you I will try not to yawn more'n once or twice."

"Ah, money," Uremáy said. "What is this? I was not speaking of the owing of money. There is nothing so singular in the owing of money. All men come to that. It is at least a clean, an honorable debt. It is when you owe something other than money that it becomes difficult to turn your face to it."

"You mean like if you are obliged to somebody," Shiloh said. "You do me a favor, then I can't rest nights till I've done you one and squared myself. The only damn trouble with that is, you're just as likely to feel you owe me one and turn right around and do me something again, and then the whole thing starts makin' the rounds like a pup chasin' its tail. It does play hell with the hind end of your conscience, don't it?"

"Now you have said it, what I wished to say. What do you think of this, Franco?"

"Well, I don't expect hardly a week goes by I don't have to pay off some obligation or other, even if it's only to say howdy to the hen lays the egg."

"You are a man of great heart, who thanks the hen. We are agreed, then, that only the man who is lacking in *sentido* would neglect the payment of his just debts."

Richards got up and walked off into the dark, out of the circle of firelight.

"Go on," Sykes said.

"I have finished," Uremáy said.

"Finished. I thought you was goin' to track out some long story for my eddyfication. You are tendin' to flounder worse than a crockheaded horse, Uremáy. I had just got my ear tuned to you."

364

"I regret it," Uremáy said. "Perhaps by this time tomorrow something will come to me. For now, I am ready to sleep."

"All right, I will match you there." Sykes put out his cigarette. "How much did you win here tonight, McLean?"

"Close to forty," McLean said. He stood up. "Too bad we ain't got nothin' to play with but beans, ain't it?"

In the middle of the cool overcast morning Richards dropped back to ride beside Uremáy. He had estimated that they were maybe thirty miles out of Fort Laramie, and he wanted to make it in by nightfall, to restock the chuck wagon. He still wasn't sure whether he was mad at Uremáy or not.

"You figure my spine needs stiffening, Tiburcio?"

"What a strange thought," Uremáy said. He did not look at Richards, and his eyes were blank and innocent.

"You figure I owe Ramón Dominguez something."

"*Amigo mio*," Uremáy said, "God forbid that I should be the man to point it out to you."

"All right," Richards said. "Maybe I have been lettin' how I feel about Ramón Dominguez stand in the way. You are right. I owe him something. I owe him a much obliged and an explanation of some kind, and a decent *adiós*. He has been *mucho hombre* to me and a goddam snake in the grass to his own, and I don't reckon I too much care whether I shake his hand again or not."

"I did not know you had thought of this," Uremáy said.

"Maybe we ought to get it straight that I think a lot of things you don't know about, then. Look, I got beat out a while ago, but I ain't dead yet."

"It was only I thought there was perhaps no room in your mind, at the moment, for anything but your own troubles. I believed that it would be kind of you to say your farewells and wish good fortune to La Morena Flor."

"Sure," Richards said, "it would do me good to go back to all these weddings and fiestas and whatall, will be goin' on down there." He pulled in the horse. "Hold up a minute, Tiburcio. I want to ask you a question, and I don't want any brush dodgin' on the answer, if you can manage it. If Quesada showed up this summer, what makes you think Cayetana ain't gone by now? And by the same token, what makes you think Ramón Dominguez stood still for it?"

"That is two questions," Uremáy said. "Do you think Morena Flor would go without me, without seeing me, without having me there? Well, I have replied with a question, I see. The answer is no. For the rest of it, what action could the *patrón* take against either of these children? Listen, they have remained faithful to each other a long cruel time." He smiled a little. "And then, of course, the hand of the Señora, that most estimable of women, will be in the matter by now, and we shall be powerless."

Richards was frowning, his face as dark and rigid as if it had been turned out of bronze. Then he said, "It ain't my nature to ride through life castin' over every stone I see. But I would surely dislike to leave one right side up and find out later there was something under it I should of got down and picked up."

"Now you speak as a sensible man. Let us say no more of this, and return to whatever awaits us."

Richards took up the reins. "I'll think about it," he said. "I got quite a few miles ahead yet, to think about it."

Yet when he tried to think of it, in the pace of the passing days, he found it hard to do so. It was almost as if his mind had shut off and confined that portion of itself which contained all that he had known of Tres Reyes. At night he lay with his arms under his head, watching the sky, and remembered small isolated things: the sound of the Señora's chair in the hall, the way Dominguez lifted his heavy gray brows at times when he spoke, the dark trapped ghost of grief which lived in the girl's eyes. It was not enough, a picture here, a word there. And when he did not wish it, when it was the one thing he fought against, he could call Avis' face into his mind as easily and clearly as if she had come out of the night to him. He felt himself begin to go obdurate as stone, and bitter, and there was a new austerity in the set of his mouth.

The autumn days of the return were long days, dawn to dark. It was not like drifting, it was a hard push to get home, and both men and horses were tired. They stopped nowhere, for nothing, spending only one night in the reverberating saloons of Ogallala, and Richards resented that, as if he had someplace to go and was late getting there. They wanted to outrun the fall rains, but that was a futile hope, and it was raining hard on the early November day they sighted the smoke of the trains, puffing off like wet gray cloud, at Dodge City railhead.

Sykes was to leave them here, until he came south again in the spring. They got in out of the weather, playing cards and drinking beer all afternoon, listening to the smashing squall of wind and rain against the windows. Late in the day a buyer who had looked at the M Bar L herd with Todd Allenby wandered in and talked with McLean at the bar, and after a while McLean came over and touched Richards on the shoulder. "Ben. Can I see you a minute? I reckon you ought to come too, Tiburcio."

They got up and went to the bar. The storm was blowing harder, and the cold wet misery of it seemed to be penetrating the building itself; the bartender was rattling around in the innards of a potbellied stove in the corner. "You remember Mr. Barnard," McLean said. "I reckon I ought to let him tell you."

Barnard was a short portly man, in a black slicker. His hat was wet. "You men are from the Three Kings outfit? I'm sorry to be the one to tell you this. I can't vouch for it, understand, but the talk in town here is that Mrs. Dominguez died during the summer."

Richards felt an instant of quick clean shock; when he looked at Uremáy he saw that Uremáy's face was twisted, dark with blood. "You are certain of this, Señor?"

"Not certain, only what I hear. I was interested because, well . . . I remember when the lady caused such a stir runnin' off to Mexico and all. Like I say, I am sorry to be the one to tell you."

Uremáy turned away. Richards said, "I'm obliged to you, Mr. Barnard. He's been with the family a long time, and he will take it hard."

"Don't mention it," Barnard said. "You boys got a way to go yet, before you get home."

"Yes," Richards said. "Quite a way."

The vaqueros had drifted in from their tables and were standing around Uremáy. The flat sound of glass striking glass at the bar, the rattle of the poker in the stove, were loud in the dumb silence. Uremáy said, "Well, I think it is time for us to go on.

There is nothing to be done, but this is not the place for us."

Richards went with them, into the sweeping storm. He did not know and now would never know, whether he had intended to or not. It was beyond the power of his choosing. They rode south in the gray gusting rain.

TWENTY

"Do you recall," Uremáy said, "how it was when you returned last year?"

"I remember somebody came out. One of the Aguilár girls, I think it was. No, first we came down along the brasada and there was Esteban bringing some horses in and he hollered his head off at us. Then the Aguilár girl came out and spotted us and ran back to the house and they all came out like we had been away for twenty years. I remember that."

"How it was in the old days," Uremáy said, "was with a certain knowledge. Someone, usually an old man, would awake in the morning, and he would say, they return today. The word would go about. When it came to the big house, one of the servants would go to don Ramón and say, they return today, and don Ramón would say, I will see them when I see them. But the old man would be seldom wrong. Do not ask me how; he knew. Then it would start with the *muchachos*, looking as if they had gone out to play for the day. Their games would lead them farther and farther away, and if they could sneak a horse, or a mule, so

369

much the better. If we were coming up from Mexico, there would be a string of them between the big house and the farthest point at which they could go without being caught by the dark. In the event that this was not the day, you understand. So that miles out we would meet some fierce-eyed little man child who would gallop away from us and go to tell the next in line, before he came to meet us and ride in with us. This was an honored place, and they fought for it, as if we were returning from some battle. God knows, I can remember such times as that, also. But there they would be, a chain of the young, running home to say that the old man had arisen that day with the light of truth in his eye and the word of it on his tongue. It was a rite, a time of celebration. Now I think there is something more seasoned in the coming and going of our vaqueros, something which has lost a little of its ease and joy and becomes more to do with the making of money. To the young, now, I sometimes think we return as cowherders, and I preferred it when they believed we were *bravos*."

In the past days, Uremáy had been withdrawn, obstinately dedicated only to returning home. Once or twice he had spoken of the Señora in a queer animated way, as if there were a hope that what Barnard had told them was not true. But he knew that it was, and Richards knew that he knew it. It was early December when they came into San Antonio, and the sun was blinding and the air had a clear cold in it. And Uremáy said, "*Simplicidad*, after all, eh, my *gringo*? Men will say to me, and where is it that you have been, old *peon*, and I will say in return not that I have been south to Ciudad Mexico and north to Montana, not even will I mention the old country; no, I will say, I have been to Tres Reyes." He put his hand up to his face, quickly. "*Ay*, Christ, the wind is rising. It blows the dust of Texas into my eyes."

Richards was reflective, riding beside him. After a while he said, "She was good to me, in that way of hers. I used to think sometimes she liked me pretty well and other times she didn't know I was alive."

"That last, it was when she suffered. She thought no one knew, but they all knew, down to the little foolish Soledad. From the time she cast away her old life for the *patrón*, she called upon, I think, a greater bravery than she needed. She would not have been told she was brave, no, she would have thought it an insult. So I will say it of her now. She was not loved, perhaps. How can you love one who outwits you at all times? But the *gente* had for her the regard, the understanding, the wish to uphold her in all her small triumphs because they admired her bravery. It may be that this is more than to be loved. The *patrón* is loved."

"Not by me," Richards said.

"No? Well, you have a hard head, full of *gringo* thoughts."

"Not so hard I ever considered takin' a machete to him," Richards said.

"Remember if you will, that the *patrón* and I were born within a week of each other, that we were children together and young men together and have become old men together. I was as welcome within the walls of his home as he within mine. And he shared with me his only child. That, perhaps, was the mistake. I never lost the knowledge that the child was not mine, and yet there were times when I deceived myself too well. Yes, I was filled with rage against him, and yet in another sense, I understood." He glanced at Richards. "And he is still my *patrón*. As I hope he will still be yours, you for whom all things must be laid out in full sight, here and here and here, so that you are so busy going from what you can see to what you can see that you see nothing which may lie between. Do you grow weary of my rudenesses?"

"To the bone," Richards said.

"You change, Ben. Let me tell you what your bitterness will do to you, if you let it. It will warp you, as the wind warps the cedar. Until all things at which you look will be twisted, and you will hear things only as you wish to hear them, and know things only as you wish to know them. Is this not true?"

"It's true," Richards said. Then he said, "Do you think she left a shadow?"

Uremáy smiled slightly. "I cannot say. First I will have to look upon the land which she has touched with her wings."

Ten miles out of Tres Reyes, Esteban Ibarra, from the watch he had kept for nearly a week, rode to meet the returning crew.

371

There was no haste in the gait to which he held his horse; his greeting was hesitant. He looked first at Uremáy, and then his eyes slid away, and Richards said, "We know, Esteban, they told us in Dodge City," and Esteban took audible breath and fell in with them.

"You see?" Uremáy said. His voice cracked. "No *muchachos* now. And I saw the day when this one was a *muchacho*. I saw the day when he was born on his mother's horse, as he says."

"We were to have married, Rosa and I," Esteban said. "Now we think we must wait."

"It will do you good, who live so agreeably," Uremáy said. "Anyway, she will keep, this Rosa of yours, it is not as if she would arise in the morning and vanish. Tell me, how is the *patrón?*"

"I do not know, in truth. Outside, he goes his way as he has always done. Inside . . ." Esteban looked at him. "He bleeds. How else can it be."

"And the Señorita?" Uremáy said calmly.

"Her soul has gone away."

Uremáy kicked his horse forward a little and reached out and took Esteban by the arm. "*Cabrone*, do you wish God to hear you? Has no one come to Tres Reyes this summer?"

"*Sí*," Esteban said, wincing. "Two *hacendados* from Sonora, to see the *patrón*. The Ranger captain with the fortunate name. The Señora McLean. Father Berrades has returned. Of whom did you wish to know?"

Uremáy let go of his arm and dropped back beside Richards and slumped in the saddle.

Other years they came home singing, Richards thought. Now there was only the silence and a little keen wind and the sound of the horses and the creaking of leather and the dust rising where the hoofs stirred it to blow away. The first person he saw was Father Berrades, standing with a small shovel in one hand and shielding his eyes from the sunlight with the other. When he saw them he put down the shovel and stood waiting. Several children ran up the outer wall and stood blank-faced and big-eyed, watching.

"I would bend down to you, Father," Uremáy said, "but these poor bowed legs of mine have been held too long to a horse."

"I am happy to see you, old friend," Berrades said. "And you, Señor Richards."

"Howdy, Father," Richards said. They shook hands.

"You have come quickly," Berrades said. "This house mourns." He made the sign of the cross, his long brown fingers moving with swift grace. "I bless you all. Your families will have cause to rejoice that you are home safely."

They came forward one by one, to speak to him and file across the courtyard. Richards and Uremáy dismounted; Uremáy held his hand across his belt buckle, a clench-fingered holding of himself, as if he hurt, and Richards looked up and saw Cayetana crossing the courtyard with that same firm light step, like a young cat, that he remembered. She went straight to Uremáy and reached out and circled his wrist with her fingers, a curious gesture, as if she knew him too well to take his hand, but not well enough to embrace him. Her voice was so husky it was almost hoarse. "*Bienvenida*, Tiburcio."

"Well, small flower of a thousand places," Uremáy said. "I come home to mourning, but the earth does not stand still for me, since you are upon it." He did not smile, and his countenance assumed a sudden, still, vigilant mask. She had turned, and Richards took a step back, in astonishment, before he felt her hand slide cool and hard in his own. "Welcome, Ben."

"Caye, I am mighty glad to see you," he said. But her stark face, with the fine plane of bone showing and the eyes as deep and fathomless as a shaft in the earth, with all the light blown out of them, stunned him. The somber little look, the child look, which had been upon her in the time of his knowing, had left nothing of itself. The child had gone away and left a woman with skin as translucent as yellow pearl and shadows like wounds under the haggard eyes. Only the deft subtle body, the quick gliding strength of the hand spoke to him of some clinging resiliency.

She had turned to Uremáy again, and this time they did not speak and Richards looked away, not wanting to know what they told each other with their eyes, with their changed faces.

Within, it was as if nothing had changed. It was all the same,

373

and when he went into the room upstairs that too was the same, even to Soledad's cheerful little greeting. Yet the house seemed to him unnaturally quiet. The noise from the courtyard, where the *gente* came to welcome their men home, was dim and muffled. After a while he went and looked catercorner across the hall, at the room with the closed door. He put up his hand and felt the rough growth of several days on his jaw, and then he lowered it and touched his own leg and a small dust came from his clothes. Staring at the closed door he was conscious that he was still wearing his hat, and he took it off.

Dominguez did not come in until dinnertime. There was a certain slope in his shoulders that had not been there before, and his face showed marked strain, but he held together. It was not until the meal was served that Richards realized there was a slow fumbling of his hands as he moved them, and a new cast in the eyes. He tried to keep away from it, but it was there: the same dumb entreaty he had seen in the eyes of dogs. And there was nowhere else to set his sights, except upon Dominguez or the composed girl who faced her father down the table, seated where her mother had been seated, with Feliciano behind her; or, across from him, the quiet attentive face of Father Berrades. He was aware that he was talking a great deal, as if he could compress the account of months on the trail into an hour or so, but there was no help for this and it was expected of him. Before the meal was over he had become grateful for several things: Dominguez' careful regard, which wandered only occasionally; Cayetana's composure; but mostly for the inspired interest of Father Berrades. It was not a comfortable time, and he knew, long before he rose from the table that he had not, after all, come home in any sense of the word, and that he had made a grave mistake in returning. He had come back because he had been swept into it, swept up by Uremáy and a cold autumn rain and a piece of bad news, and unable to prevent any of it.

He did not look forward to any seclusion with Dominguez, for he had begun to notice that there was something vague, something more than the uncertain groping of the hands, about the *patrón*, and it was Cayetana who first brought it to his attention. It was as though their roles had been reversed: her attitude to-

374

ward him was that which she might have cultivated toward a child she guided, faintly indulgent, and touched with defensiveness.

He knew too, when they had gone into the office, that Dominguez was making an extraordinary effort. Somebody, Richards noted, had done a thorough job of cleaning the place up; the walls had been freshly whitewashed and the usual clutter of the desk seemed to have been neatly swallowed up by drawers and pigeonholes, so that he knew women had been at work here, something which had not been allowed before. And he was not ill at ease, as he had expected to be. He had wondered if perhaps he might not, alone with Dominguez, consider only the thing he now knew of this man, and be unable to consider anything else. And he thought, but I would never let him know what I know, and said, "Don Ramón, I don't have any words to say how I felt when I heard about the Señora. It must of been a bad summer."

Dominguez was looking at the end of his cigar. He thought, Richards is the same to me, but now he makes no attempt to conceal that harsh watchfulness I have seen upon him before. A bad summer. How little he knows. He said, "I think it was our fault, that we were not more mindful. We knew, of course, that her heart was bad. It was, at one time, the only thing the doctors were certain of." He took a deep breath. "What I now find most difficult to believe is that life goes on, as it did before. All things are not the same, it is true, but most things are no different. If Father Berrades had not been here . . . well, it is good that he was. It helps me, now, to see you back. I am grateful to you, Ben."

"Grateful? I don't follow you, don Ramón."

"For many things. Most of all, for the fact that you have been with me two years now, and from the time you came into Tres Reyes, you have made it apparent that you looked upon it not as an employment, but as if the interests here were your own. You have been loyal; this is a thing of great value, beyond even the proving of your ability. You are discreet, and you have honor."

He's going to raise my pay, Richards thought, and bit down hard on his cigar without meaning to.

"I say this to you as my friend," Dominguez said. "I am certain that I leave Tres Reyes in good hands, when I entrust it into yours. It is because of this . . ."

"Wait a minute," Richards said, leaning forward, his eyes narrowed. "Wait, now, you're goin' too fast for me, sir. Leavin' out all the things you think I am, let's get down to whatever it was you just said."

"I go to Mexico City," Dominguez said. "The day after Christmas, if it is possible. There are many things to attend to, following doña Alicia's passing. You understand. I have had neither the desire nor the will to put my mind to this. There are financial matters, and other considerations which require my presence. I had intended, as well as I could think it out, to go when you returned."

He felt as if he had taken another burden upon himself. "How long do you reckon to be gone?" he said.

"I do not know. As long as it will take. If I should not find it to my convenience to return before spring, I have all confidence that you will prepare for the trail and use your judgment, whether or not we have a contract forthcoming."

"Sir," Richards said. But he could not say it, that he still was not sure he wanted to remain, that he had not made up his mind, that there was something in this house now which had put him at war with himself, telling him to stay and telling him to go. What he said was, "I'm sure Allenby's comin' up with something by the first of the year. I reckon the reason he didn't make me a firm offer now is that he is a born speculator, and wherever the market looks good is where he is bound to be. I wouldn't fight him, he makes money."

Dominguez' smile was thin, as if he had forced it. "This too I leave to your discrimination. I am very tired tonight. I rode a long way this day. I do not know why I make such long rides . . ." He broke off. "And what can my aching bones be compared with yours, or the length of my ride, for that matter. Whatever final affairs I leave, we shall discuss with Cayetana and Uremáy present. There is time." When Richards rose, he looked up from under the heavy gray brows, managing for the first time the old half-humorous look, or something close to it. "There is no need for you to arise in the morning. Or the morning after that, if you so wish."

"I don't expect I'll have any trouble rememberin' that," Richards said. He was done in, and the collar of his white shirt felt too loose and irked him. When he crossed the hall he stood for a time looking into the chapel. There were dried flowers and paper blossoms all over, and a lot of candles burning. He supposed they burned a good deal now, for the Señora. There was not a sound in the house, but he had a feeling Cayetana was alone in the big room, Father Berrades having gone off to talk to the vaqueros right after dinner. He looked full at Guadalupe this time, and thought, there is no sense in looking for change in you, you never change and I don't expect you ever will. Upstairs, he avoided the closed door of the Señora's room. He sat down on the edge of the bed and took stock of how easily he had been dragged down and taken in, on a perfect cast of the rope. He felt resigned. He fell asleep with his clothes on.

It was still early when somebody knocked on the door, and he was awake feeling cold and cramped, with the taste of the cigar stale in his mouth and not recalling where he was. When he opened up he saw a kid about six outside. He thought it was Lupe's grandson but he wasn't sure. "*¿Que paso?*" he said.

"*La Señora Uremáy quiera usted,*" the boy said.

"*¿Donde?*"

"*La Cocina,*" the boy said. He looked like a little brown statue, and he didn't smile.

"*Voy corriendo,*" Richards said. He ran a hand through his hair and picked up his hat. The kid streaked off ahead of him and ran down the stairs.

When he went down he heard Cayetana and Father Berrades in the big room, but the lamps were out in the kitchen. Natividad was waiting, holding a single candle. She gave him a start, with the candle held up before her impassive face. When he went up to her she took him by the cuff of his shirt. "Natividad?" he said. He still felt groggy.

She was pulling at his sleeve. "*Venga, Señor, por favor.*"

"*¿Que sucéde?*"

She hissed it at him. "Tiburcio. *Muy borracho. Vino y mas vino, esta noche. Es verdaderamente malo.*"

"*¿Por que razón?*"

"*No se nada de eso.*" She lowered the candle and he could no longer see her face. Not that he needed to. She wasn't going to tell him anything. It came into his mind that he had never seen Uremáy drunk and that there was a bare possibility Natividad never had either, since she seemed so upset about it. But instead of going back with him, she scuttled off into the night as if she planned to spend it with neighbors. As he had figured, it was not late, and there was light showing in every window, Uremáy's included.

Uremáy did not look drunk. He looked more as if he had been struck over the head, sitting with a fixed and steadfast immobility, as though he had been torn at for centuries by wind and rain and sand and had remained untouched. The house was two rooms partitioned by a curtain, with a neat smooth-beaten earth floor. There were some chairs with woven rush backs, in one of which Uremáy was sitting, at a table with a faded red cloth covering it. A little collection of statues and pictures of saints was arranged on a chest pushed back against the middle of the wall, and some dried rushes and flowers had been tucked around the frame of a Holy Child hung over the chest. There was a faint smoky smell of frying in the air.

He thought Uremáy was not drunk at all, or else so drunk he had no right to be still sitting up. It was not warm in the house, but the gray cotton shirt Uremáy wore was open nearly to the waist and the sleeves were rolled short. The strong thick upper arms, the meaty thick exposed chest were as wet as if he had come out of the river, and his hair hung down straight and wet over his eyes. His face, in the dim light, appeared to have been oiled. The gray shirt was black with sweat at the armpits, and across the ribs. But he was breathing deeply, steadily, and his voice was only a little thick. "I am pleased that you have come to take a drink with me, *gringo*," he said.

"What's the matter?" Richards said.

"Why must something be the matter? Can I not stay in my

own house, with my own bottle, and have my own drink, in my own time? Sit down. I will bring you a *cupita*."

"Never mind," Richards said. "I don't want it right now, if it won't hurt your feelings." He picked up the bottle and saw it was three-quarters gone.

"Natividad comes for you," Uremáy said.

"No," Richards said.

"Now I am pleased again, that you tell me lies to protect my wife. It is kind of you. You wish to know why I am drinking. I am drinking because Father Berrades said to me, here is a bottle of wine for you, old friend."

"He didn't say for you to drink it all at once, did he?" Richards said.

Uremáy shrugged, but it was accomplished with caution. "It may be that I accepted his gift in more good faith than he intended. You spoke with the *patrón* this evening."

"Not for long," Richards said.

"Longer than I. Why does he not come down and look at me, why does he not put out his hand upon my shoulder and say it lightens his heart to see me? Has he been much affected, by the death of the Señora?"

Richards thought about it. Then he said, "Yes. He acted to me, tonight, like he's kind of . . . well, like he relies on Cayetana."

Uremáy laughed. There was an ugliness in the sound. "I would rather talk to you than to Father Berrades. You tell me more in six words than he in an hour of endless speech."

"He couldn't of said much when he handed you that bottle."

"Do not interrupt me. Did the *patrón* tell you that it was La Morena Flor, coming up the stairs in the night, who found her mother dead in bed?"

Richards felt his chest tighten. "We didn't talk about it."

"No? What was it you spoke of, then?"

"We seem to of talked about me, although I didn't think about it that way at the time."

"Such a subject," Uremáy said. "Forgive me if it does not hold my interest."

"Tiburcio," Richards said. "What happened to Quesada?"

"I wondered when you would come to asking me that. Are

379

you certain you do not wish a small drink? No?" He tipped up the bottle and put it down again. "That was to a noble animal, a fine gray Arab that I remember, and which I do not need to close my eyes to see again, going up to Málaga he was, to greet the sun of a feast day with silk in his mane, and died that afternoon as no horse should die." He folded his arms and leaned across to Richards. "Died as Glass died. Do you remember? Yes, you remember."

"And Quesada?"

"Remained three days beyond the days of that horse, with a broken back." Uremáy's blunt coarse hand moved, kneading at the faded red cloth of the table. Water sheeted down his face. "Could you look at Morena Flor this morning, and not know? I knew. It seems to me now that I knew the day I fought with him when I slept, and I said to you, how does one fight an army, and you told me."

"You ain't blamin' yourself, are you? You ain't that drunk, are you?"

Uremáy shook his head. "I blame myself for many things, but what is the use of asking why I did not do these many things in some way other than I did? Now the *patrón* knows that I know what he has done, and does not wish to face me. Now he knows that I know Morena Flor went up the stairs of the big house with the darkness of death upon her, and found the Señora. How does one heart, one small heart, stand up to so much?"

Richards could feel the slow spreading ache of hurt, of depression, in him. But he felt something more, and he thought it might be anger. "For Christ's sake, how could they of kept that from her?"

"It would not have been withheld. Because the only way in which it can be made clear that a thing is over and done is to say outright that it is over and done, and nothing will bring it back. Nothing will change it. All this I have from Father Berrades. She only said to me, well, I have sent the little Macarena back where she belongs, with doña Mercedes, and while she was not all to me that I wish she might have been, she was so good to me for a time that I will always remember her. That is what she said to me."

380

"Listen," Richards said. "Listen, do you believe we got to pay for our mistakes?"

"If so, I shall be a long time in hell."

"Not that. I mean that maybe we got to pay for 'em while we're still here, still alive?"

"I do not know. I do not wish to believe that I must make payment here and in hell also. If you mean will the *patrón* be forced to some penance, I do not know that either. His wife is dead and his daughter might as well be. Perhaps that is enough. And perhaps that is little, beside what takes place in his mind, no? You said to me, did she leave a shadow? and I say to you, yes, I think so, and so did that other young eagle, whose eyes never looked upon this earth I call mine, but whose heart is buried here now whether or not he would have had it so. And I have exhausted all my store of knowledges and despairs and misunderstandings, and tomorrow I will arise and pick up my life in both these hands, and go on, not as if all is as it was, but as if there is something, still, beyond. What is it that you will do, or do you feel that this is no longer of any importance to me?"

"Tiburcio, go to bed," Richards said.

"Very well. Go. *Adiós. Buenos noches.*"

Richards leaned across the table and took him by the shoulder, feeling the damp cotton under his hand. "Tomorrow I am goin' to pay a visit to the M Bar L. And next week I might head out for San Antone to do some stockin' up for myself."

"Aha," Uremáy said, "You go to the M Bar L? What does this cost you, *compadrito*, if I may ask?"

"It costs me some common sense, that's all. Did you reckon I was goin' to turn my back on them, over there, like a cross-grained kid?"

Uremáy closed his eyes. "Does this mean that you are going to stay at Tres Reyes?"

"I don't see how it could hardly mean anything else," Richards said.

"Then you have found it in yourself to forgive us all?" Uremáy said.

"Forgive you?"

"It is that I remember what a fine life you had, before you

came to us. Free as the wind, without a care to cloud your mind, without a trouble to touch your heart. With nothing dependent upon you."

"And nothing to depend on," Richards said. "Also the meals weren't too steady. You are goin' to have a hell of a head in the morning, Tiburcio."

"It does not matter," Uremáy said. "You stay, and what passes in my head, that will go away."

On Sunday there was a special Mass for Alice Graves Dawes Dominguez, for the vaqueros of the trail crew. The benches had all been filled and the *gente* were kneeling on the floor and it had begun by the time Richards went through the gates of the *capilla* for the first time. He stood in the back, against the wall, but that did not seem right, so he got down on his knees, where he was profoundly uncomfortable. He kept his eyes on Guadalupe and the smaller statues which were grouped around her, but he did not look at the crucified Christ because it made him feel sick that anybody would so such a thing to anybody else. He had only a vague idea of what was taking place and his knees tortured him and he became drowsy. Six little kids in white smock kind of things did some singing and Father Berrades was going through some complicated motions, and with the warmth of the close-packed room and the small dancing lights of the candles and Father Berrades' soothing voice, he dozed off. When he came to again he thought he saw the Señora's chair in the aisle, as he had seen it so many times, but it was only a momentary idea and did not bother him much. What bothered him was the back of Cayetana's head, bent under its black drape so that he could see the smooth young curve of her neck, as exposed and defenseless as if it had been bared to an ax. He was glad when it was over, except that he wasn't sure whether he was supposed to walk out or wait at the door and shake Father Berrades' hand and tell him what a fine sermon it was, as his own father had done with the preacher after a good roaring Methodist session. Something told him not to. But he waited at the gates for Cayetana. When she came out he noted that Dominguez seemed to be leaning on her arm and he moved around figuring to help, but Cayetana looked up at him and shook her head and he stayed where he was. She went with her father to the foot of the stairs and then came back to the gate. "He says he is not well this morning."

I shouldn't wonder, Richards thought. "I hoped you would come out for a while this afternoon, Caye. I got a couple of things on my mind and I seem to think better on a horse." There was only mild inquiry in her glance. "Only if you feel like it, now."

"By this afternoon I will feel like it. It is just that at the moment . . ."

He had a feeling the service might have upset her, and figured he should make a clean breast of it. "I went to sleep," he said.

She raised her head and there was suddenly a low sound of laughter in her throat. "She would have enjoyed that. My mother. Thank you for coming, Ben."

When she moved away, across the hall, he heard the stiff rustle of her skirt and thought, It does beat all how they feel they got to go on wearing that old black mourning, like a walking mine shaft. That girl looks terrible in black, and even if it gets her sore at me I'd ought to do something about it.

But when they had ridden out past the brush spur and turned west into the clear December day, it was a long time before he could say what he had to say. Cayetana barely spoke to him, but he did not feel awkward about it, nor did he feel that she was uneasy. She was not listless or despondent; only her eyes had that stricken muteness in them, that lack of light that he thought was maybe even worse than the sadness he had never known them to be without. For himself, it seemed to him that he had become more taken up with her tribulations than with his own, and he wondered if he had not done this deliberately, so that he would have something else to think about. It was only a little difficult for him to reconcile this girl with the girl he had known through Uremáy: surely the seed of laughter and passion and small fears and shy ardor were still in her somewhere. When he rolled and lit a cigarette he passed it over to her, where she rode beside him, and reminded her of what she had once said to him. "You feel any older?"

"Centuries. And look at poor Ebano. His muzzle is getting gray."

"Did he take up smoking, while I was gone?"

"I never ask what he does when he's alone. That is his affair. Ben, are you glad to be back?"

He looked at her. "Glad in some ways, sorry in others. You don't mind I'd rather be honest about it?"

She shook her head. "I want you to be. Then we understand each other. Does my father make you uncomfortable?"

"No, but I wish he didn't look to you so much. I reckon now he can maybe switch it to me. On account of I don't think it ought to be put on you. And I expect it just takes time now, he'll come out of it all right."

"He told you he was going to Mexico City? It is the best thing, I think. He has many friends there, it will be good for him to see them."

Again he looked at her. She was practical, and yet there was a fondness, a protectiveness in her voice. And he knew it would not be in her to be any other way, ever, with her father. He said, "I maybe ought to be talkin' to him about this, but then I thought he wouldn't want to be bothered about it right now. When I was at McLeans' the other day, I took a look at the deed to the M Bar L."

She had slowed Ebano to a walk; now she pulled him in, watching Richards with something painful and curious on her face. "But why, Ben?"

"As I understand it, if anything happens with the McLeans, if there are no heirs, or if they should want to clear out, that land reverts to Tres Reyes. Is that right?"

"Nearly so. In consideration of a token sum to be agreed upon by . . . well, in this case it would be my father and Frankie. Has something happened?"

He did not look at her now. "I reckon you know Frankie and Avis are goin' to marry."

"Tiburcio tells me this. Are you saying that they do not want to keep the ranch?"

"They are all fired up about goin' out to California. Avis had a letter from a cousin, somebody out that way somewhere. Anyway,

384

it impressed her kind of hard with the idea that it was as much the golden land as they say it is, and the frame of mind they are both in now, I look to see that M Bar L land come back to Tres Reyes. The only thing they would have to do is estimate how much stock they got runnin' around over there and sell it off, send that woodcutter and his family packin', and they are free to go. I told Shiloh if he wasn't set on goin' with 'em he could come here. I didn't aim to take so much on myself, but your father told me to use my own judgment, and I reckoned I should start right now, and get the feel of it. What do you think about it, Caye?"

"I would be sorry to see them go."

"Does havin' that land mean anything to you?"

"A great deal." She was looking at her hands, clasped on the saddle horn. "In one way, it is only a piece of land, and in another it is a piece of my life coming back to me. Ben, my grandfather came here, from Seville, after his wife had died. God knows what he hoped to find, in that little pueblo of mud huts. I think he must have been ill and dejected, looking for something to hold onto again. He found my grandmother, an Indian woman who was no longer young, and he found Tres Reyes. Somehow he brought order and prosperity and built the big house and began to live again, and by then he had learned to love this land. Yes, I would wish it all back to Tres Reyes, every foot of it."

"Something to do with this idea of family tradition you all have?"

She smiled a little. "I do not wish to sound like a poor imitation of my mother, but I despise tradition. What is past is past, and I want only to borrow and preserve certain graces and beauties and comforts from it, and to build something newer and better around them." She hesitated, but only for a moment. "I would like to say this, and then I won't speak of it again: I regret what happened between you and Avis. It must have been difficult for you, to return here."

"I almost didn't," he said.

"We need you now, more than before. I would have understood, if you had not come back."

"Now you'll probly have to fire me," he said. "Say, what does Tiburcio do, anyway, run through Tres Reyes like a flash flood, handin' out a word here and a word there, where he figures it's goin' to do the most good?"

"He has always played with us all as if we were a deck of cards."

"And?" he said, waiting.

"And under all that piety there is an arch intriguer and an irreverent reformer. And very dear to me."

Richards turned the buttermilk, so that he could face her. "He has called me *amigo* just once too often for me to feel like anything else. But I don't aim to let him meddle with me any old time he feels like it. Right now I have got my mind fixed on the fact that your father's goin' to be away for a time and that I am supposed to be doin' what has to be done around here without any interference from anybody unless I ask for it. I wouldn't want to tell Tiburcio, but are we partners?"

"We are partners," she said, and smiled again. "And there will be no need to tell him, he will discover it for himself."

And he thought, I made her laugh this morning and smile twice this afternoon. That ought to count on the good side of my ledger. "Do you want to go back, Caye, or would you like to ride on some?"

"I'd like to go on. Only . . . Ben, could we just not talk to each other, unless it matters very much? For now. For today."

"Why sure. I have said all I want to say." But inside he echoed her. For now. For today. He would just as soon think what had to be thought, instead of talking, and that was that whatever dull gnawing ache persisted in staying with him now, was shot through with a dawning deliverance.

He had not been disappointed or surprised either, that when he went into the M Bar L Avis had managed to be cool and easy and totally unconstrained, or that McLean, after a few unwieldy minutes had got his feet under him quickly. There were no problems, and Shiloh wandered in and made it doubly certain. What it had amounted to, once they had all been reassured by each other's attitudes, was a couple of aroused kids caught up in the idea of starting out on a new adventure. What they were saying, and doing, the pictures they were making for themselves, could have been infectious, although Shiloh said he felt his fate was forever to ride out with the longhorns, like it was some kind of punishment, and that he didn't have any hankering for hauling up his stakes and then having to hunt up another place to dig in again. When they asked Richards' advice on various aspects of the move he gave them the best he could and tried to make it all sound good, because he knew that was the way they wanted to hear it. But he held them off on speaking to Dominguez about the ranch. He didn't think that Dominguez was in any mood to be reminded of the ranch, or how and why it had been chopped out of Tres Reyes; he and Cayetana could settle the matter when Dominguez left for Mexico. After an hour or so all the excitement spilling over in them began to make him restless, even irritable. He had forgotten that young people took their enthusiasms to heart with such blithe and buoyant vehemence. It made an unexpected clamor in his head and brought to him the knowledge that while there was a lot to be said in favor of good cheer, he was getting too settled to put up with the noise.

He had welcomed the untroubled face of the open land, the limitless cloud-bordered sky, when he left. The stillness consoled. Now he was receptive to Cayetana's imposed tranquil silence and aware of a first immanent stirring of what he hoped would bring him to a willing and peaceful compromise, with himself and with whatever lay ahead for him.

TWENTY-ONE

On Christmas Eve he went to Mass and on Christmas Day he got up early and went down the hall to Cayetana's door and stood wondering if he ought to wake her and decided not to and left the box on the floor. Where Soledad might find it first, but it didn't make any difference. Then he went down and left some cigars for Uremáy and some striped cotton for Natividad and came back through the kitchen hoping Lupe had made coffee.

She was grinding vanilla beans in a stone mortar, to put in the chocolate. But she stopped and gave him a long look and brought him some coffee that was sending up steam alongside the fire. He wished her Feliz Navidad and sat down to drink the coffee and said he was glad to see she realized that he wanted to come in the kitchen in the morning, first thing, and have his coffee, and that he hoped she didn't feel it was too high-handed of him. She told him smartly in Spanish that she did not understand a word he was saying, but after he had gone she lectured a bewildered Soledad on the virtues of preparing the coffee as soon as she had come in for the day.

He met Cayetana in the upper hall, which was what he had figured to do, not wanting to cause her any uphill moments in front of her father or Father Berrades, and she had the box in her hands and she had opened it. Before she could say anything, he said, "It was on account of I don't like you in that black thing, around your head, so even if you got to wear black, if I thought you put it on when you were all by yourself I would feel better about it."

She was touching the yellow silk as if she were afraid of it. He could not read her face. "It is very beautiful, Ben. Thank you."

He cleared his throat. "Well, don't cry about it, I didn't mean I don't like you in black, I always like you, it is only I don't like bein' reminded so much of things as they are every time I see you. And I want to say I hope you have a happy Christmas."

Her heart was breaking but she wanted to smile anyway and it was a terrifying feeling and still somehow a good feeling and it made a quivering weakness in her thighs, and her hands. She handed him the box and took the fragile stuff from it and draped it over her head and said anxiously, "Is it all right?"

"Needs a comb, like your mother used to wear," he said gravely. He thought there was something lustrous in her eyes, but it was hard to say for sure. "Did I ever tell you about the time I was supposed to of got a rifle, when I was kid? I can laugh about it now. I don't know why I like to tell that story because I was sure wallowin' in my own misery at the time."

And she said, "It is because you can laugh, now. If you were still miserable there would be no point in telling it."

He thought about that several times, later in the morning, hanging around the courtyard. The *gente* had come up for their gifts and their drinks. Tall poles had been set up, with the *piñatas*, hollow papier-mâché birds and animals, hanging from them, and the kids had a great time swinging at them with sticks to break them and let down the flood of sweets and trinkets which had been packed inside. What he thought was that the farther along you got with the business of living the more you realized that nine out of ten every crisis had its lighter side, and as time went on it had some power, when you thought of that crisis, to make you remember the more unexacting face it presented. The mind had a way of shutting out the old trials and temptations, or at any rate grinding them down to a point where they quit looming so large and overpowering.

He spent an hour with Uremáy that afternoon. Neither of them said much: he was lost to the hilt in what he was thinking about, and Uremáy knew it and was singularly uncommunicative. Cayetana was packing for her father; the house would settle to its afternoon rest, and he went into the office intending to familiarize himself with the books and ended up sitting looking at the wall and deciding it would be good to be heading out again on moonlight nights, beginning to gather in the longhorns when they came out of the brasada in the dark to water and graze. When he started to think about the longhorns he also thought, I must of come home after all.

When Cayetana came in to dinner she was wearing the yellow silk over a high silver comb, and he looked at her and gave her a single abrupt positive nod of his head, to tell her it was all right.

Dominguez left them immediately following dinner. He was to leave at dawn with a picked company of eight vaqueros, who would accompany him into the interior of Coahuila, to the *hacienda* of an old friend. A few of the *gente* were going in and out of the chapel. In the big room, Father Berrades was sitting on a deep-cushioned couch slung on a rawhide frame. Richards sat opposite him, in his shirt sleeves. Beside them, within its cave of rough gray stone a low fire smouldered and talked to itself.

Berrades was slumped on his spine, his legs crossed and his arm up along the back of the couch. He had been speaking of some long gone Christmas of his past, one which he particularly recalled for a particular reason, although to Richards the point had seemed as vague and unsatisfactory as he now realized the heart of his own Christmas story must be. Berrades was gazing into the fire, absent and meditative, until Cayetana came in and leaned on the couch behind him. He did not turn, but his hand came up and took hold of hers. "Sing me a little song, Cayetana," he said.

She hesitated; then she went and picked up the guitar and returned to lean on the back of the couch. She was frowning a little, not certain that this was right, but as it was Father Berrades who requested it, perhaps he had taken the responsibility for it. When she struck not the strings, but the wood of the guitar, Richards remembered the night of the fiesta when she had sung in the courtyard; he could almost feel again the numb stupor which Uremáy's pulque had produced in him. And as before, he did not like the harsh broken music, but he listened, watching her face where it was turned to the instrument, half-shadowed and half-glazed with copper light where the fire touched it.

> *Esta yegua lunanca*
> *tiene un potrito*
> *con una pata blanca*
> *y un lucerito.*

But she broke off, looking up and saying it softly, slowly, in English, saying it badly because it was not meant for any other tongue, as if she wanted him to understand. "The big mare has a small colt, with one white leg and a little star." Her hand came away, the fingers spread. "And that is a little song."

"Too small," Father Berrades said. "Sing 'Guadalajara, Where I Was Born' . . ."

"Father Berrades!"

"Well, what will happen, will the heavens fall in upon us, do you think, on Christmas Night?"

"They well might," she said. "Especially as you were not born in Guadalajara." But she struck the chords and Richards felt the old anguish of the *flamenca* dissolve and before she was finished Father Berrades was singing with her in a thin true tenor and he found his heel striking the floor as if it no longer belonged to him. "Now that is enough," she said. Her face was flushed, with more color than he had ever seen in it. The taut skin drawn over the bones had taken on its own fragile quince-colored glow, independent of the fire. When she had put down the guitar she came to sit beside Father Berrades.

The priest looked at her, one thick dark eyebrow raised. "Now you are saying to yourself, what will be thought of us, at such a time."

She shook her head. "No."

"Then you are saying to yourself, "I do not care what is thought of us.""

Again she shook her head. "Not that, either."

And Richards thought, Some little tough resistance that she used to have, some hard high wall she had tried to throw up, as she had done the day she told Avis that it was a fine moment when you stopped caring what people thought, maybe that was cracking around her now, and maybe not too much pressure needed to widen the breach, if it was applied in the right place.

"I believe," Berrades said, "that what would be said of us is, here are three sinners, and is it not in innocence, after all, that they wish to lighten their souls with a little music?"

She protested. "You can't include Ben."

"Include me, if you could," Richards said.

"But the idea of you as a sinner is horrifying," she said.

He laughed. "Well, I would be obliged to know you hadn't set me up in your mind as a saint."

"That is even more horrifying," she said. "Oh, excuse me, Father Berrades, that was not well put I'm afraid." Her lower lip was caught between her teeth, as if she tried to prevent her laughter, and the pale glow rose higher in her cheeks. Then he saw her face contort. She stood up. "I want to see Father off in the morning, so I will go up now. Father Berrades, would you, tomorrow . . . well, would you say something special to him, something he might think about, while he's away?"

"What?" Berrades said. There was a mock dryness in his tone. "Are you suggesting that I create some unique sermon of consolation and then offer it as if it had only come to mind at the moment of his departure?"

She bent to him. "Would that be so difficult?"

He stared up at her. "You will have the last word in this, I see. Very well. No, it would not be difficult. May I say, Cayetana, that I am pleased to see you with that pretty thing upon your head, it becomes you."

She said nothing; but she gave Richards a quick, almost shy smile, before she left the room.

He listened for the last sound of her slippers in the hall. When he could no longer hear them, he leaned forward in his chair and looked directly at Berrades. "Father, she's goin' to come through this all right?"

"It will take time. They had, as I suppose you know, a peculiar relationship, she and Alicia. It was almost as if they could not . . . could not bear to love each other."

"Father," Richards said, "I am not talkin' about the Señora. I am talkin' about something else entirely."

For a bare second Berrades' eyes darkened, with caution. But they never left Richards' and after a time he said, "I have never known anyone to die of love. I approach anger, that I must say such a thing." He ran a restless hand through his unruly dark hair. "People die from the most hideous irreconcilable causes. Great wounds. Agonizing sickness, loathesome disease. Fearful accidents. But never of love. Perhaps my thoughts upon this matter are not what they should be; that is to say that they might not meet with approval in certain high places. But it seems to me that men die, by and large, so ignobly, so without dignity."

"And you think it would be noble, dignified, to die of love?" Richards said.

"Why not? Love is the greatest gift God gives us, over and above any other. It should be quite simple, quite comprehensible, to die of it."

Richards said, "Maybe man hasn't come as far up the trail as he thinks he has."

"What you are saying is that the whole human heart of mankind has not reached the stage where it may merely cease to beat when, and where, and for whatever reason it wishes. This would hardly be a progressive development, should it come to pass, and would conflict with the will of God. We die at God's will."

Richards said, "You mean God's whim."

"I cannot conceive of God as capricious, and when you say whim rather than will it puts such a meaning upon it. You are not a Catholic, and perhaps . . ."

"Father, I am afraid that I ain't much of anything along that line. I don't have any ideas to trade with you."

"I am not at all certain of that," Berrades said. "Pardon me, for I do not mean to sound in any way as if I were leading into

393

an attempt at conversion. It is only that I noticed you have come to two Masses now, and I questioned it."

"What kind of an answer did you come up with?"

"That you felt a profound and honest respect for this family, and that you could not do otherwise."

Richards got up and took a cigar from the box on the table. He stood lighting it, watching Berrades, with his teeth clamped on the cigar and his eyes assessing. "That's part of it. To tell you the truth, I feel all right when I get in there. I don't mean I come out like I had been born again or anything, it's only it lets me put my guard down for a while. What I don't like is that I seem to take something out of it, but I don't reckon I bring much to it."

"Is this important to you?" Berrades said.

"I don't know if it's important. I thought of it, is all. I suppose it is like every other proposition you get handed in this life: if you don't do anything but take you can end up poorer than when you started out. And if you go to meet it and try to put something of yourself into it, sometimes you come out in the end with a little less of it but a lot more of yourself."

Berrades was silent, his brows lifted. Then he said, "Your convictions or lack of them aside, is there no spiritual schooling in your background?"

"Did I go to church, you mean? As a kid, to one of those no smoke, no drink corporations. Then I got trapped into the revivalist thing, hellfire and brimstone from the time they set up camps, not a real shoot-out success unless all the old ladies had passed out and were laying in the aisle like they had been shot by the time it was over. It was kind of like the old song about the girls, you know, the more you make love to 'em the wilder they get. I never really thought of it as goin' to church."

Berrades coughed, twice, behind his hand. "So that you feel no particular pressure . . . no need, is that it?"

"I got needs, and pressures, just like any man. It is just that it raises my hair when I find out how many things there are in this world, so small I couldn't even get up enough sap to give 'em the time of day, that you people consider a sin."

"When I was very young," Berrades said, "studying what con-

394

stituted human sin and learning what penances I, as a confessor, would have to impose once I had classified those sins, I went through a trying time. There were all the evils of the earth laid out for me, so naked, so ugly, so utterly execrable, that I could hardly bear to read them, much less admit their existence. The knowledge that every hour, every minute of the day, someone, somewhere had, if you will forgive me, that entire endless list to choose from, was almost too much to encompass. I choked on the sins of mankind, Richards, as precisely as if I had a bone in my throat. And I wanted . . . I wanted . . ."

"You wanted to go out and save everybody," Richards said.

"I was too humble for that, although I knew young men who were not. No, I wanted merely to swallow my bone and hope that the horror of it would eventually be mitigated by hard work and the healing powers of time."

"And?" Richards said.

"And there came a day, when I had moved for a long time in the world of men, when I had begun to acquire some understanding of man, when the realization came to me that a very high percentage of those same abominable sins which I had looked upon with such despair and loathing, were now becoming positively alluring. Do not misunderstand me: although I have had my share of temptations, I am not speaking personally. But once sin became something more than words set forth for my training and instruction, much of that ugly nakedness began to clothe itself in delicate colors, to take on substance, flesh and blood, to become more human than anything I had imagined possible. And when the hungers, the appetites, the desires, had become real to me they no longer seemed so appalling. Because, you see, once they had taken life, once I had seen them contained in all humanity itself, they became tempered by all the great goodnesses which are also in man: tenderness and compassion, honor and courage, faith and endurance, benevolence and generosity. And love, the greatest of all, and the strongest. Not soft, and weak and languishing, as we tend at times to think of it, but hard as flint, strong as steel, yes, and bright as diamond." He was looking into the fire. "I do not feel so pessimistic concerning sin any more, because I know the forces which are at work against it."

Richards' cigar had gone out. He got up and went and threw it into the fire and stood braced, his arm against the chimney. "It seemed to me she always saw things different than anybody else. Like it was somehow more real than it ought to be. Tiburcio said to me, how does one small heart stand up to so much. Can you answer me that, Father?"

"The human mind is capable of many things which are beyond our power to reason. There are always imponderables. Things which should, unconditionally, destroy the mind itself. The simple fact of human behavior enters into it, of course. By which I mean that man has learned, since he came out of his cave, to conduct himself well before other men, and when he has mastered this he begins to build a new strength in himself."

"Pride?" Richards said. "And pride is one of your sins?"

Father Berrades leaned back, smiling. "And is not the candle worth the game?"

"But how do you know if the time is right? How do you know when to do what you want to do, and when not to do it?"

"Rules would be of inestimable assistance, but all we have is uneasy risk. Are you troubled, Richards?"

"Father, do you think Cayetana would have me?"

After a while Berrades said, "I do not know. I do know this: that out of grief there sometimes arises a deep need for sympathy, and out of sympathy affection, and out of affection a deeper bond . . . yes, I will say that word once more, love. We are so made that there are many complex and subtle shifts of our emotions under stress. All these that I identify are closely interwoven. To expect some pure passion to emerge from them might be a mistake, but the facets of love are so many, so varied, that it is beyond my power to put a name to any single one, or to the whole and complete . . . and very possibly, totally rare . . . thing which may arise from them."

"I am tryin' to be practical."

"Practical? In heaven's name, if you wish to approach this in a practical manner, I urge that you give it further consideration."

Richards said, "Father, I want that girl."

Berrades sighed. "Now that is more to the crux of the matter. Much more encouraging than what you have been saying."

"You are makin' it hard for me, Father. I know how I am, and that I probly won't ever be much different."

"And what is wrong, with the way you are?"

"No future, no money, no youth." He turned and looked at Berrades. "Some God, but not as much as you would probly like."

"Self-pity is also a sin," Berrades said, "although I hesitate to bring it up at this moment. May I ask how long you have felt this way, concerning Cayetana?"

"I couldn't say. Sometimes I think I always felt this way, and sometimes I think I only began feelin' this way the day I rode into the courtyard again. Because in between I had got myself into such a snarl I hardly knew which was day and which was night, and now that I have got that straightened out I ain't at all sure I'm not worse off than I was before. And I don't want it to seem . . ."

"You do not wish it to seem that you are buying Tres Reyes," Berrades said pleasantly.

"I thought of that, too."

"Of course, a man with your practical turn of mind would undoubtedly have thought it before he thought anything else. What does Tres Reyes mean to you?"

"More than I like to admit, even to myself. She makes it mean something."

"Then let us eliminate, entirely, the remainder of these practicalities of yours. They are all negative, and more, they are unimportant."

"Not all. I reckon I left out the biggest one."

"Cayetana," Father Berrades said.

"Cayetana. Because probly I am no more what she needs now than . . . than another black scarf."

"I wonder if either of us are in any position to judge that. What a queer allusion, Richards. What made you think of it?"

"I gave her the yellow one, this morning."

"And you find nothing amazing in what a piece of silk, and a song, might effect in the mortal soul? Indeed, Richards, I am concerned about you, but not for reasons you might think." He

397

rose and went to stand before the fire, looking at Richards steadily, sympathetically. "I say this to you. You have my approval, for what it is worth. More, my blessing, which I like to believe has its wellspring in some higher place than my own heart. But you said to me, I want this girl, and I wish to know that this is what you meant. Or did you mean something more?"

"I thought I wouldn't say love to you," Richards said then. "You know too much about it, more than I do."

"To the contrary," Berrades said. "Love can be, must be, known in many different ways. I only wished to be certain that I had placed the correct interpretation upon what you said. Personally I find love a pretty word, full of promise, and security, and hope. A dauntless word. I would not hesitate to use it, at any time."

"I said what I wanted. What about what she wants?"

"My friend, if you intend to stand passively, attempting to learn something which she herself can hardly know the answer to, I anticipate a long time of waiting. How did you propose to go about this, may I inquire?"

Richards put his head down on his arm, where it still braced him against the warm stone. "I don't know," he said. "I have never known how to do anything in my life, except just by doin' it when I had to. That's all I know how to do."

Juan Antonio Berrades reached to the table and selected a cigar. "Then the only advice I can offer you is that you do not, under any circumstances, attempt to alter your methods."

A hushed dawn still veiled the day, chill and silvery, when Dominguez came out of the house. No bird sang. He glanced at the sky, dark at the high arc of its crescent, and let his eye follow the darkness downward, until it came at last to a wide border of nascent paleness in the east. In the west a few stars still burned with a faint frosty glow.

Father Berrades' last private words to him had touched him, but he was not at all certain that he could call them to mind again, if he needed them. When he turned to the face of the house he wished that he had had the outer lamps lit, that he might take away with him every shadowed hollow, every intricacy of texture, every intimate detail of washed adobe, shuttered window, solid carved doors. But they had not been lighted, and he could barely identify Lupe and Feliciano and Soledad; their forms looked to him cold and forlorn. This house. Well, the heart had gone out of it. The heart and the soul and the backbone. In the years since that heart had been smashed, coming to meet him, there had been, quietly, other women; he was no sanctimonious monk. But his strength had been the strength of the crippled woman.

He could hear the mount string and baggage horses stamping and snorting, outside the gates. Someone had put the bridle of his sorrel horse into his hands, and the horse nuzzled at him and he felt its soft lips, soft breath. But he did not mount. He had put his arm about Cayetana and then taken it away, for it had seemed heavy to him and he thought that it might seem so to her also. Perhaps when God took He also granted: like this forbearing child, this miracle in his life, who not only forgave but tried so hard to give him now of her own small store of strength, knowing his was gone.

He noted the sky again and wished that the day would begin to break and looked back to his own courtyard and saw that Richards was crossing to him and thought, No, I cannot consider, after all, that what I did was ill advised. I only offered protection to a friend. Bonaventure had understood that. He said, "There was no need."

"I wanted to wish you a good journey, don Ramón," Richards said.

"Where is Uremáy?"

"Here, *patrón*," Uremáy said. He came up out of the gray light, rolling a little on his bowed legs, with his straw hat on the back of his head and his hair standing up thick and stiff, like bristles.

"I may not see you before the spring," Dominguez said.

"It presents ample time," Uremáy said.

"Which you will spend to good advantage, of that I am sure. Now I dislike this moment of my leaving. Cayetana . . ."

"Yes, Father?"

"Care for yourself, you are all that I have."

"Now, Father." She stood up on the tips of her boots, to kiss

399

his cheek. "Don't tire yourself, and return when you feel you can. I will think of you."

"And I of you," he said, looking at her, wishing again for the first light to touch the day. "Juan Antonio."

"Go with God," Father Berrades said.

"Uremáy. If there is word from Gómez, or even from Verdugo, remember, the best, only the best of horses for this season."

"Yes, *patrón*. So you have told me three times now, *patrón*. I will not forget."

Dominguez turned and mounted. He was wearing a big *charro* hat, and a pistol in a holster worked with silver. "So you have my fond *adiós*." He could hear the vaqueros filing down the outer wall. "Remain in health, until I come again."

And I shall come again, and lie beside my father, in the land which was his, and which he gave to me.

He rode out through the open gates. Until they were swallowed by the darkness Cayetana stood against the wall and did not turn to the house again.

Father Berrades had gone in. "I happen to know there might be some coffee made, in the kitchen," Richards said.

Uremáy yawned expansively. "*Ay de mi*. One would think it is *my* head which grows empty, the way he repeats to me what it is that I must do. What makes you think there is coffee, at this hour?"

"New set of house rules."

"With the *patrón* hardly through the gates, I see. Have a caution, Ben."

"I have had my last warning from you," Richards said. "I hope he comes back in a better state of mind."

"*¿Por que?*" Uremáy said softly, his eyes squinted, as if the sun had already risen, and blinded him. "You, who speaks to me of making penances here, upon this earth. I too hope so, but I do not believe it. His spirit is gone. It is . . ." He stopped. "No. I am sorry I said that to you, *amigo*, that the day of the *hacendado* will soon be over."

Richards turned, eyes as narrow as Uremáy's. "And what if it is? What's wrong with it bein' over? What's wrong with something just as good or maybe better to take the place of it?"

For a moment Uremáy was startled. Then he said, "Christ's wounds. I see what my lot will become. Starved and unwatered, brutally beaten, like an old work horse, because I cannot bear the load you impose. I believe that I knew you better when you had begun to set yourself so bitterly against us all."

"I don't reckon I'm to blame. That was another of your damn warnings."

"My flesh is very tender this morning," Uremáy said complacently. "Wait, I wish to speak with Morena Flor."

"Don't do it," Richards said.

"Do not speak to her? Why so, in the dawn, when she looks as if she needs a word or two?"

"And maybe doesn't," Richards said.

They had reached the back entrance. "I thought it would hearten her to say that as soon as I have heard from my *mesteñeros* we shall arise one fine day and be off across the border, and that she will come with us."

"Not this time," Richards said.

"*Hui*, I become deaf, in addition to all my other afflictions. What was it that you said?"

"I said, not this time."

Uremáy stood looking at him. "Now you are telling me something. I wish I knew if it is because you wish to, or because you become weak in that *gringo* head of yours. This tone of command you are taking upon yourself . . ."

Richards said, "I only aim to use with you, because you always seem to be standin' right where I want to put my feet. Just so we understand each other, Tiburcio."

Uremáy took off his hat and rubbed at his head, almost angrily. "At last, it seems, we do understand each other, which is a great deal. That is to say, that while at certain times you have understood me, I have understood you at all times. Of course, God in His wisdom did not make it difficult, this last."

"*Gracias*," Richards said.

"It is no trouble, be assured," Uremáy said.

Pedro Navarro, who had been cutting wood for the M Bar L, was coming down through a similar dawn a week later, at a time when the morning star had flared at its brightest and disappeared. He was cutting some miles from where his family was camped, and having run short of necessities, had arisen early to return to the ranch. While he was normally indolent, he saw no point in returning emptyhanded; when the first light showed itself, he brought in his donkey and loaded her with cut wood, stacked in hide slings. Then he picked up a stout stick to kill snakes and set out for camp, where his wife and children would still be sleeping.

There was a cold wind blowing, and he walked with his head down, occasionally rubbing the dust from his eyes. The brim of his hat flatted up in the wind, and he shivered under the frayed greasy old serape. He thought that when he reached the camp the day would be full upon the land and his woman would be making tortillas before the fire, and it would be for him a little time of contentment.

The wind was so strong he could hear it breaking off the brittle thorny branches, in the long arm of the brush which he followed. Here at least the brush protected him, but when he came again into the open land he was forced to lean into the wind, to lean even upon the rope by which he led the donkey. When the rope snapped from his hand he turned and raised his head and his hat blew off and went away on the roll of its brim and the curses came into his mouth. The rope snaked from him when he bent to it, as the donkey shied and broke away. Navarro looked up and saw in the gloomy morning light the dark looming shape with its massive horns coming out of the arm of the brush, and felt the curses in his mouth turn to a cry of fear.

He began to run, where the donkey was running, and the fear told his feet where they should go and by some marvel he would call upon heaven to witness, he managed to grasp the matted hair of the donkey's rump and scramble up, upon her back, between the two stacks of wood.

On the same morning, at nearly the same time, Esteban Ibarra was coming down the opposite arm of the brush spur some miles away, riding a big powerful work horse and leading a mare which he had spent two days attempting to locate. She would foal in the spring, and since he believed the stud to be a half brother of

Ebano he was interested in the foal and wished to keep the mare in the *casa* corrals until she dropped it. He rode slowly into an uncertain sunrise, thinking of Rosa Benítez, and when he came to the end of the spur saw that there was a man sitting hump-shouldered on the ground some distance ahead. The man did not look up until Esteban had ridden within a few feet of him and said, "What passes, man?"

Then Navarro raised his eyes, hatless, with his dusty black hair hanging.

"It is you, Navarro," Esteban said.

"It is I," Navarro said.

"Why do you sit here, in the wind? Your donkey wanders."

"I have had a great fright," Navarro said. "A devil came out of the brasada, and chased me."

"Speak more softly," Esteban said, glancing around him. "When did this happen, man? Are you hurt from it?"

Navarro shook his head. "I am not hurt. He came out there, back there, looking at me and running a distance, before he returned."

Esteban dismounted, keeping the mare's rope in his hand. He squatted on his heels, beside Navarro. His voice was very low. "How did he appear? Do you say he has gone into the brasada?"

Navarro got to his feet, drawing the serape around him. "A devil of great size, who had taken the form of a steer, or a bull, I could not tell. I could not span its horns with my arms if I were to do so from now until old age comes to me. And just as I said the last thing I was to say in this life, which was to Christ, I turned to look at it, for I could not help myself, and the sun was appearing, and I saw this thing was red as my own fire in the night and as I looked, it turned and went back to where it had come from, and I was spared."

Esteban stood up, his lip curling a little, his handsome dark head thrown back derisively. "And you have maybe had too much from the bottle which warms, this cold morning, eh? To look anywhere upon this land and see no thing of horn and hoof would be the strange passing. Go home, Navarro. Your donkey goes off with the food from your children's mouths, upon his back."

He went to mount. Navarro stood stolidly and saw Esteban

turn again. "A moment, Navarro. A red steer, you say, with very large horns?"

"You spat out my words as if they contained no truth," Navarro said. "Why now should I . . ."

But Esteban's hard strong hand was gripping his arm. "Rojo," he said. "Was it Rojo?"

"I do not know what you are saying."

"Forget this, it does not matter. Well, you have been chased by a devil, and you are a most fortunate man, and it would seem to me to your profit if you would go home and speak to no one of this. Here, I will catch up your donkey for you."

He watched Navarro plod away, hump-shouldered and disconsolate. Then he tightened his saddle girth and checked the two ropes he carried, one a heavy work rope, the other a tough braided rawhide *reata* of eight strands. The labor of two days was lost, but he saw no help for it: he turned the mare loose.

When he went into the brush he carried the work rope. And he thought, If I could do this, do this one thing, I do not think I would ask to do anything more in all my days, and I will bring more *peloncillo* to that blue ox Constante than he has ever seen before, more and more, until he runs sweet slobber with it.

A spiny branch slashed him across the forehead, full of the cold white pain of the knife and the hot burning pain of fire, and he felt his blood running. He wiped it away impatiently, with the back of his hand, taking the work horse deeper into the interlaced trails the longhorns had made, in the brasada.

TWENTY-TWO

He knew the man came for him.

He knew now a great deal of men, and of horses, as he knew his own kind. When men came into his secret places, into the brush, the calves would betray, bawling for the cows. He knew also that one night soon there would be many men moving abroad, when the winter sky cast all its white light upon the earth, full and clear as day, and that there would be small safety when that time began. The leaves had dropped; the brush lay bare to the eye but little more accessible. All day the longhorns would hide in it. On moonlight nights, when they came out to grass and water, on the open land, the men and horses would be waiting.

He had gone a long way, and returned a long way. Another single wrinkle ringed both mossy horns, and his maturing weight was settling, forward, into the heft of his huge chest and withers. He was more vigilant than he had ever been. Only when men came within the sight of the luminous black eyes did he summon an instinctive recall: he associated men and horses with the long time of captivity, with the stubborn blue ox and the confinement of the corral and, ultimately, the long northern trail, when he had walked in the lead.

He had come back to his own domain. At times he came quickly; frequently he waited for days where there was luxuriant grass, and in the country he traveled, returning, he saw men and horses and passing herds. The old disciplines were in him; he had not forgotten retreat and evasion. But he lifted his head to the south, when the late summer winds blew some warm moist fragrant thing to his nostrils which smelled of remembrance. He stood for long periods, knee-deep in grass, puzzling the remembrance, moving on when the pull of it grew strong in him. He followed no trail, and seeing the herds come out of the morning, as he had done, he went wild-eyed to the nearest refuge of hills, trees, rocks, canyons. That wild light was often in his eyes, except when the winds of remembrance and the surge of ancient impulse drew him south again.

When the leaves were fallen in the brasada he came to his own country of chaparral and prickly pear, of catsclaw and retama, of cactus and yucca, of acres of grassland steadily shrinking under the advance of the dense encroaching mesquite. He knew when he had come home, standing again under the old hackberry trees, scouting the wind he had raised his head to a thousand miles and more away. When the weight of his horns was heavy he went to work them in the wet earth along the river and, fed and watered, to lie beneath the winter stars before he went back to the old trails in the thickets.

The man persevered, methodical, heedless of the tearing thorns, as though compelled to search every trail in the hundreds of acres which comprised the long, ever-widening arm of the brasada. There were cows starting up in panic where the man passed, taking their calves to some other pocket of defense. Steers and bulls raged and ran in a bursting crash and crack of brush.

Together they moved, man and longhorn, pursuer and pursued. They faced the conflict with cunning, patience, respect, and with the inherent knowledges of the land itself. They wearied together and they endured together, alert not only to sound but to silence. The wind died and the day wore on, and once, for a flashing second they glimpsed each other through a tangle of impenetrable branchings, like a taunt, like a reassurance, before they were lost to each other again.

On the river side of the brasada, the man emerged at nightfall and built himself a fire and consumed his *carne seca* and a handful of parched corn. Still staunch and unspent, taking moisture from the succulent prickly pear, the red steer hid himself in the barricades of the brakes. The man slept fitfully. When the light bloomed in the morning sky, he rose unrested and took the work horse to water, and entered the brasada for the second day.

Coming up from the *acequia* with a bundle of laundry on her hip, Rosa Benítez paused to speak briefly to her prospective mother-in-law, with her pretty brows drawn together, like the wings of bees. "Esteban is gone four days now, Señora."

Uremáy, walking down from his own house with a coil of maguey rope over his shoulder, stopped to listen.

"Four days, is this the world?" Esteban's mother said.

"Four days is much, Señora."

Uremáy noted appreciatively the swing of Rosa's hip as she shifted the bundle. "You learn a very good lesson early, all impatience," he said. "Accustom yourself. Whenever it is a question of horses you will do much counting of days before that *caballero* returns."

The tears sprang to her eyes. She stamped her foot at him. "What is it that you know of such matters, Tiburcio?"

After a pause Uremáy said, "You are quite right, little one. I beg your good humor for an old man who knows nothing about anything."

He passed on.

The quiet of the house, which from the time of his return had been a disturbed and heavy quiet, had changed. He had believed, the day Dominguez left, that perhaps the going out of both the Señora and don Ramón would only add to the sense of oppression which lay in the atmosphere, so thick he might have gathered it up in his hands. He never stepped out of his room that he was not conscious of that closed door, and inevitably, at certain

407

hours, Feliciano, waiting outside Cayetana's room as he had once waited for the Señora.

Yet that same day he heard Soledad singing and a burst of gunfire invective from Lupe, in the kitchen, all more normal than he could have asked.

He had gone through the days of his return working himself as if the whole enterprise would collapse without him. The evenings weighed upon him the most, although since he had talked with Father Berrades he had struck up a further acquaintanceship with the sense of compromise which had come to him earlier; now a certain hollowness seemed to have left the house, and a certain stable accommodation to have taken its place, as if it too had learned and accepted reconciliation.

Sometime long after dinner, when he had had a conference with Uremáy in which he did most of the listening, he came back to the house and found it silent and shadowed, and went to the big room but got no farther than the doorway. One lamp was burning, casting such small illumination that it only served to affirm the darkness of the room. The fire had gone low and he saw that Cayetana was down upon her knees before it, with her hands busy in one of two big straw baskets. While he watched she drew out several papers, glanced through them, and put them into the fire. She was totally absorbed in what she did; one thick black loop of hair had slipped out of the coil which bound it and lay in the curve of her neck. When the fire flared, taking the papers, he saw the muted flash of the little hammered silver pendant that swung between her breasts. Twice more she fed the fire with the contents of the basket, and then she looked up and saw him and did not speak, but he moved into the room and stood looking down at her and said, "Whatever you're doin', are you sure it's the right thing?"

She shook her head, emphatic. "Father has kept every receipt and record and transaction and scrap of paper that ever went through his hands." She was scanning a page from an old ledger. "There are things here from Grandfather's time."

He was watching her bent head. "Caye, if you feel that way, why don't you toss it all in at once and get it done with."

"It doesn't make me sad," she said quickly, glancing up at him.

"It's nothing I regret doing, it should have been done long ago. The useless accumulation of the years. So many years it almost seems another age."

"It was another age." He sat down and reached into his shirt and rolled a cigarette and handed it to her. He felt a nagging unidentifiable fear. "Have you got to go through it all?"

"Why do you do that?"

"Do what?"

"Give me your cigarette. It's nice." She lowered her head, feeling the color rise in her face. "You used to say I should be taken to the corncrib."

"That was when you were a little girl."

"You are confirming that it did make me grow older."

"No, I reckon that was only the natural passing of time, and circumstance. Are you sure you don't want any of this stuff? None of it has any value?"

"None of it," she said firmly.

"But you don't have any idea in your mind that you can just burn up the past."

She straightened and slumped back, resting on her heels. The lock of loose hair slid forward and the flash of silver disappeared again into the little glistening hollow at the round of her dress. "Oh Ben."

"All right," he said. "I just wanted to make sure." He got up and came and picked up the basket and turned it upside down in the fire. They drew back from the sudden surge of the flame and when the papers had gone to ash he upended the second basket and again they drew away from it. "I got a feeling that in another ten years you will have managed to save up twice that amount and we will be doin' this all over again," he said.

"But it's a clean beginning, at least. And I have good intentions. What would it be like if everyone carried out all their good intentions?"

"I don't expect there would be anything very exciting goin' on anyplace."

"Ben, you make me feel . . ."

"How?" he said.

"Conspiratorial."

"Well, we burned some papers together in near the dead of night. I reckon that is kind of conspiratorial."

"And plotted to do the same ten years from now."

He took back his cigarette from her. "The idea that we might be doin' anything at all together ten years from now doesn't strike you as bein' too improbable?"

A still watchful look shadowed her face. "I didn't think . . . Were you making a game?"

"No, I quit playin' games years ago. Or tried to. I have never liked games very much, because when you begin playin' them it means you got to go by some kind of rules."

"And what happens when you want to play the game and not stay within the rules?"

"You get hurt, mostly. And the world doesn't stop for you."

"Then what do you do?"

"Well, I expect you can always crawl into a hole somewhere and go blind in the dark and live for quite a time feeding on all the misery you can lay mind to. Or else you can take another look at the rules and pick the things that matter out of the mess around you and start over again: the things, the words, Father Berrades says all the time, words I like and would like to use, because I think they mean something, but I am not a priest and maybe when I say hope and dignity and freedom and courage and love they don't sound the same."

"You can't take the meaning away. Why are people afraid to use those words?"

He shook his head and stood up, leaning back against the stone with his arms crossed. "Because they are not easy words to use. Maybe because they are so big that when you say them you got to have something just as big to set your sight on, as if you could look out and see the whole world, or up and see the whole sky. And even if I came to use that one word, love, and looked up at the sky while I did it, I don't reckon I could see it all and would have to look back and see what you thought about it."

She was so still he could hear her breathing. Then she rose and stood before him. "And what else?"

"Only that I reckon I am as hard-headed as Tiburcio says I am, and that all the while I was workin' so hard to stay that way it was you I loved, on account of you had surely put yourself into the back of my mind and I couldn't seem to move you out no matter what else I happened to be thinkin' of. And all the time I thought I was only sorry for you, sorry about . . . since the day I picked up that letter."

"Stop," she said quietly. "And what am I to say to you, now?"

"You do not have to say anything to me, now. If you mean do you have to tell me anything, no, because I already know what you think you might have to tell me."

Her voice was still quiet, but she had gone very pale. "And would you want me, then, with other images in my eyes?"

"I don't see anything in your eyes," he said. "Except way down inside there is a kind of a light showing, not very bright, I will admit, you couldn't find your way home by it or anything. But I think sometime it might come up again, and if it does I would like to see it, because then I think your eyes would be almost the color of that yellow scarf. Which I guess is how come I settled on that color."

She put both hands up over her face. And he said, "Caye, if you would look at me, you would maybe see that while I would not exactly like for you to expect that I am aiming to remain entirely harmless, I have got good intentions too." And she took her hands away and saw that he was holding his arms open to her. The time of hesitation which held her where she was hurt him, but it was no more than he had expected. One moment more of it and he would have been beaten, but she moved into his arms and was holding to him as if she had had nothing else to hold to before in her life. Her skin held the fire's heat and sunlight and cold blue air and the deft resilient little body was fused along him and the quiet lips broke apart as if wind was tearing away petals and he went from that first instant of defeat to one of elation, knowing that he had been right, that the warmth and response and intensity were only sleeping behind that protective sheltering wall of her own building.

Then she was shivering, mutely, with what he thought might be appeal. "Now wait," he said. "Wait."

He could hardly hear her. "When Tiburcio said you almost did not come back it was another emptiness."

"You have got to stop thinkin' about what was and what could be and think about what is," he said. "Don't shiver like that or I will get to suspecting you are afraid and that is the last thing I want you to be. Here." He swung her up in his arms and crossed to the chair again and held her cradled against him, but not as a child. "Now tell me."

"Only that I think . . . I think I have so much to give."

"Sure you do. I never doubted it."

"But suppose that even if . . . suppose part of me never changes, that part of me is always the way I am now."

"Suppose so? Is that what you're afraid of? When nothing stays the same? When people change all the time? Whatever's buried down inside you, Caye, you'd ought to do what's necessary, talk about it and think about it and feel about it how you want."

"And you don't believe the risk is too great? For you?"

"Whatever is worth having is worth riskin' for. You don't listen to me very good, do you? If we go lookin' for problems I expect there will be no difficulty findin' 'em."

"Do I sound negative, then?"

"Some. But you don't look it." His arms tightened around her. "And you sure don't feel it. And you doubt yourself too much. Any more questions you want to ask?"

"Yes. What if I could see the whole world and the whole sky, as you said, and still could not say that word love back to you? Or even find another word to take its place at this moment?"

"Then I ought to warn you ahead: I am a very patient man, but I have got my limits. Also I do not look to be accepting any substitute words. I have noticed that when people, women mostly, can't decide what to do next they always ask for time."

"Time? No, when it's gone you never get it back. I don't think we have any to waste."

"Now that is more like it. You seem to be learnin' how to say the right things. I always suspected if somebody encouraged you you might come to it."

"I didn't know how good it is, to be encouraged. Do you think you can keep it up?"

"I aim to try," he said.

412

Her head had fallen back on his shoulder. "Ben, it doesn't seem right to say it, but I am so tired."

"All right. Go to sleep then. I won't let you fall. Not ever, if possible." He had already sensed her weariness, sensed even some tangible, nameless relief. Her breathing was quiet and steady; the draining tension had left her boneless and yielding, surrendered to something more than sleep. After a while he looked up and saw in the dim light that Father Berrades was standing in the doorway.

When he moved into the room his face was suave, without question. He looked first at the two empty baskets and then at the sleeping girl and then at Richards. When Richards stood up, lifting Cayetana, he snapped his head brusquely at Berrades. Berrades bent and picked up the lamp and followed him.

Without speaking they ascended the stairs. In the hallway Father Berrades opened the door to Cayetana's room and raised the lamp. There was not a break in the rhythm of her breathing when Richards put her down on the bed and drew the big striped Saltillo blanket up to cover her. When he turned he shot one uneasy glance into the corner. The golden Virgin was gone, as Uremáy had said, and the niche was as bare as the rest of the room. He was glad, and yet he thought that there should not be that much emptiness; that, for her, there ought to be something there.

Outside, still holding the lamp, Father Berrades said, "I try at all times to be unobtrusive. That is, it gives me a certain vicarious pleasure to materialize as if out of thin air when I am needed. And likewise to circumspectly disappear when I am not. It is none of my affair, of course, but may I ask what horrendous blunder you have committed, to put her to sleep?"

Richards grinned at him, but there was something tight in it. "Father, that girl is used right up."

Berrades nodded. They started down the hall. "Emotional exhaustion. Weeks of it. Much more difficult to remedy than simple lack of sleep, or even the effects of hard physical labor. As a rule, it requires a monumental deliverance to break the pressure."

"Like some kind of blunder?"

413

"Forgive me. I intended only to feel my way, so to speak, without questioning you too directly."

"I would as soon you asked straight out. You are startin' to sound like Uremáy."

Father Berrades was amused. "In that event, you did whatever it was you had to do?"

Richards stopped and looked at him thoughtfully. "Actually, I reckon only about half. It kind of surprises me that it was enough."

"It gratifies me, since your half is surpassing more than the whole of everyone else in this house. I would have looked for more joyousness in you. You seem rather strained."

"I am all wound up like a watch spring. Father, what do you think don Ramón is goin' to say about this?"

"My dear Richards, I would look forward to his return with some disquietude if it occurred to me that you had not learned something from the manner in which he dealt with a previous and similar contingency, and that you would permit him to entertain any but the most acquiescent attitude."

"He will probly hate my guts, if you will excuse me."

"Not at all. He will remain what he is, a weak and charming gentleman who will have discovered that the sun does not arise in the morning at his discretion. And at any rate, you are holding in your hand at this moment that most potent force in the world. You remember that we spoke of it? Surely you do not believe one self-centered and very mortal man can stand up to it . . ."

"He did it once before," Richards said.

"Permit me to finish. I was about to say, under the present circumstances." Berrades looked up at the ceiling, where a wavery pool of light was reflected. His face was innocent, almost pious. "At any rate, when I have finished with him, he will be in that chapel daily, thankful to count his blessings."

Richards stared at him. Then he laughed, once, a short, harsh sound. "Are you sayin' that along with everything else, I now got the Lord on my side?"

Father Berrades winced. "Please, my friend. What makes men imagine God would condescend to taking sides? I hear this everywhere I go, as if we were all engaged in some heavenly tug of war in which God would eventually add His weight, on the end of

His own choosing." He looked at Richards. "However, if I as His instrument, am enabled to perform some perfunctory arbitration, it is in no way an affirmation of His espousal, or lack of it. Do I make myself clear?"

"Right on the nose," Richards said.

"There are times," Berrades said, "when I must stop and remind myself that I am only forty years old. I feel that surely I have sprouted a long hoary beard and my bones often seem to be growing brittle. It is to do with dealing with a simple and superstitious and tractable people, of course. It makes the task easier in one way, and in another difficult beyond measure because they tend to attribute all things, great and small, to God. Lack of common sense is what it comes to. And if you are so wound up, as you express it, may I remind you that the chapel gates are open?"

"You have got a big strong hand there, Father," Richards said. "Would you do me the kindness to take it out of the middle of my back?"

There was a small silence. Then Berrades laughed. "Very well. I give you my word, Richards, that I will keep both hands at my sides when I am in your presence. And since you will not allow me to be overt, I will even dispense with resorting to the devious. You have no objection to my praying for your, and Cayetana's, good fortune and peace of mind?"

"I would be much obliged to you. And by the way, Father, I meant to say that I am not only glad I came back, but that you did."

"I wish I could say the Lord sent me, but I cannot. I seem to move freely and of my own will, and I felt no particular call to return to Tres Reyes at the time I did. It was a fortunate accident. Well, if you will not join me, I shall say good night to you, with the hope that you manage to unwind yourself before morning." He started down the hall; then he turned. "Richards, one matter. Do not expect too much of her, for a while."

And Richards only stood there, watching him evenly. "No, Father. If you can see your way to it, you take care of your share of this and let me take care of mine. On account of I expect a great deal of her, right away."

Berrades inclined his head, slowly, in a gesture which was graceful, dignified, and submissive. But he took pains to lower the lamp, not wanting Richards to take note that he was smiling.

Rosa Benítez came to the rear entrance of the big house early in the morning and stood in the doorway, seeing that Lupe was busy at the fire and Señor Richards sitting on a stool with his boot hooked through a rung and a cup in his hand. She was afraid of Lupe and uncertain as to whether she should call attention to herself or wait until she was discovered. As it turned out, Señor Richards solved the problem for her by wishing her *buenos dias*; then she came in diffidently and said she wished to see the Señorita.

Richards shook his head. "She's not up yet and I don't reckon she will be for a spell. You're one of the Benítez girls."

"Yes, Señor. I am Rosa." She caught Lupe's disdainful eye and straightened her shoulders. "But the Señorita always arises early." She had turned away when Richards said, "Anything I can help with, Rosa?"

She stopped and faced him. He was always so courteous, and she did not think he would take the liberty of teasing. "I do not know, Señor. It is about Esteban."

Lupe snorted. Rosa's face flamed. "You are all as bad as Tiburcio. He teases me so that I cannot even speak to him of this. No one will listen to me."

"Whoa now," Richards said. "What's Tiburcio got to do with it? And why won't anybody listen to you?"

"They will not listen to her," Lupe said, "because she is a silly lovestruck *niña*, that is why."

"Well, before I pull in my head here, Lupe, I wish you would remember that you have not always been so old as however old you are, and if you think about that hard enough you will be too busy to say anything. Rosa, are you the girl is going to marry Esteban?"

"Yes, Señor. Now he does not come back."

He saw the tears in her eyes and was discomfited. This was nothing for him, after all, but he didn't see his way clear to duck out now. "You mean he's gone off and left you, Rosa?"

That seemed to pinch her. She frowned. "Oh no, Señor, he

went . . . it is five days this morning, he went to look for a mare he wished to bring into the corrals."

"Well, maybe he is havin' trouble pickin' her up."

"Something is wrong, Señor. I feel it is wrong."

He breathed wearily. "Just you feel it? What do you suppose could happen to a big strong full-grown boy like Esteban?"

"I think many things could happen. Never mind, Señor, I will wait for the Señorita to awaken."

"No, wait a minute. What do you want to do, send out a search crew?"

"Would you do that, Señor?"

"Sure, why not? And how do you think Esteban is goin' to feel if you shame him like that, when maybe all he is doin' is takin' a little time off for himself?"

Her face was obstinate. "Señor, when Esteban says he will come home within three days, he will come. He does not tell lies."

Lupe banged a frying pan. Richards finished his coffee and stood up. "All right, I'll tell you what I'll do, Rosa. I will take a look myself, today, and if he ain't back by sundown, we'll head out in the morning and cover Tres Reyes. That suit you?"

"I would be very thankful, Señor."

When she had slipped out, Lupe turned to Richards. "It is not my place to say it, Señor, but if you continue to give your ear to silly lovestruck girls, so silly that even Tiburcio Uremáy can offer nothing but his laughter, you will soon find yourself unable to attend to the affairs of the day."

"I appreciate your good wishes," Richards said. "At the rate you are goin', you and me will be gettin' right fraternal before long." He went out into the morning. He felt good. It was cold and clear, although a thin layer of wispy cloud had hazed over the pale bluish-white of the sky. Esteban Ibarra could be anywhere. He was not alarmed, but he figured to head out and see if he could pick up any trace of him. Lupe was probably dead right about the Benítez girl, and Esteban would be back before nightfall.

In the open clearing, closed off at the end of the trail and not more than thirty feet long, they faced each other for what seemed an endless time, as if they took each other's measure, and

417

with a mutual deference. Trapped in the blind clearing, from which no trail led out again, the red steer had turned at bay. In the morning light his eyes were almost mild in their weariness, yet he gathered himself to charge. The man spoke aloud. He said, *Mother of God, guide my hand,* and the work rope made a solid loop in the air, casting out strong and true, before it settled.

He felt it at the base of his right horn. He tried to wheel. His head tossed wildly against the pull, and he sprung his weight and balance to run, forward, but the man and the horse were not there. The horse had swung away, into the brush, and he felt the rope draw, tearing at his head, and he braced against it. He could hear the breaking of the brush, where the horse maneuvered. Then the rope was circling a stout trunk of black chaparral, and there was no slack between his horn and the tree.

Fresh blood was welling on the man's face and hands when he came back into the clearing, and the horse also was torn and bleeding across withers and flank. The eyes were savage now, watching, while the man cast again. This time the *reata* settled upon the left horn and was taken off in the opposite direction, and he could do nothing but brace against its pull as he had done before. When the man was done, he could not move his head, between the two ropes.

Again the horse moved into the clearing, and again the man sat and looked at him. When he rode out, back down the trail in the brush, he was slack in the saddle, and the horse carried its head low, in exhaustion.

At midday, nearly within sight of the walls of Tres Reyes, Esteban was met by Juan Sanchez and his oldest son, a boy of thirteen. *"Caramba,"* Sanchez said, "when I first see you coming I think it is some survivor of a terrible battle. What has passed with you, Esteban? Your face, it will not be the same as it was."

Esteban told him. The victory he had wished to see acclaimed felt stale in him; he was too tired. He gestured at the boy, with a hand upon which the blood had darkened and congealed. "Go and tell them, at the house," he said. And the boy kicked his pony in the ribs and was off, scattering a band of horses as he went.

Juan Sanchez shook his head and raised a hand to his unshaven face. "Ay, Esteban. They laughed at Rosa because she felt anxiety for you, gone so long. All but Señor Richards . . . he went early this morning to look for some sign of you."

"I hope he has not gone far," Esteban said.

"No matter. Let us bring the red steer into the corrals, and when he returns he will see what he will see."

Esteban said, "No. I think it is for him to say. Who knows what he will think? This red steer walked in the lead of the Tres Reyes herd last summer, did he not?"

When Richards rode in early in the afternoon Uremáy and Esteban were waiting for him. He took one look at Esteban's lacerated purple face and said, "Looks like Rosa was right. What'd you tangle with, a panther?"

They were standing near the rear wall, to get out of a rising wind. A plume of dust snaked around the entrance and blew straight up in the air and disappeared. "Señor Richards, I have this morning taken Rojo," Esteban said.

Richards looked at him, and then at Uremáy. Uremáy shrugged; his face was expressionless.

"Two days I have been upon his track," Esteban said. "Two days to find the mare, and then I must let her go and spend two more smelling behind this son. We tired each other, at the last, and I thought when I threw my rope that I could not take him, there was so little space to cast. But there are two ropes on him now, Señor, one upon each horn. I believe the work rope would have held him, but I feared that he might snap a horn in his rage and escape again."

Uremáy was staring at a point somewhere beyond Richards' left shoulder, his eyes almost vacant. Then he smiled slightly, unnaturally, showing his lower teeth. Richards felt the touch on his arm and turned and saw Cayetana had come up behind him. His face softened; he took her gloved hand for a moment and then turned back to Esteban. "How far out, Esteban?"

"Perhaps eight miles, I would say, Señor. Shall I bring up Constante, and some of the *manso* steers?"

Richards was biting at his lower lip. Then he shook his head. "No." He saw Uremáy's eyes flicker to him and slide away again.

"All right. So he led the herd, and he did a great thing, he walked all the way home again. But I remember something else. He killed a man and he killed my horse and now he has got no more savvy than to come back and I reckon the time has come to get it done and over." He turned on his heel and went toward the house.

"Tiburcio. Stop him," Cayetana said.

"I?" Uremáy said. "No, Morena Flor. If you do not wish him to do this thing, it is you who must not permit it."

She ran toward the back entrance and into the house. Uremáy's mouth had a small bitter smile upon it. *Well, fool of a red steer, I give you your freedom, for nothing, and this is how you spend it. I am in no position to give it to you again, nor do I know that I would wish to. The occasion is not the same. I see already that something passes in this house which does not surprise me, so that if you are spared now it will be a more persuasive voice which provides for it than the voice of this old peon . . .*

She burst into the main room. He had opened the gun case and taken out his Winchester and was putting a handful of shells into his pocket. She wanted to run to him but she held herself where she was and she kept her voice steady. "Ben, no."

"Yes," he said. "I'm through with all that. I was glad when he got away, on the Cimarron. I never looked to see him back."

"Ben, give him a chance."

"He didn't give Jonah a chance. Or Glass. What do you mean, give him a chance?"

She crossed to him and put her hands on his arms. "I mean a choice. Give him a choice. Bring him in."

"And then?"

"Let him make up his own mind. It's not fair this way, Ben. You know it isn't. You had a great deal of feeling for him, once. I think because he was free as the wind. I know what he did, what he might do again. But to rope him and tie him and leave him no defense and walk up to him and shoot him . . ."

He watched her. "We all come back to Tres Reyes, don't we? Even that red steer." He put the rifle down. "I have surely been disarmed since I came into this house. In just about every way I can think of." They stood locked together for a long time; then he said, "You keep out of the way."

She saw them go out with Constante, and six Judas steers. Then she sent Juan Sanchez' son to saddle Ebano.

"I believe Constante remembers this one," Uremáy said. On the narrow side of the brush the vaqueros were chopping with machetes, to widen the trail.

"He'd ought to," Richards said. "Rojo near choked him to death."

"How is it that you listen to Morena Flor and do not come armed to the execution?" Uremáy said.

"How is it that you never learn to mind your own damned business?"

"Every day I pray to change, but it accomplishes nothing. If I make a confession to you today, will you be very angry with me?"

"Probly," Richards said. "Anyway, that is Father Berrades' line of work, not mine."

"I wish to tell you that it was I who chased Rojo off from the herd, that day of the stampede, when we were bringing in the drifters."

After a minute Richards laughed.

"You do not believe me," Uremáy said testily. "Believe what you will, or will not, then. It is nothing to me. What is so strange in my coming upon this fine brute, with his nose in the grass and a look of freedom all about him, and not wishing to see him brought to the end of his days by an insignificant child such as Franco?"

Richards said, "I would not feel that was so strange. What are you tellin' me now for, and expectin' me to swallow it whole?"

"*Bueno*," Uremáy said. "*Bueno*. It pleases me more than I can say that you do not believe me. Morena Flor knows it is true."

"Yes? Let me give you a word of advice, in exchange for what you been passin' out to me. There is no reason now for you to be goin' to bed at night and gettin' up in the morning with the idea in your head that you're holdin' any reins up at the big house. Is that plain enough for you?"

"I am to be relieved of my duty?" Uremáy said.

"You made up that duty for yourself. Nobody handed it to you. You did all right, while you were doin' it. And I recollect something you said, and now I am goin' to throw it back to you. You said it was hard for you when she didn't need you any longer. You had better start gettin' yourself used to the fact that day has come around again."

Uremáy made a small bow, from the waist. "In that event, I wish you all good fortune. What am I to call you now: don Benjamín?"

"*Amigo* will do, like always," Richards said.

"I will bring you some pulque, and we will observe this as it merits," Uremáy said blandly, and moved his horse forward into the clearing where, for the second time, Rojo stood necked with the blue ox Constante.

Once he had cleared the brakes he ran Constante for perhaps ten minutes. The Judas steers stood patiently, waiting until the race was over; then they were driven up to surround ox and steer. He allowed himself to be taken away from the brasada.

It was nearly sundown when they approached the slope which led into the fields and corrals of Tres Reyes. The wind had died and a pale silver green light lay low in the sky. Cayetana came up on Ebano to meet them and they started down into the dying day.

Behind him, Richards heard Esteban curse softly and rounded and saw the Judas steers had walked ahead and that Rojo was standing, without apparent effort, protesting the thrust of the powerful ox. Constante made a complaining sound and strained forward, but he could not move the *ladino*. The red steer stood like rock, looking down the slope at the ranch.

Richards leaned from the saddle and tipped up Cayetana's face with one hand and held her wide trusting gaze. "Now do you reckon he has made his choice?"

"Not yet. Cut him loose, Ben."

He dismounted and called to Esteban. "Will your rope reach that tree, Esteban? Take it over. Not too tight, give him room to move. And cut him off Constante."

Two work ropes went around the hackberry, holding him. The

moment he felt himself free of the ox he went to the ground, with deliberation, and lay facing down the slope. Esteban was standing, the knife still in his hand.

"But, Señorita, what is it that he can do now?"

"He can come down and walk in the lead of the Tres Reyes steers for as long as he lives, Esteban," she said.

Uremáy was sitting loose, his hands on his thighs, his squint appraising. He said, "No, small gray dove, he will not do this thing that you wish of him."

"You think not?"

"I am certain of nothing, but he speaks to me, this one. With the way he lies, with the bearing of his head, he speaks to me. I have known this before. Not often, but it comes to pass. I thought this of him earlier, when Franco took him. That he would die first. Is this not true, Ben?"

"Now and again, I expect," Richards said reluctantly. He wanted Cayetana to win this. And he thought, Berrades was wrong, maybe; if an outlaw steer can will himself to die, why can't man do the same . . .

"He considers," Uremáy said. "It may be that he will spend a long time in this consideration."

Cayetana said, "At least the decision is his." She watched Rojo, with compassion, but his eyes were detached and turned away.

When night fell he had not risen. He lay on the slope and saw the lights winking in the dark, and scented water. The water was where man was, where the corrals were. There was grass around and under him, but he did not lower his head to it. He could hear the sounds of men, carried in drifting waves, laughter, voices, the music of a mouth organ, the clashing of gates by which man hoped to close out that same night which sheltered him.

In the morning he felt thirst, and the dawn smelled fresh and wet to him. When it was light, men, and the children of men, came to look at him, but he only lay with the same detachment in his eyes. He was comfortable, in the sere winter grass; the earth beneath him was familiar. There was no wind and the sun felt warm upon him. By the middle of the day men no longer came to stare at him, except for two who stood watch over him, and whom he ignored.

With the dark of the second night he changed his position slightly, and once put his muzzle to the grass, hoping to find moisture. As he had done before he watched the lights below, and a mild wind from the south blew the smell of water to him. He knew that there would be water, and grass, all he would ever need, and that he had only to rise to his feet again.

When dawn came a brown verdin alighted in the grass near him. It was an old friend, who had its winter nest in the chaparral. Along that very arm of the brakes where he had hidden, the small bird would have dropped the golden seed of the granjeno, planting a living fence to add to the sheltering islands of the brush.

At the first touch of the sun, when the sky flushed clear in the east, he looked down once more at the white walls beginning to wash amber with morning, at the bending river where the glittering light lay, at the prison of the corrals. His vision was no longer detached, but serene with reflection of the old, known sanctuaries of the brasada, the tall cool grasses and clear waters of the north country. He lifted his great head to the day. But his free heart was alive only to release; it could not will him to rising, and he felt it go quietly to the last shattering stillness.

The verdin flew suddenly, low in the grass, straight out before him, going home. With the last of his sight, he followed it.